WAKE

WAKE

JOHN HUBBARD

Commonwealth Books Inc.,

ACKNOWLEDGMENTS

My sincere thanks to the proof readers (in alphabetical order) of preliminary versions of this novel—Aaron, Gay, Guy, Jack, James, John, Parker, Shane, Tara, Taylor, Tim, and Tom.

Woe to those who call evil good and good evil.
(Isaiah 5:20, NIV)

A Commonwealth Publications Hardback
WAKE
This edition published 2021
by Commonwealth Books
All rights reserved

Library of Congress Control Number: 2021947758

ISBN: 978-1-892986-29-0 (Trade)
ISBN: 978-1-892986-30-6(E-PUB)

This work is a novel and any similarity to actual persons or events is purely coincidental.

First Commonwealth Books Hardback Edition: September 2021
PUBLISHED BY COMMONWEALTH BOOKS, INC., www.commonwealthbooks@aol.com
www.commonwealthbooksinc.com

Manufactured in the United States of America

The first bullet, fired forty-five minutes before dawn, instantly killed Special Agent Linda Ogleby. The commander of the FBI raid, Special Agent Titus Warren, heard the shot and saw her body fall limp twelve feet in front of him. He immediately dived to the ground and slid behind an old, red pickup for cover.

When he peeked around it, he was momentarily stunned by the pool of blood spreading around her head. His team proceeded with caution to the warehouse buildings, and Agent Ogleby made no mistakes. He never lost an FBI agent under his command before, and the weight of it hit him hard.

Taking a deep breath, he spoke more calmly than he felt into his head mic. "Agent Ogleby down. I repeat, Agent Ogleby down. Did anyone see where the hell that shot came from?"

"Gun flash from the third floor of warehouse of Building B-1, second window from the left," replied the senior sniper perched in a loft well behind the advancing team of FBI agents and SWAT support. "I see the shooter and have a shot if...."

Before he could finish, gunfire erupted from the second- and third-floor windows of the warehouse.

Warren cautiously peered around the truck again and grimaced when he saw Ogleby's body jerk twice, as bullets struck her lifeless form. He pulled back barely in time to avoid more bullets flying past his head.

"Return fire at will," he ordered. "I repeat, return fire at will. Snipers, take out those gunmen. Washington, deploy Brave Team to the back of B-1 when able to do so. Report when your team is in position for an assault."

Determined no one else would be lost that day, he added, "Proceed with caution. I repeat, proceed with caution."

"Yes, Sir," Special Agent Earl Washington responded.

As the snipers homed in on the shooters' positions, the terrorists' shots slowed to a trickle. Warren knew Ogleby was dead, but he couldn't leave her body in the open to be riddled by more bullets. With no recent gunfire near him, he crawled to her, grabbed an arm, and pulled her body to a protected area.

Once safe behind the truck again, he saw the kill shot went through her right eye and exploded out the back of her skull. He'd seen worse in the Army, but it was still unsettling. He momentarily closed his eyes and cleared his head. There was no time to think about Ogleby.

As he waited, the area around him became eerily still. Moments later, he heard, "Bravo Team in position."

Warren immediately snapped out orders. "Snipers, I want all intact windows on Building B-1 shattered on my command. Three, two, one, fire!"

The sound of rapid gunfire and shattering glass pierced the night air.

"Bravo Team, prepare to breach the building from rear entry points. Do not proceed until my order. Alpha Team, prepare to advance on the front and side entry points on my command."

All agents and SWAT officers replied they were ready.

"Once inside, be sure of your targets," Warrant warned. "Do not fire if any laboratory facilities might be hit. I repeat, do not fire if any laboratory facilities might be hit. All units advance on my signal." Taking a deep breath, he gave one last cautious look around. "Three, two, one, breach!"

Flash grenades were fired into the front and back of the warehouse, lighting up the interior. Several members of Alpha Team burst through the front door using a steel battering ram, while others crawled forward and went in through the shattered side windows.

Warren ran into the building, past metal drums, boxes, and large wooden crates. Shards of glass crunched under his boots, as he looked for cover and enemy combatants. Shots rang out.

The lights were off, but between night-vision goggles and bright gun flashes, two terrorists were quickly spotted and taken out by Alpha Team. Other terrorists retreated up wide metal stairs to the second floor.

Warren moved to the downed terrorists and knelt to check for a pulse, finding none. Both males appeared to be Middle Eastern, one in his forties, the other not over sixteen.

After securing the ground floor, Alpha Team slowly followed their targets up the stairs, with Warren leading. Bravo Team simultaneously advanced up a back metal stairway equally wide. Surprisingly, after only a few minutes of shooting, the sound ceased from the second floor.

Warren reached the second floor and looked around. No one was visible. "They must've abandoned this floor for higher ground," he warned his team. "Collins, Smelly, and Caine, secure the second floor and watch our backs. The rest of Alpha Team will proceed up to the third floor.

"Bravo Team, proceed up the back steps. We'll have them pinned in a crossfire, so move slowly and methodically." Warren moved toward the stairs. "Alpha Team, on me."

As he crept up the stairwell, he pressed his back tightly against the wall and looked for targets. Suddenly, his team came under heavy fire. Three bullets struck the wall inches from his head. Chips of plaster flew into the side of his face before he could duck. His NVGs broke, but at least they protected his eyes from flying debris.

He disconnected and tossed the worthless goggles to the floor, wiping blood off his face, and returned fire. The intense gunfire stopped abruptly after two combatants were hit. Their bodies tumbled down the steps toward them.

Warren moved over the lifeless forms and bolted into the room at the top. Bullets slammed the floor near his feet. He lurched right and down behind a large wooden crate. As soon as he could, he peered around the corner and returned fire.

Other members of his team followed him, found cover, and returned fire.

It didn't take Warren long to run out of ammo. As he paused to reload his Glock 23, he said, "Secure all exits and stairways on the third floor. If possible, take remaining targets alive. I repeat...."

Before he could finish, someone moved at the corner of his eye. A terrorist ran at breakneck speed toward a door leading to the roof. Without considering the possibility of other gunmen trained on him, he raced after the man.

The panicked man was fast, but Warren was faster. In seconds, he tackled the man from behind. The terrorist's face struck the concrete floor hard, and his weapon slid across the room.

Warren, grabbing an arm, tried to slap cuffs on the man, who kept violently twisting and turning. Eventually, the enraged terrorist somehow twisted and managed to thrust a curved knife at Warren's neck.

Seeing it coming, Warren caught the man's wrist before the blade struck. In a swift blur of instinct and adrenalin, he squeezed and wrenched the man's wrist so hard he heard bones crack.

The terrorist screamed in pain, and the blade fell harmless to the floor. He writhed and bucked until Warren gave him a vicious head butt to his already-broken nose. Blood splattered both men, and the terrorist passed out.

CHAPTER 2

When the fighting was over, eight terrorists were dead and three captured. One, a young Black woman, was seriously wounded in the chest and left leg. Shortly after the FBI agents stabilized her wounds, a medical team arrived, gave her more complete emergency treatment, and transported the prisoner to a nearby hospital under heavy guard.

Warren checked on his team members. In addition to the loss of Agent Ogleby, one SWAT officer was wounded in the thigh. Everyone else suffered only minor scratches and contusions. He set guards around the building and had local police lock down the entire block. Crime-scene investigators were called in but given specific instructions not to enter the building without Warren's permission.

Special Agent Cynthia Cook came over to Warren when she saw blood smeared on his face and clothes. "Are you all right?"

"I'm fine," he said dismissively.

Holding his chin to keep his head still, she examined his facial wounds. "Hold still. Let me take a look."

"It's just a few scratches. I can take care of them later. We have a lot of work to do."

"Don't be stupid, Sir. Blood running down your face won't help you do your job. Give me two minutes to clean those wounds." She pointed toward a wall. "There's a first-aid kit over there. You wait here."

Reluctantly agreeing, he sat on a wooden crate. It was easier to cooperate than argue.

Cook, pulling on latex gloves, wiped blood off Warren's face with sterile wipes. There was so much grime and blood on him, she didn't have any idea of the wounds were deep or superficial.

As she worked, Warren said, "You did a good job today."

"Thank you." After a thoughtful pause, she added, "I didn't see her go down, but I'm sorry about Agent Ogleby."

He nodded silently.

"Word has it you risked your life dragging her body away from the gunfire after she was already dead. You shouldn't have done that."

"They were using her for target practice. I wouldn't let them."

Cook grimaced at the thought. "I see something larger embedded in your forehead. I need to get it out. Bear with me a little longer."

He nodded.

Using forceps, Cook gently grabbed the foreign object sticking out from the skin and pulled. It didn't budge at first, but with a bit more effort, she removed a piece of plaster from under his skin that was one-inch long and about a quarter-inch wide.

She cleaned all his wounds with facial wipes and Steri-Stripped the larger wound closed. "You're good to go for now, but be sure to have a doctor look at these as soon as possible to be sure I got everything and prevent infection. That large wound might need stitches, OK?"

His mind was already on the mission. "OK. Thanks." Turning his com set back on, he asked, "Has anyone found the lab yet?"

"No, Sir," members of the team responded.

"Keep searching. We won't go anywhere until we get what we came for. Notify me immediately if you find anything even remotely suspicious. Touch nothing that looks like it might've come from a lab. Also, stay on guard for more combatants. There are plenty of places for someone to hide in this building."

Teams of three began carefully inspecting the enormous warehouse. The building was even larger than it appeared from the outside. With a PhD in molecular biology from the University of Virginia, Warren knew exactly what to look for, but the other team members didn't have his expertise.

He quickly realized the first floor served as a warehouse to distribute hotel supplies, such as linens, towels, dry food, and various toiletries. That must have been the front for their organization and also furnished the terrorists with living supplies. The second floor was primarily living quarters with beds, personal items scattered about, and a galley-style mess with two refrigerators and three round kitchen tables.

"You should come take a look at this, Sir," one of the FBI agents said over the com system. "I think I found their command and control center."

When Warren got there, he saw several smashed computers, a conference table, and recently burned debris scattered on the floor that was probably documents the terrorists hastily destroyed. There was also an area with eight monitor screens displaying the surrounding neighborhood of the front, back, and sides of the building. Some had night-vision capability.

"So that's how they spotted us so fast," he muttered. To the agent who found the room, he said, "The cameras for those must be well-hidden. I didn't see a single one, damn it."

"None of us did, Sir."

"Stay here and keep everyone else out. Leave everything as it is for CSI."

"Yes, Sir."

Ten minutes later, Agent Cook announced she found a laboratory facility in a back room on the top floor. Warren sprinted up the stairs, eager to find what they came for.

When he arrived at the doorway, he said, "Follow me and don't touch anything."

Entering the room, he held his breath and scanned the interior. He saw propane tanks, glass flasks, burners, scales, ph strips, aluminum foil, and other equipment thrown about. Within moments, his shoulders slumped, and the intensity of his expression faded.

"Damn it. This is just a meth lab. I don't see what we're looking for."

"That's what I thought, too, but I wasn't sure," Agent Cook replied.

Special Agent Washington, joining them, looked around. "This is probably how they financed their operation."

"Yeah, at least in part," Warren said. "I get the feeling this is a really big, well-funded group. I wouldn't be surprised if they had outside money as well. We'll know a lot more once we start interrogating the prisoners."

Washington nodded. "We've got a lot to learn about this group."

"Let's split up and keep looking," Warren said. "There has to be another lab around here somewhere."

Within ten minutes, Agent Washington found a large metal door set back in a corner of the top floor with a sign over it that read *No Entry! Authorized Personnel Only!* Trying the handle, he found the door locked.

"Sir? I think I found something."

Warren asked quickly, "Got something?"

"I don't know, but I have a funny feeling about this. It's off-limits to most personnel, and the door's locked. All the other doors were open. I thought you might want to be here before I break in."

Warren drew his gun. "Let's take a look. You open it up. I'll go in first."

Washington swung a battering ram at the door, which fell open after a single crushing stroke.

Warren cautiously stepped inside, followed by Washington, who also had his weapon ready. It was dark. Warren, groping for a light switch, flicked it on.

The room lit up to reveal a locker room with two showers, a changing area, and several protective laboratory suits. No one was there.

"You may have found something, Washington," Warren said. "I'll bet this is a changing area for a microbiology lab." He walked over to peer through a single small, thick window set in another door. Inside was a modern microbiology lab with laminar flow hoods, incubators, microscopes, an autoclave, and other equipment.

Seeing no one inside the lab, he holstered his gun. "Bingo. This is no meth lab. Send someone to grab our protective suits from the van. I won't touch theirs, and I sure as hell won't go inside without one."

When they finally entered the lab, Washington was momentarily mesmerized and even a little intimidated by the intricate equipment. He was no moron, but it was well beyond his realm of experience. Warren felt right at home.

"Start taking pictures for the Deputy Director," he told Washington. "He'll want to see a few preliminaries right away. CSI can give him the detailed stuff later. Remember—touch nothing. I'll look for a container that might house the vials."

"I'm not sure what I'm taking pictures of, but I'll do it."

After five minutes, Warren saw a special temperature-controlled container of liquid nitrogen, something often used to store and transport dangerous pathogens. Pulling on special gloves, he cautiously opened the container.

Washington looked at him, gasped softly, and whispered, "Is that it?"

Warren, not answering, took a closer look inside at three small vials. Carefully lifting one, he read the numbers on the label. Those were the pathogens they came for. The vials contained lethal, genetically engineered bacteria stolen from Fort Detrick in Maryland, where the Army housed much of its biological defense program.

He smiled and sighed in relief. "We got 'em."

Washington took several pictures of each vial, as Warren carefully held them up one-by-one and then replaced them in the container.

Warren methodically searched the rest of the lab before calling his boss, Deputy Director Rafael Otero, of the Washington, DC, Counterterrorism Office.

"We have the vials, Sir," he reported.

"Thank God. Had they started to replicate the bacteria yet?"

"I see no evidence of that, Sir. They had a very sophisticated laboratory, and I'm sure they were planning to do it right here in DC."

CHAPTER 3

Despite the praise he received from Deputy Director Otero at the debriefing, Agent Warren felt unsettled, as he worked on his FBI after-action report. A deadly terrorist cell was taken down, and heaven only knew how many lives were saved, but Agent Ogleby was killed, and her family weighed heavily on his mind. The mother of two small children, she had a loving husband.

He was still in the middle of his report when he heard a tap on his door. Expecting it to be a member of his team, he didn't look up, as he said, "Enter."

The door opened, and he heard the footsteps of at least two people enter the room. After a moment, Warren raised his head and was surprised to see the Deputy Director. With him was a tall, silver-haired man in his sixties he didn't recognize.

Warren immediately stood. "I'm sorry, Sir. I thought it was one of my agents. How can I help you?"

Deputy Director Otero, removing his glasses, wiped the lenses clean with a small cloth before replacing them on his face. "I know this isn't a good time, Agent Warren, but I have someone with me who wants to speak to you right away. He says it's quite urgent."

Warren wasn't thrilled about being disturbed with so much to do, but he looked at the tall man, nodded, and smiled politely.

Otero pointed to his companion. "Agent Warren, this is Seth Miles from MI-6." He turned to Miles. "Seth, this is Special Agent Titus Warren I told you about."

Miles grinned and shook Warren's hand warmly. "A pleasure."

"Mine as well." Warren gestured to two chairs in front of his desk. "Why don't you both take a seat?"

As Miles slid into his chair, Warren instinctively began to take the man's measure. He looked intelligent, was impeccably dressed in a dark-gray suit and blue tie, and had a calmly confident look about him that made him seem typically British. Given his age, Warren suspected he held a senior position at MI-6 and probably worked as a liaison with U.S. law enforcement agencies.

Simultaneously, Miles formed his first impressions of the FBI agent. Warren's shaved head, muscular build, and bandaged face gave him a rugged appearance. He looked like someone from an action movie and slightly resembled a young Jason Statham. More importantly, he saw the intelligence behind Warren's piercing blue eyes. Miles knew of the man's short, stellar career as a Delta Force officer and his accomplishments with the FBI's Counterterrorism's Division, and he was acutely aware of Warren's science background, which might be useful.

Warren sat, rested his forearms on the edge of his desk, and clasped his hands. "How can I help you gentlemen?"

Before answering, Miles turned his gaze to the Deputy Director. "Rafael, if you don't mind, I've changed my mind. I'd like to speak to Special Agent Warren alone."

Warren, finding Miles' English accent pleasant, was amused by an outsider telling his boss to piss off in his own building. He watched curiously to see how his boss would react to the strange request.

Otero looked blindsided, yet Warren sensed no indignation. The two radiated friendly familiarity.

"As I said previously, what I wish to discuss is very hush-hush," Miles continued. "The fewer the people in the loop, the better, and all that rot. I have a feeling only Agent Warren may be needed right now. You understand, don't you?"

Otero coughed to clear his throat. "No, I don't, and I don't like it." He gave Warren an appraising look before turning back to Miles. "I guess I'll trust your judgment on this. I wouldn't do this for anyone else, Seth."

Miles smiled in appreciation. "Splendid. Thank you, Rafael. You know I would include you if that were in everyone's best interests."

Otero nodded slightly and looked at Warren. "I want you to give this man your complete cooperation. He apparently has something very important to discuss and says he needs your help right away."

Warren, totally perplexed by the Deputy Director's immediate compliance to Miles' request, was genuinely curious what the Brit had to say. "Yes, Sir."

Otero saw the subtle, questioning look on Warren's face. "Miles and I go way back. We worked together in joint operations for military intelligence in Afghanistan. Since then, we've worked on other joint operations in our civilian roles. Miles is as good a man and as good an operative as you'll ever meet. I trust him with my life." He looked at Miles, then back to Warren. "He saved it on more than one occasion. You should consider his requests as my orders. The responsibility is fully mine if something goes sideways."

Warren scratched his face where one of his wounds itched. "Yes, Sir."

Otero stood and looked at Miles. "Bring me onboard if you think I can help. Will you do that, Seth?"

"Of course. Thank you, Rafael."

Otero nodded to Warren before giving Miles a look as it asking, *Why didn't you tell me this before?* Then he left the room.

Miles' attention returned to Warren. "You have a wonderful Deputy Director. You'll learn a lot from him."

Warren nodded. "I already have."

"From what he told me, he has a great deal of respect and confidence in you."

"Thank you, but let's cut to the chase. Why are you here, Mr. Miles?"

"Call me Seth, won't you? I'll call you Titus, if you don't mind. I'm here, because I think I can help you."

Warren sat back in his chair again and crossed his arms. "Oh? How is that, Mr. Miles?"

"Call me Seth, please. First, I want to congratulate you on your takedown today. Brilliant work. They were a very dangerous lot. I understand you ran down and apprehended one of them yourself."

"My team did a great job," Warren replied coolly, avoiding being sucked in by the compliment. "As for the one I got, well, it wasn't that hard. He wasn't shooting at me, just running way."

After a moment, Warren continued, "I assume you're here about the terrorists. I was planning on interrogating the two we brought in today as soon as I finish some paperwork. That'll be in twenty minutes or so. You're welcome to observe if you like. A third prisoner is in surgery. You can watch that interrogation, too, when she's able to talk."

"I'm certainly interested in what they have to say, but that's not the main reason I'm here."

"No? Then why *are* you here?"

Miles clasped his hands in his lap. "I'm here about you."

Warren's head jerked subtly back in surprise. "Me? I thought MI-6 would have a great deal of interest in a bioterrorist group as sophisticated as the one we stopped today."

"Indeed, MI-6 is interested in them, but we already know quite a bit about the group, you see."

Warren's eyebrows went up. "You do?"

"Quite so. That's what I thought I could help you with. One of your prisoners is Aabis Abdeljour. *Aabis* means lucky. I guess his luck ran out, wouldn't you say?"

"Ha!"

"Anyway, his job was primarily to recruit vulnerable youth in America into his radical Islamic group. That's the one you personally apprehended."

Warren, taking out a pen, began writing notes. "Go on."

"Your other prisoner is Zaad Wafa. He's one of their muscle men, an enforcer. Zaad's not involved in the bigger scheme of things. He doesn't have much upstairs, if you know what I mean. However, I wouldn't be surprised if he was the one who killed one of your agents today. He's an expert marksman, top notch I understand." After a short pause, he added, "I'm very sorry about your agent, by the way."

"Thank you. If I find out Zaad took the shot that killed one of my agents, I may have a private word with him when the cameras are off." Warren shook his head, as if trying to clear his thoughts. "I'm sorry. That was out of line. I haven't had time to process her death."

Seth nodded. "I understand. I probably would be thinking the same thing if I were you."

Warren rubbed the stubble on his chin. "You seem to know a lot about this terrorist group. What's your take on the woman in surgery? Do you know who she is, as well?"

"She goes by the name Aafreen Khalaf. Her birth name, before converting to Islam, was Shakima Harris. Basically, she's a malcontent from New York City who failed in school, failed to keep a job, and, I suppose, was looking for something. Maybe she was trying to find herself. Who knows? I'm afraid she found trouble."

Warren nodded.

"Now she'll pay heavily for her choice. As best as we know, she's been in this group for less than three months. She doesn't have much of a role, really, except for being one of Dr. Mabrouk Dada's playthings."

"Dr. Mabrouk Dada. Is he the scientist behind their operation? We had very limited intel before the raid."

"Precisely. The late Dr. Dada was an instructor of microbiology at the University of Maryland who arranged for the deadly bacteria vials to be stolen from the Army laboratory. He caught MI-6's attention when he lived in London two years ago."

"The late Dr. Dada?"

"Yes. He was unfortunately killed in the raid today. I've already identified his body."

Warren, stunned that Miles knew so much more than he did about the terrorist cell, tried not to show his surprise. "It would've been nice to interrogate this Dr. Dada, but I won't lose sleep over his death."

"Nor will I."

Warren slowly tapped his pen against his desk and considered his two options. He decided to come clean. "To tell you the truth, Deputy Director Otero got the tip only yesterday that they were the ones who stole the lethal bacteria from Fort Detrick. We knew very little about them before we struck this morning. Given the threat level, there was no time to waste. We knew only that the information came from a reliable source."

He paused, rubbed his head, and grinned. "Of course. How could I be so stupid? Our reliable source was you, correct?"

Seth smiled and shrugged. "Who's to say, hmmm? However, international collaboration in battling terrorism is part of my job. That's why I'm officially here to see you."

"Well, thank you." He paused again. "That's why you're officially here to see me, but there's clearly more. The other reason is why you sent Deputy Director Otero away, correct?"

Miles cleared his throat with a cough. "Quite so."

Warren waved his hand to indicate the man should continue.

"You're the lead investigator on another important case, are you not?"

"All of my cases are important." He rubbed his chin and stared at the man. "Which one are you talking about?"

"Unbeknownst to the general public, there are two U.S. congressmen who are missing at this time. You're trying to learn what happened to them. Is that not correct?"

Warren, wondering how much Seth knew about that case, said slowly, "Perhaps."

"Come now, Titus. I hope you have realized by now that nothing much is a secret anymore, especially from MI-6. One congressman is from Northern Virginia, a divorced, ex-Naval officer who is a Republican and who serves on the powerful Appropriations Committee. The other fellow is an openly gay civil rights lawyer from San Francisco, who is a rising star in the Democratic party. They have little in common, but both disappeared under mysterious circumstances within weeks of each other. That's why you're heading up both cases, correct?"

Truly stunned, he wondered if Miles knew all that on his own or had been told by Deputy Director Otero. "I can't say if any of that is true or not. If it were, why is MI-6 so interested in U.S. congressmen?"

"Good question. The answer is I believe your case and the one I'm working on are the same."

Warren stood and walked to a small refrigerator to take out a bottle of water. He looked at Seth. "Want one?"

"No, thank you."

He returned to his desk and sat down. After drinking from the bottle, he eyed Miles and felt very curious. "Go on."

"You'll need to follow closely, because things are a bit murky, even to me. You see, I believe there's something much bigger going on than just two missing American congressmen."

His eyebrows shot up in surprise. "I'm sure I'm way down the national pecking order from you, Seth, but it seems to me that two missing congressmen is a pretty big deal."

"I'd normally agree with you, but I believe there's a more-ominous and widespread problem, I'm afraid. You see, there are other prominent people missing all around the world, including three from Great Britain."

"We both know there are always people missing somewhere in the world. I assume you think they're connected somehow. Have you found a pattern?"

"Not exactly, but I *have* found what you might call a common denominator."

"A common denominator. OK. I'll bite. What common denominator."

"A man named Dr. Dao Lin."

CHAPTER 4

Titus slowly swiveled his chair from side-to-side, pondering the name. "Dr. Dao Lin? I've heard that name before, but where? I can't quite place it."

"You probably heard it on the telly. He's a business tycoon who's been in the news quite a lot lately because of his humanitarian work."

Titus' eyes widened. "That's right. I remember now. He's a rich businessman who donated medical supplies to third-world countries or something. Isn't that right?"

"That's him."

"He sounds like a really good guy." Titus' brow furrowed. "Is he missing, too?"

Seth chuckled. "No. You may want to wait to decide whether you think he's a really good chap or not after I give you some additional information about him."

"OK. Shoot."

Seth scratched his head. "Before I do, perhaps I could trouble you for a drink? Maybe something stronger than the aforementioned water?"

Titus thought it was pretty early in the day to ask for liquor. "I wish I could, but I'm afraid I don't keep alcohol in the office. When we're in this building, special agents like me always have to be ready to go into the field on a moment's notice. I hope you understand."

Seth looked a bit embarrassed. "Yes, of course. What was I thinking? You're an active field agent. I've been hanging around too many desk jockeys in my old age. They always have special refreshments on hand."

"If you say so."

"Yes, well, getting back to Dr. Lin. Let me begin by saying he's a third-generation Chinese-American who started his career as a PhD-level pharmacologist from the University of California at San Francisco. He quickly moved into the business side of pharmaceuticals and eventually became an entrepreneur par excellence who started and owns Dynasty Pharmaceuticals. It did reasonably well but wasn't much to write home about."

Titus nodded.

"Then, about eight years ago, Dynasty Pharmaceuticals suddenly grew exponentially and is now just one part of an international corporation called Dynasty Enterprises. Consequently, Dr. Lin not only became a multibillionaire but one of the wealthiest men in the world."

Titus leaned back in his chair. "Wow. Dynasty Enterprises is owned by one person? It's huge."

"It is."

"What exactly led to the transformation of an average pharmaceutical company into a corporate conglomerate?"

One of Seth's eyebrows shot up. "That's an excellent question, but I remain quite vexed about it. What concerns me is that they did it without producing any new blockbuster drug. His company's wealth seemed to shoot up dramatically after he started a consulting division called Dynasty Consulting, or DC, for a very select group of clients.

"What the division does, however, I'm not sure. It certainly makes a lot of money, and the missing people all paid Dr. Lin large amounts for DC services, and then they donated additional money to his humanitarian organization, Dynasty Global Foundation, or DGF."

"Who are these select people?"

"His clients are a virtual who's-who list of power and success—Wall Street investors, OPEC leaders, military generals, lawyers, doctors, CEOs, journalists, financial managers, professional athletes, politicians—you name it. It's quite remarkable, really."

"Were the missing congressmen paying for Dynasty Consulting services?"

"Indeed, they were, and donating to DGF like all the others. That's why I said our investigations might be one and the same."

As Titus rubbed his chin in contemplation, there was a knock at the door. He raised a hand to stop Seth's conversation for a moment and said, "Come in."

Jamie Kramer, Titus' administrative assistant, peeked around the door. "Excuse me, Sir. Agent Washington says he's ready to interrogate the prisoners if you are."

Titus looked at Seth and decided he needed to sort out what the man was telling him first. "Tell Agent Washington I'm still occupied. The prisoners can stew a little longer. Hopefully, I can join him in an hour or so."

"Yes, Sir."

"Thanks, Jamie." He saw a look of gratitude on Mile's face.

"Thank you," Seth said. "I'll try not to keep you much longer."

"You were telling me that this Dr. Lin has a consulting service and foundation that the missing people are all connected to, correct?"

"Quite so."

"Perhaps that's important, and perhaps not." He kept his tone noncommittal. "You say you don't know what Dynasty Consulting actually does for its customers despite the large sums they pay?"

"I haven't a clue." Frustration showed in Seth's tone. "I've approached several of them, but they were very elusive or even denied any affiliation with Dr. Lin. It seems to be some sort of big secret. His clients were successful before getting DC services but were much more so afterward. That's true of your congressmen, too."

"Could he be supplying them with illegal performance-enhancing drugs, like steroids, human growth hormone, stimulants, or something like that? You said he was a pharmacologist."

"I thought of that. The only problem is that no PED has shown up in urine drug screens for any of his clients. The professional athletes are particularly screened, but others have been, too, for various reasons. I don't see how one PED could help people with such different professional needs. Everyone, from lawyers to NFL players, all benefit significantly from whatever Dr. Lin does for them. It's puzzling."

"If it's not a PED, I'm at a loss."

Seth ran a hand through his silver hair. "I am, too, I'm afraid. I do have one interesting lead. Charles, my IT man, discovered that shortly before Dr. Lin began Dynasty Consulting, he began communicating with an industrial spy in China. You know the kind, a cyber-spy who hacks into companies' digital data and communications."

Titus sat up straighter. "Now that's interesting."

"I'm sure you're aware of the massive amount of industrial espionage the People's Republic of China does to boost their economy and defense programs by stealing innovative technologies from the West."

"Of course. We lose hundreds of billions of dollars from it. You think this Chinese cyber-spy provided information that led to Dr. Lin's inexplicable success?"

"That's my theory. We discovered that Dr. Lin secretly paid this fellow a few million dollars, so the information must've been quite valuable. That's how we discovered the spy, by following the money, not that it was easy. It was very difficult, even for Charles. The transactions were covered up extremely well. Dr. Lin is no one's fool. Charles was eventually able to piece it together, and Dr. Lin's sophisticated cover-up only added to my concerns about him."

"Do you know who the spy is?"

"His name is Li Cheung. We also know after the payoff, he fled China and now lives in Paris, France. Charles says he currently goes by the name Mu Wong."

"Sounds like this Charles guy is quite an asset."

Seth nodded. "You're quite right. He's a high-tech genius. Fortunately for me, we've been friends since we were young lads at Cambridge."

Titus tapped his hand lightly on the desk. "Do you have any idea what sort of information Cheung sold to Dr. Lin?"

"Not at all. That's the question, isn't it? I think that's where we begin."

Titus smiled. "We? You want me to help with your investigation?"

"That's why I'm here."

Titus knew they finally reached the point of the meeting. "I heard what Deputy Otero said, but I can't recall agreeing to anything just yet. I have a lot of work to do around here. We just brought down a major terrorist cell, and we have to milk these people for all the information we can get before it loses its value."

Seth nodded. "Yes, of course. Why don't you tidy up things here while Charles and I confirm where Cheung is living? I'd like you to speak to him and find out exactly what information he gave Dr. Lin. Rafael assured me he'll cover for you whenever you need to go out on an assignment for me."

Titus, silently considering the request, sighed. "Something doesn't add up. Why me? Why not someone at MI-6?"

Seth grimaced. "Yes, well, that would seem the thing to do, wouldn't it? That's where things get a bit, well, sticky, I'm afraid."

"Sticky? What do you mean?"

Seth stood and slowly walked around the room. You see, Titus, I'm here of my own accord."

"What do you mean?"

"My investigation into Dr. Lin isn't a sanctioned MI-6 operation, nor is it approved by the FBI, CIA, or any other governmental organization. Not even Rafael knows why I need your help."

Titus stood and walked closer to Seth. "You're saying this is a rogue operation?"

Seth, taking a deep breath, knew his efforts would pay off or collapse in the next few moments. "I'm afraid so. My agency thinks I'm here about the terrorists, nothing more."

Titus' expression became even more perturbed. "Is Rafael aware you want me for an operation that's off the books?"

"He does. I told him that much before we gathered."

Titus eyed him curiously. "He's OK with that?"

"He is."

"You know I'll check with him."

Seth shrugged. "Of course. I would expect nothing less."

"Why isn't this a sanctioned mission?" he asked apprehensively. "Is it because Dr. Lin is wealthy? Is it because he has friends in high places?"

"That's part of it, but there are other considerations as well."

Titus' mind raced with questions. "Why can't you use someone from your own organization, even if it's off the books? You hardly know me."

"Come now, Titus. As you Americans say, this isn't your first rodeo. I think you know exactly why."

He stared at Seth for a moment and slowly nodded. "You don't trust them—any of them. You're a spook, but for some reason, you're the one spooked."

Seth grimaced again. "You're quite right, I'm afraid. I have reason to believe that MI-6, the FBI, the CIA, and Homeland Security may all be compromised. I trust no one except for a handful of very highly selected people, and no one in my own organization except for Charles."

"You realize that makes you sound a bit paranoid." He was only half-joking. "Do you have proof that you can't trust your own people or those in the other organizations?"

"In my world, there's scant proof of anything, Titus. Spooks like me, as you say, must often act on instinct and speculation alone. We live in the shadows, so there are usually missing pieces to every puzzle. In this case, I know there are top-level people in each of these organizations who are linked to Dr. Lin. Whenever I opened an investigation into Dr. Lin or Dynasty Consulting, I was quickly and forcefully shut down. I won't bother you with the details, but it was so forceful that I'm lucky I still have a job."

Titus didn't reply.

"That has never happened on any other cases in my many years of service. This operation is off the books, because *it has to be.*"

After a moment's thought, Titus said, "It sounds like you're taking a huge professional risk to still be investigating this guy."

"Very much so. The more pushback I get from my superiors, the more I'm convinced something is terribly wrong."

Titus nodded.

"Do you believe in intuition, Titus?"

"Sure."

"I know something very big and very wrong is going on with this Dr. Lin. I don't believe he is who he appears to be. I know in my gut that he has something to do with the missing people. They are all ambitious people with little to no connection with each other. They come from different countries, so the connection between them isn't obvious. I can't count on someone else to investigate. They'd probably be shut down, too."

Seth's calm demeanor was slowly eroding, revealing a lot of frustration.

"You should also know that my home and office computers were bugged during my last attempt to investigate Dr. Lin. I could never find out who did it, but it confirmed for me that something is wrong. Perhaps I'm getting paranoid in my old age, but this situation scares me." He looked seriously into Titus' eyes. "I don't scare easily."

Titus, sitting down, considered the situation carefully.

"There are too many powerful players, too many missing people, and too much industrial espionage and overt cover-up." Seth shook his head slowly. "Something big is going on, and I can't just let it go. My problem is I don't have a clue what it all adds up to, and I'm very limited in what I can get away with in the field without raising suspicion. I desperately need a covert operative to help me with this investigation."

Titus sat back in his chair, his mind still sorting things out. "Why didn't you ask Deputy Director Otero to help you instead of me? You two are obviously tight and have worked together before."

Seth, sitting down, slowly regained control of his emotions. "I considered that. I trust Rafael completely, but what I really need right now is a talented field agent. He hasn't been a field agent for some time. Given his position, he wouldn't be readily available much, anyway. It wasn't feasible to use Rafael, but, when I described the kind of person I needed, he pointed me directly at you. At the last minute, I decided to keep my old friend entirely clear of this operation, since I didn't need his help, anyway."

Titus saw Seth look at a photo of himself standing armed with two other members of Delta Force at a training base.

"With your Delta Force and FBI experience, I know you can handle yourself in the field. Rafael says you're as good a field agent as he's ever seen." Seth chuckled. "Not that you heard it from me."

Titus smiled, unable to conceal his pleasure at the rare compliment from his boss. "Heard what?"

"Reading between the lines, I'll bet you did some black ops with Delta. There are too many gaps and vague explanations in your record for all the medals and awards you received, including a Silver Star. A person with black ops experience is exactly what I'm looking for. On top of that, you got a PhD in molecular biology after leaving the Army. You went to the University of Virginia, I believe. That makes you even more valuable to me."

Titus nodded.

"Why did you do that, by the way? Get a PhD."

He thought about the unexpected question for a moment. "I wanted a career change and thought the life of a college professor looked pretty nice. Even before the ink was dry on my diploma, Deputy Director Otero showed up and recruited me to this position. The PhD took four-and-a-half years, and I guess I missed the action by then, so I took it."

"I need someone with your skill set I can trust. Rafael trusts you completely, which means I do, too. You're also off the radar with no prior connection to me. We have the perfect cover to meet regularly in our antiterrorism efforts. You can see why I'd love to have you onboard, if you're willing."

Titus said, "Rogue missions are dangerous things to get involved in. I don't do such things lightly."

"I understand, and I won't lie to you. You'll be investigating a very rich and powerful man. I know how powerful people can be. They can be ruthless, well-protected, and dangerous. Many will stop at nothing to get what they want and protect what they have."

Titus nodded.

"This could be extremely dangerous for you if anyone catches on that you're helping me."

As he listened, Titus tapped his fingers lightly on the desk.

"No matter what Rafael said, I won't bring you onboard without your being aware of the danger and fully willing to accept the risks." Seth waited anxiously. He had nowhere else to turn.

"OK," Titus said. "I think you're onto something important that may even be connected to my missing congressmen. If Deputy Director Otero trusts you enough to give you a blank check with my time, then count me in."

Seth sighed in relief. "Bravo. Thank you. Please believe me when I say it doesn't make me happy that I might be putting you in harm's way. I would...."

Titus raised his hand to stop him. "I understand the risks. If anything happens to me, it's on me, not you."

Seth smiled. "Thank you for that. Rafael told me you were a stand-up chap. I see he was right."

Titus nodded and grinned. "I doubt he'd call me a chap, but I hope I can help."

"I'm sure you can, but we must be careful. We can't underestimate our foe. We should assume there are prying eyes and ears everywhere. I can't emphasize that enough."

Titus agreed.

"We must stay totally off the grid. We'll have no electronic communication about this whatsoever. We will communicate at secure locations in person or use national and international untraceable burner phones. I'll get you plenty to use in the next few days. If anyone else joins our little team, they'll communicate only with burners, too."

"That's the way I want it."

"Charles is our primary source of information. The computers he uses to investigate Dr. Lin are highly sophisticated, his own, and utterly untraceable. Your first assignment will be to go to Paris to question Cheung and find out exactly what information he sold to Dr. Lin."

"What are the rules of engagement?" he asked curtly.

"Use whatever means necessary to get the information we need, no more and no less. Cheung was a Chinese spy, a traitor to his country, and our only lead. He'll be on his guard and possibly dangerous, but we need to know what he knows. Can you do that?"

Titus smiled. "I can."

CHAPTER 5

When Titus returned to his apartment, it was late, and he was exhausted. The apartment was small, but he loved it for its wonderful location in Alexandria, Virginia, with a view of Arlington Cemetery.

He went to the bathroom to tend his facial wounds. Ammo, his Bengal cat, jumped onto the edge of the tub and purred. Titus rescued Ammo after a hurricane, when attempts to find the owners failed. It was just him and Ammo, and she was immediately at his side whenever he got home.

Titus knew exactly what she wanted. "OK, OK. I hear you." He turned on a slow stream of cold water from the bathtub for her to drink. "There you go, Little Beauty."

Ammo always insisted he pet her first, then she took her time before her first drink.

Titus peered at himself in the mirror. He looked like he'd been in a bar brawl with all those cuts and bruises, which made him remember when he did such things and laughed at his youthful foolishness.

He took off the Steri-Strip and was thankful the largest wound held together without stitches. After he washed all the wounds, he applied topical antibiotic on the cuts and finally replaced the Steri-Strips on the wounds that needed them. He promised Agent Cook he'd have a doctor examine his face, but that wouldn't happen unless an infection set in or the larger wound separated.

He waited for Ammo, who took her time. Finally, she moved on, and he turned off the water. He felt a sudden sharp pain in his right shoulder. He thought it was from scuffling on the concrete floor when he took down the terrorist who ran. He hadn't slowed down long enough to notice the shoulder pain before.

Titus moved the arm enough to loosen it and assure himself no muscles were torn or bones broken.

After he was satisfied that the pain wasn't anything he had to worry about, he took off his shirt and went to his workout room. It would have been a small dining room for most people, but he had no need for one. Instead, he set up a bench press with weights nearby, attached a pull-up bar to a doorway, and had a crunch apparatus. There were also weights for biceps curls.

He felt a bit hungry but thought he'd get in his exercise before eating. He did most of his regular routine except for the pull-ups because of the sore shoulder.

Afterward, he walked into his kitchenette and made a vegetable shake with added protein. As he stood by the kitchen counter to drink, he noticed a light blinking on his landline phone. He wanted to ignore it, but he decided to make sure there was nothing important, given the day's events.

The first two messages were from organizations asking for money. He had his own favorite charities and erased them before they finished speaking. The third was a political message, which was also erased.

The next message was a sweet female voice with an Indian accent that he immediately recognized.

"Titus, this is Sabri. You're late. Call me when you can."

The final call was from her, too.

"I assume you forgot about our dinner date tonight. I'll eat and probably go to bed early. I hope everything is OK. 'Bye."

Her tone wasn't angry, but neither was it particularly friendly.

"Damn," he mumbled.

He quickly returned the call, hoping she hadn't gone to bed yet. She didn't answer until the fourth ring, and he wasn't sure she would answer at all.

"Hello?"

"Sabri, this is Titus."

"Titus? Titus who?"

"Yeah, I know. I messed up." He ran his hand over Ammo's head, who came up beside him on the counter. "I deserve that, and I'm sorry. It's been a long day. I forgot about our dinner tonight. I'll make it up to you. I promise."

"I heard on the news there was a shootout between the FBI and some drug dealers today. Was that you? Were you there?"

He knew he couldn't reveal too much, but he said honestly, "Yes. I was there."

"Are you OK?"

"Yeah, I'm fine, just some cuts and bruises."

"Thank goodness. Reporters said some people were killed, but they didn't give details."

"One of my agents was killed, along with several suspects."

"Oh, no! One of your agents?"

He sighed. "I'm afraid so. I've already spoken to her family, so I guess I can tell you now. That's one reason I was so distracted at work, not that I have any excuse for not calling you. We worked late, and I really didn't think about our dinner date until I heard your voice on the phone."

Her tone softened. "Can I bring you something? I've eaten, but I have some leftover lamb curry. It's good, if I do say so myself."

He was tempted, but he said, "That sounds great, but I think I'll pass. I walked in a few minutes ago and haven't even showered. Also, I have a lot on my plate tomorrow, so I better go to bed early tonight."

"Of course. I'll let you go then. Good night, Good Lookin'."

He smiled. "Good night, Beautiful. I'll see you soon."

After he hung up, he carried Ammo to the sofa to give her some attention before bed. He thought about Sabri, as he petted his cat. She was a beautiful woman with long, black hair, a nice figure, and dark-brown eyes who was in Washington, DC, with a trade delegation from India. He met her by chance at his favorite coffee shop and struck up a nice conversation about local history after he saw her reading a book on the Civil War. They went out only a few times but seemed to have some chemistry. He knew he better enjoy her company while he could, because she would fly back to India soon, and he didn't know if he'd ever see her again. That was typical for many people living in the DC area.

He also thought about Ogleby's death and the conversation he had with her distraught husband. He reviewed every detail of the operation repeatedly, wondering if her death could have been prevented.

"Well, Ammo, what do you think? Could I have done anything differently today to save her life?"

Ammo, rubbing her head against him, purred.

"Yeah, you're probably right. I can't think of anything either. Sometimes, bad things happen. I'll miss her, though." He stroked the cat's head some more. "Thanks, Ammo. What would I do without you?"

The last thing he did before going to bed was text his younger brother, Steve, who was on vacation but had a cattle ranch an hour west of Nashville.

How is Rosemary Beach?

Love it. U need to come next year.

Why would I do that? Except for no beautiful beaches, soothing Gulf water tides, cool sea breeze, and pretty women in bikinis, DC is almost identical to Rosemary Beach.

LOL. Think about it. You haven't been on a real vacation in years.

Will do.

After a little more catching up, Titus went to bed. Unfortunately, he tossed and turned all night. Old nightmares returned of Army buddies he saw killed in battle and the faces of those he killed in combat. The nightmares had almost faded, but Ogleby's death brought them back.

The following day, Agent Warren met with Deputy Director Otero and discussed Seth's request for him to fly to Paris.

He concluded by saying, "I wish I could tell you more, but...."

"I understand. He already told me about his request," Otero replied from behind his large desk. "I meant what I said yesterday. You have my permission to do whatever he needs you for. Just let me know when you have to be away, and I'll cover for you here."

"Thank you."

The director ran a hand through his salt-and-pepper hair. "I want to be clear that I'm not forcing you to work with Seth. As you said, this is off the books. There are inherent dangers in that sort of work. Just do what he asks if you think it's right. That's all I ask."

Warren nodded.

The Deputy Director saw the concern on his agent's face. "I know you're worried about your work here. Don't. Retrieval of the vials was the most-critical part of the mission, and you did a great job. The rest is cleanup. Agent Washington will take charge whenever you're away. I'll tell your staff that you're on special assignment here and there for a while. That's all they need to know, and that's all you need to tell them." He paused. "Are we good?"

"Yes, Sir."

"Good. I said a lot of good things about you to Seth, so don't make me eat my words."

Warren let a small grin come to his face. "I won't let you down, Sir."

"You'd better not."

As Warren left the office, he stopped abruptly and turned back. "You mentioned that Mr. Miles saved your life."

"That's right."

"May I ask how?"

Otero hesitated, then motioned Warren back into a chair. "As you know, some things aren't easy to talk about, but I'll tell you this once, OK?"

"OK."

"Seth and I were in several firefights together, but one was particularly bad." He studied the top of his desk for a moment, then took a deep breath. "When I was a young officer in Army intelligence, Seth was my counterpart in the British Army. Eventually, we were assigned to work together in Afghanistan. Our job was to find Afghans in the country who were willing to feed us intelligence."

"Sounds dangerous."

Otero nodded. "It was, for both us *and* our informants. My greatest fear wasn't to die but to be captured by the enemy. I heard some pretty gruesome torture stories, and I wasn't sure how well I'd hold up. I even had nightmares about it." He paused. "I still do."

Warren nodded. He heard the same horror stories.

"I was very lucky to be working with Seth. He was more experienced and just plain smarter than I was. He taught me a lot."

Titus leaned forward in his chair. "So what happened?"

"One of my so-called informants sold me out and led me right into an ambush. Before I knew it, five heavily armed Afghan tribesmen surrounded me, and we got into a wicked firefight. I was wounded and running low on ammunition. Slowly and methodically, they began closing in on me. I was absolutely terrified."

"Holy shit," Warren muttered.

Otero took a deep breath before continuing. "Fortunately, Seth came out of nowhere before they got to me and started blasting away. I wasn't much help. I was out of ammo, so I threw rocks. I did whatever I could to distract them until I could find a weapon. Seth had the drop on them, but he was outnumbered. It was a ferocious shootout."

Warren was almost on the edge of his seat.

"With little or no help from me, he killed them all and got me out safely. He took a bullet in the arm. If we'd lost that firefight, we both would have been captured and tortured. Ever since, Seth drinks too much, and I rarely get a good night's sleep."

Titus nodded, remembering his own nightmares and excessive drinking after he first left Delta. "I understand. I'm very happy he saved you, Sir."

"I owe him my life. I'm forever in his debt. Since then, we've worked many assignments together. We trust each other like brothers. Seth knows the important work you do here. If he has something for you to do that he thinks is even more important, well, it must be pretty damn important."

CHAPTER 6

Dr. Lin stood behind a black podium outside the Lin Grand Hotel in Manhattan. A tall, lean man, he reeked of confidence. He was well-dressed in a dark-gray Armani suit and black tie. Microphones from camera crews for numerous TV and cable networks surrounded him, as he began speaking.

The billionaire smiled as he surveyed the growing crowd. Seeing a host of enthusiastic reporters and camera crews present, he cleared his throat to begin.

"Thank you all for coming today. It's good of you to be here. As you know, for the last few years Dynasty Global Foundation ships have provided medications to sick children in poor countries in Africa, South America, and Southeast Asia. I'm here today to announce a new humanitarian initiative by the Dynasty Global Foundation. Specifically, DGF will donate one billion dollars to the United Nations to combat climate change."

Cheers and applause broke out from the spectators and several reporters.

One reporter from a large cable network asked enthusiastically, "Dr. Lin, did you really say one billion dollars?"

"That's right—one billion dollars. The world has given much to me, and I feel the need to give back to the world community."

Most of the reporters beamed with delight, as they furiously tried to ask more questions.

"I believe climate change is the single most-important danger to mankind today. We can't let this imminent threat continue any longer.

We must take more-aggressive and immediate action. It's my sincere hope that this money will not only help combat climate change but also bring about world unity, as we fight against this horrific danger as citizens of our planet, Earth."

More applause and cheers erupted. His words were broadcast live on many stations in the U.S. and worldwide.

One reporter from a local New York station asked, "When do you plan to distribute the money to the United Nations?"

"I'm making the final arrangements with the UN. It will probably be made in quarterly distributions over the next year."

He fielded several more friendly questions.

The last question came from an attractive blonde woman who hadn't been applauding the announcement. "Dr. Lin, Fox News has discovered information that shows that the Dynasty Global Foundation has raised many billions of dollars worldwide and yet only a small fraction of that money goes to the poor it was meant to help. Can you comment on that?"

He didn't look at her or reply.

"We've also found documents showing that large amounts of DGF money has been spent on lavish conferences, high staff salaries, expensive DGF office buildings, and other extravagant administrative costs. Can you tell us why so much donated money is being spent on those costs instead of being used for the people it was meant to...?"

Before she could finish, he waved good-bye to the crowd and walked away. With a big smile, he shook hands with the Mayor of New York City and the Secretary General of the UN. Neither the questions asked by the skeptical reporter, nor his lack of response, appeared on most mainstream TV or radio stations.

Fa Shen, Dr. Lin's gigantic six-foot-seven-inch personal bodyguard, took his arm and guided him through the excited crowd into the plush hotel. In addition to Fa Shen, several more bodyguards were stationed nearby. All were large, muscular men, wearing black suits, who were well-trained in armed and unarmed combat. Competency, secrecy, and complete loyalty were required off all Dr. Lin's bodyguards, as well as his other staff.

They went up the elevator to the penthouse suite, where he stayed whenever he visited New York. His business empire hired people of every race and nationality, but his personal staff were quite different. They were exclusively of Chinese or Southeast Asian descent.

Once inside the suite, Mei, the senior female household servant, immediately came up to the billionaire and bowed respectfully. She wore a traditional form-fitting Chinese *cheongsam.* "Is there anything you need, Master Lin?"

"I'll have tea over by the balcony window."

She bowed again. "Of course. I'll arrange it immediately." She signaled Biyu, one of her subordinates, to fetch his favorite Camellia tea quickly.

Like Mei, Biyu and many others of Dr. Lin's household staff were snatched from severe poverty, often from slums in Southeast Asia. His strict demands and their limited freedom were never questioned or considered a heavy burden. Most considered themselves to be extremely fortunate to work for a rich American who gave them food, shelter, and safety from the dangers of life on the street.

"Would you like a change of clothing?" Mei asked softly.

"No. I'll change after I've had my tea."

Mei bowed politely.

When Biyu returned with the tea, Dr. Lin was already seated on one of his plush, leather seats looking out at the New York City skyline. He took the tea and stared out the massive window without acknowledging the servant.

His penthouse, occupying the entire top floor of the Lin Grand Hotel, was paid for by Dynasty Global Foundation funds. The décor was immaculate, with valuable Chinese weapons, books, rugs, and paintings. All were carefully chosen by his buyers to remind him of the Chinese empires of the past and the powerful men who ruled them. He cared nothing for the communist government that currently ruled

China and from which his grandparents fled. Even so, he traveled to China often to do business and visit the ancient historical sites he loved.

He wore Western clothes in public, but the traditional Chinese *changshan* at home. He loved ancient Chinese culture. Secretly, he longed to grow a traditional Fu Manchu mustache with a long, goat-patch beard, but he was a practical man who knew a clean-shaven face appeared infinitely friendlier to Westerners.

He relaxed with a contented smile. His grand plan just reached the next level. Several more carefully executed steps were needed, but great rewards never came easily. Anything or anyone who got in his way would be removed.

He motioned for Jinjing, one of his most-competent administrative assistants.

She hustled across the room as quickly as she could. "Yes, Master Lin. How can I assist you?"

"There was a reporter at the press conference who questioned me about Dynasty Global Foundation's finances."

"Yes, Master."

"I want you to find out who she is and send a surveillance team to monitor and record her activities. I want them to find evidence of wrongdoing—accusations of racism, taking bribes, or perhaps abusing drugs."

"Yes, Master Lin. Nothing would damage a reporter's career more quickly than accusations of racism or bribery, but may I be so bold to say, I believe drug abuse may not have the same affect. People accused of such things merely go to rehab and then are right back at work. It usually does no permanent damage." She tapped a finger to her lips, thinking. "Perhaps accusations of sexual perversion might be useful."

He shook his head. "No. Such accusations are as ineffective as drug abuse. There are no sexual boundaries anymore in America. I want her disgraced and her career permanently destroyed. Do you understand?"

"Yes, Master Lin. What do you want done if they find no such damaging evidence against her?"

"Then set her up, of course. Record a tempting bribe or coerce her to make a racial comment. Use false witnesses if you have to. My agents are free to use whatever means are necessary. I don't want her killed, but her career must be destroyed quickly. I don't need reporters like her at my press conferences or investigating my finances."

Jinjing bowed. "Yes, Master. It will be done as you ask."

After Dr. Lin finished his tea, a household servant helped him out of his suit and into a long, yellow *changshan* shirt and black pants. The yellow color represented his Chinese heritage, which his mother told him about often when he was growing up. She repeated many times that his blood was that of past Chinese emperors, and his family was nothing like the despicable communist leaders who made their family flee China. The stories of his ancestors always filled his imagination with excitement and wonder as a child.

He made some phone calls to his investment staff. After forty-five minutes, he summoned his meeting coordinator. "How many interviews do I have today?"

"Only twelve today, Master Lin," she replied. "The last is scheduled for three o'clock in the morning. Seven are new recruits, and the rest should be ready to take their next step of Commitment in the Society of the Wake."

It wasn't a society in the usual sense of the word. Except for his immediate advisors, members never met together. It was a secret organization of his clients, whom he categorized in his mind according to their level of usefulness and trust.

"Who's first on my schedule today?"

"Her name is Janet Clayton, a lawyer with Welch, Banks, and Stein here in New York City. She's been receiving treatment for nearly two years. Here is her file." She paused to let him review it quickly. "She's been in the waiting room for about two hours."

He continued reading. The file was impressive, and it was indeed time for her to take the next step. He dismissed his scheduling coordinator and walked into the room where Clayton waited.

She sat on a couch with her eyes fixed on a large TV screen on the wall, listening to a cable channel that featured a commentator and several guests discussing Dr. Lin's huge donation. Clayton turned off the TV the moment Dr. Lin entered the room.

"Good day, Ms. Clayton."

She stood, smiled, and offered her hand. She was slender, of average height, with stringy brown hair. Not particularly attractive, she stood straight and confident.

He ignored her hand and sat in a large, comfortable chair across from her.

Clayton shrugged off the slight and sat down. "It's nice to see you again, Dr. Lin. It's been a long time."

"Yes, it has. I trust you've been receiving your medication on time."

"I have, thank you." After a short pause, she added, "I've been making my payments on time, just as you asked."

"Including to the Dynasty Global Foundation, I assume."

"Of course."

He clasped his hands in front of himself and leaned comfortably back in his chair, quietly studying her.

She felt his dark-brown eyes seem to penetrate her soul, but she didn't flinch. She'd been around the superrich before, and she assumed his stare and ignoring her hand was part of a power trip. Neither impressed her.

"You have a beautiful place here," she said. "I love your Chinese décor. It's very elegant."

"Thank you. I find reminders of ancient Chinese culture most inspiring."

"I was just listening to discussions on the TV about your incredible donation. The commentators are beside themselves with your generosity and concern for our planet."

He smiled politely. "You think my performance went well?"

"Oh, yes. Your performance was excellent." After a moment, she added, "We both know it was complete bullshit."

His eyebrows shot up. "What did you say?"

"I said we both know it's complete bullshit."

His expression revealed nothing but a hint of curiosity. "Why do you say that?"

Clayton sat back nonchalantly in her chair, as if she confronted billionaires every day. "Because we both know those reporters are idiots. They reflexively support anyone who says what they want to hear. You obviously wanted to befriend them in a serious way, so you told them something they loved to hear."

"You think so?"

"I do." Although she was confident, she shifted in her seat a bit. "I understand that a billion dollars is a huge sum, but by supporting one of their precious causes, like global warming, they instantly became your friends." She smiled. "In fact, you just became one of the best friends most will ever have, given the amount of money you plan to give away."

He didn't reply.

"I believe your donation, however, was a means to an end. Now they'll never ask you the tough questions and will even protect you against negative publicity. You made most of them your protective allies. I mean, well I should say I assume, this is all one big PR stunt."

He still didn't reply.

Her green eyes stared deeply back into his. "I don't know you well, Dr. Lin, but I know how you value money. You'd never waste so much on environmental apocalyptic hysteria unless you had an ulterior motive."

He stared at her without expression, tapping his index fingers tip-to-tip.

Clayton, taking a deep breath, felt her heart rate increase, as she wondered if she estimated him accurately. Still, she continued, "I don't see you as a climate-change doomsayer."

Slowly, a faint hint of a grin came to his face. "You're quite right, Ms. Clayton. I'd hoped it wouldn't be so obvious."

She sighed in relief, glad he hadn't been angered. "Don't worry. It wasn't. I'm just a damn good lawyer. I question what everyone says, especially when there could be ulterior motives. Those reporters you spoke to...."

She shook her head. "Let's just say, not so much. As I said, the talking heads on cable news are going on and on about your great humanitarian effort. Hell, they might start calling you Saint Lin, the man who saved the planet."

He smiled.

The bold young lawyer knew she took a risk, but it paid off. She felt euphoric and more confident. She was actually bonding with the great Dr. Lin. "Do you actually plan to donate all that money to the UN?"

He waved his hand dismissively. "Of course I will. I've publicly made myself accountable for it."

"They will absolutely love you for it. Just think about all the public figures who rail on and on against global warming and were glorified for it. They didn't give away any money, much less a billion dollars."

He eyed her curiously. "What would you say were their real motives?"

Clayton knew he was testing her. "Obviously, like you, they do it mostly to help themselves. Media outlets make money on their countless stories about global warming. Liberal politicians get votes and financial donations for fighting for the cause. Entertainment celebrities get precious publicity for their phony outrage. None of them are scientists or know a damn thing about climatology other than what they read or tell each other."

"I agree. Don't forget the climatologists themselves managed to pull themselves out of obscurity, and they benefit from large research grants, easy publications, and mandated jobs."

Clayton grinned. "It's all so obvious. I can tell you, Dr. Lin, I have countless friends who are blind to it. They just accept what the mainstream media tell them, hook, line and sinker."

He smiled broadly. "That's exactly what I'm counting on. Climate change is the perfect enemy for heroes like me."

She laughed. The conversation was fun. "Funny you should use the words 'climate change' instead of 'global warming.' I always thought that change of wording was pure genius."

"Why is that?"

"Because that slight change of wording made the scientific findings and arguments against global warming meaningless, because change *always* happens. Climate change enthusiasts will claim to be right no matter if world temperatures get warmer or colder." She raised her hands in feigned excitement. "Wow! They said it would change! How smart they are!"

He couldn't help laughing, something he rarely did.

"I try to tell them that climate change began when the earth began, and it will end when the world ends. The earth has gone through cycles of cooling and warming repeatedly." She shrugged. "They don't listen."

Dr. Lin realized he was spending too much time with her and hadn't yet touched on the purpose of their meeting. "I must confess that part of me hates getting up in public and speaking nonsense, even if it does bring me the PR I want." He shrugged. "But I do what I have to do, and I guess psychologists would say that my confessing my true thoughts to you is cathartic." He grinned. "I do feel better now, but let us move on. I'm impressed with you, and I have exciting plans for your future."

Clayton leaned forward in her chair. "What exactly do you have in mind? You've already been a big help to my career."

"A couple years ago, I selected you as a client into what I call the Society of Wake. As you know, it's a carefully chosen group of talented people who have already achieved a lot, but I felt they could do more with my help. I picked you, because I saw your accomplishments at Northwestern University and then at Columbia Law School. You're doing quite well at your law firm, are you not?"

"Oh, yes. Very well. My colleagues can't believe what I've been able to accomplish. By literally working day and night, I've left them all in the dust."

"Good. I invested in you, Ms. Clayton, and I hope you won't disappoint me, as we move forward."

She shook her head. "I won't. I assure you. I'm at the top of my game, thanks to you. What do you have in mind?"

"It's time for you to move up to the next level in my exclusive organization."

"I'd be honored. What would that entail, exactly?"

"You know that I run a very large organization with many busi-ness interests. I need many talented lawyers like your to help me with corporate contracts, lawsuits, public relations, and so on. That's espe-cially true here in New York City, where many of my financial transac-tions take place."

She nodded enthusiastically.

"I want you personally to handle all the business I send you. The amount of work I have in mind will require you to make me your sole client. In return, I'll see to it that you become the youngest part-ner in the history of your law firm and very wealthy. Does that interest you?"

A broad smile spread across her face. "Yes, of course! Thank you for your confidence in me. What do you mean by sole client?"

His expression of joy quickly vanished, and his usual harsh ex-pression returned. "Are those words difficult to understand? It means all of the work you do from this point on will be for me alone. Even without sleeping, you'll have no time for anyone else. I'll expect the usual payment for the Wake Formula, but you'll be expected to increase your donations to the Dynasty Global Foundation from five percent to ten percent of your take-home pay. Obviously, you can write off such donations from your taxes, and the amount of money you'll make will far exceed the increase in donations."

Clayton sank back into her chair. "That's a lot of money, Dr. Lin. I have other clients I'd like to keep. It's never a good idea to have all your eggs in one basket."

Dr. Lin didn't reply.

Seeing disappointment on his face, she felt like a child who failed a parent. "I promise I'll do a lot of your work myself and see to it that my personal interns and other lawyers in my firm take good care of you. I could increase my donations to DGF to seven percent, I suppose."

His expression became stone cold. "That's not the response I wanted to hear, Ms. Clayton. I'm happy you're a tough negotiator, but now you're negotiating with me, and I don't negotiate."

She refused to be derailed. "Maybe I can make it eight percent for the foundation, but I can't promise you more than fifty percent of my work time. I don't believe having one client is in my best interests or something I wish to do."

"You must not have heard me say that I don't negotiate, Ms. Clayton. If I don't have your complete cooperation in this matter, your treatments with us are completed, and your inclusion in the Society of Wake is over."

She raised her hands in mock surrender. "OK, OK. You win. If you must have ten percent, then I'll give it to you, but as I said, I must have fifty percent of my time for other clients. I think that's a fair deal. Don't you agree?"

He stood. "I do not agree. I hired you, because you're smart and a tough negotiator. You apparently aren't smart enough to know that no one negotiates with me. Your treatments are now ended. You'll tell no one about the medication you have received, about our society, or even about our conversation today. If you do, there will be severe consequences from which you will never, *ever,* recover. Do you understand?"

Clayton was so stunned, she couldn't speak. Everything changed in an instant.

"I demand total cooperation and total loyalty from every person in the Society of Wake. I thought I made that quite clear from the beginning."

Her shoulders slumped, and her face turned pale, "But, but...."

"You're dismissed. I have many other lawyers to see today." He motioned to one of his bodyguards. "Please escort Ms. Clayton out."

Her eyes widened in shock. "Please, Dr. Lin! I didn't mean to...."

The large guard grasped her arm before she could finish and led her from the penthouse to the street.

The billionaire called his administrative aide over. "Ms. Clayton will ask to see me in a few weeks. Do not agree to a meeting right away. I want to break her completely before we rebuild her confidence and renegotiate terms of our agreement."

"Yes, Master Lin."

"When she begins begging to see me, arrange for her to meet me at my estate in Texas." He rubbed his chin. "I find that my home is the best place to clarify my business relationship with stubborn clients."

"Of course, Master Lin."

"Who's next?"

"Federal Judge Aaron Holden. He looks very weak and is now in a wheelchair."

"Is he ready to take the next step?"

"I believe he's ready to do whatever you ask, Great One."

CHAPTER 7

Except for some mid-Atlantic choppy weather, Titus' flight to Paris was uneventful. Upon arrival at Charles de Gaulle Airport, he took a taxi to a nondescript hotel a few blocks from where Cheung lived.

Shortly after checking in, he changed into running clothes. He planned to observe Cheung long enough to discern his daily routine, identify his contacts, and estimate potential dangers. He would grab the man, extract the information he needed, and leave France as quickly as possible.

He expected Cheung to be cautious. A person didn't escape the People's Republic of China, especially if he was an industrial spy, without constantly looking over his shoulder, so he expected Cheung to be armed and his residence to be well-secured.

Titus didn't shave for several days before his trip to help obscure his facial features. Before he left his room, he put on a black baseball cap with an Eiffel Tower logo and pulled it down over his eyes. He looked at his reflection in the mirror. He looked like any one of hundreds of American tourists in Paris. He left for a run to begin his reconnaissance.

With the information from Charles, Titus found Cheung's first-floor flat without any problem. The shades were down, and he had the impression no one was home. He was tempted to look inside but decided it wasn't worth the risk of someone noticing him.

It was almost dinnertime, and he saw several small cafés in the area. He casually walked around, checking menus that were posted outside, while also watching for Cheung. He took his time but didn't see anyone come or go from the flat. Eventually, he became hungry and chose a small bistro for dinner with a clear but distant view of Cheung's building.

Titus ordered beef bourguignon with garlic mashed potatoes and a glass of wine. He ate slowly, enjoying the meal, taking as long as possible to finish another glass of Pinot Noir. After he finished, and with no sign of Cheung, he paid his bill and moved on.

He circled several blocks before returning to the same area from the opposite direction. It was dark, and he took time to read several outdoor menus again. Eventually, he chose a café that had several unoccupied outdoor tables from which he could observe the flat. Titus, sitting at a small table, ordered chocolate mousse, eating it slowly, acting like a tourist enjoying a beautiful night in Paris. Listening to live music coming from inside the café, he watched attractive women walk by, like any other single man would.

After lingering as long as he could, he reached for his wallet. Before he could take it from his pocket, he saw Cheung coming toward him from a side street. He held the hand of an attractive woman, although neither spoke. Her blue dress was cut low at the top and high off the bottom, revealing an excellent figure.

Titus shoved the wallet back into place and brought his water glass to his lips to obscure his face. The two walked right past him without paying him any attention. The couple didn't stop at any cafés but went straight to Cheung's residence.

He paid his bill and walked casually around the area again. Forty-five minutes later, the woman came out alone and walked back the way she came. He considered following her but didn't want to complicate the situation. With his target's location confirmed, it was only a matter of figuring out when and where to intercept him.

For the following two days, Titus watched Cheung from a discrete distance. His reconnaissance revealed two things. First, Cheung had no obvious routine other than he frequented the same strip bar every evening. Second, the woman he saw with Cheung was one of the strippers at the bar.

Once or twice, Titus had the uneasy feeling he was being watched. One time, a Chinese man seemed to look toward him a bit too often. At another time, a different Chinese man perhaps too quickly looked in the other direction when Titus glanced at him. Was this part of Titus' battle-hardened instincts, or had Seth made him paranoid? He couldn't decide.

He was more comfortable with Army reconnaissance, using camouflage and looking through high-powered binoculars, but this was different. He was in the open, trying to remain hidden merely by looking like everyone else. He was left feeling vulnerable, so he had to stay on high alert. If trouble came, he had to be ready.

Assuming Cheung's flat would have a state-of-the-art security system, Titus decided to seize the man one night on his way back from the strip club. He carefully assessed Cheung's usual route and chose a location near a Dumpster where several abandoned buildings gave plenty of places for a quick interrogation.

He inspected each building. One was locked down tight. Another was potentially useful but looked structurally unstable, with holes in the floor and ceiling.

He was more fortunate with the third building. Breaking the lock easily, he discovered a deserted office that seemed structurally sound and perfect for the job. He scoped out two escape routes in case of trouble. Cheung was an industrial spy, not a field operative, so Titus felt confident he could abduct him without too much trouble even if Cheung was armed. Still, he had to be careful.

The opportunity came the following night. It was raining, which meant fewer people on the streets and limited visibility. Both were to his advantage. Cheung headed home alone from the strip bar right on time. No one else was in sight. Titus wouldn't get a better opportunity, so he slipped on a nylon mask and waited.

As Cheung passed the Dumpster, Titus silently sneaked up behind him, grabbing his right arm and twisting it forcefully behind his back while covering his mouth with the other.

In French, Titus whispered, "Come with me quietly if you want to live."

Cheung struggled for a moment, but Titus' grip was too strong.

"Stop trying to get away," Titus growled in French, "or I'll break your arm."

He guided the man into the abandoned building. As he closed the door behind them, Cheung twisted and tried to free himself again.

Titus reasserted his hold and raised Cheung's arm higher.

"Ahhh!" he moaned in pain. His face twisted in fear when he saw Titus wore a nylon disguise.

Terrified and defeated, Cheung stopped struggling but shook with fear.

Titus, quickly frisking him, found a switchblade hidden in his boot but no gun. He slipped the blade into his pants.

Nervously, Cheung asked, "What do you want? Take my money. I don't have much, but you can have it all. Just don't hurt me."

"I don't want your money," Titus replied in English. "Keep your voice down. I know who you are, Li Cheung. I know you speak English, so drop the French."

Cheung's eyes widened, and he said in French, "My name is Mu Wong. I am but a lowly businessman from Taiwan. You have the wrong person. I have nothing of value. I swear it. You have the wrong person!"

Titus slammed a knee into the man's groin, sending him to his knees. He yanked him back to his feet. "I don't have time for this. You speak English, German, French, and Chinese. You were an industrial spy for the People's Republic of China. I know everything about you, Cheung, so stop wasting my time. I told you to speak English."

"OK, OK. I speak to you in English, but my name is Mu Wong. Look at my driver's license. Maybe I look like someone else. I know you Whites think all Chinese...."

Titus punched him hard in the stomach, and Cheung crunched over, trying to breathe.

"Listen carefully," Titus said between clenched teeth. "Just like they say in the movies, we can do this the hard way or the easy way. Every time you lie to me, I'll hurt you. Each time will be worse than the one before. I don't want to do this, but I will. Do you understand?"

"Yes, yes," he gasped.

"Good. I have only a couple of questions. If you answer honestly, I'll let you go unharmed. Each time you lie, I'll hurt you."

"Who are you? You are American, are you not? Are you CIA?"

"I'll ask the questions, but I'll tell you who I'm not. Fortunately for you, I'm not CIA, and I don't work for the Chinese government, although I'm sure both want to get their hands on you."

"Why are you after me, then?"

"I'm here for my own reasons. I just want the answers to a few questions. That's all."

Some of the terror left Cheung's face, and his body relaxed a little. "OK, OK. What do you want to know?"

"You had correspondence with a Chinese-American named Dr. Dao Lin just before you left China. He paid you a lot of money for information. I want to know what information you gave him."

"I don't know a Dr. Lin," he said frantically. "I left China because of political persecution. I swear, I...."

Titus broke the little finger on Cheung's right hand. He screamed in agony, as his finger bent sideways at an odd angle.

Titus covered his mouth to stifle his screams and whimpering. In an almost-growling, muted voice, he said, "Shut up. You have nine more fingers. Every time you lie, I'll break another one. I can break them fast and easy like that time, or I can do it slowly and much more painfully. You can't stop me. I will get what I want from you one way or another. It's up to you how much pain you go through before you talk, understand?"

"Yes, yes," he moaned.

"Good. Now what was the information you gave Dr. Lin that was worth so much money?"

He was about to speak when Titus heard laughter and covered Cheung's mouth with one hand, holding his arm with the other, as he listened to several people walk by, clearly drunk.

After they passed, he eased his grip a little. "Choose your next words carefully. You spied on my country and betrayed your own. I don't like you, and I won't hesitate to break more fingers. Now talk."

"OK, OK. I'll tell you what you want to know."

"Were you or were you not an industrial spy for the Chinese government?"

"My job was to hack into foreign pharmaceutical companies' digital files and communications for the Chinese government."

"In other words, you were an industrial spy."

"That was my job. That was what the Chinese government trained me to do. I didn't care about it. I had excellent language and computer skills, so they trained me for that. No one asked me if I wanted to spy on other countries. I was told to do it. It was my duty to obey. Your country has spies, too."

"Go on."

Cheung momentarily thought of Dr. Lin. How he envied the American millionaire. Cheung had been excited at the thought of escaping China and starting a new life in the West.

"I said go on," Titus said, snapping him from his thoughts.

"Our government was looking for new drugs to copy. I met Dr. Lin many years ago at an international pharmaceutical conference in Beijing. He told me he owned a pharmaceutical company in America, and we spent a lot of time together at that meeting."

"Why?"

"It was my job. At first, I planned to spy on his company. Eventually, however, I became fascinated by the wealthy American and discovered we had many interests in common. We even shared some distant ancestors."

"What interests and ancestors?"

"We both have a love for the old, imperial China and respect our ancient forefathers. He talked about it for hours and discovered we were both taught that we were descendants from the royal family of the Tang Dynasty. It was one of the greatest Chinese dynasties. I didn't say anything right away, but eventually, I trusted him enough to hint what I did for the People's Republic of China."

"Go on."

"He was excited and said he would pay me a lot of money if I sent him promising information that led to new drugs. We worked out a scheme how I could secretly get the information to him and how he would pay me. I told him I wanted to leave communist China and thought it was my way out if I were paid a lot of money for a new drug. I'd seen western Europe once at a pharmaceutical meeting and dreamed of living there ever since."

"What information did you give him?"

"We discussed several research drugs, but he showed little interest in most of them. He was only excited about information concerning a sleep drug. I sent him all I had on that, including email, scientific data, and recorded conversations with the scientist and his family. That's the drug he paid me so much for. I eventually gave him everything he needed, and he gave me enough money to sneak out of China. Now I live here."

"A sleep drug? You want me to believe he paid you millions of dollars for information about a sleep drug?" He slowly began bending another finger backward.

"Stop! Stop!" he screamed. "It's true. I have no reason to lie anymore. I'm telling you everything I know!"

Titus stopped before he damaged the finger.

"He was interested in the sleep drug. I swear it! I don't know why it was of such value to him. Maybe Americans can't sleep. I don't know. He wanted every piece of information I could find on it. He was very excited. He became obsessed over it."

"What was it called?"

"It had no name. Most drugs don't get names until they go to market, but the scientist sometimes referred to it as WF."

"What company was developing it? Who did you steal the information from?"

Cheung hesitated, then said, "It didn't come from a pharmaceutical company. The formula was taken from a scientist named Dr. Burrus. I'll always remember that name—Dr. Frederick Burrus at the Burrus Research Institute in Frankfurt, Germany."

"Why was this sleep drug so valuable?"

"I don't know, believe me. I really don't. I'm a linguist, a computer expert, and an information specialist. I'm trained to understand just enough medical information and basic science to guess what might be profitable to China. If I discovered something interesting, I passed it on to my superiors, and they passed it on to our scientists. I know only that the information had something to do with sleep. I didn't and probably couldn't analyze the data myself."

"That's it? That's what you want me to believe?"

Cheung nodded emphatically. "Yes, I swear it!"

"What are you not telling me?" He began bending another finger.

"That's all I know! I wanted enough money to leave China and live peacefully in Europe! Please, let me go! I told you everything."

Titus slowly released his hold on the man. The story was so odd, it rang of truth. "If I find out you lied to me or withheld any information, I'll be back for you. After I'm done with you, I'll turn you over to the CIA or the Chinese government. Do you hear me? Think again. Is that all you know?"

"Yes, I swear it."

Titus didn't know if the information was valuable, but he sensed he'd get nothing more from Cheung and so released him. "Go."

Cheung tore out the door and ran down the street. Titus watched him fall on the wet sidewalk. He got up, looked back to see if he was being followed, and darted off again.

CHAPTER 8

As he walked back to the hotel, Titus broke the switchblade and tossed it into the gutter. The last thing he wanted was to be caught with a weapon in a foreign country. He kept watching for trouble, but none came.

Once back in his room, he called Seth on one of the international burner phones and told him everything Cheung said.

Seth was clearly underwhelmed by the information. "That's it? That's all he had to say?"

"That's it."

"You're sure you got everything out of him?"

"As sure as I can be. The conversation became a lot more believable after I broke one of his fingers."

"Yes, I guess it would. OK. I have no idea how this fits into our investigation, but Charles and I will look into it." He paused and added, "I probably don't need to tell you this, but now that you made your move, assume the worst and leave Paris as quickly as you can. We'll meet when you're back to discuss things further."

"What do you mean, assume the worst?"

"At least one person knows you're there and knows about Dr. Lin. Maybe he doubled back and followed you to the hotel. It's happened to me before. Cheung may want to take you out. Dr. Lin has contacts everywhere."

"Ten-four."

"See you soon."

"Yeah."

After a quick shower, Titus lay on his bed and looked up at the ceiling, thinking about the night's events. He didn't like breaking the man's finger, but it would heal, and it had to be done. No matter how he thought about it, he couldn't fathom how the information might help anyone. Perhaps the relationship between Dr. Lin and Cheung was interesting, but it was a dead end. Maybe Seth and Charles would find something.

Either way, he wouldn't figure it out that evening. He would catch a flight out of Paris first thing in the morning and get back to his job trying to squeeze all they could from the terrorists they caught.

He reached over to turn off the light beside his bed. He was about to roll over and go to sleep, but Seth's warning came to mind. He got up to take a last peek out the window for caution's sake. Nothing moved. It was quiet down below on the street, and the rain stopped.

Just as he was about to turn away, he saw a Chinese man tucked inside a doorway almost out of sight. Had he seen him before? He might have on the second day he surveilled Cheung's flat.

Titus barely peeked through the blinds, cautiously watching the man. What concerned him most was that the man repeatedly glanced at Titus' window before ducking back into the doorway to stay out of sight.

Seth was right, he thought. *Maybe I am exposed.*

He quickly threw his few possessions into a small duffle bag, pulled on a thin, waterproof jacket and the black Eiffel Tower baseball cap, and carefully looked out the shades again.

The Chinese man was still there, intermittently looking up at Titus' window in the dark.

He turned the light on near his bed and left the room. With a suspicious man out front, he decided to slip out another direction, taking the steps to the basement before looking around until he saw what he wanted. The building had a loading dock in back, and a hotel employee was standing on it, smoking.

After a minute, the man tossed the butt to the ground and went back inside. Titus slipped onto the street. When he looked around without seeing anything of concern, he began walking.

He quickly noticed another Chinese man tucked into a clothing store doorway across the street. Pulling his baseball cap lower over his face, Titus slowed, wondering if he should continue or turn around. There was nowhere to hide for at least half a block.

Watching for a moment, he saw the second man studying the hotel, then he suddenly turned toward Titus. Their eyes met, and Titus saw recognition in the man's eyes before he turned away.

Lowering his head, he increased his pace, reached the end of the block, and turned the corner. Moments later, he heard the man's footsteps following, so he walked faster.

So did his pursuer.

Titus turned another corner, but the man turned the corner, too, and began running, his footsteps splashing on the wet sidewalk.

When the man was close enough, Titus spun to face him and asked in French, "What do you want?" His expression and stance weren't of fear but of defiance. He hoped to scare the man off.

The Chinese man stopped and stared at him without speaking. Titus, seeing he carried a small club in one hand, resembling a nightstick, wished he still carried the switchblade.

Suddenly, the man raised the club and rushed him, swinging violently. Titus ducked with a speed that surprised his assailant. A second swing knocked off Titus' hat, but he kicked the man's side, then added a follow-up kick to his groin.

The groaning man dropped to his knees. Titus' fist slammed against the man's left ear, and he fell senseless to the ground. Titus stood over him, watching for a moment, as rain began falling again, dripping off his head and clothes. When he saw no other movement, he checked the man's pockets for a wallet or gun without finding either.

He wished he could interrogate the man, but he was out cold. He picked up his wet hat and pulled it over his soaked head. A quick glance around showed no one else.

He walked briskly for several blocks, making many twists and turns, before he hailed a cab for the airport. On the drive, he booked a red-eye flight from Paris to London, where he would catch another flight to Washington, DC. He glanced out the back window a few times without seeing anything suspicious.

When he got out of the cab, he called Seth and told him what happened.

"That's interesting," Seth said. "It gives me more hope than your first call. If people were watching you and came after you with harmful intent, perhaps we're onto something."

"I'm happy my being attacked pleases you," he said with mock sarcasm. "It's concerning to think they had at least two people watching me when I barely got started on this."

"This is how the mission has gone for me all along. We must constantly be on the alert for enemies we know nothing about."

"I'll find my way back as soon as possible. You find out what you can about the information Cheung gave me."

"I will. Stay on guard."

"I'll take precautions."

As soon as he got off the phone, Titus ditched the hat, found a restroom, and shaved, tossing his jacket and shirt in the garbage. From his duffle bag, he pulled out a white shirt, thin black tie, and black-rimmed glasses that had no magnification. Putting them on, he checked his reflection in the mirror.

"Not bad," he mumbled.

We went to the terminal waiting area, where there were more people waiting for the flight than he expected, but he saw no one of concern. He sat directly across from a young woman trying to manage a baby in a stroller and two adolescent children who were tossing a small yellow ball back and forth.

"You have quite an entourage with you," he said in French to the flustered woman.

"They're all eager to get home and see their papa," she replied. "Please let me know if they're bothering you."

"They're no problem at all." He settled back in his chair.

Shortly before boarding, he saw two Chinese men come into the terminal. One was the man he saw below his window. The other was someone he didn't recognize.

Titus winked at the oldest child. "Throw me the ball."

The child complied, and they played catch. He played and laughed with the children, as the two men neared.

Boarding was called. When the woman stood, he walked over to her. "Let me help with your bags. You push the stroller."

The woman smiled and agreed. Together, they looked like one big happy family. The plan and disguise worked perfectly, because the men barely glanced at them before moving on.

The long flight home gave Titus plenty of time to think. He was watched and then attacked. Why? Who were they? Were they connected to Dr. Lin, or were they Chinese agents after Cheung to whisk him back to China? Did they know who he was? Had someone in the States compromised his mission?

He had many questions, but unfortunately, no answers.

CHAPTER 9

"Here he comes," the pharmaceutical plant Operations Manager said to his assistant, as Dr. Lin stepped down from the helicopter. "The big man himself."

"You mean here comes trouble, don't you?"

"Yeah, that's exactly what I meant. God, I hate these inspections."

The plant was only thirty minutes from his west Texas ranch by helicopter, but Dr. Lin rarely visited there anymore. The inspection was unannounced, and every division director was asked to drop everything and attend him.

An entourage of administrative assistants, security guards, and plant executives surrounded Dr. Lin, as he toured the plant. Every eye stared at him wherever he went. He didn't mind. He loved the attention.

He asked many astute questions in each department but revealed nothing of his inner thoughts. His expression remained stone cold. Occasionally, he whispered to one of his personal assistants. As designed, the overall effect was quite unnerving to everyone at the plant.

Dynasty Pharmaceuticals produced more generic drugs than any company in the world. The only non-generic drugs the company sold were developed by other pharmaceutical companies before DP acquired them. Dr. Lin briefly considered having a more-intensive research division, but he decided that the tens to hundreds of millions of dollars needed to produce even a single new medication and get it through the FDA wasn't worth the effort or the financial risk. Besides, the only research he was truly interested in was hundreds of miles away in a hidden underground facility at the far edge of his vast estate.

The multibillionaire smiled to himself, as he recalled that owning such a large pharmaceutical facility had once been his life's dream. Now it meant little compared to his ultimate ambition. He occasionally inspected the company's largest properties, but mostly only to remind those who worked there he was boss. Today was no different.

At the end of the tour, Dr. Lin held a private meeting with each division director to discuss productivity, costs, plans, and shortcomings. The directors were unanimously amazed at his knowledge and insights, especially considering they knew he had so many other properties and business endeavors.

At eight o'clock that evening, Dr. Lin held an executive conference with the division directors and other senior executives. He sat at the end of the long mahogany conference table with a large brass logo of Dynasty Pharmaceuticals on the wall behind him. On the opposite was a large painting of the company's founder, himself. He enjoyed seeing that painting. It showed him staring intently straight ahead with the Great Wall of China in the background.

Everyone's eyes were on him, and it was relatively quiet in the room, with tension dampening out the usual banter and small talk that occurred before most conferences when he wasn't there.

After the last person arrived, Dr. Lin opened the meeting. "Thank you for coming. Overall, production at this facility is functioning at an adequate level. We continue to be the largest producer of generic medications in the world, and this particular plant continues to be profitable."

Heads nodded around the table, and several of them grinned. His opinion carried a lot of weight, so any compliment from him meant a great deal.

After discussing the financial aspects of the facility in greater detail, Dr. Lin said, "I have only two major administrative changes to make at this time." He gazed around the large table until he saw the two people he was looking for. "Mr. Howell and Ms. Berry, your services will no longer be needed at Dynasty Pharmaceuticals."

Both employees were stunned. The room fell silent, and faces became expressionless.

James Howell, the Director of Sales and Marketing, spoke first. "I...I don't understand. Are you saying I'm fired?"

"That's correct," he replied matter-of-factly.

"But sales are good. As you said, we still lead in the generic medication industry."

Dr. Lin remained impassive. "As I told you at our meeting earlier, Mr. Howell, I have the highest standards. We are indeed leading all of our competitors, but several are catching up in percentage of sales. Dynasty Pharmaceuticals must not only be expanding its total sales but also extending its lead in percentage of the market. That won't happen without innovation and fresh ideas in sales and marketing. I'm sure you understand. Thank you for your service."

Sweat beaded on the man's forehead. Looking around the large table for support, he found none. Most of the other executives lowered their gazes to avoid his eyes or turned away when their gazes met. Their fear of Dr. Lin was far greater than their loyalty to any coworker. No one wanted to be next on his list.

"And me?" Ms. Berry, Director of Human Resources, asked in a squeaky but angry voice. "What exactly have I done wrong?"

"Human Resources spending is excessive, Ms. Berry. The unnecessary waste of funds is your responsibility, as we have already discussed at our divisional meeting."

"You did, but I never thought that meant you would fire me. I can make the changes you insist upon. You don't have to let me go."

He placed his hands flat on the table. "I'm sorry, but I do. You should have considered cost reductions before you needed to be told. I do not appreciate people spending more of my money than necessary on things that reap no return. Thank you for your time at DP, but I will no longer need your services."

"You can't do this!" she said in indignation. "I had no warning of being let go, and I did nothing wrong. Don't you know that the financial rewards of Human Resources is indirect and comes from employee contentment?"

"I know more than you think, Ms. Berry. I also see how differently we view things. You say you've done nothing wrong after I carefully explained earlier that you're wrong. You spent my money in ways I don't agree with. You'll receive three months' severance pay, but you must go." He turned to Mr. Howell. "You will receive the same severance pay."

The room was eerily silent for what felt like hours but was only a few minutes. No one moved.

Finally, Dr. Lin said, "You are both dismissed from this meeting and should clear out your offices immediately."

Ms. Berry was the first to stand. "You'll be hearing from my lawyer. This is sexual discrimination."

"Is that what you think, Ms. Berry? Then what about Mr. Howell? Perhaps he is really a female, too? Gender can be so complicated these days."

Her face reddened with anger, and her emotions seethed.

"No, I don't think he is," Dr. Lin said in a sarcastic tone. "So I must conclude that you think I discriminate against both males and females? Is that right? If I discriminate against both, I wouldn't have much of a workforce, would I?"

Looking at him in disgust, she crossed her arms over her chest.

Dr. Lin looked around the table. "Has anyone here ever heard me say a word against employees for being female or male?"

Heads obediently shook.

"I'd like each of you to answer that question verbally for the record. State your name and if you've ever heard me say anything discriminating against females or males."

They all did as they were told.

Berry fumed with increased anger each minute. "They have to say no, because you're a controlling dictator. You're a tyrant! We all know it. This isn't fair. You'll hear from my lawyer."

He coolly tapped his fingers on the beautiful table. "That is fine, Ms. Berry. For every lawyer you hire, I will hire three. The battle will take years, cost you a fortune, and you will lose. I suggest that you spend your time and money on finding another job rather than trying to fight me. Now, any recommendation you might have received from Dynasty Pharmaceuticals is forfeit. I don't tolerate insults from my employees."

"You bastard!"

He ignored her and looked at Mr. Howell, who hadn't moved. "Do you wish to complain about discrimination as well, Mr. Howell?"

Stunned and frightened, he stood to leave on shaking legs, barely able to utter the word, "No."

"That's good. Perhaps we'll provide you with a recommendation to help you find new employment."

"Thank you."

Dr. Lin waved his hand. "You may both leave now. The rest of us have work to do."

Howell walked out, but Berry stood with arms crossed, her eyes bulging in fury.

Dr. Lin looked at Fa Shen and nodded toward the woman. The huge Chinese bodyguard came over, took her arm, and walked her to the door.

Even in her rage, she couldn't free herself from his grip. "This is abuse! He's hurting my arm! You can't do this!"

Dr. Lin chuckled. "Be gentle with her, Shen. I don't want to hear complaints about physical brutality from her lawyer." After a moment's pause, he added in a playful tone, "And Ms. Berry, please be gentle with Shen. I'm sensing an inner hostility about you that I didn't realize existed before our little chat. Please do not become violent and hurt him. He's really just a big Teddy Bear. Your behavior is obviously very threatening and will be documented as such."

Dr. Lin sighed and shook his head in amusement after Berry was escorted from the room. He gazed at the others, who seemed startled and were as quiet as church mice. Even the plant's Executive Director looked abashed.

Dr. Lin looked amused. "Don't look so frightened. No one else will lose his job today."

Seth Miles and Charles Newman couldn't imagine how a stolen sleep formula could explain anything, but they didn't let their prejudice interfere with doing a thorough investigation of the new information.

After living behind a panel of sophisticated computers for several days, Charles found something very interesting. He told Seth about it, who quickly arranged a meeting with Titus.

Titus chose to meet in an old, family-owned bookstore in Arlington that he frequented often. Books surrounded them at the back of the store, as they faced each other for a private discussion. Only a few other people were in the store, all of whom Titus recognized from earlier visits.

"First of all," Seth began, "we haven't found any novel insomnia medication produced by Dynasty Pharmaceuticals or any of its affiliates. They manufacture the common insomnia medications but nothing special."

Titus grimaced. "I knew Cheung's story didn't make much sense, but it was so unbelievable that I believed him. You know what I mean? He could have come up with something a lot better than that if he wanted to lie to me. He stuck with the story even under serious threat." He sighed. "Maybe I was too soft with him. I fell for his whining and begging. Now I have to go back to Paris and get the truth out of him, and this time, I won't be so nice."

Seth smiled knowingly, remembering his own impatience when he was younger. "Hold on. Your enthusiasm is impressive, but let me finish. You Americans are much too impulsive."

Titus fidgeted in his seat and rubbed his chin in thought, fighting the urge to return to Paris immediately.

"You see," Seth continued, "we took a good look at this Dr. Burrus fellow."

"Anything come of it?" he asked hopefully.

Seth smiled. "Indeed."

"So tell me. I'm all ears."

"Actually, there's quite a lot to tell. First of all, his full name is Dr. Frederick Caver Douglas Burrus."

"That's a mouthful."

"It is. He's a very interesting chap. He earned both a PhD in neuroscience and an MD from the medical school at the University of Tubingen. If you aren't familiar with European schools, Tubingen is a world-class institution in Germany."

"I've heard of it."

"Anyway, after he completed his formal education, Dr. Burrus moved to the States and spent four years of training in the psychiatric residency program at Duke Medical School in North Carolina."

"Awesome creds."

"Indeed. Afterward, he became a professor of psychiatry and neurology at nearby University of North Carolina Medical School. He stayed there a few years, during which time he married an American geneticist named Isabella. The two moved to Germany, where he became a senior neuropsychiatric researcher at the newly established Burrus Research Institute."

"Did you say the Burrus institute, as in Dr. Burrus?"

"Quite so. The institute was founded by his parents. He came from a remarkable family. His father is a very accomplished physicist, and his mother is an American-born and trained neurosurgeon."

"Wow. Nice lineage."

A woman came their way, looking through the stacks. The stopped talking and glanced at a couple of books they took off the shelf. The customer must have just come in, and Titus didn't recognize her. He gestured Seth to be on guard.

After a few minutes, the woman looked at Titus and smiled warmly. He looked into her eyes and smiled back, then looked down at his book.

She slowly moved away. Titus watched her carefully. Soon afterward, she seemed to find what she wanted, paid for two books, and left the bookstore.

"Were we made?" Seth asked softly.

"I haven't seen her here before, but I didn't get that impression. I think we're good. If I'm wrong, I'm carrying."

Seth nodded. "So am I."

"You were saying Dr. Burrus came from a rich family?"

"Quite so. And if brain power wasn't gift enough, his father made millions from patents based on his research in new forms of energy production. With some of that money, they started the research institute that bears the family name."

"Anything particularly helpful to us about this Dr. Burrus?"

Seth leaned forward. "He just happened to have written a number of research papers on, of all things...."

"Let me guess. Sleep."

"Bingo."

Titus leaned forward. "That's interesting. If I'm not mistaken, you seem to be speaking of him in the past tense. Is he dead?"

"I'm afraid so. That's where the story gets even more intriguing. Dr. Burrus was murdered."

Titus' expression stiffened in surprise. "Murdered? The plot thickens."

"Indeed, it does. From the reports Charles found, it appears that a powerful bomb blew his laboratory to bits, and everyone in it was killed. What's most interesting to me is that this happened one week after the transfer of money from Dr. Lin to Cheung's secret account."

"You think the bombing had something to do with the information Dr. Lin obtained from Cheung? It seems he didn't want anyone else to have the same information."

"Exactly. The two events must be related. The timing of the money transfer and the murder are too perfect to be a coincidence. Not long after Dr. Burrus' death, Dynasty Consulting was formed, and Dr. Lin's personal and corporate fortunes increased exponentially. To make matters even more compelling. Dr. Burrus' wife and children seem to have vanished, too."

"Do you mean lost or killed?"

"I don't know, nor do I know what it means."

Titus leaned back in his chair with a sigh. "I wish I could have spoken to him. He could be the key to this whole investigation. What do we do now?"

"I'm not sure. I suppose we do the next best thing."

"Meaning?"

"Perhaps we should speak to his parents. After all, they founded the Burrus Research Institute and knew him best. They should have some idea what he was working on and why all these myste-rious events happened."

"We could also ask some pointed questions of his closest pro-fessional colleagues."

"All of his direct laboratory collaborators died in the explosion. We could check to see if there were other scientists he corresponded with who might offer some information. The problem remains that we must be very discreet. We can't take a shotgun approach. No one must understand what we are investigating and why. No connection can be made with Dr. Lin."

"So what does that mean, exactly? Do we ask questions or not?"

"The secret nature of our investigation makes interviewing peo-ple about Dr. Burrus ten times more difficult than it would be other-wise. We must disguise the enormity of our inquiry and be very selective who we talk to and what we say."

Titus nodded. "Good point. Perhaps we should just start with his parents for now."

"That's probably best."

"Do you want to speak to them, or should I do it?"

"Neither just yet. Given how tricky this step may be, Charles and I want to investigate our options in more detail before we proceed. I'll update you as soon as possible."

CHAPTER 10

Dr. Lin's Chinese-style mansion was in the middle of his 700,000-acre Texas ranch. Thousands of cattle were watered by several large ponds and three flowing rivers. The isolation of the lush estate gave him the privacy he insisted upon, as well as a feeling of mastery over everything he could see. The ranch was almost totally self-sufficient with repair shops, storage facilities, administrative buildings, and housing for staff. Other auxiliary buildings included luxurious lodges for guests. The ranch even had its own massive slaughtering house far enough away from the mansion to avoid disturbing the beauty of his home.

Beautiful large trees provided shade for the mansion from the hot Texas sun. The complex resembled a high-end resort with tennis courts, a nine-hole golf course, and extravagant swimming pools, all designed by master architects. The largest pool included waterfalls, tunnels, slides, and a water bar. The children's portion had a dragon slide, which was very popular on hot summer days. The staff and their children used a more-modest pool.

One secluded, luxurious pool, called the Emperor's Aquatic Kingdom, was restricted to use by Dr. Lin, specially invited guests, the billionaires' many concubines.

He was working in his main office behind an enormous sandalwood desk with intricate Chinese carvings when a senior administrative assistant knocked on the door.

"Yes?"

"Excuse me for disturbing you, Master Lin. Your Director of Security and Surveillance is here to see you."

"Send him in."

The assistant bowed and escorted General Chen into the study. The retired general stood six-feet-one-inch tall, with wide, sloping shoulders and a large gut hanging over his belt, still an imposing figure even in his sixties.

"General Chen, how are you?"

"Not very good, I'm afraid."

"Oh? Why is that?"

"I received disturbing news from our Paris operatives."

"Go on."

"They report that a man was seen on multiple occasions over several days near Li Cheung's apartment. The man appeared to be covertly observing Cheung and his movements. They didn't see the man make direct contact with Cheung, but they could not be certain if he did or did not speak with him before he left town."

"And why not?"

The general looked disgusted. "They said they didn't have enough manpower to observe him 24/7, and they were watching other people, too. They attempted to interrogate him, but he overpowered one of our agents and got away."

Dr. Lin shook his head. "All my Paris operatives have to do is keep an eye on our regional clients and Cheung, yet they failed at the simple task of apprehending and interrogating one suspicious man. Is that what you're telling me?"

The general sighed. "That is correct. There is no excuse."

"Did they at least photograph him?"

"No. They said they planned to do so, but they were still trying to decide if he was important enough. They say people of concern come and go almost daily in Paris, with many new faces each day. They described him as White, muscular, six-feet tall, wearing a black Parisian baseball cap."

"Wonderful," Dr. Lin said sarcastically. "What else did they say?"

"I had them interview people in the area about this man. A waitress at a nearby café thinks she remembers him. She felt he was American."

Dr. Lin's keen intuition sensed the general wasn't finished with his report. "I doubt you would concern me about a suspicious man in Paris who got away from our operatives if there were no other concerns. Is there something else you wish to tell me, General?"

"Yes, I'm afraid. The day after this man was last seen, Cheung made a large withdrawal from his bank account and left Paris."

"Where did he go?"

"Our agents watched him board a flight on Linas Aereas de Espana headed to Madrid with two large suitcases."

Dr. Lin took a deep breath. "That may be of concern, and maybe not."

"I agree. I had them break into Cheung's flat and search the entire residence."

"What did they find?"

"It appears he took most of his personal belongings. They suspect he left Paris permanently and is now on the run."

Dr. Lin leaned back in his chair. "How do I tolerate such incompetence?"

"We can't," General Chen said with equal disappointment.

"I would immediately and permanently eliminate the operatives who were watching Cheung, but we may need them to identify the man they saw. Right now, we must find Cheung. Who knows? From Madrid, he may have taken another flight elsewhere, which will make finding him much more difficult."

"Yes, Master Lin. My men are checking into it. We will know soon. What are your orders in the meantime?"

"It seems this unknown agent scared Cheung enough to leave his home. That concerns me. I'm afraid Cheung's time in this world must come to an end. I should have killed him years ago." After a moment of reflection, he added, "But we share distant ancestors, and I tend to be too merciful when it comes to family, no matter how distant."

The general wanted to agree, but he had to choose his words carefully. "I'm sure you had many good reasons to let him live, Master Lin. You never make such important decisions without consideration of all the ramifications."

Dr. Lin grinned. "You're quite right, General. In truth, I also thought he might become a useful bargaining chip with the Chinese government should the need arise."

"You think many steps ahead of anyone else, Master Ling."

He nodded. "Use our technical support team and all of our operatives in Spain and throughout Europe to locate Cheung. When they do, I want you to go there personally to question him."

"It will be my pleasure."

"Find out if he made contact with this mysterious man. If so, what did the man want? What did Cheung tell him? Find out anything he said that might be used against us. Be certain he tells you everything. If he spoke to this man or anyone else, I want to know every single word that came from his mouth."

"How merciful do you want me to be with Cheung? I ask only because of your distant connection."

Dr. Lin frowned, then shook his head. "He means nothing to me now. Use whatever means necessary to get the information I seek. I'm done playing games with him."

"Of course. Afterward, what should I do with him?"

"Kill him, of course. If he betrayed me, do it slowly and painfully. If not, kill him quickly. Either way, he poses more risk to me than any benefit. Report back to me once your mission is complete."

"Yes, Great One."

After General Chen left the office, Dr. Lin called in an assistant to have a personal indoor shuttle brought to him. He and a bodyguard took the large, electric shuttle from his office to his family living quarters. He gave much thought to what his Director of Security told him, as the shuttle moved through the gigantic estate.

Nearing their destination, he forgot about the Paris incident and focused on his family. Only when he was with his children or concubines did his mind ever leave his work. He agreed with Confucius, who encouraged strong family ties. Although Dr. Lin didn't have a traditional family through marriage, he considered his many children, and, to a limited degree, their biological mothers, to be his family. His concubines were for pleasure only and weren't considered part of his family unless they bore him a child.

The well-guarded family area of the mansion included a large dining area, gymnasium, indoor swimming pool, classrooms, lounging areas, and computer rooms. There were luxurious bedrooms for each of his twenty-one children and their mothers. The security guards, teachers, and other servants slept in comfortable, though far-less-ornate, dorms near the house.

When he walked into the education facility, all the children stopped their activities and ran to him. Many gave him warm hugs, which he returned. The teachers stayed where they were, and the mothers waited nearby.

The mothers bowed deeply in greeting, but none dared approach him without being invited. None were. Except in rare circumstances, the mothers no longer shared intimacy with Dr. Lin, nor were they allowed intimacy with anyone else. If they did, there were severe consequences. Their job was to nurture, teach, and help raise his children. It wasn't a free life, but most of them found it more fulfilling than being a concubine. To be the mother of one of his children was a great honor.

Dr. Lin swept up the smallest child in his arms, as he asked the group, "How are my little emperors and empresses today?"

He'd been out of town recently and hadn't seen them in over two weeks.

All talked simultaneously, each vying for attention. He loved their adoration, but he eventually clapped once and said, "Quiet, quiet."

There was instant silence in the room.

"Now line up by age."

They lined up as they did many times before, and he surveyed the group. They were a reflection of him, and his expectations were high. Overall, he was pleased.

To three, he said, "Stand up straighter." To one of the small boys, he said, "Look more confident. You look like a wet cow. Here. Watch me." He showed him a confident stance and fearless expression. "You're a child, but you're *my* child."

The six-year-old changed his stance and expression to mimic his father.

Dr. Lin watched, and a small smile of pride came to his face. He patted the boy's back. "Much better."

"Thank you, Father."

"I will see what you have learned since I saw you last." He settled into a plush judge's chair on a small platform at the end of the room. No one else ever dared sit there.

All the children knew exactly what he meant. They would be vigorously tested, academically and physically. Those who did well would be rewarded. Those who did poorly would be punished, along with their mothers and tutors.

The previous year, one of his sons, who was doing poorly in several areas, was diagnosed with autism by his family physician. The child and her mother were sent away. No one knew where they were exiled, and it was forbidden to speak of them again.

The teachers handed Dr. Lin worksheets for each child showing what he or she had been taught, since he last saw them. From those worksheets, he would base much, but not all, of his testing.

He settled deeper into his elaborate, throne-like chair, as the children arranged themselves before him. Teachers and mothers watched from the periphery of the large room with anxious anticipation. The comprehensive examinations lasted several hours. First came math, followed by science, reading, computer science, world history, Chinese history, Chinese philosophy, and family heritage.

As testing proceeded, each child stepped before him to answer his numerous questions. The other children listened to the answers.

That took great patience for all of them, but it was particularly difficult for the younger ones. Dr. Lin knew that, and teaching patience and discipline were part of his educational plan. They weren't being trained to be ordinary people. He wanted them to be emperors and empresses someday. They would be extraordinary in all ways. None had yet received the Wake Formula from him, which would start when they reached adulthood.

The last question of each child at the end of their academic testing was always the same. "What is the goal and destiny of our family?"

"To rule," was the simple, yet powerful, answer from each child.

Except for his extremely gifted children, most were greatly relieved when the testing ended. The parents and children moved to the large dining hall. Servants quickly and efficiently delivered food in ornate bowls to the massive antique table, with Dr. Lin sitting at the head, and his children arranged on both sides. The mothers sat at nearby tables. Teachers watched and listened, as they stood at the periphery of the room. They would eat in the staff dining room after Dr. Lin left.

No one took a bite until Dr. Lin gave his reflections on the day's academic evaluations. Testing results for each child were pronounced for all to hear. Most of the children did well. Those who didn't were assigned various punishments according to the level of Dr. Lin's disappointment. Several had minor deficiencies, which meant less play time and more required study hours. The punishments might last for a few days or until the next testing session.

He glared at one of his seven-year-old daughters. "Changying, I'm very disappointed in your math skills. You did poorly the last time I tested you, as well."

"I'm sorry, Father." She kept her head down. "I tried my best."

"You won't be allowed lunch for one week. During lunchtime, you will have extra math tutoring. When I test you again, I will expect much improvement, or your punishment will be much harsher."

The little girl's head fell even lower in disappointment, and she started to whimper. "Yes, Father."

When Biyu, her mother, heard the punishment and saw tears on her daughter's face, her heart sank. She ran to the table and fell to her knees beside Dr. Lin.

"Great Master, please have mercy on your child. She has been doing her best. She just isn't good at math. Some people are not. I am not. Her reading and other skills are good or excellent."

Dr. Ling didn't look at her, as he placed his hands on the table before him as if to steady himself. "If you're saying she is intelligent but not learning her math, then you tell me that the blame is on her teacher and yourself. Is that correct?"

"We're all trying our best, Master. I am merely saying that some children are not good in all things. Not eating during the middle of the day will not help her learn math. It will only make her hungry and learning more difficult. A hungry child does not learn well over the sounds of her growling stomach. Please, I beg you. Punish me, but do not punish her."

He finally looked at her. "It will be as you wish in part. Your punishment, and that of her teacher, will be worse than I planned due to your insolence. Changying's punishment is unchanged, because I'm merciful. Go to your seat and never lecture me again on how to train my own children. I will deal with you and her teacher more fully later."

Biyu didn't move and began crying at his feet.

"Go, or I'll change my mind about Changying," he snapped, annoyed by her blatant disregard for his simple house rules.

She returned to her seat with muffled sobbing. Her outcry hadn't helped and put her at risk for the punishment she most feared—forced separation from her child. She saw that happen before to other mothers who displeased Dr. Lin.

Ju, the child's tutor, stood motionless, although she was furious inside at the child for being so incompetent at math and her mother for making matters worse. What had *she* done to deserve more punishment? Would it mean grueling manual labor, removal of access to staff recreation areas, reduction in salary, or even dismissal. Irate with Biyu, she would find a way to get revenge, although she didn't know how.

After dinner, everyone was allowed to relax in one of the lounge areas. Dr. Lin enjoyed watching his children play and attempt to impress him. After the two-hour recess, he clapped his hands, and everyone moved to the gymnasium for physical testing to begin.

First, the girls danced for him. They performed both individual and group dances. All wore ancient Chinese costumes. Their performances pleased him.

The boys demonstrated their skills at martial arts, starting with dance-like katas, then they broke boards. Finally, for the older children, there were combat competitions.

Children eight or older put protective gear on their heads and hands before being paired off for sparring. The highly skilled black-belt instructor was there, as well as the family physician in case of serious injury.

That was Dr. Lin's favorite part of the day, and the children put on a great show. They fought with skill and intensity. No child was seriously harmed, although one had a hard time getting back up after a furious kick to the abdomen. Many left with minor bruises, which they considered badges of honor.

Time was no object to Dr. Lin. He enjoyed testing the children well into the night. While he watched, his mind was obsessed on the thought that one day, they would lead the new world he was building.

CHAPTER 11

One week after their previous meeting, Titus and Seth met again at an old, unassuming brick coffeehouse for breakfast. Titus ordered an open-faced egg and avocado sandwich with black coffee, while Seth ordered Earl Grey tea and a cranberry scone. They sat at a table in the back, where they had more solitude and could watch the people who came in and out of the store.

Seth was in good spirits. "Charles has done some brilliant work, and I have exciting information."

"What did he find?"

"For one thing, we now know who is by far the best person for us, or rather you, to interview about the information you got from Cheung."

"Who?" he asked, sipping hot coffee.

"Dr. Frederick Burrus."

"Dr. Frederick Burrus? Is that Dr. Burrus' father?"

Seth grinned. "Good guess, but no. I'm talking about the actual neuropsychiatrist Cheung mentioned—that Dr. Burrus."

Titus sat back in his chair, puzzled. "I don't understand. I thought you said he was dead."

"I did, but I was wrong. It appears that his death was a ruse, a hoax."

"You're saying there was no explosion at the lab?"

"Oh, no. It blew up all right. Everyone inside was killed. Well, I should say almost everyone. We've since discovered that Dr. Burrus survived the blast and has been in hiding ever since."

Titus leaned forward, excited. "That little dog. That's great news. Where is he? How'd he survive the blast? Why did the reports say he died?"

Seth took a bite from his scone and sipped tea before answering. "Slow down, Old Boy. I'm glad you're happy about our discovery, but let me answer one question at a time. First, we don't know how he survived the explosion. Charles found out he's alive and is hiding right here in the States. He's a professor at a small liberal arts college called Sewanee, or the University of the South in Tennessee."

"I've heard of it, but I don't know much about the place."

"My guess is that's the point. Don't get me wrong. I understand that Sewanee is a wonderful college. However, it's very small, with less than 2,000 students, and it's rather isolated, sitting on a hill near the Alabama border."

Titus rubbed his chin. "I need to speak with him right away. Maybe we can find out what this is all about."

"I agree. He presently uses the name Dr. Erwin Welkener. That's all we really know. Go there and talk to him as soon as possible. I've already cleared your schedule with Deputy Director Otero. You can fly into Nashville and take a rental car from there. It's only ninety minutes."

As Titus drove up the steep, winding road to the Sewanee campus, he realized it was a great place for the missing scientist to hide. Other than the campus, there was nothing around except for trees and a handful of homes, some in the Victoria style, which he found quite charming.

He drove around campus until he found the admissions office, where he saw two people speaking with an elderly receptionist. Titus took a course catalog, sat in a chair, and flipped through it.

"May I help you?" the receptionist asked, after she finished with those ahead of him.

Titus shrugged noncommittally. "I'm fine. I was just checking out your school for my daughter. She's interested in possibly applying here. I wanted to look through the course catalog before I looked around the campus.”

"Of course. Let me know if you have any questions.”

A few minutes later, he stood and walked toward her. “Actually, I just remembered that a friend of mine asked if I could say hello to a professor named Dr. Erwin Welkener. They’re old friends. Could you tell me where his office is?”

"What department is he in? I’ll look him up on the computer.”

“I’m sorry, but I don’t remember. Biology, maybe?”

“That’s OK. Just give me a moment.” She typed commands into the computer and looked up. “His office is in the science building a couple buildings away.” She pointed in the direction he needed. “The computer lists him as a professor in biology and chemistry.”

“Great. You’ve been very helpful.”

“You know, that’s the first time I ever heard of one of our faculty having an appointment in two different science departments.” She sounded impressed. “He must be very smart.”

“That’s what I’ve been told.”

“Perhaps his being in two departments is why you couldn’t remember which one he was actually in.”

Titus smiled warmly at her. “You’re probably right. Thanks again.”

“You’re quite welcome.”

He walked to the science building, where he was greeted with another warm smile from a young, attractive receptionist with long, reddish-brown hair and green eyes. “Hello, I’m Tammy Vick. How may I help you?”

“I’d like to speak to Professor Erwin Welkener, please.”

“May I tell Dr. Welkener who’s asking for him?”

“Just tell him I’m a concerned parent who wants to discuss why his son is struggling in Dr. Welkener’s class. Is he in? I’d like to speak with him as soon as possible.”

“I believe I saw him come in a little earlier. Give me a moment while I call his office.” As she placed the call, she glanced to see if the handsome man's hand had a wedding ring. She saw none, which brought a subtle smile to her face. She'd been divorced three years, and there were few prospects for dating in the area. "It's ringing now."

After a moment, she heard, "This is Dr. Welkener."

"Hello, Doctor. This is Tammy. Sorry to disturb you, but there's a parent here of one of your students who'd like to speak with you as soon as possible."

Titus overheard the man's reply in perfect English with a noticeable German accent. "That's fine. What's the student's name?"

"The name of your child?" Tammy asked, continuing to gaze at Titus.

"Just tell him I'm a concerned parent. I don't want any repercussions to my child because I came here. He doesn't know I'm doing this. I just have a few basic questions about the class and the grading. If the professor doesn't mind, I'd like to remain anonymous for the moment."

"I see." She passed on the message.

Dr. Welkener didn't like the suspense, but he said, "OK, send him my way. I'll see what this is about."

Tammy pointed Titus toward the offices. "It's four doors down on the left. His name will be on the door. Let me know if there is anything else I can do for you, Mr...?"

He smiled at her playful attempt to learn his name. "Thank you, Tammy."

Finding the office with the nameplate *Dr. E. Welkener*, he knocked. A deep German voice inside the room said, "Come in."

As Titus walked into the office, he did a subtle double-take. The professor with the German accent wasn't what he expected.

Dr. Burrus noticed the newcomer's surprised expression and smiled. "You look puzzled. Were you expecting someone else?"

Titus laughed at himself. In front of him was a large Black man ten years his senior who looked like he could have been a defensive lineman on the Alabama football team in his youth. "I'm sorry I heard your German accent, and, well, you don't look very German. You look so, so, American."

"You mean, I look Black, don't you?" The professor's face became stern. Folding his arms across his chest, he seemed upset.

Titus, embarrassed, tried not to show it. "To be honest I was subconsciously expecting you to be much smaller, with crazy white hair sticking out in all directions, and a pipe in your mouth. I wasn't expecting an African American who looks more like Tyler Perry than Albert Einstein."

The professor regarded him coldly for a few seconds, then he smiled and chuckled. "That's a good one, but to tell the truth, I'm not African American."

Titus' eyebrows rose. "Oh?"

"No. I've never been to Africa, and I'm not an American. I'm German."

Titus grinned, amused by the spirited quip. The man obviously enjoyed good banter and was getting the best of him.

"I got my skin color from my Black, American mother, and my accent from my White, German father." He thought back to his boyhood and chuckled. "Some of my schoolboy friends called me 'Halfrican.'" He shook his head in amusement. "Some people would probably get all wigged out about it these days, but I thought it was pretty funny. You didn't come to hear me discuss my heritage. How can I help you?"

Titus offered his hand. "Let me start over. Nice to meet you, Professor. I'm sorry for my preconceived notions about you."

The professor chuckled again. "No harm, no foul. It happens to me all the time when people hear my voice before laying eyes on me." He shook his head. "I find it very amusing."

"You were messing with me when you acted all defensive?"

"Of course. I'm not a politically correct snowflake. It gets boring around here, and I need to have some fun when I can."

Titus was coming to like the man very quickly.

"I'm Dr. Erwin Welkener, and you are?"

"Titus."

"Why don't you have a seat, Titus?"

They looked around the office for an empty chair and found none. The two guest chairs had stacks of books and journals piled on them.

The professor looked a little embarrassed. "Please excuse the mess. Let me clear off a chair for you. I assume Titus is your first name?"

"Yes."

"Your last name is...?"

"Titus is fine for now."

The professor stopped straightening books and looked at his visitor. "Still keeping secrets, are we?"

Titus shrugged.

After the professor removed some books, he pointed at the empty seat, and Titus took it. The professor sat behind a simple wooden desk.

"So how can I help you, Titus? I understand you have a child in one of my classes who has a complaint about me. Is that correct?"

"No."

He leaned back in his chair and studied Titus curiously. "Oh? That's what I was told. If not that, why are you here?"

"I'm here to see Dr. Frederick Burrus."

Titus saw the professor's previously calm, confident face tense up for a second, only to smooth out again.

The professor took a deep breath, stood, and walked calmly to the door, looking outside to make sure no one heard his visitor before closing it slowly. He turned and stood with his back to the door, one hand on the knob.

"Who are you, and what do you want? I don't know any Dr. Burrus."

"Of course you do. You're Dr. Burrus. Don't try to deny it. I know who you are."

He didn't move, keeping one hand on the doorknob. Part of him wanted to run. The other part needed to know who managed to find him.

Titus raised both hands to ease the tension. "I'm here only to ask you a few questions, nothing else. You have nothing to fear from me."

The professor looked him over carefully, sizing him up. Titus looked potentially dangerous, but he was acting friendly. "Who are you?"

Titus stood and took out his badge. "I'm Special Agent Titus Warren of the FBI."

The professor took the badge, studied it, and returned it. "What do you want with me, Agent Warren?" His tone was serious and definitely not friendly anymore.

"I want to know about the research you were doing in Germany."

"I had many different research projects in Germany," he replied indignantly. "I was a scientist there for many years."

"I want to know what you were working on just before your laboratory in Frankfurt blew up."

Dr. Burrus glared at Titus guardedly. "I want to know why the FBI is interested in my research in Germany. Has America become a totalitarian state?"

Titus ignored the provocative question. "Listen, Professor. We already know that several years ago, you were a scientist at the Burrus Research Institute. After the explosion in your lab, you were listed as dead. Now we find you quite alive and living in the U.S. under a false identity. Why? What's going on? Why did someone want to kill you and destroy your lab?"

"You're correct that I have a new identity here in the United States, but it's not for sinister reasons. I'm here quite legally. Your State Department allowed me and my family in through a back door. As far as *why* I'm here and using a different name, I think that should be obvious even to the FBI."

Titus sighed. The man sure liked to argue. "I assume you're using a false identity, because you're worried someone will try to kill you again."

"That's correct. You're not so naïve after all. It's for my safety and that of my family." He paused. "To tell the truth, when you mentioned my real name, I thought for a moment you were here to kill me."

Titus softened his expression and posture as much as he could. "I'm sorry. I didn't meant to frighten you. Please accept my apologies."

"When I didn't see a gun in your hand, I knew you weren't an assassin, but I'm still in hiding, and I don't want my cover blown. I like it here, and I prefer not to be forced to move and change my identity again because of someone like you."

"Again, I'm very sorry. Your secret is safe with me."

Dr. Burrus, taking a deep breath, returned to his chair. "Thank you."

"How'd you end up here?" He hoped the simple question would ease the tension.

"After the explosion, we hoped the assassins would be found and brought to justice quickly, but that didn't happen. No one was ever charged with those murders. I had to find a place to hide and make a decent life as a scientist. I knew Europe wasn't safe, so we came to the U.S."

Titus nodded.

"My mother grew up not far from here in Birmingham, Alabama. She was familiar with Sewanee College, because one of her friends graduated from here and always spoke fondly of it. It was her idea that we come here."

"From what I can tell, I think it was a good idea. This is a nice place, and it's certainly off the beaten path."

"My parents are very wealthy and well-connected. It wasn't difficult to get the German authorities to cooperate with us to fake my death and help arrange with your State Department to allow me and my family to come here with new identities. We were told it was arranged with only a handful of high-level people knowing my whereabouts."

He paused, then added, "We became convinced no one would ever find us," he said with a sigh, "but here you are. Here *we* are."

"Yes, here we are. I'm not trying to put you on the spot, but I'm curious. How is it that you alone survived the blast?"

He looked down despondently and shook his head. "I've asked myself that question many times. Why did I survive when others did not? That question can be asked on many levels and brings both happiness and sadness. The happiness is for myself and my family. The sadness is for the others."

Titus nodded. "I understand. I've lost friends, too."

Dr. Burrus locked gazes with him. "Are you a religious man, Titus?"

He shrugged. "Not particularly. Maybe a little."

"Well, I am," Dr. Burrus said firmly. "I believe God has other plans for me. He didn't intend for me to die that dreadful day. To answer your question from a pragmatic point of view, I was in the laboratory cold room getting supplies when the blast went off. The cold room was built with thick, highly insulated walls. It acted like a bomb shelter for me."

"You were very lucky."

"No, I'm very blessed. I thank God every day that I'm still alive, and I pray for the souls who were lost."

"That must've been very hard."

"It was and still is. I woke up a week later in the hospital. A rescue team dug me out of the rubble, and I was carried out unconscious on a stretcher. I had cuts, bruises, several broken bones, and a major headache, but I was still alive."

"I see."

"When my parents learned someone tried to kill me, they quickly came up with a plan to protect me from further attempts. They're a very intelligent couple. They publicly announced I was in a deep coma before passing away from my injuries. With the exception of my wife, my other relatives and friends were told I was dead. A closed casket and private burial helped with the deception. Other funerals were also happening because of the blast, so mine was one of many.

Titus nodded.

"They thought the assassins would be caught quickly, but that didn't happen. They had people they could trust help me and my family disappear. I won't bore you with the details except to say it was quite costly and complicated. They aren't fond memories."

"Of course."

After a short pause, the professor asked, "Now tell me what you really want, Agent Warren. Why are you asking about my work in Germany?"

Titus paused. "Specifically, I want to understand what you were working on that was so interesting that someone tried to kill you."

Dr. Burrus sighed. "I see." He stared up at the ceiling before answering. "I was studying sleep, trying to develop a new medication for insomnia."

Titus looked at him curiously, although he wasn't totally surprised. "A sleep medication? I don't mean to be rude, but why sleep? I know a lot about you. Your medical and scientific credentials are impeccable. Unlike many scientists, you were financially free to study anything you wanted. Why not brain cancer, or Alzheimer's, or something like that?"

Dr. Burrus crossed his arms on his chest. "I understand your question. You aren't the first one to ask me that. My parents wondered the same thing at first."

"So why?"

"I wanted to know more about the human brain. It's the most-complex, fascinating, and powerful object in the physical world. I thought sleep research was a novel way to explore it."

Titus was still baffled. "Sleep?"

He sighed, as if he were tired of explaining it to ignorant people. "Why not sleep? It's quite fascinating, if you think about it. People spend about eight hours of their lives every twenty-four-hour cycle shut down to the world in what we call sleep, yet we know so little about it. Obviously, something important must be going on for the body to give up so much time and make itself highly vulnerable to attack during those hours. I wanted to know what made sleep vital and hoped it would give insights into the brain. It's as simple as that."

Titus cocked his head. "Actually, it does make some sense."

"Thank you for your heartfelt support," Dr. Burrus said sarcastically. "While other medical problems, like brain cancer and Alzheimer's are absolutely worth studying because of the severity of those illnesses, others are worth the research effort because of the frequency of the problem. Insomnia is very common, you know."

"I didn't mean to insult you, and I'm sure it is."

"There are only a handful of sleep medications available, and many people have side effects from them, like morning drowsiness, amnesia, bad taste, abuse, and so on. Inability to sleep disturbs a person's day as well as their night."

"I see."

"My mother suffers from severe insomnia. It probably comes from her extremely long work hours as a neurosurgeon. She's one of those people who gets side effects from the currently available insomnia medications. I thought it might be helpful with her insomnia while trying to unlock some of the mysteries about the brain. That might sound goofy to some, but it's true."

Titus shook his head. "It doesn't sound goofy at all. It sounds pretty cool. Why would anyone want to kill you over a new sleep medication? Is a new sleep drug worth that much?"

Dr. Burrus laughed. "I have no idea. I wasn't interested in the money, and I never discovered a new sleep medication, anyway."

Titus eyed him. The man was a total enigma. "What? I don't understand. What's this all about, then?"

Dr. Burrus opened his mouth to speak, then stopped himself. After a pause, he asked, "What do you know about sleep, Agent Warren?"

"Not much, really. I know we all need sleep. I also know from my military days that prisoners can be tormented with sleep deprivation. Some even become temporarily psychotic, that sort of thing."

"That's true. Psychosis from sleep deprivation makes it all the more interesting, don't you think? Why would the brain react like that if sleep weren't so important?"

Titus knew it was a rhetorical question, but he answered, "I don't know."

"Agent Warren, before I answer your questions any further, I want you to understand the basic neurophysiology and physiology of sleep. What I have to say about my work will only make sense when you understand those to some degree."

"I'm not just an FBI field agent, Dr. Burrus. I don't have your level of research expertise, but I have a PhD in molecular biology. I should be able to follow you.

"Do you have a background in the neurophysiology and biochemistry of sleep?"

"Not specifically, but...."

"Of course you don't. Very few people do. You've probably never even thought about the neurobiology of sleep, have you?"

"No, but I...."

"Tomorrow, I'm scheduled to give a lecture on vision to my upper-level neurophysiology class. However, for your sake, I'll change the next couple of lectures to the neurophysiology and biochemistry of sleep."

"Please, Dr. Burrus. I need answers. I'd like to get them as quickly as possible and return to DC. I don't need to hear anything about...."

"Do you have children to get back to?"

"No," Titus admitted, "but I have other investigations to work on, and I have a cat."

Dr. Burrus chuckled and shook his head. "I'm not a fool. Cats can take care of themselves for many days if you leave them food and a little water running. Did you leave your cat running water?"

Titus nodded sheepishly.

Dr. Burrus slapped his hands on the desk. "It's settled, then. If you want more answers from me, you have to get them my way. It has taken years for anyone to find me. What does another day or two matter?"

Titus started to speak, but Dr. Burrus raised his hand in objection. "No. My mind is made up. I can be quite stubborn on important matters—just ask my wife. If you want my help, I'll see you at my eleven o'clock neurophysiology class in room 106 in this building tomorrow."

"I haven't even told you why we want the information," Titus said, feeling a bit frustrated but also intrigued.

"No, you haven't, and I don't want to know right now. I'm sure you'll tell me all about it soon enough. A day or two to bring you up to speed won't matter."

It was clear there was no way to change the man's mind, so Titus stood to leave. "OK. I'll be there."

"People around here know me as Dr. Erwin Welkener. Remember that. Never use my real name around here again. Agreed?"

"Understood, Dr. Welkener. I'll see you tomorrow."

As Titus was going out the door, Dr. Burrus asked, "Where are you staying?"

"I don't know. I just got here and wasn't planning to stay overnight. Any suggestions?"

Dr. Burrus smiled. "Yes. You can stay at my house. I'll text my wife, Isabella, and tell her to expect you."

Titus shook his head. "Oh, no. I can't do that to you and your wife."

"I insist. She's a wonderful person and a great hostess. She would love to have you stay with us. Besides, we don't get much company out here compared to living in Frankfurt. It would be our pleasure. Just keep the FBI thing to ourselves for now until we sort things out. Agreed?"

Titus grinned. "Agreed."

"I'll tell her you're a visiting molecular biologist from Washington, DC. That's true enough."

Titus nodded."

"The college gets visiting faculty now and then. Your presence won't seem too strange to her."

"It's very nice of you to invite me. Are you sure?" He was already looking forward to it. It would mean more time to get the answers he needed, and Dr. Burrus appealed to his scientific side. He enjoyed a bit of science banter at times. Solo trips were sometimes isolating.

"Yes, no problem. We have a guest bedroom you can use. We'll see you at six. Isabella and I will have dinner waiting. Do you like steak?"

"Of course."

"Good. Then it's settled." Dr. Burrus wrote his address on a piece of paper and handed it to him. "In the meantime, I suggest you relax and take a nice walk around the campus. It's quite lovely here."

On his way out, Titus stopped to thank Tammy for her help.

"How'd it go with Dr. Welkener?"

Titus smiled. "Pretty well, I think. I liked him."

"He's a good man. He and his wife, Isabella, are wonderful people."

Titus nodded and turned to go.

"If you need someone to show you around campus, I'd be happy to." She wrote something on a small piece of paper and handed it to him. "Here's my cell number if you want to take me up on the offer."

Titus gazed into her beautiful green eyes. "Thank you. I might do just that. It looks like I'll be here for a day or two."

CHAPTER 12

Cheung sensed something was wrong when he walked into his quiet apartment in Madrid. Where was Tiger, the guard dog he recently purchased? Why hadn't he started barking the moment Cheung entered the apartment? What was that strange smell?"

Standing near the entrance, he considered turning around to run, but nothing seemed terribly wrong. Maybe the dog was sick.

To be safe, he drew his 9mm Sig Sauer from a jacket pocket. After his scare in Paris, he always carried a gun and a knife.

He reached out to turn on the hall light switch. When the lights came on, he saw nothing unusual, but he remained on high alert.

"Tiger!"

There was no response.

"Tiger!"

After a few silent seconds, he thought he heard a noise and raised the gun. "Is someone here?" He hoped to sound intimidating, but his voice was higher than he intended.

"I have a gun. If anyone's here, come out with your hands up, and I won't shoot."

He heard nothing.

Against his better judgment, he cautiously walked down the small hall toward the dark living room. His heart pounding, he clutched the gun in two shaking hands.

Suddenly, he stepped on something sticky and looked down. When he saw blood, his heart almost leaped from his chest. A closer look showed the blood was smeared toward the living room. He wanted to run, but he was too frightened to move.

"Put down the gun, Cheung," a voice from the darkened living room said. "It will be no use to you."

He jumped and aimed at the voice. "Get...get out of my apartment whoever you are. I have a gun. Leave now, and I won't shoot."

His wrists exploded with pain, as a baseball bat slammed down on his outstretched arms. He screamed, and the gun fell to the floor. The bat struck his legs next. He crumpled to the floor, moaning in agony.

Cheung saw two sets of boots in front of him. Seeing his gun only a few feet away, he frantically reached for it. A boot slammed down hard on his fingers, and he screamed again.

"Pick up his gun," the calm voice said again. "Stand him up."

Strong arms lifted Cheung's injured body to his feet, but he couldn't stand. One or maybe both his legs were broken. Intense pain roared through him.

"I don't think he can stand, General."

"Then lay him on the floor and hold down his arms and legs."

Cheung was flung down. Footsteps came toward him. A moment later, he saw a large, older Chinese man, probably the General, hovering over him. Cheung's heart sank at the thought that the Chinese government finally caught up to him. What would they do?

"I was forced to leave China," he said desperately. "I was kidnapped and only recently escaped. I was trying to find a way home, but I wasn't sure how."

The general laughed and shook his head in amusement. Saliva dripped onto Cheung's torso from the laughing man. The large man took out a knife and showed it to Cheung.

Cheung gasped and whimpered, struggling to free himself only to make the pain worse. "Please, don't hurt me! I beg you! I'm in terrible pain already!"

Taking a deep breath, he tried to sound convincing. "I'm a loyal officer in the Army of the People's Republic of China. I'm in Army intelligence and was kidnapped."

"Hmmm," the general said. "Kidnapped? That's interesting. By whom?"

"An American."

"Oh? Who is this American?"

"Dr. Lin. His full name is Dr. Dao Lin. He owns a pharmaceutical company in the United States. He hired people to kidnap me, because I had valuable information he wanted. I was an industrial spy for our country, and he wanted information I stole from the Germans. Look him up on my computer. You'll see I'm telling the truth. Ask your superiors about me. Please, you'll see I'm telling the truth. I'm with Army intelligence."

"That's very interesting," the general said, still amused. "Go on." He waited for the man to hang himself with his own words.

"They took me out of China and held me captive. I only recently escaped. The information he wanted is still of value to my superiors, and I need to give it to them right away. Harm me anymore, and they'll be extremely angry with you. I'm an intelligence officer."

"I see. So I should be afraid of you, then?" The general rolled the knife in his hands and kicked Cheung's ribs.

Cheung moaned. "No, no! I'm just saying I have important things to report. We're on the same side."

The general walked to the TV and turned it on with the volume set very loud. "Hold his arms and legs still."

"What are you doing? You're making a grave error. You have to believe me. I have valuable information for the People's Republic of China." He started sobbing. "I'm a spy. I have things to report. Don't you hear me? You could be in big trouble if you hurt me anymore."

"Yes, I hear you very well. Now let me tell you who I am. Do you want to know?"

"Yes. Tell me. I'll make a favorable report about you if you let me go."

"I'm General Chen."

"General Chen, my superiors will be very pleased you found me. I have important scientific information they want to hear."

"Yes. I've heard you say that so many times. I certainly want to hear the information you have, but you should be quite interested to know that I don't work for your despicable communist government in China. I'm a retired American general."

"What? You aren't from the People's Republic of China? Why are you here?"

"I report to Dr. Dao Lin."

"What?"

General Chen smiled, but his eyes filled with hatred. "Yes, the man you so quickly turned against. He sends his greetings, by the way. Yes, he'll want a full report on what you have to say."

"What? You work for Dr. Lin?" Cheung's mind raced. Had he just blundered into a deadly error by mentioning Dr. Lin's name? Could that be a good thing? Certainly, a pharmaceutical owner would be easier to deal with than the People's Republic of China. He just wished he kept his mouth shut about being kidnapped by Dr. Lin's people.

The general played with the knife where Cheung could watch.

"Well, that's wonderful," Cheung said quickly. "Dr. Lin and I are old friends. Ask him."

The general nodded, but his sinister expression didn't change. "That's what I was told. He took good care of you, has he not? He paid you a great deal of money for the information you sold him, didn't he?"

"Yes, he did. I'm very grateful. Please tell him that."

"He also paid you to keep silent about him. Now I see how easily you give him up and break your agreement."

Cheung twisted but wasn't able to break free. The intense pain didn't matter anymore. "No! I would never betray him! I was just saying that to buy time."

General Chen smiled. "Just as you are now."

"No, wait! I thought Chinese government agents found me. They would have tortured and killed me for escaping, for giving information to Dr. Lin. I'm here, because I helped Dr. Lin."

"So you did it all for Dr. Lin?" the general asked mockingly. "How nice of you. Do you fear him less than the Chinese government?"

"Yes. I mean, no." Cheung didn't know what to say. "You're confusing me. Dr. Lin and I are old friends. He'll be very angry with you if you harm me any more. Now let me up."

"Are you threatening me again?" General Chen growled. "I find that amusing. This has been amusing, but now, it's time for business. We're here, because Dr. Lin's agents in Paris observed a man following you before you fled the city. He wants to know who the man was, and if you spoke to him."

"Dr. Lin's agents? A man in Paris? What are you talking about?"

The general's expression became sinister. "Dr. Lin has eyes and ears everywhere. Did you think he would just say good-bye and good luck to you? He's much smarter and more powerful than you can ever imagine." He played with the knife more quickly.

"Please just put down your knife and take me to him," Cheung pleaded between whimpers. "I'll explain everything to him."

"No. You'll speak to me now. Let me show you what will happen if you don't tell the absolute truth to every question I ask." He bent down to cut open Cheung's shirt.

"No! No! You don't have to hurt me!"

"But I do." He slowly cut off a six-inch strip of skin from Cheung's abdomen.

Cheung screamed, as blood seeped from the superficial, painful wound.

"That is how tonight will go if you don't cooperate fully," General Chen said. "Now answer my questions, and be completely honest, or this will seem like child's play."

CHAPTER 13

Instead of going on a walk, as suggested, Titus changed into running clothes and started a pleasant jog around the quad of the Sewanee campus. It was a cool spring day, and flowers of all colors blossomed in the crisp air. He gazed at the secluded campus, with its green common areas and lovely stone building. The All Saints Chapel in the center of the small campus caught his eye, and he decided to go inside. He found lovely multiple arches and beautiful stained-glass windows. Choir practice was starting, so he didn't stay long.

As he jogged, he watched the students moving about. Some walked to class, several played Frisbee, and others hung out in small groups. It looked so pleasant and reminded him how much he enjoyed his long runs around the beautiful campus of the University of Virginia when he was a grad student there in molecular biology. As he ran, it felt like a vacation from the hustle and bustle of Washington, DC, and his job at the FBI. He also decided to meet Tammy the following day.

After eight miles, he slowed and stopped. As he did his post-run stretching, he wondered what life would have been like if he followed his original plan after leaving the Army and became a college professor. It might have turned out well. *Colleges are beautiful places, students are fun, and professors certainly have more free time than I do at the FBI.* However, the Bureau suited him, too. As long as he was young and healthy enough to be in the field, he would stay.

Perhaps, he thought, *I'll teach college after I retire.* The idea brought a smile, as he stretched more and enjoyed the weather.

Later that evening, Titus arrived at Dr. Burrus' house, a lovely, two-story home with white picket fence. He checked his watch and saw it was almost six o'clock.

As he walked toward the front door, he heard laughter in the backyard and smelled charcoal burning, so he changed direction and peeked over the fence. The professor was there, starting the grill, tossing a Frisbee to a beautiful German shepherd.

Dr. Burrus laughed at the dog when Titus called, "Hello, Professor!"

The professor took the Frisbee from the dog's mouth and looked toward him. "Titus! It's good to see you. Come on back and join me."

As he walked through the gate, he noticed a swing set, trampoline, and a large backyard. The German shepherd barked at him, but Dr. Burrus quickly calmed her. She ran over to sniff his legs, as he walked.

"Hello, Dr. Welkener."

"Please, call me Frederick here. Remember, only here."

"Got it."

An attractive woman with shoulder-length blonde hair, who looked ten years younger than Frederick, came out of the house to join them.

"Isabella, this is Dr. Titus Warren. Titus, this is my first wife, Isabella."

She smacked his shoulder. "Very funny." She offered her hand to Titus. "Hello, Dr. Warren. It's nice to meet you."

"The pleasure is all mine."

She looked at her husband again with feigned jealousy. "My first wife, eh? Well, if you find someone better than me to look after you. I suggest you snag her as quickly as possible."

Frederick chuckled and hugged her. "You know there's no one better than you for me."

She gave him a look that said, *Maybe I'll keep you.*

"Is the little man asleep?" he asked.

"Yeah. He was running around, playing. The next thing I know, he's asleep on the floor. I decided to let him be for a bit." She reached down to pet the dog, who was still at Titus' feet. "This is Winnie. I think she likes you."

Titus bent to pet her. "Hello, Winnie."

"I see you snuck into the backyard."

He grinned. "Sorry. I should have knocked on the front door first, but I smelled the charcoal and heard noise back here, so I couldn't help taking a look."

"I'm teasing. We're happy you're here."

"Winnie's a beautiful dog. She seems very well-behaved."

Isabella smiled. "She's like my husband. She can be good when she wants to be."

Titus returned the smile.

Frederick grabbed a Heineken from an ice bucket. "Want one?"

"Sure."

Isabella gave Frederick a quick kiss. "I have more dinner preparations to do inside. I'll see you fellas after the steaks are done." To the dog, she said, "Come, Winnie." Glancing at her husband, she added, "I'll put her downstairs until after we eat."

"Thanks, Babe."

Titus watched Isabella and Winnie go inside. "Isabella seems very nice."

"Too good for me, that's for sure."

"Where'd you two meet?"

"We met at church when I was a young professor at the University of North Carolina, and she was a graduate student at Duke in genetics. Soon, we discovered we shared a deep love for Jesus, science, and eventually for each other."

"Sounds like a good way to start a relationship."

"The best. As they say, 'Those who pray together, stay together.'"

Titus smiled and looked around the spacious yard, as he drank his beer.

"Not long after we married, my parents created a research institute in Frankfurt, Germany, so we decided to move there. Isabella and I were scientists at the Burrus Research Institute for several years, though we had different interests and worked in different labs. After we had children, she chose to stay home and become a full-time mom. She loves it."

A beautiful little girl ran up to Frederick. Titus guessed she was five-years old.

"*Vater, Vater! Hol much ab!*"

Frederick picked her up, as she requested, and tossed her up and down over his head, while she squealed with laughter.

When he put her down, he said, "*Was habe ich gesagt? Als gaste sind hier wir sprechen Englisch.*"

"Yes, Daddy." She turned her attention to Titus. "Who are you?"

Titus offered his hand to shake. "I'm Titus."

"Dr. Titus," Frederick corrected.

"Daddy says I have to speak English around you, because you probably don't know German, but I know how to speak German and English."

"You must be a very smart young lady."

She beamed. "I am."

"Don't be a bragger," Frederick warned.

"Yes, Daddy."

"We usually have the children speak German at home, so they'll know at least two languages fluently, but they always know to speak English when we have guests over."

"What's your name?" Titus asked the girl.

"Leeza."

"Hello, Leeza. What a beautiful name you have."

"Thank you."

Soon, she ran to Titus and hopped up and down. "Can you toss me up in the air, Dr. Titus?"

He smiled broadly and said, "Well, you're quite a big girl, but I'll try."

She launched herself into his arms, and he tossed her into the air many times. A couple of times, she went so high, Frederick flinched.

Leeza laughed so hard, she almost wet herself.

When Isabella glanced out the window and saw how high Titus was tossing Leeza, she ran out the back door and called, "You boys be careful with that child! She's not a sack of potatoes!"

"I'm sorry, Isabella." Titus carefully set the girl down. "Don't worry. I'd never let this beautiful girl fall."

"*Wir warden, Mutter,*" Frederick said to his wife, as she went back inside.

Leeza looked at him sternly and pointed her finger at him. "Talk English, Daddy. We have a guest here."

He laughed and picked her up. "You're right, Sugar Plum. Thanks for reminding me."

Leeza giggled and said, "Dr. Titus threw me higher than you did, Daddy. He wins!"

Frederick chuckled. "What? He wins? That's not fair. Dr. Titus is a show-off, Baby."

Titus laughed. "That's true. Look how big your daddy is. I'm sure he could throw you higher than me if he wanted to."

Leeza rocked in his arms in excitement. "Do it, Daddy! Do it!"

"No, I can't. Do you know how much trouble I'd get in with your mother? She's right. You're too precious to take chances with."

She frowned. "Oh, Daddy."

Frederick, setting her down, turned to Titus. "How do you want your steak?"

"Medium-rare would be great."

Soon, the steaks were on the grill over the hot coals. Frederick placed them on a big serving pan when they were ready and covered them with aluminum foil. "Let's all go eat while the steaks are hot.

Why don't you grab another beer for yourself and one for me, too, if you don't mind?"

"Sure."

Leeza took Titus' free hand and led him inside. Once they were in the house, she pointed to a place on a long bench at the dinner table. "You sit here next to me."

"I will. Thank you, Leeza."

"Did you have to wake the little guy?" Frederick asked Isabella.

"No. Fortunately, he woke up on his own."

"Good. He's less cranky that way."

After Isabella had the children situated, food was passed around the table.

Titus cut his steak and was about to take a bite when Leeza held his hand and stopped him.

"Wait, Dr. Titus. Daddy hasn't said the prayers yet. If you take a bite before he says prayers, then you have to say them."

Titus smiled at the sweet little girl. "Oh, my. You're right, Leeza. I should wait for the prayers. Thank you for saving me."

"Now fold your hands and bow your head like this." She assumed a pose.

He set down his fork, folded his hands, and bowed his head.

"Heavenly Father," Frederick said, "thank You for this food, my family, and our time with Dr. Titus. We pray that You bless us and draw us ever closer to You in faith. We thank You for Your guidance, protection, and provision. It's in Jesus Christ's name we pray. Amen."

"Amen," Leeza and her mother said, while Titus crossed himself.

Soon after they began eating, Isabella said, "This steak is wonderful, Frederick. You boys did a good job out there despite all the beer drinking and horsing around I saw."

"Thank you, My Love."

"Leeza is a German name, isn't it?" Titus asked. "Is she named after a family member back in Germany?"

"We call her Leeza, but her real name is Condoleezza," Isabella said. "She was named after Condoleezza Rice."

"Really? That's wonderful. She was an outstanding Secretary of State and is a remarkably humble person for someone so talented and successful."

"I agree. Unfortunately, I don't think she gets all the credit she deserves."

Frederick wiped his mouth with a napkin. "It seems that Blacks have to be liberals to get the credit they deserve. Freedom for us to choose a political party for ourselves isn't acceptable in America according to the mainstream media. If she'd been a Democrat, they'd be going on and on about how awesome she is."

"We also thought of her," Isabella said, "because she's an academic, like Frederick and me. She has a master's degree in political science from Notre Dame and a doctorate from the University of Denver in international studies. She was also a provost at Stanford University."

"Nice résumé," Titus said.

"She doesn't use the race card for political gain, either. When politicians do that, it really annoys us. She even took a lot of heat for being against the use of affirmative action in tenure decisions at Stanford. That took a lot of guts, especially at a California school."

"In my opinion, being Black or mixed race like myself," Frederick said, "I think affirmative action is insulting. It treats me like a dependent child who can't succeed without special advantage." He thought, then added, "Don't you think you would be insulted if the government gave you an extra ten points per game in college basketball, because you were White?"

Titus chuckled. "No. I wouldn't like that."

"Affirmative action might have been needed at one time, but now Blacks can be, and do, whatever they want. Just look around. Affirmative action is just a nice word for government-sanctioned racism, and everyone knows it."

"Seems that way to me."

Frederick wiggled a finger at him. "Don't say that out loud. Even I can't say it without being harassed." He shook his head. "Affirmative action doesn't foster self-respect for those who get it or earn respect from those who can't. I often worry that when people find out I'm a doctor or scientist, they must wonder if I truly earned my position or was moved ahead of more-qualified people, because I'm Black. The system makes it harder for me, not easier."

Titus found his ideas interesting. "What about prejudice against Blacks? Are you saying that's not a big deal?"

"Of course it is, but let's be adults. Prejudice exists everywhere. Some Whites are prejudiced against Blacks. Some Blacks are prejudiced against Whites. There's prejudice against fat people, skinny people, ugly people—you name it. No one is free of prejudice. We've all got to put on our big-boy pants sometimes."

It was truly refreshing for Titus to speak to someone in academics with such common sense. It wasn't usually the case. "What about your being the descendant of slaves? Doesn't that change the equation?"

"Why should it?" Frederick asked matter-of-factly. "I was never a slave. In case you didn't get the memo, slavery was abolished in America about 150 years ago. That's not last week. Slavery was a terrible tragedy. When this country was founded, it had already been going on for thousands of years around the world. America didn't invent it."

"The Roman Empire and the Vikings enslaved countless White Europeans for hundreds of years," Isabella added. "The Babylonians enslaved the Jews. Indians enslaved captive Whites or members of other tribes. Africans even enslaved other Africans or sold them to slave traders. It goes on and on. We're all descendants of slaves, you, me, and Frederick."

"You make a good point," Titus said.

"What irks me is how victimization is embellished in today's culture," Frederick added. "What we really need to do is embrace thankfulness. Do you ever hear civil rights leaders say how thankful they are that hundreds of thousands of White people were severely wounded or died freeing the slaves in the Civil War?"

Titus thought a moment. "No, now that you mention it."

"My family tree is well-documented," Isabella said. "One of my relatives fought with Grant and was killed at the Battle of Shiloh. Another lost his left leg fighting at Petersburg. Yet another fought for the Confederates but never owned a slave in his life. Where does that put me in the eyes of White-guilting liberals?"

Frederick said, "If you think that's good, consider this. My mother was descended from American slaves, but my father is German. Germans enslaved and killed Jews. Should I benefit from my mother's heritage or be held accountable for my father's?"

"I have no idea," Titus said.

"You have no idea? Of course not! Being taught you're a victim because of the color of your skin is corrosive to the soul. People from India often have darker skin than me, but do they ask to receive special benefits? Do they do well despite the color of their skin? Of course they do, if they work hard."

Titus nodded.

"Personal responsibility is what I was taught by my parents, and that's what Isabella and I teach our children. That's how you earn respect and gain self-respect. That's where people of my race find motivation."

"You continuously surprise me, Frederick."

"Thank you...I think."

Isabella wiped Martin's froth of milk before adding, "We like to say that Condoleezza Rice transcends race. Our children are also biracial, and we want them to be like that."

Titus nodded and worked on his ear of corn on the cob.

"I'm four!" Martin suddenly announced.

"Wow!" Titus said, excited. "You're a big boy!"

Martin grabbed for his cup of milk but knocked it over. A wave of milk splashed across the table into everyone's laps.

"Martin!" Leeza said. "You got milk on me!"

Martin started crying.

Isabella immediately stood and began cleaning the mess. "It's OK, Martin. Accidents happen." Turning to Titus, she said, "I'm sorry."

He wiped a small amount of milk off his lap. "No problem."

As Isabella wiped up milk with paper towels, she mumbled rhetorically, "What is it with males and messes? If I'm not cleaning up after Martin, I'm cleaning up after Frederick."

"Guilty as charged," Frederick agreed with a laugh. "I'm a bigger mess than my kids most of the time. I don't know how she puts up with me, Titus, but I'm glad she does."

"My mother said the same thing to me and my two brothers, Michael and Jim," Titus reminisced.

Isabella sat down and began finishing her meal. "Are you married, Titus?"

"No, never have been. After seeing your lovely family today, I think I'd like to be someday."

She smiled. "I'm sure you have plenty of ladies interested in you."

He grinned. "I was engaged once, but it didn't work out. I was in the Army, and she didn't like the thought of leaving her law practice to follow me around the world. I couldn't really blame her. Now I just date here and there. It's fine."

"Well, when you're ready, remember the Lord said, 'Ask and it will be given to you; seek and you will find; knock and the door will be opened to you.'"

"I'll do that."

"Isabella has a Bible quote for almost every situation," Frederick interjected, "for better or worse."

"Hey!" She feigned irritation. "You can never have enough gospel in your life."

He smiled and put an arm around her. "You certainly can't." After giving her a quick kiss, he turned to Titus. "Actually, her faith is one reason I love her so much."

Isabella eyed her husband with amusement. "And here I thought it was my legs."

Frederick laughed. "Well, I can't deny that, either."

Titus looked at her. "Your faith reminds me of my mother. She went to Mass at least twice a week and quoted plenty of scripture to me and my brothers when we needed it. She was a very devout Catholic, God rest her soul."

Isabella reached out to touch his hand. "She sounds lovely."

"She was."

After dinner, Titus started to help clean up. Isabella tried to stop him, but he insisted. As the three adults and Leeza cleaned the table, Titus remarked, "You told me where Leeza got her name, but how about Martin? Is he named after anyone special?"

Before they could answer, he snapped his fingers. "I got it. Martin Luther, right? He was German and a holy man, a monk. I believe. Am I right?"

"Good guess, Titus," Isabella replied. "Martin Luther it is."

"I knew it." He acted so pompous, Leeza laughed.

Frederick laughed, too. "It's the wrong Martin Luther. We named him after Martin Luther King. You seem stuck on my German heritage."

Titus lowered his head and stuck out his lower lip in feigned disappointment. "Of course. Martin Luther King. I should have known." He hoped Leeza would laugh again, but instead, she became very concerned.

She rushed up and grabbed Titus' hand. "It's OK, Dr. Titus. Don't be sad. Everybody makes mistakes."

His frown turned into a smile. "Yes, they do, Leeza. You're a smart girl, and a caring one, too."

Isabella smiled at the two of them. "Martin Luther King wasn't a German monk, but he was a minister. He believed all people should be treated equally under the law just as we do."

Like many academics, Frederick liked to drive his point home. "You can't legislate the way people feel about one another. They have a right to their own thoughts and feelings, good or bad. Both individuals and governments should treat everyone equally, with no special favors to either one."

Titus chased Leeza around the kitchen table. "Needless to say, you two have beautiful children who have excellent namesakes."

"What about you?" Isabella asked. "Titus isn't a very common name. Did your parents name you after someone special?"

He thought about that. "Sort of yes and no. One night, my dad asked my mom what she wanted to name me, if I were a boy. She happened to be lying in bed, reading the Book of Titus in her Bible, so she asked, 'How about Titus?' My dad thought that sounded pretty good, so they went with it. Not much to that one."

"That's a wonderful story," Isabella said. "You're named after a book in the Bible."

After the table was cleared, Frederick asked, "Want to play a little catch, Titus? It's not Isabella's thing, and I don't usually have another grown-up to throw the ball with. Since coming back to America, I've really gotten into baseball."

"Sure. That would be great. I play on a fast-pitch softball league in the summer, and I need to start getting ready."

Frederick went to the garage, grabbed two gloves and a softball, and hustled back to throw the ball with Titus. Slowly, they drifted farther and farther apart, testing each other's arms. Eventually, they were so far apart, Titus couldn't throw the ball all the way back to Frederick.

"Good Lord, Frederick. You have a hell of an arm. Not many people can out throw me."

"Thanks. It just comes naturally."

"If you lived in DC, I'd recruit you to my softball team for sure."

"That would be fun. Unfortunately, there's no adult league around here, so I don't know if I'd be any good."

"I have no doubt you'd be a star. With your size, you're probably a long-ball hitter."

Isabella glanced out the window and saw Frederick was backed up all the way into the neighbor's yard. She stepped outside to yell, "Frederick, keep the ball in our yard, please. Just because the Holloway family isn't home this week doesn't mean you can use their yard without their permission."

"They won't mind!" he yelled back.

"You don't know that. Bring it back into our yard, please."

Frederick's expression resembled a disappointed little boy. "OK."

As she stood on the porch, watching the two men laugh and play, she had to smile. Her husband hadn't had that much fun in a long time.

When they wound down, Frederick said enthusiastically, "Tomorrow, we should get up at five o'clock sharp."

Titus wondered if he heard correctly. "What?"

"I said we should get up at five sharp."

"Fine with me, but I didn't take you for a runner."

Frederick laughed. "Me, run? For heaven's sake, no. I'm not talkin' about running. Come and see what's in my garage."

Titus tucked his glove under his arm and jogged to the garage with Frederick.

Frederick opened the door and pointed, his face in a big smile. "Isn't she a beauty?"

"Wow! That's a fine-looking boat."

"A glitter purple Nitro Z-21 bass boat with a 250hp Mercury engine. I love it. I'll set us up with four fishing poles apiece in the morning, if you're game for fishing."

"Absolutely, but why so many poles?"

Frederick's smile turned mischievous. "I guess you haven't been bass fishing before."

"Once. The friend who took me said I couldn't catch fish at a grocery store."

It was an old joke, but Frederick laughed, anyway. "Don't worry. I'll show you the ropes, and I guarantee you'll catch some fish. The poles have different lures, so we save time finding out what they're biting. It's not the same every day."

CHAPTER 14

United Nations delegates from around the world gathered to celebrate Dr. Lin's generous donation to combat global warming and climate change. The gala was hosted at Dr. Lin's massive Texas estate, and the entire extravaganza was paid for by the Dynasty Global Foundation.

Fu Wang, Dr. Lin's Director of Finance, coordinated transportation and kept a close watch to ensure everyone arrived smoothly. The isolated estate had two runways for small jets, two helicopter pads, and a small terminal. It was a busy day, but so far, everything went as planned.

While pouring coffee in the break room, Wang remarked to one of his female staff members, "Isn't it interesting that so many delegates who want to regulate other people's so-called carbon footprints arrive in their private jets? So far, I've seen a Gulfstream, three Lear jets, two Hawkers, and an Eclipse fly in, and more are coming."

She laughed. "Indeed, especially; since they had the option to arrive by commercial flights and take a shuttle here at no expense. I guess it was too inconvenient for such important people."

Wang shook his head as if unable to believe what he already knew to be true. "Yes. The jet-setting environmentalists are all quite amusing, whether they are rich celebrities, politicians, or these UN People."

"If by amusing you mean hypocritical, then I agree."

The first day of the celebration was orchestrated by Fu Wang and Dr. Ling to be fun and a time for the delegates to converse. Dr. Lin was strategically absent that day to allow the guests time to relax, mingle, and talk freely without his presence being a distraction.

Some delegates lounged around the beautiful guest swimming pool, while others played golf, tennis, shuffleboard, putt-putt, or took advantage of free body massages. Dynasty Global Foundation staff gave supervised horseback rides for novice riders, while those more skilled were invited on longer rides to see parts of the large cattle ranch surrounding the estate. Strolling musicians added to the festive atmosphere with joyful music.

The American delegate, Tara Ruggerio, mingled with other guests at poolside before enjoying a massage. Earlier, she walked around to absorb the ambience. She'd never been anywhere so spectacular. Paths were lined with flowers lit with Chinese lanterns at night. The sculptures of Chinese emperors, dragons, and tigers were grand in size and excellent in quality. Numerous decorative ponds with quaint bridges added to the grounds' tranquil splendor.

Chinese kites of birds, turtles, tigers, and dragons added color to the sky, as skillful staff flew them. A young female staff member flew a green and yellow turtle kite when she saw a sixty-something-year-old man in tan shorts, green shirt, and teardrop shades staring at her nearby. She smiled and called, "Would you like to give the kite a try?"

He looked around and playfully pointed a finger at himself. "Me?"

She laughed. "Of course, you."

"Sure." He ran over to stand beside her, subtly checking her out, as she explained how best to fly the large kite. He loved her long black hair, shapely legs, and smooth skin. He found her attractive from a distance, but she was even more stunning up close.

"Here you go." She handed him the line. "Do you have it?"

"Got it."

"I am Luli Sun."

"Hello, Luli. I'm Robert Hyde. You can call me Bobby."

She giggled at the idea of calling an older man by such a boyish name. "Nice to meet you, Bobby."

At first the kite flew well in his grip, but, when the wind died, he struggled to keep it aloft.

Luli took the line from him and ran around to catch the breeze just right. "Here, like this!" she called, still running.

Bobby enjoyed watching her run. She was beautiful.

After the kite stabled again, Luli gave him the line.

He did as she advised, and it worked well, but he wasn't as young or as fit as she, so after a few minutes, he stopped to catch his breath, and the kite struggled again.

She giggled pleasantly at his panting for breath, took the line, and helped him get it flying again.

Bobby, his hands on his knees as he bent over to catch his breath, said, "Thank you. I'm not in the shape I used to be."

"You're doing fine."

"Not really, but thank you for saying so. Can you believe I used to be a high-school ice hockey star? Now look at me."

"You look just fine. I can tell you used to be an athlete. You just haven't run for a while. You probably have more-important things to do. Are you one of the United Nation delegates?"

"Guilty as charged," he said proudly, standing up straight again.

She smiled sweetly. "We're honored to have you here. Your work must be very interesting."

"It can be, but it's usually pretty routine, to tell the truth."

"I bet it's amazing and very important work. Your wife must be very proud of you."

"That's nice of you to say." After a short pause, he added, "She used to be proud of me, but she doesn't seem to care much about what I do anymore."

"Oh, I'm so sorry."

"Don't be. The truth is the truth. She just likes to take my credit card and shop all day. I'm used to it."

"Perhaps she's buying you nice things," she replied pleasantly.

He chuckled. "Right. No, she likes dresses, purses, hats, shoes, and then more dresses, purses, hats, and shoes."

"I see. Well, all of that must make her look very pretty."

Bobby shrugged. "I guess so. She used to be very pretty."

"What country do you represent at the United Nations?"

"Canada."

Luli looked up at the sky, as she talked. "I've never been to Canada. I hear it's very beautiful."

"It is." He almost added, *Like you,* but thought better of it. He usually needed a few drinks to flirt properly.

Luli, savvy in the ways of men, knew exactly what he was thinking by the look in his eye. Purposely stringing him along, she asked, wide-eyed and excited, "What did you do before you were a United Nations delegate? It must have been something very special for you to be selected to represent your country."

"I owned an advertising business. I have to say it was very successful. We have offices all over Canada and the United States. I backed away from active management when I took the UN gig, but I'm still co-owner."

"Wow! An advertising business. How exciting. I always dreamed of being a model for an advertising business. Do you hire models?"

"We do, as a matter of fact. Yes, you're pretty enough to be one of our models." He felt more comfortable around her.

She bounced up and down on her toes in excitement. "Do you mean it? Do you really mean it?"

He appraised her openly, as she turned and posed for him. She was so child-like, cute and innocent. "Sure, I mean it. You're quite beautiful."

She looked at him shyly. "Thank you. You're so sweet." After a moment, she added, "You must be a very caring man to give up your business to work for the United Nations."

His chest expanded with pride. "You do what you must when your nation calls. Sure, you can never have enough money, but I do fine. The United Nations has its perks, like this trip. I have a feeling it will be a lot of fun, and very important, of course."

"Have you had a good time so far?"

"Yes, of course. It's been great." After a moment's hesitation, he added, "Even more so now, thanks to you. I never knew kites were so much fun."

Her pleasant smile grew wider, and she kissed his cheek. "That makes me happy. I like making people happy."

He smiled back and wondered if she was truly being seductive or was just a tease. Did she actually like him, or was she after his connections to get a modeling gig? Then again, what did it matter? If she was after a modeling job, that was OK with him. He could play that game. It happened several times before. He could string her along without making any promises.

The possibilities excited him. "What do you do here, exactly?"

"I'm on the entertainment staff. I set up for the parties and help make sure everyone has a good time. Dr. Lin entertains visitors here often, although few are as special as delegates from the United Nations."

"Well, you do a very good job. The relaxing atmosphere around here is amazing."

She put a hand gently on his arm. "You're so sweet. Thank you, Bobby." Her hand lingered just long enough to see his excitement build, then she pulled away. "Do you like to dance?"

"A little. Why?"

"There will be music and dancing later tonight. I, and all the other entertainment staff, will be there to dance with guests. We help them break the ice, if you know what I mean. I could look for you if you wish. Perhaps we could dance together."

"I'm afraid I'm not much of a dancer," he said sheepishly.

"Then I'll show you how. I'm a good teacher. That's why I'm here, just like with the kite. It'll be fun. Promise me you'll be there. I'll enjoy it, too."

Bobby smiled broadly. "OK, then."

"Then it's a date?"

"It's a date."

She gave him a smile and a cute wink. "I guarantee you'll have a good time."

He smiled with eager anticipation. "I know I will."

Luli saw the kite falling again and took it from him.

Like other delegates, Bobby had a job to do. Mostly, he wanted to know how, when, and where Dr. Lin intended to spend his money. Everyone knew that prior to his announcement, the United Nations reluctantly agreed to give him almost total control of how the funds were spent, as long as it was in their name. Bobby had a lot of mingling to do to ensure Canada got its fair share.

After another five minutes, he said, "This has really been fun, but I'm afraid I have to go."

"So soon?"

"I have to meet with other delegates and discuss United Nations business. I hope you understand."

"Of course. You're an important man, and you have important work to do. Thank you for hanging out with me for a while, Mr. Hyde. I had fun meeting you."

"It's Bobby."

She smiled, brushing hair over her shoulder with a coy expression. "I had fun meeting you, Bobby."

"So I'll see you later?"

"Oh, yes. We'll have a good time together."

He looked around for transportation options. He took a charming man-pulled rickshaw earlier, but there were none in sight. After a few minutes, an electric golf cart with *DGF* on its side came by, and he hailed it down.

Luli smiled and waved, as he pulled away. He waved back, closed his eyes, and fantasized about being with her later that night.

CHAPTER 15

The evening meal was a banquet of some of the finest delicacies from around the world. Small flags beside each dish described the food and its country of origin. Even those delegates who stuffed their plates couldn't come close to sampling all the dishes available. Wine, beer, cold drinks, and water were all available as beverages, and pleasant music filled the air without interfering with conversation, as the delegates mingled.

After they ate, some delegates returned to their prior leisure activities. Others went to their rooms to relax, nap, make calls, and change clothes. Bobby Hyde stripped down to his underwear and went to bed to take a nap before the evening fun.

First, he called Missy, his wife. It was best to get it done early.

He listened patiently, as she told him about the new clothes she bought at a French boutique that day and the lunch with her best friend, Kelly. Bobby told her about Mr. Lin's beautiful estate and upcoming meetings. He neglected to mention all the fun he had flying a Chinese kite with Luli or about the casino party later.

"I'll be doing some reading tonight," he said. "In fact, I'm already in bed." That was true, at least, and he planned to read his email.

"Oh, Honey, all work and no play is no fun. At least watch a movie or some TV before going to bed."

He sighed. "We'll see. I'll call you tomorrow."

"OK. Love you."

"Love you."

After the brief conversation, he read his email, replied to a few, and lay down for another nap. Hopefully, it would be a long night of drinking and fun. His last thoughts were of Luli running around in the field, flying the kite.

A few hours later, delegates began arriving at the covered outdoor entertainment facility that hosted the casino party. The atmosphere reminded some of their college spring break parties. Few could remember when they had such fun. Spouses and families weren't invited, so delegates danced with entertainment specialists or each other. Some didn't like the idea of dancing without their spouse, so they gambled, drank, and socialized.

When Bobby woke, he looked at the clock and said, "Shit!" He forgot to set an alarm and overslept by two hours. He quickly showered, dried off, and donned khaki pants, a white shirt, and blue blazer before running outside to hail a DGF rickshaw.

When he arrived, he took his $250 in casino chips and looked for Luli. She wasn't in the casino area. Instead of gambling, he looked on the dance floor. After ten minutes, he found her, and his heart sank. She was dancing with a young, nice-looking man.

He went to the bar and ordered a cocktail. After downing his first drink quickly, he ordered another and found a table where he could watch Luli.

She was beautiful, moving smoothly and seductively, as she danced. He sighed. Would she even want to dance with him anymore? Had she ever wanted to? Her low-cut, thin, white dress clung tightly to her body. Bobby fantasized what she looked like without it and what she would be like in bed.

He had a third drink before she looked his way. To his delight, she smiled and waved at him. He smiled and waved back.

When the song ended, Luli excused herself from the younger man and came toward him. Bobby pushed himself up from his chair to greet her. A crackle in his left knee made him groan with a twinge of pain. Embarrassed that she heard it, he said, "My damn arthritis. Hockey's hard on the joints."

"Oh, you play hockey? I heard it's a very rough sport."

"I do. Well, I used to play when I was younger and more fit."

"You look fit to me." She reached for his hand. "Would you like to dance?"

He took her hand. "I wasn't sure if you still wanted to. Aren't you dancing with that guy?"

"Don't be silly. Of course I want to dance with you. I didn't see you until now, then I came over as soon as I could." She leaned over to whisper, "Men his age are too immature for me. I like grown men. Come on. Let's dance."

Smiling, he followed her to the dance floor, where he was a bit hesitant and self-conscious, but he learned quickly.

The dancing and open bar lasted long into the night. When Bobby and Luli were tired or too hot, they took breaks to gamble. With her help, he gambled away the money he received very quickly and had to buy more chips. When that was gone, he bought more.

Bobby couldn't remember when he had so much fun. He knew she was working, so he was pleasantly surprised when she spent all her time with him.

He drank slowly but steadily. Eventually, he was so drunk, Luli almost had to hold him up, as they slow-danced.

Her body felt soft and wonderful against his. She glowed with faint perspiration, which only turned him on more. She laid her head on his shoulder and wrapped her arms around him.

Slowly, his hand slid down her back until it came to her butt. It stopped there for several moments before he raised it again. She didn't seem to mind, so he did it again.

Eventually, he whispered into her ear, "You're quite beautiful, you know."

She lifted her head off his shoulder to look at him. "You're so sweet, Bobby. I find you charming as well."

He looked into her dark-brown eyes. He wanted her then and there. "I think I've had too much to drink, but I'm not sure I can get back to my room by myself."

Luli giggled. "Do you need my help?"

"If you don't mind."

"Of course not. Let me grab my purse. I'll be right back."

While she was away, he downed another quick drink. He definitely felt his alcohol—not to mention being hopeful. The night turned out better than he could have imagined, and who knew what might come next?

Bobby's gait was wobbly, so he leaned on Luli all the way back to his room after they got off the DGF transportation cart.

She laughed, as she helped him get his key card into the door. She carefully guided him onto the bed, making sure he didn't fall to the floor.

"There you go." She giggled with intoxication. "All safe and sound."

Bobby leaned on the edge of the bed. "Thank you."

To his disappointment, she walked slowly to the door and looked back before opening it. "Will you be all right now? Do you need anything else?"

"Actually, I was hoping you could stay awhile and keep me company. Maybe we could dance some more in private. I have some great music on my cell phone."

She gazed at him as if struggling with a difficult decision.

"I promise I won't bite." He chuckled. "Much." He turned on some Al Green.

Luli laughed at the joke she heard many times before, locked the door, and walked toward him.

He stood to take her in his arms to slow-dance. They swayed slowly back and forth to the music.

He softly kissed her neck several times. They didn't even finish the song before they were taking off each other's clothes.

She stayed with him for two hours. Luli was prepared to stay longer, but it wasn't necessary. By the time she left, Bobby's carnal desires were fully satisfied, and he snored in the bed.

What she knew but he didn't was that the entire bedroom encounter was being watched and recorded by prying eyes. Tiny audio and visual surveillance devices were hidden in every guest bedroom, lounge, dining area, and restroom.

In an underground floor of the main security building, teams of surveillance and analysis staff hovered over computer consoles, monitoring and recording the delegate's conversations and activities. Their work began as soon as delegates began arriving and wouldn't stop until the last one left the estate. The huge surveillance room rivaled NASA's Command and Control Center in the number of monitors and the complexity of the operation.

The staff listened for any revealing personal information, such as opinions about Dr. Lin and Dynasty Global Foundation, political stances, and other matters of potential use for extortion and manipulation. All the data was organized, categorized, labeled, and tagged for future review and use by Dr. Lin.

Retired General Hui Chen, Director of Security and Surveillance, ran the operation himself. He walked from monitor to monitor, observing how the operation was going, musing over what he witnessed. Delegates who gambled heavily were labeled as having a possible gambling addiction. Those who turned in their chips for personal cash were tagged for possible financial problems. Those who used illicit drugs in their rooms were noted as drug abusers. Those who had sex with the entertainment staff or each other were marked for potential sexual blackmail.

The staff was well-trained, well-paid, and knew exactly what Dr. Lin wanted to find.

CHAPTER 16

Dr. Lin arrived late in the afternoon of the following day. He flew in at noon on a Gulfstream G650 that he named *Dynasty One*. There was great fanfare and excitement when the jet's landing was announced. Many delegates rushed to watch him deplane. A portable podium and acoustic system was quickly set up by a well-trained crew near the landing strip.

Dr. Lin waved to the enthusiastic crowd like a famous celebrity when he stepped from the jet. More and more guests and staff gathered around the podium. A few cheered, as he walked to the microphone.

Tara, the American delegate, commented softly to the Israeli delegate nearby, "I don't think his arrival could have been more dramatic if he were the President of the United States."

"Or a visitor from outer space," he joked.

At the podium, Dr. Lin continued waving a greeting. "Thank you. Thank you. Thank you very much for your warm welcome."

The cheers increased, but he motioned with his hands to calm the applause. "Thank you. Thank you. I'm so happy to have delegates from the United Nations here at my humble home. I hope you're all having a good time."

The applauding delegates cheered loudly.

"I'm sorry I couldn't be here before today, but I unfortunately had pressing business concerning vital upgrading of two GDF ships used to provide medications to needy children around the globe." He shook his head. "Such work cannot wait."

An entertainment staff member began chanting, "Dr. Lin! Dr. Lin!"

A chorus of people joined in.

He basked in their cheers but eventually waved his hands to quiet the crowd. "Thank you. I have a few important matters to attend to right now, but I will be with you at the banquet this evening. Until then, please continue to relax, mingle, and enjoy yourselves. I hope to meet each one of you before the celebration is over. Don't hesitate to ask me, or any of my staff, for anything you need. We are your servants."

Placing his hand over his heart, he bowed his head in humility. When he looked up again, he said, "Thank you all again for coming. I hope to make our time together something you will always remember."

He gave one final wave before getting into a DGF transportation cart.

Once in the private wing of his mansion, Dr. Lin removed his suit and tie and immediately slipped into the large Jacuzzi waiting for him. He was in a joyful mood after such an enthusiastic welcome.

The water felt good. Four concubines were summoned to join him. They removed their clothes and got in. After twenty minutes of relaxation and water play, he pointed at two of them.

"You two have pleased me most. You may come to my bed. The rest of you must entertain our guests."

After sex with his concubines, Dr. Lin dressed and went to his main office to work. He made multiple calls to investors and various administrators of companies he owned, and then he read through a number of profiles on potential clients and email. Finally, he asked an attendant to bring General Chen to him.

When the general arrived, Dr. Lin beckoned him to a seat. "Tell me, Hui, what are the guests saying so far?"

"Many things, Master Lin. First, they are most impressed by the grandeur of your estate and their accommodations."

"As well they should be."

"Some were concerned that you weren't there to greet them as they arrived. Many were worried you wouldn't attend the festivities at all."

Dr. Lin grinned and leaned back in his chair. "It's good to keep them guessing, Old Friend. It has more impact when they finally see me."

"You're most wise in the ways of showmanship."

Dr. Lin nodded. "Yes. I was pleased with the response at my arrival. Showmanship wins half the battle before it begins."

The general nodded.

"What else do you have for me?"

"Many spoke less about celebrating your generous donation than concern that you give their country some of the money."

"Of course." He nonchalantly waved his hand. "The important thing is that they're here."

"Surprisingly to me, many don't think a billion dollars is enough to go around—unless most of it goes to their country."

Dr. Lin shrugged. "They're right, General. A billion dollars isn't as much money as it once was, but it's enough to get everyone's attention, and we did."

"That's true."

"What else did they say?"

"Interestingly, given your great wealth, a few plan to ask you for personal favors." He stood to hand Dr. Lin some papers. "Here is a list of those people and what they plan to ask of you. I also listed those with serious personal problems that you might be able to exploit."

"Well done. This will be very useful. I'll read it shortly and be ready for them."

The general handed him more documents. "Here is our other surveillance information. Some will be of great interest to you, I'm sure. You'll find summaries of important conversations, a list of audio recordings you may want to listen to later, and some videos that you'll enjoy watching. Some are very funny."

"I can't wait," Dr. Lin said, excited. "It sounds like you and your staff did a thorough job."

The general bowed his head in acknowledgement of the rare compliment. "I must say, Master Lin, your plan seems to be working perfectly. We have already gathered an incredible amount of information we can use to achieve our goals."

Dr. Lin skimmed through the reports. "Of course it's working, General." As he read, he muttered softly, "So what are my guests up to, I wonder?"

A few moments later, he laughed. "I'm pleased that several delegates have already found pleasure with my concubines."

"Oh, yes. Your entertainers are doing a wonderful job of enticement."

"They should. They've been very well-trained, and a generous bonus awaits them if they bring a guest to a compromising situation."

After reading more, he laughed again. "A few of them found pleasure in the arms of each other, I see. They must think that what happens in Texas, stays in Texas." He chuckled. "They'll soon find out that's not the case."

The general laughed with him.

"I assume you know the names of their spouses or significant others."

"Of course. You should have heard their innocent conversations with them."

Dr. Lin scratched the back of his neck. "There's nothing like the threat of exposing a sexual affair to get the full attention and cooperation from those who need extra prompting."

General Chen grinned and nodded.

"What fools they are."

"Look here." The general pointed to a page farther down in the report. "One of our female guests fell prey to one of the concubines, as well." He laughed. "She's married, no less."

Dr. Lin laughed so hard, he almost cried. "This is all too easy, General. See to it that the concubines who were successful in their seductions are rewarded."

"Of course, Dr. Lin."

"Give the one who seduced the married female delegate a double bonus."

The general nodded. "Such rewards will encourage even greater efforts from our entertainers." After a moment, he added, "We also have information on a couple of delegates who used drugs in their rooms."

"Excellent." Dr. Lin set aside the papers and looked at the general. "Keep all the videos and reports in your securest vault. I'll review them in short order."

"Of course."

Titus enjoyed the beautiful sunrise and surrounding woods, as he and Frederick maneuvered the boat on the Tennessee River a short distance from campus. The fresh morning air was wonderful, and a break from his normal routine with the FBI felt great.

Frederick didn't have much luck with top water baits but did better when they switched to plastic worms. He watched Titus' technique and wasn't impressed. "Cast your line, so your lure moves with the current. The bass are waiting for fish to swim to them. Your lure needs to act like the fish they're used to."

"Will do." Eventually Titus landed one large bass and two small ones.

Frederick pulled in several smaller fish and six keepers. The small ones were thrown back. "Not a bad morning," he said with a smile when they prepared to leave. "We'll have just enough for a fish bake tonight. Bass aren't the best fish to eat, but they're fun to catch, and they'll do."

"Sounds good to me. I'm just happy I caught something. I haven't done anything like this in years."

On their way home, Frederick stopped his SUV at a small shack in the middle of nowhere and got out. "Wait here a minute. I'll be right back." He opened the back and grabbed the cooler full of fish, taking out the largest and putting it in a bag.

Frederick walked to the small house that looked ready to fall down with a strong breeze, then he knocked gently on the door.

A few minutes later, an elderly Black woman answered. She was thin and short, with snow-white hair, and she wore a blue nightgown with pink slippers. A metal cane with three prongs at the base helped her stand. "Well, hello there, Dr. Welkener. How you doin' this fine morning?"

"Hello, Ms. Green. I'm fine, thank you. I hope I'm not disturbing you too early in the morning."

"No, no, of course not. The place is a mess, but come on in. I've been up for over an hour. Do you want some coffee? I'll warm up some for you."

"That's very nice of you, but I can't stay long."

She looked at the bag in his hands. "What you got dere?"

He slid part of the fish out to show her. "How would you like a nice, big bass for dinner?"

"Oh, my, but that do sound wonderful. I'll fry it up tonight for sure. Thank you so much for bringin' it. I 'ppreciate you and your lovely wife always lookin' out fer me. You know, Miss Isabella brought me some pie yesterday."

"She did?" After a brief pause, he added in amusement, "So that's where it went."

Instead of laughing, her eyebrows went up in concern. She pointed at a small refrigerator inside. "I still have some left if you want some. I didn't know it was for you."

"No, no. I was just teasing. Please forgive me. She made it just for you, Ms. Green."

"You sure?"

He placed a hand over his heart. "I promise."

"OK, but you're welcome to it."

Frederick shook his head and backed toward the door. "Good to see you, but I have to go. It's a workday." He waved good-bye. "Enjoy the fish and have a blessed day, Ms. Green."

"You, too, Dr. Welkener. God bless you."

When Frederick was back in the car, Titus asked, "Who is she?"

"Just a poor widow Isabella met in the grocery store about six months ago. She was having a hard time loading her groceries, and Isabella helped her out. Then Isabella followed her home to help her unload."

"That was nice of her."

"They got to talkin', and Isabelle found out she lost her husband to cancer a few years back. Now she lives alone in that tiny house."

"Does she have any children?"

"One son who lives in Nashville and rarely visits. To tell the truth, I haven't seen him here."

Titus nodded.

"Anyway, she doesn't have much, so Isabella and I try to check on her when we can. She loves fish." He took a last look at the shack. "I got to get back over here sometime soon and fix that porch."

Later that afternoon, Titus slipped quietly into the back row of the neurophysiology classroom just as Dr. Burrus was about to begin his lecture. Sewanee's class sizes were small, so everyone knew each other. Several students noticed the new, older guy and wondered who he was. An attractive brunette with an oversized Sewanee sweatshirt sitting in the same row unexpectedly gave Titus a big, almost alluring smile.

He smiled back but immediately looked away. He had no interest in college-age females.

Frederick tapped the mic. "Good morning, Class."

"Good morning," a few students replied.

"I hope everyone picked up the class handout, as you came in the door. As you can see, I've changed the lecture schedule a bit. The next couple of lectures won't be about vision as previously planned but will focus on sleep. I apologize to any of you who read ahead on vision, but I promise we'll return to that after we discuss sleep."

The students stirred in their places, and Dr. Burrus sensed some disappointment. "I realize that to some, sleep doesn't sound very exciting, but I believe the more you learn about it, the more fascinating the topic will be. It certainly has become that to me."

A few heads nodded.

"Let me begin by asking you, 'What is sleep?'"

At first, no one replied.

"Come on. Don't be shy. This isn't a trick question, and there are no wrong answers."

A student in the second row raised her hand.

"Yes, Victoria?"

"It's a state of unconsciousness that happens every night."

"OK, that's a good start. Sleep is indeed a naturally occurring state with decreased consciousness to stimuli that occurs in a cyclical time frame of about every twenty-four hours for human beings. For most people, it occurs at night, but not for everyone. The reduction in consciousness is significant but not absolute. For example, it's not as deep as being in a coma. Agreed?"

Heads nodded.

"There are other changes that also take place during sleep." He turned off the room lights and put up a PowerPoint slide. "As you can see, there are changes in muscle tension, breathing, heart rate, eye movement, and significant alterations in brainwaves. These brain wave changes can be monitored by an electroencephalograph, simply called an EEG."

Students took notes, as he spoke.

The next slide showed someone with electrodes on his head during a sleep study. "The EEG studies show that brainwaves change when a person goes from a waking state into light sleep, then at various stages of deeper sleep."

Another slide showed actual EEG tracings and information about each stage of sleep.

The students' eyes darted back and forth from their handouts to be sure the information they had was the same in both formats. Some still felt a bit uneasy at the sudden change in schedule.

"As you can see, the 8-13 Hz alpha waves of wakefulness transition into the 4-7 Hz theta waves as light sleep begins. This is called Stage 1 sleep. As sleep becomes deeper, Stage 2 begins." He changed to the next slide. "That's shown here with 11-16 Hz sleep spindles and K complexes."

He waited, as some students struggled to keep up with their notes.

The next slide came up. "In Stage 3, or deep sleep, brainwaves slow to 3-5 Hz, referred to as Delta activity. Some texts include a Stage 4 as well, but many simply combine Stages 3 and 4 into just Stage 3."

Students' heads nodded, as they showed increased interest.

The next slide came up. "Rapid Eye Movement, or REM sleep, is associated with dreaming and has high-frequency EEG waves resembling wakefulness. As implied from the name, the sleeping person's eyes move as if he were watching something, but of course, the person is totally asleep."

"Excuse me, Dr. Welkener, but I've always wondered. Why do we need sleep?" a dark-haired student wearing a University of Georgia football shirt asked from the first row.

"Great question, Austin. I was just about to ask the class that very thing. What do all of you think is the purpose of sleep?"

"So the body can rest and refresh itself," someone replied from the middle row.

"True. I'm sure that takes place, but you can rest without sleeping, can't you?"

"True," a few mumbled.

"So if the body doesn't have to sleep to rejuvenate itself, what's going on?" Frederick asked.

"It's a brain thing," a young woman with reddish-blonde hair called from the back. "It must do something for the brain."

"You're onto something, Amelia. Sleep must have more to do with the brain, or the mind, if you will, than just the body itself."

"I'll bet it sort of reboots the brain," a young blonde woman in the third row said.

"That's a good way to think of it, Emmalyn. Surely, the brainwave changes coincide with significant neurochemical changes or renewal that we might call rebooting."

Heads nodded.

"The famous Austrian neurologist and psychoanalyst, Dr. Sigmund Freud, thought the purpose of sleep was what he called 'dream work.' He suggested that dream work entailed mentally dealing with the residue of the day's activities, as well as subconscious conflicts."

Titus sat up straighter in his chair. He knew about Freud, but he didn't know the man's perspective on sleep.

"Dr. Freud believed that insomnia was a failure to achieve adequate dream work concerning unresolved, disturbing, and often sexually oriented subconscious conflicts, such as the Oedipus complex."

"Dr. Welkener, animals sleep," an athletic blond young man in a soccer shirt said, "Are you saying that male horses sleep in order to resolve their subconscious desire to have sex with their mothers and kill their fathers?"

Laughter erupted in the room.

Frederick smiled. "Landon, as usual, you pose an interesting question. It's a very valid point, and I can tell you've already had a class or two in psychology."

Landon smiled. "Last semester."

Frederick nodded. "I said Dr. Freud proposed those things, not me. I brought him up mostly for historical purposes. I'm more of a biological type of thinker myself. By the way, Dr. Freud was a biological thinker, too, but he understood the neurochemistry of the brain was poorly defined and of limited use during his lifetime to explain much. He turned to psychologically oriented explanations. Our limited knowledge about the brain is still true today, but science has advanced a great deal since Freud."

Titus enjoyed the lecture more with each passing slide. It was awhile since he took a college lecture, and he was glad Frederick invited him to come. The students seemed young, eager, and ready to take on the world of ideas and thoughts. It made him miss his own college days, when anything was possible, and he wasn't quite so hardened by the real world. Back then, he saw the world with a wide-open mind, just like the students around him. Later, he came to view the world with suspicion, waiting and watching for the next tragedy to occur.

"Of course, today our emphasis is focused on the need for neurochemical resetting, or rebooting of the brain, as Emmalyn suggested. I think that would explain the need for sleep even in animals, Landon."

Landon nodded, pleasantly surprised that what he said mostly as a joke led to a legitimate discussion.

"Most people sleep around six to eight hours a day. Without it, many bad things can happen. Who wants to name a few consequences of not sleeping?"

"I get cranky," Victoria admitted.

"I feel tired all the next day," a skinny student named Jim said, cleaning his glasses.

Tom, one of the brighter students, added, "My cognitive abilities aren't as sharp after a bad night's sleep."

"Those are all excellent answers," the professor said. "Many other consequences can occur."

The next slide came up. "Body aches, inability to complete tasks, heart abnormalities, worsening of all sorts of mental health disorders, and even increased mortality risk can occur with severe insomnia. Sleep is truly an important phenomenon. It's not the benign phenomenon many people think. Does anyone have an idea which groups of people are at greatest risk for insomnia?"

"The elderly," Kinley called from the back row. "I worked at a nursing home last summer, and insomnia was a terrible problem with many of the residents."

"Yes, that's true. The elderly are at risk. Shift workers, alcoholics, drug abuser, divorcees, widowers, lower socioeconomic people, those with anxiety problems, and pregnant or menopausal females are also at increased risk for insomnia."

Titus chuckled to himself at the irony that one of the students in front of him was nodding off during a lecture about sleep. He felt the student was probably in the partying and excessive alcoholic risk group.

"So how does sleep happen? In other words, what's the neurophysiological mechanism of sleep?"

No one responded.

Dr. Burrus looked around the room and saw the student in front of Titus sleeping. "What do you think, John Neubert?"

John woke, startled, trying to remember where he was.

"So what do you think, John?"

"Sorry. I missed the question."

"I see. Fortunately for you, we'll discuss the neurophysiological mechanism of sleep tomorrow."

CHAPTER 18

After the delegates finished their delicious evening banquet, Dr. Lin walked to the elevated platform to address the crowd. He took a moment to look out at all the eyes beaming up at him, treasuring their expressions of awe and admiration. Several assistants helped hush the crowd until there was total silence.

In a benevolent tone, Dr. Lin began, "Delegates to the United Nations, thank you again for coming and sharing this celebration in my humble home. It's important that we relax and enjoy ourselves, because we have much work to do. The world, the earth itself, is dying and desperately needs our help."

Heads nodded throughout the assembly.

"Our time together isn't just a celebration of the billion dollars I will donate to the United Nations to fight global warming and climate change, but also to start planning the exciting work ahead. History will remember this moment, and you'll be remembered for the important contribution you played in this great fight for the survival of our planet."

Applause erupted in excitement, as did many of the egos listening.

"The money I have donated isn't the last, just the beginning. I hope to do much more. The vast job ahead will need all our best ideas and efforts. Each of you has the responsibility to convince the citizens and leaders of your country that the United Nations needs greater authority and more financing so world problems, primarily global warming, can be dealt with effectively."

Intermittent applause continued.

"We currently live in a world of many distinct nations. Each nation selfishly looks out for its own special interests. There is no overseeing authority with power enough to solve international disagreements, stop wars, care for the ill, feed the hungry, and prevent climate change." He pounded lightly on the podium. "This, my friends, must not continue."

The applause was enormous.

Dr. Lin, a student of oratory, allowed the applause to go on for a full minute before he continued.

"One global authority must be able to override an individual nation's petty interests. The United Nations should have that authority. It must oversee and control carbon emissions. It must be able to levy taxes, enforce stiff financial penalties, and issue harsher sanctions against nations that do not comply with the important mandates from the United Nations. We must think like one global community, one global family, like one village, if we are to correct global problems."

The applause was so thunderous, he had to wait a long time before he could continue.

"The United Nations must also have the strongest military force on the planet to do its job. That military force must be under no other authority than the United Nations itself. After all, who else can we trust?"

"No one!" someone shouted, quickly echoed by others.

"Only, you, the representatives of the United Nations, understand what the world needs. Only you can save the planet from the thoughtless actions of so many countries, including my own. Only you can bring enough power to the United Nations to stop those who don't understand or don't care if they destroy the planet. Yes, *you* are the key. You have the power. You're the chosen few with the wisdom and influence to solve the great problems of the world."

Egos swelled with such pride that some delegates jumped up and down, applauding in excitement.

"I urge you to exert your influence in your home countries. Whatever leadership and support I can provide in this great cause, I happily give to you. Tonight, and until you leave, I'll endeavor to get to know each of you to find out how I can help."

Applause continued.

Dr. Lin waved his hands for silence, then he smiled and lowered his voice. "For now, please relax and enjoy the celebration. Thank you, My Friends. I hope you have a wonderful time."

They gave him a standing ovation. Excitement was everywhere—almost.

Tara Ruggerio was quite concerned about what Dr. Lin said. She whispered into the ear of Moshe Cohen, the delegate from Israel, sitting beside her, "We need the UN just like we need the World Health Organization, but do these delegates understand what he said? Does he really want to give a single global bureaucracy so much unchecked power?"

"That's what he says, and that could be very dangerous. Israel has many enemies in the United Nations."

Ruggerio crossed her arms over her chest. "Every nation takes the best care of itself. Self-responsibility works for people and for nations. Otherwise, you become a dependent country, begging for the UN to take care of you. If they don't, there's nothing you can do."

Given the crowd's reaction to the speech, they kept their voices low.

"His persona uses climate hysteria as a means for power," Cohen said. "As I've heard some say in your country, 'Green is the new red.' It's true. If we aren't careful, we could end up with a one-world government. Do you know what the worst thing is about such a government?"

"I could think of many things, but I'll say no."

"There's nowhere to run."

Dr. Lin spent the evening mingling with as many delegates as possible. Aides whispered information to him about each person, but he also had an excellent memory and reviewed biographies about the guests before the gathering.

When he met with Delegate Viktor Petrov from Russia, he gently pulled him aside to speak privately. "It's come to my attention that your wife has bone cancer. I'm so sorry to hear about it."

"Yes, thank you," Petrov replied solemnly. "I fear for her greatly."

"Of course you do." After a brief pause, he added, "I'd like to give you the name of the best bone oncologist in the United States. He practices in nearby Houston. If you like, I could set up an appointment for your wife with him. I've helped him in the past, and he owes me a favor."

"That's very kind of you," Petrov said somewhat suspiciously, "but I'm just an old soldier and not a wealthy American like you. We have excellent doctors in Russia, too."

"Forgive me for saying it, but there's none better in the world than the one here in Houston. I can probably persuade him to take your wife's case at no charge if you wish. It would do no harm and might be a great help."

He still eyed Dr. Lin suspiciously. "Why would you do that for me? What do you want in return?"

Dr. Lin, taken aback, spread his arms and looked around the beautiful ballroom. "As you can see, I have all that I need, but I do have humanitarian projects that are very dear to me. We must all work together against global warming."

Petrov didn't reply.

"I ask myself how you can help us with that effort if your mind is on your wife's health? If you want me to make the arrangements, I will. If not, that is your decision. I'm only trying to help your wife and build international teamwork for a common cause."

The Russian delegate scrutinized Dr. Lin for a moment, then he patted the billionaire's shoulder. "Please take no offense. Your offer is most generous. I would be very grateful if you make such arrangements. I'm afraid it's a very aggressive cancer. She has little time. I almost didn't come to this meeting because of her illness."

"Of course. That's what I mean." He called an assistant over and whispered in her ear. She nodded and walked away.

After she left, Dr. Lin said, "My assistant will call the doctor tomorrow in my name. She'll let you know what arrangements can be made for your wife before you leave the conference. Just let me or her know how to contact your wife."

The Russian smiled. "Thank you, but I have a confession to make." He leaned closer and whispered conspiratorially, "I care nothing about this global warming. In fact, if it's real, it may help Mother Russia's climate and agriculture." He smiled and gently touched Dr. Lin's shoulder. "I'm tired of being cold."

Dr. Lin smiled and shook his head.

"My wife will be very excited to have another expert opinion on her cancer. Maybe he can help her. Who knows? As you say, it's worth a shot. Thank you. I love her very much."

Dr. Lin looked at him as if he suddenly had a new idea. "Viktor, I started out in the pharmaceutical business. I know how expensive medications can be, especially for cancer. If new medications are needed but are too costly, let me know. Dynasty Global Foundation will help pay for them. Again, I want nothing from you."

Petrov's eyebrows shot up. The cost of new medications had already occurred to him, but he hadn't wanted to say anything. "That would be most generous. I must admit I was concerned about that. I'll remember this, Dr. Lin. I'm in your debt no matter what happens. Thank you."

As Petrov walked away, Dr. Lin felt pleased. He'd been worried about gaining Russia's cooperation before that conversation.

As he continued mingling, he noticed Delegate Hagi from Mozambique and recalled the man had a gambling problem. Dr. Lin's sources indicated Hagi's debts were well over $100,000. He had an aide casually mention in Hagi's earshot that Dr. Lin sometimes gave personal loans to colleagues in need.

As Dr. Lin hoped, Delegate Hagi soon found his way over to him to congratulate him on an inspiring speech.

After some small talk, Hagi said, "Life has been so hard and difficult on my family this last year, Dr. Lin."

"I'm so sorry. Why is that?" he asked. concerned.

"My mother is getting old, and end-of-life care is so expensive these days. My daughter wants to go to college in America. That, too, is very expensive, I'm afraid."

Dr. Lin nodded without speaking.

"I have no idea how I can pay for either. I mention this, so you'll know if things don't improve, I'll have to return to my business and leave the United Nations. It was my hope to help you with our crusade to save the planet from climate disaster, but I'm afraid I may not be able to manage it with so many financial problems."

"I'm very sorry to hear about this," he said sympathetically. "You must not leave the United Nations, My Friend."

The delegate lowered his head without replying.

Dr. Lin patted his shoulder. "Our work is much too important to let money get in the way." He leaned forward and whispered, "You may not know this, but I sometimes give loans to special people in need from my own abundant resources."

Delegate Hagi looked shocked. "Really? I didn't know that. What sort of loan could you make? I'd love to do this vital work if I could."

"How much money would it take to help your family?"

He hesitated over the amount. If he asked for too much, he would lose his chance. Too little, and it would be a wasted opportunity. "I hate to say it, but I believe that $150,000 American dollars would be just enough, if it came at a low interest."

Dr. Lin smiled to himself, appreciating the man's shrewdness. "How does $200,000 at no interest for two years sound? I want to help those I can trust and who want to work with me to make the world a safer place, people like you."

"That would be most wonderful, Dr. Lin! Thank you! If there's anything I can do for you, just let me know."

Dr. Lin called over an aide and told her to arrange a contract for a loan. "If the loan isn't paid off within two years, the interest rate will be 22% compound interest." He knew if the man repaid him, he would still owe Dr. Lin a huge favor. If he didn't repay the loan, the compounding debt would quickly put the man in such straits that Dr. Lin would completely control his life.

As the evening went on, Dr. Lin made many more new, grateful friends. Several delegates suggested that he be named the official delegate to the United Nations from the United States. Many didn't like Delegate Ruggerio.

"No, no," he replied humbly. "The President already has his delegate, and I must support my president's choice and help in other ways."

The delegate from Mexico said, "Dr. Lin, you're smart, wealthy, and generous. The businesses you brought to my country are very much appreciated. You should run for President. If you don't mind my saying so, the person in office has no vision of global unity, and, of course, denies global warming. You've becoming very popular. I believe you could win the next election."

Dr. Lin , smiling, shook his head. "No. I'm not worthy of such an honor. I have no ambition to be the President of the United States. Thank you for your kind compliment."

As the Mexican delegate walked away, the personal assistant to Dr. Lin whispered, "The presidency doesn't wield nearly enough power for your greatness."

Dr. Lin smiled at her insight. "That's true. It doesn't."

CHAPTER 19

The Society of Wake comprised many levels of inclusiveness. Dr. Lin called his innermost circle of directors the Supreme Council. It was the only level that met together as a group. Due to his concealed but constant paranoia, Dr. Lin didn't allow other members to be acquainted with each other unless necessary. He knew very well the intoxicating addiction of power, and his greatest fear was that his society of superhumans would one day turn on him to gain more power and wealth for themselves.

The four members of the Supreme Council gathered in an elegant underground hall with Dr. Lin. The room was lit only by flaming, wall-mounted torches that flickered eerily across the faces of those present. The room was both imposing and mediaeval-looking, with its expansive gray stone walls and beautiful ancient Chinese tapestries. That was the place where Dr. Lin felt most like the grand emperor he desired to be. Stationed around the periphery of the room, Fa Shen and five other of Dr. Lin's most-trusted bodyguards stood watch. Each was extremely well-armed.

The directors dressed in traditional Chinese robes and sat on intricately carved wooden chairs along two side of a central aisle carpeted in red. They included the Director of Security and Surveillance, the Director of Finance, the Director of Planning and Propaganda, and the Director of Research and Medical Affairs.

When Dr. Lin entered the room, all the directors stood. He wore an elegant yellow robe and mian-style emperor's hat. After a brief moment looking around the room, Dr. Lin slowly and ceremoniously walked down the center aisle toward a beautiful throne covered in gold plate and studded with precious stones.

After he slowly settled in his seat, he gestured for the others to sit. His eyes scanned the room and gazed upon each director before he spoke.

"Members of the Supreme Council, with a mandate from heaven and with the help of our ancestors, the time is nearing when we shall bring great glory to ourselves and order to a chaotic world. It will be a world under my singular rule. You who have helped me most will share in my greatness and power."

All the members of the Supreme Court nodded graciously.

"Great achievements are never won easily and take a great deal of time and effort, but we have patiently and systematically accomplished much. The foundation upon which we shall build our empire is already in place." Pausing for effect, he gazed around the room. "As you know, like the four legs of a stool, our grand plan consists of four major components. The first was my desire to obtain the enthusiastic approval of the media and thus the public at large. We have achieved that goal and will easily maintain it."

Heads nodded.

Liang Lee, Director of Planning and Propaganda, was a short, thin man with black glasses. Although not intimidating in stature, he was Dr. Lin's most-valued member of the council. Lee took pride in knowing it was he who promoted the idea of using global warming and climate change over other possibilities to bring the mainstream and social media into their grand scheme.

"Secondly and simultaneously, I'm promoting a more-powerful United Nations as the only world organization that can effectively fight climate change." After a pause, he added, "Already, their authority is increasing."

Heads nodded again, but no one spoke.

"Thirdly, I will soon become the Secretary-General of the United Nations and usurp the authority of that organization. The current Secretary-General has agreed to support me. He is an elderly man who seeks only money in his old age. He has already received two payments and will receive two more once I occupy his office. Of course, the reason for these money transfer appear benign if anyone investigates. My best money handlers are certain of that."

Several directors wanted to add their support but held their tongue, as they hadn't yet been asked to speak.

"As Secretary-General, I will continue to increase the organization's legal authority, wealth, and military power. It will eventually rise above any national power on Earth."

The others nodded again in silent agreement.

"Finally, through our continued manipulation, coercion, and control of the media, I will eventually be asked to become the permanent leader of the United Nations." He chuckled. "I will hesitate, of course, but then reluctantly accept for the good of world unity and the Earth's environment. Afterward, I will transform the UN into the most-powerful empire the world has ever known." He paused for his words to sink in. "What say you?"

"You will, indeed, rule the greatest empire in history," Liang Lee commented enthusiastically. "I suggest that international laws be passed that make speech against you or the United Nations illegal as hate speech, because it weakens global solidarity and threatens the planet's well-being. From that point on, you'll be untouchable."

Dr. Lin smiled and nodded.

General Hui Chen, who was forced to retire from the U.S. Army due to abuse and bullying of fellow soldiers, as well as sexual abuse, didn't look as exhilarated as the others. "I agree with what you said, Dr. Lin, but I received some troubling news."

"What is this news?" Dr. Lin asked.

"Permission to speak freely?"

"Of course, General. This is a critical time in our society's history, so I must have your truthful input."

"We have two problems. First, I recently learned that Dr. Burrus is alive."

Dr. Lin's brows furrowed, and he leaned forward. "Was he not in the laboratory when it was destroyed?"

"He was, but he survived nonetheless. His death was a fabrication."

Dr. Lin fell back against his seat truly stunned. "What? Dr. Burrus has been alive all this time? How? This can't be."

"I'm not sure how he survived the blast, but he did. He's been living right here under our noses in the United States these many years."

Dr. Chao Liu, Director of Research and Medical Affairs, anxiously chimed in. "That means he could produce the Wake Formula. Possibly, he has already done so. The monopoly we so richly enjoy would be seriously challenged at any time if he is making his own."

"This could not have come at a worse time," Fu Wang, Director of Finances, added with alarm. "For the first time in our history, more money is going out than is coming in."

Dr. Lin felt upset, but he wanted no panic in the ranks. "Silence!" he said, standing.

Silence filled the room.

Dr. Lin spoke in a commanding voice. "If we have a problem, we face it and destroy it. Remember how powerful we already are."

The room remained deadly quiet. Embarrassment showed on several faces.

Dr. Lin glared at the general. "What is the second thing, General Chen? You said there were two. I must know everything."

"Secondly," the general began, "we know from Cheung's interrogation that he told someone about the information he sold you. We don't know who the man was or who he works for. We think he's an American. We must assume some government agency, perhaps the FBI, CIA, or Homeland Security, knows about the Wake Formula."

"Was Cheung dealt with appropriately for his treachery?" Dr. Lin asked in anger.

"Of course. He suffered greatly before he was killed."

Dr. Lin's fingers tapped on the arms of his chair. "We have eyes and ears everywhere, including the CIA, Homeland Security, and the FBI. What have you heard from them?"

"Our spies have heard nothing, but they have been placed on high alert. If we can discover who this man is, we can deal with him before any real damage is done."

"And we must terminate Dr. Burrus," Liu added.

Dr. Lin seethed. "Both must be captured, thoroughly interrogated, and then terminated. Double your efforts, General Chen. Follow every lead with every resource at your disposal. This is top priority. Report any new developments to me immediately."

The general nodded.

Dr. Lin looked at his Director of Planning and Propaganda. "Lee, we must use all the sensitive information we discovered about the United Nations delegates right away to ensure their full cooperation. Bribe them, threaten them, or use whatever means are necessary to bend them to our will. They must push hard for me to be elected Secretary-General of the United Nations."

Lee nodded.

"I understand that the news reporter who questioned my finances has been disgraced and is no longer a thorn in my side. Is that correct, General?"

"Yes." General Chen had a sly grin. "We needed only to get her drunk and prompt her to use disparaging language against a colored colleague. We recorded it and put it on the internet with angry indignation about her racism. Her career as a journalist is officially over."

Dr. Lin nodded and looked at Lee. "The news outlets, social media, and internet must be continuously abuzz about imminent climate catastrophes we predict. Highlight every tropical storm, hurricane, tornado, flood, and warm spell anywhere in the world day or night. We must make people truly frightened. Mothers must fear for their children."

His fist struck the arm of his chair. "Fear is our greatest ally. The common masses must become hysterical and in need of a savior. Without prodding, the media will proclaim me to be that savior."

"I will work on it twenty-four hours a day until it becomes so," Lee responded. "Stories of climate disaster will hit the media with the force of a tempest."

"Excellent."

Fu Wang realized Dr. Lin wanted answers, not weaknesses. He stood. "Although our financial situation is dwindling, we will spend whatever money is needed to make this happen. Our clients will simply have to pay more for the formula and donate more to the Dynasty Global Foundation."

Dr. Lin, sensing anxiety in his Director of Finance, motioned him back to his seat. "Sit down, Fu Wang. I still see concern in your eyes, but don't worry. We have a plan, more money than King Solomon, and the media behind us. All that we've worked for will transpire."

Wang nodded and sat.

Dr. Lin held up a fist. "Think of it. Soon, we'll seize control of the world without anyone noticing we did it. The money we're spending is a drop in the ocean for the kind of prize we seek."

Fu Wang smiled. "Yes, Master Lin."

"At the right time, I'll announce the donation of another billion dollars to fight our great enemy, climate change. That will again bring all eyes to me and ignite in people around the world their hope in me."

"Your genius is an inspiration," Lee said.

Dr. Lin leaned forward. "There's no time to waste, Directors. We must act boldly. Act now. I'll hold another banquet soon. This time, I'll invite world leaders themselves to my home to bend them to my will."

"I don't think you should invite the actual national leaders here, Master Lin," General Chen said with some hesitancy. He didn't want to appear negative, but the words had to be said.

Dr. Lin regarded him in surprise. "Why is that, General?"

"Their protective services are too thorough. They would surely discover our surveillance devices no matter how we try to hide them."

"That's a good point, General, but perhaps we won't use them at the banquet." He tapped a finger against his chin. "We could just invite high-ranking representatives from each country, a person from their innermost circles."

"I like the second plan better, Master," the general said. "We may be able to discover valuable information from them during their stay if we continue using our hidden surveillance devices."

Dr. Lin turned his gaze to Lee. "Begin making the arrangements immediately."

Lee nodded.

CHAPTER 20

At Frederick's insistence, Titus stayed a second night in the house. Earlier that day, he took Tammy up on her offer, and they had a pleasant stroll around the campus. Titus asked her about Dr. Burrus and his research interests, but she knew less than he did. He also asked about her.

He learned she was a Sewanee grad in English and was two years divorced after her husband had an affair with a coworker. She had been a teacher but returned to the college a year earlier to find some peace and work in a new situation. Titus liked her very much and decided to stay in touch.

That evening, Isabella made a wonderful dinner of sauerkraut with German sausage and fresh bread. After dinner, they relaxed on the front porch.

"Your home is lovely," Titus said. "I'm not usually keen on Victorian homes, but you pull it off nicely. The detail on the exterior and interior is amazing."

"Thank you," Isabella replied. "If you can imagine, the house was originally light blue, but I think painting it gray with white trim worked pretty well."

"Would you like a Heineken or Beck's?" Frederick asked.

"A Beck's sounds good."

"So what university are you with?" Isabella asked.

He hesitated. "Georgetown."

"Really? That's a good school. Who's on the faculty there now? I may know a couple of them."

He realized he made a mistake. He should have done his homework and prepared a story. Backtracking, he said, "Actually, I started only recently, and I'm just part-time. I don't really know the other faculty very well yet, but I hope to soon."

"I see," she said, surprised. "Well, where were you before that?"

He swallowed beer and realized he had to get his story on solid footing. "The Army. I did classified research at a lab in Washington on lethal pathogens."

"Interesting. I thought there was something military about you."

Sensing Titus needed a diversion, Frederick asked, "Where are you originally from, Titus. Growing up, I mean."

He was glad to change the subject. "Baltimore, Maryland, the Highland Town area to be specific."

"Baltimore's an interesting place, for good and bad. At least, what's what my mother always said. On the positive side, it has an attractive inner harbor, and interesting history, and the medical school at Johns Hopkins is one of the best in the world. That's where she did her neurosurgery residency. On the negative, it has a lot of crime, violence, and racial turmoil."

Titus nodded. "I agree."

"What did you like most about Baltimore?" Isabella asked.

Frederick, glad she took the bait, moved away from academic questions.

"For me, the best thing about Baltimore wasn't anything you mentioned," Titus said. "It's a great sports town and has been for a long time. I'm still a big fan of the Ravens and Orioles."

"I love American baseball," Frederick said. "American football, well, I'm still getting used to it."

"What did your parents do?" Isabella asked.

"My father was a union dock worker, and my mother was an LPN at Mercy Hospital, a Catholic hospital in Baltimore."

"Was your family Catholic?"

"My mother was a devout Catholic. She went to Mass at least twice a week. My dad never really got into religion. He wasn't against it, but he just wasn't into it."

"Well, we're not into religion, either," she replied.

Titus was surprised. "I don't understand. You seem like very religious people."

"Our focus is on faith in Jesus, our Savior. That's what's important to us, not a religion," she explained. "Whosever believes in Him shall not perish but have everlasting life."

Titus drank from his beer. "John 3:16. It was one of my mother's favorites. She quoted the Bible a lot."

Isabella was pleased by his response. "Too often, people become disappointed by religions and the flawed people who run them but never by Jesus."

"My mother would've liked you, Isabella."

"I'm sure I would've liked her, too. How about you? Are you a devout Catholic like your mother, or uninterested in matters of faith like your father?"

"I'm what my Catholic friends called a Cheaster."

"A Cheaster?"

"Someone who goes to Mass only on Christmas and Easter."

She laughed and shook her head. "I see."

"What about your parents?" he asked. "Were they spiritual like you?" He hadn't been around people of strong faith for a long time and felt curious.

"Oh, yes. We went to nondenominational gospel teaching church. My parents were mighty prayer warriors. They've both passed to a better place now."

"I'm sorry they're gone." Still curious, he eyes Frederick. "What about you?"

"I'm afraid my upbringing was more complex than Isabella's. My mother's a full-fledged, gospel-singing, devout, Black Southern Baptist from Birmingham, Alabama. My father's a full-fledged, devout atheist from Frankfurt, Germany."

Titus raised his eyebrows. "Wow."

"Yes, wow. They're a bit of an odd couple, but they somehow made it work. My mother prays every day for my father to find faith, and my father thinks she's a nut who needs to put her faith in science."

Titus grinned.

"I like to think I take after her in faith and him in science."

Titus scratched the side of his head. "How do you merge the two? Don't they say science and religion don't mix?"

"I don't know who they are, but they don't know what they're talking about," Frederick said firmly. "I love science. It allows me to understand and do interesting things. I don't worship at the feet of the science god. Scientists often act like science knows or will know everything. How many times have scientific facts been disproven later?"

"Bunches," Titus said.

"Exactly. No, I worship at the feet of the one, true living and loving triune God, the God who truly knows everything and created the wonders that science uncovers."

Titus nodded.

"In fact, the more my science knowledge expands, the stronger my faith in God. This world is so incredibly complex and so magnificently designed, it has to have a Creator."

"Or did it just happen by accident over a very, very long time?" He had to ask just to give Frederick a hard time. It was a bad habit that he couldn't seem to stop. He and his brothers ribbed each other constantly.

Frederick took the bait and sat up straighter. "No way. It's all too perfect, too well-designed, no matter how long time existed. There must be a creator—a designer, if you will. Just consider the design of only one thing. Let's take eyesight for example.

"First of all, the eyeball has to be perfectly designed to let in light. That means it must have almost clear tissue as lenses. Is that accidental? No way. Then it purposefully and perfectly directs light to a film we call the retina to record the light. The lens is focused by tiny, perfectly placed muscles. Is that also by chance? No."

Titus knew where the lecture was going, but he was happy to listen.

"Then the retina transforms the light into electrochemical signals that pass all the way from the front of the brain to the back. In the back of the brain, there's an amazing, complex computer called the occipital cortex. It just happens to be there to analyze the detailed images from the light signal and communicates with all the other areas of the brain and body about what is being seen. It's simply unfathomable."

Titus smiled and nodded.

"And it all happens in the blink of an eye."

He grinned at the joke.

"If sight isn't clearly a designed, multi-step process with a clear purpose, then I don't know what is. Patterns occur throughout nature, but purposeful creation needs a Creator. That's just what happens superficially with just one small part of the human body. No words can possibly describe the full majesty and complexity of God's creation; it's just too much for the human mind to comprehend."

Titus laughed. "I agree."

Frederick couldn't help adding, "Some people say that great lengths of time can lead to anything, but really, left to time and chance, the physical world tends toward chaos, not order and design."

"You mean the Second Law of Thermodynamics. Left alone a system's entropy always increases. That is, disorder always increases. Even the best built car will fall into rabble someday."

"You got it." Frederick smiled. "Purposeful order needs a creator."

CHAPTER 21

As Frederick and Titus prepared for a second fishing trip the following morning, Frederick paused.

"Titus, I just had an idea."

"What's that?" Titus laced up his boots.

"I don't mean to impose, but would you like to give me a hand starting to replace Ms. Green's porch instead of fishing today? A project like that really needs two people. I have some wood we can use, and I don't have anyone else to ask." He paused. "And you'll be gone soon."

Titus looked up and grinned. "Sounds like a great idea."

When they reached the house, Frederick introduced Titus and told her they came to repair her porch.

"That's very kind of you," she replied, "but you don't need to do that. It's just fine the way it is."

"Actually, I don't think so, Ms. Green. Look." He pushed down on several planks, and they bent under his weight. "These are due to break soon, and I'd hate to see you hurt. I noticed this when we were here the other day."

She took a deep breath. "Oh, my. I never noticed that. You really think they might break under my weight. I don't weigh much more than a feather."

Frederick smiled. "They might not for a little while, but if you ever got hurt, and I could've prevented it, I wouldn't be able to forgive myself."

"Oh, I wouldn't want that. If you two really want to replace it, I guess I won't try to stop you." She put a shaking hand to her mouth, as if she didn't want to say more but had to. "I have to be honest. It might be a couple months before I can save enough to pay you back."

He placed a hand on her shoulder. "No, Ms. Green. This won't cost you a thing. It's our pleasure to help. Call it our good deed for the day."

Titus, seeing how excited the woman became, gently nudged Frederick in the stomach. "You can see that a little exercise would be good for the professor."

She knew he was teasing but said, "I think he looks just fine, Young Man."

"So we can get to work?"

"Yes, of course." After a pause, she asked, "Can I get you some coffee and biscuits with homemade blackberry jelly before you start?"

"No, we're fine," Frederick replied. "We ate on the way, but thank you."

"Thank you," Titus said. "I'm good."

The two took tools from the back of the SUV and got to work. First, they used sledge hammers to demolish the old porch.

"This thing falls apart easier than I thought it would," Frederick mentioned.

"It wasn't going to last much longer," Titus said. "When I was in high school, I did some construction work on weekends. I'm sure my employment was off the books, because they paid below minimum wage and always in cash, but I enjoyed it. I always said my favorite part of construction was destruction."

Frederick laughed. "I know what you mean. This part is fun." He pointed to a spot at the side of the property near a trash can. "Just throw the rotten wood into a pile over there. I'll haul it off another day if the trash men won't take it." He indicated a different location on the side of the house. "Let's set the good wood over there, and maybe I can use that for something else later."

"Sounds good."

After the old porch was demolished, the work was harder. They had to dig post holes. Frederick took the opportunity to get to know Titus better.

"You say you were in the Army, right?"

"That's right."

"Were you military police?"

"I was for a short time, but I didn't care for it. Most of the work was boring. I moved on to Airborne, Rangers, and ended up as an officer in Delta Force."

Frederick wiped sweat off his forehead. "I've heard of Delta Force, but I'm not sure what it is."

"It's a Special Forces unit for counterterrorism, hostage rescue, and some of the most-difficult reconnaissance operations. It's sort of the Army's version of the Navy SEALs."

Frederick looked up at him. "Impressive. Did you like it?"

"Usually."

"Were you ever in harm's way?"

"Definitely."

"Can you tell me about it?"

"Nope. We liked to say we let the SEALs do the bragging while we did the killing."

"Why'd you leave? You're still pretty young and obviously fit."

Titus sighed. "Believe me, that wasn't an easy decision. To tell the truth, I was fed up with the politics associated with the Army back then."

Frederick looked at him, confused. "I thought the Army was a great place to escape politics."

Titus let his anger show by using the post hole digger harder than necessary. "Are you kidding me? There's always politics in the military, and I don't mean the ass-kissing type to get promoted or for good assignments. It was the big picture that got to me."

Frederick kept digging. "What do you mean, the big picture."

"I mean the military gets tossed up and down like a Yo-Yo according to who's in the White House. Think about. We've had some great administrations who supported and truly cared about the military, but we all know how some other presidents couldn't have cared less."

Frederick nodded.

"When the Commander in Chief doesn't support his own troops, guess who suffers?" Titus didn't want for an answer. "Our military suffers, despite the fact that soldiers are often still left fighting in some far-off place and risking their lives. I was one of them."

"I see."

"Those presidents have no idea what to do except try to buy off our enemies, often with literally billions of dollars."

"Yeah, I've noticed that."

Titus shook his head. "It's outrageous to give that sort of money to countries whose leaders hate America and will use the money to kill Americans. I wasn't going to risk my life any longer for an administration that didn't have my back, so I got out. A lot of other good soldiers did the same."

"I understand."

Titus fought his way around a large rock. "Now if President O'Malley was president back when I was in, I'd probably still be in the Army."

"Didn't you just trade one dangerous government job for another?"

"Yeah, probably, but the decision wasn't about the danger. It was about feeling betrayed by our so-called leaders. To add fuel to the fire, I don't appreciate the liberal media who support our troops after the U.S. has been attacked, then make American soldiers out to be villains when they complete a mission. On the other hand, since the deep-state stuff was exposed, working for the FBI hasn't nearly been as influenced by politics as it once was. Politicians on both sides of the aisle want people like me to protect their asses back home."

"I'm sure that's true."

"Enough about me. Are you ready to discuss your research yet?"

"Have a little more patience, My Friend. Ask me after the lecture today. That's all I ask. Besides, we're having fun, aren't we?"

After setting the posts for the porch, they returned to Frederick's house to clean up.

Later that afternoon, Titus once again sat in the rear of Frederick's classroom for advanced neurophysiology.

"Good morning," Frederick said with noticeable enthusiasm. "Today, I'll be discussing some of what we know about the neurochemical mechanism of the sleep/wake cycle."

Heads nodded politely.

"There are two basic physiological drives in the human sleep/wake cycle. One is called the 'homeostatic process,' which is the increasing need for sleep, or what is sometimes called sleep pressure, as the day proceeds. The other is an endogenous circadian clock set to a twenty-four-hour rhythm. This so-called Master Biological Clock is located in the suprachiasmatic nuclei, or SCN, of the hypothalamus in the limbic portion of the brain."

He showed a PowerPoint slide of the brain with the location of the hypothalamus and SCN outlined. "This circadian clock has its own endogenous pacemaker and can function pretty well on its own. It's influenced, however, by environmental cues called entrainment. Of course, light is the most-important component of entrainment. That is, light acts as a signal that it's wake time."

A student in the front row asked, "Does artificial lighting affect the circadian clock?"

"Super question, Victoria. The answer is yes. It affects the brain and wake cycle similar to sunlight. In fact, artificial lighting in homes, TVs, and even the light from computer screens probably contribute to the high frequency of sleep disturbances in modern society."

A look of *so that explains it* showed on the faces of many students.

"Within the circadian cycle is another cycle called the ultradian process. This cycle controls the stages of sleep I told you about in the last lecture."

Heads nodded, although a few students looked lost.

"Each of these systems have biomechanical mechanisms to control them. For example, light stimulates glutamate release. The glutamate, in turn, binds to N-methyl-D-aspartate receptors to promote wakefulness. These receptors are more simply referred to NMDA receptors and are in the SCN.

"As light decreases, melatonin is released from the pineal gland. Binding of melatonin to melatonin receptors in the SCN is part of the biochemical mechanism of the circadian cycle to induce sleep."

From the fifth row, Austin asked, "How does caffeine affect all this? I know you're not supposed to drink it at bedtime, and some coffee drinkers have a terrible time waking up in the morning without their coffee."

Frederick smiled. "Thank you. I was just about to get to that."

A new slide appeared.

"If you recall, the homeostatic process is the drive to sleep. Adenosine, a breakdown product of the body's chemical energy ATP, acts as an inhibitor of wake, stimulating neurons in the basal forebrain. During the course of the day, adenosine accumulates in certain areas of the brain, which increases sleep pressure. Caffeine blocks the action of adenosine and thus promotes wakefulness."

Titus mumbled, "Cool," and thought that would make a great trivia question for his geeky friends.

The professor went on to discuss the roles of other chemical modulators in the homeostatic process, such as interleukin-1, prostaglandins, and even growth-hormone releasing hormone. Titus particularly enjoyed learning about hypocretin-1 and hypocretin-2.

"Hypocretin-1 and hypocretin-2 are produced by neurons in the hypothalamus and receive input from the SCN. Levels of H-1 and H-2 can be measured from cerebral fluid and are high during waking hours. H-1 and H-2 are highest during forced sleep deprivation, possibly the body's attempt to counteract the homeostatic process."

That was particularly interesting to Titus, as forced sleep deprivation was part of his Delta Force training and was used to interrogate prisoners.

Before the professor concluded, he said, "Most of you probably know that most antihistamine drugs, like Benadryl, are associated with sedation in most people, right?"

Heads nodded.

"Why?" When no one responded, he asked, "Any guesses?"

No one spoke.

He put up another PowerPoint diagram. "The fact that these drugs are anti-histamines led to the understanding that histamine itself is another chemical in the brain that promotes a wake state. Histamine-releasing neurons originate from the posterior hypothalamus and project to many other areas of the brain, all of which help keep you awake."

Students took furious notes, as he continued.

Near the end of the lecture, Frederick said, "As you can see, there's a very sophisticated coordination of numerous chemicals affecting both wake and sleep states. The ones I discussed today are just some of the major players."

By the time Frederick ended the lecture, Titus realized he hadn't known anything about sleep, as Frederick suspected. He was also pleased to hear another lecture. He felt a bit sad to think it might be the last day he saw his new friend. He came to like the man very much.

As the students filed from the classroom, Titus asked Frederick, "Can I treat you to lunch?"

Frederick hesitated. "I don't know. I have papers to grade before a chemistry class later today."

"Come on. You have to eat, anyway, and we need to discuss the purpose of my trip here. Besides, I owe you a meal or two. Is there anywhere you like?"

"OK, OK. You convinced me."

"Where would you like to eat? Don't say the cafeteria."

Frederick chuckled. "I know a small country barbecue shack thirty minutes away in Winchester."

"Perfect."

CHAPTER 22

Titus and Frederick chatted about the lecture, as they drove. Neither mentioned the professor's research or the explosion at his old lab.

Once they arrived, they ordered the day's special of smoked pork ribs, coleslaw, potato salad, and drinks.

After they were served, Titus said, "I really enjoyed your lectures on sleep. There were interesting and informative. You certainly know your field, and I learned a lot."

"Thank you," Frederick replied after his first bite of barbecue. "Actually, there's a lot more known about the neurochemistry of sleep, but nothing I felt was needed in an undergrad lecture."

Titus smiled. "There's always more." After swallowing a bite of coleslaw, he asked, "So can we talk now about why I'm here and your research in Germany?"

"Of course, but you go first." He liked Titus and wanted to trust him, but he wasn't sure how much he should reveal. "Exactly why are you here? What are you interested in knowing about?"

Titus explained everything he could about the Chinese industrial spy and their suspicions about Dr. Lin. He didn't say anything about Seth Miles or that the investigation was off the books.

As he spoke, he watched the professor's face closely, seeing concern but no shock or surprise.

"OK," Titus finished. "That's what I know. Now it's your turn. What's this all about, Doc?"

Frederick wiped his mouth clean of barbecue sauce and coughed to clear his throat. He decided to tell the truth. "As you probably know, I grew up rather well-off with my mother being a neurosurgeon and my father a successful physicist. While I was in medical school, my parents became much, much wealthier from my father's work."

"What do you mean?"

"He made many millions of dollars from a couple of lucrative energy-related patents. The money kept coming in year after year from stock options, various ways the patents were being used, and the interest on all that money. My parents literally didn't know what to do with it."

"Must be a nice problem to have."

"You'd think so, but the money caused a serious rift between them. My father wanted to bank the money. My mother said they didn't need it and began giving more to charities, churches, and family members."

Titus nodded and kept eating. "Since my father was an atheist, he was upset about the money she gave to churches and some Christian charities. Plus, he thought some of her family members were taking advantage of her."

"I see."

Anyway, they started arguing a lot about it and came close to getting a divorce over the whole thing. Thankfully, cooler heads eventually prevailed, and they reached a compromise. They're both good people, and both love science and medicine, so they decided to start and maintain the Burrus Research Institute for medical research with their extra money."

Titus wiped barbecue sauce off his mouth with a napkin. "That was a great idea."

"I think so, and it certainly resolved the rift between them. They set up the institute so worthy medical scientists could study whatever they wanted without the distraction of applying for grants or having to fulfill teaching obligations. As long as the work was considered useful, the scientists wouldn't have to worry about publishing for the sake of promotion or to keep their jobs."

"That's awesome. Publish or perish and the time it takes to write grants were common complaints among my professors when I was in grad school."

"It's almost everywhere in academics. Anyway, my parents asked me to join their institute as the director and as a scientist. I was happy where I was, but I eventually agreed. Perhaps that was part of their plan, too."

Titus was puzzled.

"To lure me back to Germany. They knew unfettered research time would be very appealing to me."

"I see."

"As a psychiatrist and neuroscientist, I naturally wanted to focus my research on the brain."

Titus nodded. "I don't blame you. It's a fascinating topic."

"Fascinating? It's the most-intriguing and complicated object in the known universe."

"Perhaps."

Frederick looked incredulous, but he realized Titus was teasing. "Anyway, I wanted to do something special, discover some new insight into the brain. You know—make a difference."

Titus, nodding, drank from his iced tea.

"After dabbling in a few research areas, I always came back to the same topic."

Titus grinned. "Let me guess—sleep."

"Yes, sleep. It enthralled me. It seems we spend so much of our time sleeping, yet we know so little about it. We just accept it. It's a great mystery hiding in plain sight. Sleep research isn't very well-funded, so I began to focus more and more of my time on that until it was all I did. Some of the information I discussed today was the result of research I published early on in the project."

Titus asked, "OK, but what exactly happened to precipitate an attack on your lab?"

"Hold on. I'm getting to that." He took a mouthful of tea. "As you heard from my lectures, sleep is about two complicated and competing systems."

"Sure. One is sleep promoting, the other is wake promoting."

"Correct. I thought I would try a different approach to studying sleep by primarily focusing on the biochemical processes of the wake state."

Titus sipped his drink. "OK. What happened? Did you develop some sort of super insomnia medication by cutting off the wake state that's so good it's worth killing for?"

"Good guess, but not even close. My attempts at developing a new insomnia medication were disappointing at best, but my research on the wake cycle proved to be quite, well, intriguing."

Titus was still confused. "I don't understand. What's this all about? Did you make some sort of breakthrough in understanding the wake mechanism that has importance in some way?"

With a smile and nod, Frederick said, "I did."

Pieces of the puzzle slowly came together in Titus' mind. "In other words, you found ways to maintain wakefulness by enhancing wake-promoting chemicals such as hypocretins, histamine, and glutamate while minimizing the effects of the homeostatic chemicals, such as adenosine and melatonin. Is that what you're saying?"

Frederick slapped his hands on the table. "Yes, that's basically it, although the mechanism of sleep is about a hundred times more complicated than what you heard in class. It took a lot of brain extracts to get some of the biological components I needed. We also had to develop drug delivery systems to make sure those components safely reached the brain."

"Things are always more complicated than we first imagine," Titus said, nodding.

"I'm glad you listened to my lectures. Just as Sir Isaac Newton said, an object in motion stays in motion unless another force opposes it. Once started, a strong wake state will stay that way unless more-powerful sleep processes stop it."

Titus tipped his head to either side. "That actually sounds, well, sort of interesting."

Frederick laughed. "Thank you...I think."

"What was the reaction of other scientists in the field?"

Frederick shrugged. "Heaven only knows. I never published my most-important findings. I didn't think the data was quite ready, and I wasn't sure how or when I wanted to release it to the public."

Titus nodded and reached for more barbecue sauce, dousing it on ribs and taking a few bites.

"Once I realized it was the wake state, not the sleep state, that was my most-likely breakthrough, I focused all my time and energy on it. I eventually developed what I call the Wake Formula. It was a long, difficult process."

"I can't imagine."

"The formula became more and more powerful with each new discovery and adjustment."

Titus saw the excitement on Frederick's face. "That must've been a very exciting time."

"It was. My lab animals stayed awake longer and longer. I had no idea what I'd do with the discoveries and the ever-evolving Wake Formula, but I was having a great time with my research."

Titus leaned forward and whispered, "So what happened?"

"Eventually, I fine-tuned the formula to such a degree that my animals didn't need sleep at all. I was amazed. I didn't think that was possible."

"That's amazing. A true wake drug."

"Exactly. It's a wake formula, really, because it contains so many different biologicals and other components. I called it the Wake Formula, or WF for short. First, I used it in rats. Then I developed formulas for larger animals like dogs and monkeys."

"Did it work on them, too?"

Frederick wiped his hands clean of barbecue sauce. "With some tinkering, it eventually did. Each species had its own dose adjustments and some component variation. It wasn't too hard to figure out from the basic formula. I had ten monkeys and twelve dogs that hadn't slept in eleven months before the explosion."

Titus shook his head in amazement. "Incredible. Did you ever try it in humans? I mean, even a little bit?"

Frederick shook his fork at him. "Oh, no, no, no. I wasn't going in that direction until I had absolutely all the data I needed. I still had a lot to learn about the safety profile in animals with long-term use, and it would've taken a lot more time and money. Even my parents' foundation didn't have that kind of cash for human research. We would have needed to collaborate with a large pharmaceutical company, and we weren't sure we wanted to do that."

Titus' mind raced with questions. "Other than your laboratory staff, who knew about the Wake Formula."

"Only two people I know of, my mother and father." He knew where that line of questioning was going. "I communicated with them frequently about my research."

"Could your staff have told anyone?"

"I truly doubt it. That was absolutely forbidden. They knew it was a highly secret project, and they would lose their jobs if they told anyone, even family members. We emphasized that often enough. Besides, if I didn't trust them completely, I wouldn't have hired them."

"How'd you communicate with your parents about the formula?"

Dr. Burrus stared down at the table for a moment. "Sometimes in person, but they were usually busy with their own thing. I'm embarrassed to say it was more often by cell phone, email, and text—all the usual ways."

Titus' eyebrows went up, revealing his feelings.

"I know now that was all the wrong ways," Frederick admitted. "I should've known better. Investigators speculated later that my phone and computer communications were hacked."

Titus didn't reply.

"As you probably know, we scientists often live in our own worlds," Frederick explained. "I certainly did. I was so excited about my research, and my parents were such good scientists, I wanted to tell them everything and bounce ideas off them. They were often a big help."

Titus shrugged. "I understand."

"In my defense, my parents owned the Burrus Research Foundation. They were also my employers."

"True."

"Evidence indicated three lab workers were killed, and my laboratory computers had been stolen, right before the blast. There wasn't a trace of any of the computers in the wreckage. We quickly deduced the killers were after all the information we had on the Wake Formula. They had to be. It was the only thing we'd been working on for a while. I still feel guilty about what happened."

Titus. seeing the anguish on Frederick's face, felt bad for him.

"Every day, I regret not being more careful. I had no idea someone might be eavesdropping, much less an industrial spy from China, as you said. I'm an academic. My head was in the clouds, and my carelessness got people killed."

"I'm sorry, Frederick. However, you didn't kill them. Assassins did, and the people who sent them."

"From what you've told me, it certainly sounds like this Dr. Lin is using the Wake Formula to enhance the human potential in his clients."

"How, specifically? Do you think just staying awake longer could make such a huge difference in his clients?"

Frederick was astounded by the question. "Are you kidding? You're an ex-athlete. Isn't victory often achieved by only the smallest of margins or advantage? A tenth of a second can determine if an Olympic sprinter wins the gold medal, honors, and millions of dollars in endorsements or the silver medal and is quickly forgotten. A few extra points on an ACT or SAT exam could mean a scholarship or none. The examples are endless."

Titus didn't look overly impressed. "I guess it could be true."

"Think harder. A slight edge could give a lawyer, a stock bro-ker—you name it—the advantage he needs to win a case or make more money. If the smallest edge can make such a difference, imagine what a larger advantage might mean."

"Is staying awake really such a large advantage?"

Frederick was losing his patience. "Of course it is! Imagine having six to eight hours more each day, every day, compared to other people. A person on the Wake Formula could become...."

Suddenly, Titus' eyes widened. "Almost unbeatable," he fin-ished. "How'd I miss all the implications?"

Frederick smiled and excitedly smacked his hands against the table again. "Exactly! Now you get it. A person would not just get the extra points on an exam, he would be better prepared for every test. You could practice piano or tennis for hours longer than the competition each day."

Titus smiled, as the possibilities came into focus.

"You could watch stock market data all day and night, or pre-pare for a law case twenty-four hours straight. The added time results in a 25%-33% advantage in whatever way you decide to use it."

"Wow!" Titus said, excited. "Dr. Lin didn't choose lazy people, either. He chose ambitious, talented people who are usually single and could more easily conceal the fact that they don't need sleep."

"Interesting. You're probably right. That makes a lot of sense."

Titus sank back into his chair, thinking fast. "You know, early on, we considered that Dr. Lin might be using a performance-enhanc-ing drug, but we dismissed the idea, because no illegal drugs were ever detected, and no single drug could help in so many different types of people. No one knew about the Wake Formula, so no one tested for it specifically. It would certainly give a major advantage to anyone."

Frederick nodded. "Exactly. It would remain completely un-detected by any drug screen, and who would be suspicious that some people weren't sleeping due to a drug?"

"That's why your Wake Formula is worth killing for."

Frederick nodded.

"Holy shit," Titus whispered. "Militaries could create better soldiers. Good athletes could become superstars. Business people could destroy their competition. People would make a fortune on your formula."

"From what you've told me, it looks like this multibillionaire fellow and so-called philanthropist, Dr. Dao Lin, is doing just that."

Titus gazed into space, as he thought furiously. The pieces fit, but he quickly had other questions. "Are you doing any more Wake research now?"

Frederick held up both hands. "Hell, no. No research discovery is worth risking my life and that of my family and coworkers again. I keep a low profile, quietly teaching and trying to keep my family safe." After a pause, he added, "It's the price we've had to pay for my stupidity."

Titus said nothing.

"In the beginning, we hid in France for a while, then Switzerland. We changed identities several times. Eventually, Isabella and I decided to leave Europe permanently when it appeared the authorities weren't making any progress finding the assassins."

"Did you tell the police or other agencies about your research?"

"As little as possible. We trusted no one."

Titus nodded. "You were smart about that."

"I didn't want to leave science altogether, but I had to leave big-time research behind. A small college in the United States seemed the best option. Since my mother knew Sewanee, we ended up here."

"I think it was a grand idea. Sounds like she's a smart woman."

"She is. She thought she could also visit me without suspicion when she went home to Alabama if anyone was keeping tabs on her."

"All of that must've been extremely difficult to work out."

"It was, but with my parents' money and influence, they had the cooperation of people in Germany and the United States to make it happen."

Titus nodded.

"I stay current in my neuropsychiatric interests, and this small college has been a wonderful place for us to live."

"Sounds good."

"Yes. God is good to us." Frederick paused for a moment. "My wife and I always thought the day would come when someone would find us." He sighed. "It's hard to hide forever."

Titus nodded. "You say you hadn't done any human trials with the formula, right?"

"That's right. Human trials take hundreds of millions of dollars, approval by regulatory agencies, and so on. There was no way I'd attempt that off the books or in a Third-World country."

"You think it could be used in humans?"

"I don't see why not. From what you've said about Dr. Lin and his clients, I'm sure they're using it."

Titus nodded. Finishing his iced tea, he stood. "I need a refill. You want one?"

"No. I'm good."

As Titus walked away, Frederick sat back, thinking. He reflected on everything that happened and what they discussed. He wanted to be sure he hadn't left out anything that might be important.

He didn't notice the two large Chinese men walk into the restaurant.

Titus did.

Titus stood frozen for a moment when he unexpectedly saw the two Chinese men enter the restaurant. His instincts immediately told him they were trouble. The expressions on their faces was that of predators, not patrons. He also noticed slight bulges under their black suit jackets, indicating they were carrying.

Titus glanced at Frederick and saw he had no clue about the potential danger. Titus, casually gulping tea. studied the men, as they gazed around the room, clearly looking for someone. They quickly recognized Frederick.

Slowly, the two men moved toward the professor, their hands slipping under their jackets.

With hardly a conscious thought, Titus moved toward them without rushing. He smiled and waved at a couple sitting behind the men. When a .22 Sig cleared the first man's holster, Titus moved swiftly.

He jammed his cup of iced tea hard into the man's eyes. It wasn't the most-lethal move he ever made, but it was all he could think of at the moment.

The intruder, totally taken by surprise, grabbed at his face out of the instinctual fear he'd been blinded by acid. At first, he didn't realize it was only iced tea.

Titus slammed his fist into the man's throat. He dropped his Sig to the floor and fell to his knees, holding his throat and still worrying about his eyes.

The other man grabbed Titus' arm and swung him around to take a punch. Titus kicked hard into the man's left shin. He bent over, clutching his leg and writhing in pain.

Bystanders who moved away from the fray were mesmerized.

Someone shouted, "A gun!" and everyone ran for the exits.

Titus pulled the second man's head up by the hair and slammed his knee into his chin. The man fell to the floor unconscious.

Despite the screaming and confusion, Titus caught a small sound from behind, and instinctively dived and rolled. The man whose throat he crushed fired twice. One shot shattered a window, and the other barely missed a woman.

Titus looked up, ready to attack, when he saw Frederick hit the man in the head with a chair.

"Hurry, get the gun!" Titus said. "There could be more...."

Before he could finish, a third Chinese man burst in through the back door, gun in hand. Scanning the room, he faced Frederick.

Titus dived into his friend, knocking him down, as bullets flew past. They quickly crawled for cover around the corner of a hall leading to the restrooms.

Titus pointed down the hall. "Frederick, get out of here! Find the back way out. Go!"

Bullets rang out again, as the third man moved closer. Fortunately, he was cautious, moving from cover to cover, not sure if his targets were armed. Titus regretted not bringing his Glock with him, but he wasn't totally unarmed.

He reached down for the .22 Ruger he kept in an ankle holster, then he edged low around the corner and fired at the approaching shooter.

The man ducked back for cover. Titus' bullet missed and hit the wall behind him.

Frederick ran back and crouched beside Titus. "I got a window open in the women's bathroom. Come on. Let's get out of here."

"You go. I'll hold them off."

"I won't go without you," Frederick said forcefully.

Titus' next shot grazed the man's shoulder. He fell back, nursing a superficial wound. Normally, Titus would've rushed him to finish the job, but one of the first two men recovered his weapon and was firing at him, too.

Titus nodded to Frederick, who was wide-eyed. "Let's get out of here."

As Frederick squeezed out the window, Titus fired two more rounds to hold them off and shimmied out. Frederick ran for the can, as Titus watched their retreat, then he ran, too.

Before Titus got in, he scanned the parking lot without seeing any more of them. "Get in the car and start it." He tossed the rental keys to Frederick. "I'll watch your back."

Only a few cars remained in the lot. Titus eyed a large SUV parked a few spaces away. "Wait here."

"Where are you going?"

Titus ran to the SUV and saw it was a rental. He shot out the two front tires, then two shots rang out from the front window of the restaurant, hitting the dirt near his feet.

"Come on! Let's go!" Frederick shouted.

Titus fired back and ran toward the car. "Go!"

Tires squealed, as they sped away. More shots rang out but hit nothing.

As they drove back toward Sewanee, Titus reloaded and held it out to Frederick. "Take this."

Frederick took it. "What about you?"

He pulled his Glock out from under the seat. "I'm good." He checked the mag.

"Who were they?"

"I never saw them before, but I'm pretty sure they're Dr. Lin's henchmen. Who knew we were here?"

"What do you mean, here?"

"At the restaurant. Who knew we were there?"

"No one."

"No one?" he asked skeptically.

"Well, just Tammy at the office."

"What about Isabella? Did she know where we were going?"

"No, only Tammy." He finally understood the meaning of the question. "Crap! I'll call Tammy and see if she's all right."

"Do it."

Frederick called, listened, and hung up in frustration. "No answer."

"Is she usually there at this time of day?"

"Yes," he said with tension in his voice. "She takes a late lunch."

"Damn it, call home! Tell Isabella what happened. Warn her you're probably all in danger. Let her know we're on our way, and the entire family has to leave as soon as we get there. Tell her to bring nothing but her purse. We have to leave town fast."

Frederick nodded.

"If those men weren't hurt too badly, they'll get another vehicle and will be after us soon. They probably already know your address. Men like that won't give up easily."

Frederick dialed. "Isabella, the day we feared has come. Titus and I were just attacked by three gunmen."

"Are you all right?" she asked frantically.

"Yes. We weren't hurt."

"Is Titus OK? He must be freaking out to be caught in our mess. Did you tell him who we really are?"

He hesitated.

"Did you tell him people have tried to kill you before?" she demanded.

He didn't know what to say.

"Tell her," Titus said.

Frederick sighed and said, "He knows. He's an FBI agent."

"What? FBI? Did you know?"

"Yes," he said sheepishly.

"And you didn't tell me? Why didn't you tell me?"

"Because we were in the process of figuring out who knew what and what might be going on. I didn't want to scare you until I knew the entire situation."

"Well, you're scaring me now. You should've been truthful with me."

"You two don't have time for this right now," Titus said. "She has to get ready to go."

"I'm sorry, Honey, but there's no time to argue. You and the kids could be in danger. Just get ready to go. Hurry. Grab our emergency bags and money. We have to leave immediately. We'll be there soon. There's no time to waste. You can chew me out later. Love you."

After he hung up, Titus said, "I thought I told you to tell her to bring nothing but her purse."

"We've been packed for this emergency for years. It won't take a minute."

"I'll have to take your word on that. Try Tammy again. I'm worried about...."

He stopped mid-sentence, as he avoided hitting a slow-moving car after he took a curve in the road. "I'm worried about her."

"I'm worried about your way of driving." Frederick braced himself against the console.

"Just call. I'll drive."

After several rings, Frederick said, "Still no answer."

"Damn. There's a phone under your seat. Give it to me."

Frederick searched and found the phone, then he handed it to Titus.

Titus hit speed dial. "Seth, we have a problem."

"What's wrong?"

"A team of three armed Chinese men just tried to assassinate Dr. Burrus. I assume they were sent by Dr. Lin. I was with the professor, and we got away, at least for now. We're headed to get his family. The men were injured but still alive. I expect them to follow us soon. I need you to find us a safe house until we figure out what to do next."

"Bloody hell. Was Dr. Burrus hurt?"

"No. I'm fine, too. Thanks for asking."

"Thank God."

"I disabled their car to buy us some time, but I expect them to come after us once they lick their wounds and get another car."

"I agree. Assassins are tenacious people who won't stop until they're dead. After you pick up Dr. Burrus' family, drive east toward Virginia. I'll find them a safe house."

"OK."

"I'll call back once I have something."

"Hold on. We have to assume there was a leak. Someone knew Dr. Burrus was at Sewanee, and the timing looks like we led them here."

"I'm afraid I must agree. Did you tell anyone where you were going?"

"No."

"OK. I'll check to see if the leak came from my end. Drive east until I call back."

"Will do."

Frederick patted Titus' shoulder. "You saved my life. Thank you."

"You're worth saving. Thanks for your help back there. You really walloped that guy good."

Frederick smiled. "I didn't tell you I can hit a baseball as well as I throw one."

Titus grinned. "No, you didn't."

Frederick rubbed his sore shoulder.

"You OK?"

"I'm fine. It's just a couple bruises from your tackle."

"I'm sorry. I had to do it. I'm also sorry I brought this trouble to you. Your being attacked has something to do with my visit. I must've led them here somehow."

"This mess started years ago, Titus. This day was bound to happen sooner or later. It's here. I'm just glad you're with me. If they came for us in the middle of the night, well...."

"Don't think about it, and this isn't over. The trouble has just begun."

As soon as they pulled up to the house, Isabella ran outside with the two children. They carried little bags, while Isabella had weapons and a large bag slung over her shoulder. Winnie ran up to the rental car, barking with excitement.

Titus got out and watched for trouble, while Frederick helped his family pile into their SUV. Just as they finished loading, Titus saw a car racing toward them.

"Give me that rifle and some bullets," Titus said calmly.

Frederick complied without a word.

Titus loaded the weapon and looked at him. "What are you waiting for? Go! Head east and don't stop. I'll catch up with you. Go!"

Wheels squealed, as the SUV raced off. Titus got behind a tree, watching the approaching vehicle through his scope. Once he recognized the driver as one of the men who attacked them in the restaurant, he fired at the tires but hit the front grill. He wanted them to stop, but he didn't want to leave any dead bodies behind. Soon, a tire blew, and the car went off the road into the ditch.

Titus almost ran toward the car, then he thought better of it. He had no idea how badly the men were hurt from the crash, if at all. Instead, he ran to his own rental and sped off.

Only a quarter-mile down the road, he saw Frederick walking toward him with a shotgun in his hand. Titus slammed on the brake.

"What the hell are you doing?" Titus demanded. "Are you leaving your family alone?"

"Isabella has a rifle, and she can shoot. We won't leave you, Titus."

"Damn, you're stubborn."

"That's what I've been told. Where are they?"

"In a ditch near the house. I shot out a tire. Now get in. I'll take you back to your family. I have no idea how long it will be before they come after us again."

When they reached the SUV, Titus saw Isabella crouched behind a tree, her rifle ready. Frederick ran up to her, and they hugged.

"You and Isabella have to crush your cell phones and toss the parts into the woods," Titus instructed. "Then get in the SUV and follow me."

"How will I call Tammy?"

"You can use one of my burner phones." Titus reached into the car and handed Frederick two burners. "From now on, we communicate only with these. Got it?"

"Got it."

After they destroyed their phones, Frederick and his family got into their vehicle and headed east behind Titus.

A few minutes later, Frederick called him. "I never reached Tammy, but someone found her tied up in a closet. They beat her up. I guess they found out where we were from her, not that I can blame her. Those bastards!"

"Damn. How badly was she hurt?"

"They took her to ER. She's got multiple bruises, maybe a fractured rib, and she lost a tooth. I told my chairman to tell the president it wasn't about her, but that my parents were very wealthy, and the thugs probably wanted me for ransom. I added that we had similar threats in the past, and I had to go into hiding for a while."

"Good thinking. Will Tammy be all right?" he asked.

"They think so."

"I hope so. We took a stroll around campus together. She's really nice."

"Yes, she is. She likes you, you know."

"What?"

"She told me she thought you were cute. She wanted to know more about you, especially when I said you were single and staying with us."

"Really?" Isabella asked. "We're running for our lives, and you boys want to talk about this now?"

Titus smiled. "After we get out of this mess, I'll take her to lunch."

"I'd say you owe her dinner at a very nice place after all this," Frederick shot back.

Isabella grabbed the phone and said, "*Two* dinners. Now let's please focus on getting to a safe place, OK?"

After a moment, Frederick said, "I saw how fast you reacted back at the restaurant, Titus. I'm impressed."

"It's from my football days. I played safety at West Point. In situations like that, I go into autopilot. It's all instinct. I see what's in front of me and move without thinking, just like in football."

They hung up. Fifteen minutes later, Titus received a call from Seth, who had an address for him of a safe house in the backwoods of West Virginia. "I'll arrange for a more-permanent place for them as soon as I can. I'm still trying to figure out what happened. Keep them safe until I can get you more help."

CHAPTER 23

The safe house was anything but easy to find in the mountains of West Virginia late at night. They took many winding, hilly back roads with lots of switchbacks. Some of the roads were quite treacherous for those unfamiliar with them. They also had to watch constantly for sign of pursuers. Titus and Frederick devised a plan to respond to any suspicious cars they encountered, but it never happened. Nonetheless, the drive was nerve-wracking, even for Titus.

Eventually, they arrived at the entrance to their destination in the middle of nowhere. A large *Private Property—Do No Enter* sign was posted threateningly near the locked gate. Titus got out and prayed the combination Seth gave him would open the lock. He sighed in relief when it did.

They slowly went up the long driveway over coarse rocks that made loud, crunching noises under their tires. One hundred yards down the road, they arrived at a dumpy two-story cabin. Titus knew the sound of gravel would alert anyone of their presence, but no lights came on. He also knew the gravel would serve equally well as an alarm for them.

As he got out of the car, he heard thousands of insects singing. The night was pitch black. He drew his Glock and whispered to Frederick, "Wait here."

He eventually found the door key hidden under a rock as Seth said. Slowly, he approached the cabin and unlocked the door, stepping inside cautiously. He wasn't expecting trouble, but he wouldn't take any chances.

What he saw surprised him. Although the cabin looked like a wreck on the outside, the inside was updated with every modern amenity anyone could ask for. Thoroughly checked all the rooms, he found no one had been in the house for a long time.

Titus brought the family inside.

Exhausted by the drive, they were pleasantly surprised when they saw the interior. Isabella, overjoyed by the unexpectedly modern kitchen, was also happy to find the cabinets stocked with canned and boxed food, including dried milk. They were tired and hungry, so she set to work getting something to eat for everyone.

While the family settled in, Titus initiated a preliminary outdoor perimeter check. He liked the cabin's location. It sat on a hill that gave an excellent view in all directions. There were no lights for miles around.

He sat on the front porch to eat cereal, analyzing how assailants might attempt to assault them. Although anything was possible, he was mostly concerned about a night raid. They could sneak up quietly on foot and would be difficult to see in the dark.

Titus saw only a couple of lights around the house, but additional ones could be added. The second floor would serve as a lookout post manned 24/7 by the adults. He intended to use Winnie as a guard dog, especially at night.

The following day, he found the Burrus family adapted surprisingly well to their new situation. Frederick and Isabella treated the event more like an adventure for the children, not the potentially lethal situation it was. The kids understood they were in some sort of vague danger without knowing details. They were told never to leave the sight of at least one adult.

Frederick kept a shotgun within easy reach at all times. Isabella carried a 9mm pistol in the small of her back, and her rifle was always nearby. The discipline, love, and calm the family showed impressed Titus, making his job of protecting them much easier.

After breakfast, he helped clean the dishes. Frederick stood guard upstairs. Titus saw a mischievous expression on Isabella's face.

"What's that about?" Titus asked.

She grinned and handed him a plate to dry. "I thought there was something odd about you, Agent Warren."

He chuckled. "I've heard that many times before. In which way do you mean?"

She smiled knowingly. "Whenever my husband is around one of his science colleagues, all they discuss is their research or interesting things they've read in the latest scientific journals. You two talked about everything except science. I found that unusual, and not knowing the names of the other professors in your department was a little disquieting."

He grinned and nodded. "Those are accurate observations. I actually have a PhD in molecular biology, but I could've played my part better."

"I still can't believe you two lied to me." She raised her voice as if trying to reach Frederick upstairs.

"It was my fault," Titus said. "I hated being deceitful, but I didn't want to scare you until Frederick and I sorted out a few things."

She crossed her arms. "How smart did that turn out to be?"

"Not very, I admit. I wasn't the only one keeping secrets, though, was I?"

She smiled. "You got me there."

"In fact, is Isabella even your real name?"

"It is. I wanted to keep a little of my identity."

He nodded and dried the last dishes. "I don't blame you. It must've been difficult spending all these years in hiding. Now I feel bad that I made things worse. If I hadn't come here, those would-be assassins might never have found Frederick."

"Maybe yes, maybe no. We thought someone would eventually find us. Frederick and I are fortunate you were there when it happened. He says you saved his life."

"Well, he probably saved mine, too."

"This isn't your fault, Titus." She raised her voice again. "It was my husband's stupidity that caused all this years ago, what with using email and cell phones about important work!"

"I heard that!" he called back.

"Who did you think you were, Frederick, to be using unsecured communications so carelessly, the Democratic Secretary of State?"

Titus laughed.

"We've been through this many times," he replied. "Let's not do it again in front of Titus."

"Yes, but how can you be so stupid for someone who's so smart?"

He didn't bother replying.

Isabella felt she may have pushed her point a little too far and softened her voice. "But I love you, Frederick. Yes, I'll move on from this now. I just had to scold you about this one more time. That's what wives do."

"Love you, too," he called back.

"I'm tired of hiding, anyway. I'm Mrs. Burrus, not Mrs. Welkener."

Titus nodded and walked toward the door. "I'll make my rounds and will be back shortly."

Later that evening, Frederick and Titus sat on the deck, drinking coffee and discussing the situation. Titus tried to find any other dots he could connect to the picture.

"This Dr. Lin promotes himself as a great humanitarian battling global warming and other high-profile causes. Does that mean anything to you? Have you done any work related to that?"

"No. My work has nothing to do with global warming or what they call climate change."

"I didn't think so, but I thought I'd ask just to see about possible connections."

Frederick shook his head.

After a moment, Titus asked cautiously, "So what do you think of people like Dr. Lin, pushing for billions of dollars more to be spent on global warming or climate change?"

"Personally, I'd like to see that money spent on things I know would make a difference, like feeding hungry children or cleaning up foul water."

Frederick was a smart man. Titus wanted to dig a little deeper. "What do you think about global warming?"

He shrugged. "I have no real opinion about it."

Titus' brows furrowed. "Really? You're a scientist. I thought for sure you'd have an opinion about such a popular topic."

Frederick glared at him. "Not really. There's not enough accurate data for me to have a worthwhile opinion."

Titus looked at him curiously. "Are you telling me you're a climate change denier?"

Frederick looked back at Titus as if he were an idiot. "What does that even mean? That term is used to bully people who don't get onboard with what their group think."

Titus chuckled at his success in riling up his new friend. "Just messing with you, Professor. Actually, I thought there was plenty of data on climate change. Most of the talking heads say there's no question about global warming."

Frederick laughed. "Yeah, yeah. How many times has science said they knew something for sure, and later had to admit they were wrong when new data came in?"

Titus shrugged.

"Many, many times, I assure you. How can people be so certain in this case? The data is weak. Maybe the world's temperature is warming now, but for how long? Are there cycles to these things?"

"What do you mean?'

Frederick rubbed his chin. "The earth has been around for four to five billion years, right? How long has man been accurately measuring temperatures, maybe a couple hundred years? That's a blink of an eye in the life of a planet. Even if the temperature data is accurate, which is debatable, the data is infinitely small for the time frame concerned to reach an accurate conclusion. Temperatures may rise for a time, then fall again. Micro patterns can be found, but no one can predict long-term temperature. There are too many factors involved. It's like the old question of a blind man describing an elephant if he's only holding onto the tail."

"Good point."

"The data we have is that the earth's climate has always changed. Common sense indicates it always will. We also know that many, if not most, of the climate-change models and predictions have been shown to be grossly inaccurate."

"Do you think man is affecting the climate?"

"Sure, but many things do. How significant is it? There isn't even a clear correlation between carbon dioxide levels and climate like many want you to believe. By far, the most-important factor in climate isn't man. It's the sun."

"The sun? I never really thought about that."

"The sun's radiation isn't as constant as people think. There are changes in the frequency of solar flares, shifting of the sun's interior plasma, and even wobbling of the earth's axis."

"Interesting."

Frederick paused in thought. "What about the influence of volcanoes?"

"Volcanoes? You think they're significant?"

"They might be. Underwater volcanic eruptions that we never hear about can push temperatures upward by warming the oceans. The vast amounts of dust from a large eruption on the surface could significantly block radiation from the sun and cause cooling for a long time. There are countless variables being ignored by the media to keep people stirred up."

Titus found Frederick's insights fascinating.

Frederick's expression became disgusted. "Unfortunately, too many of the so-called climate scientists act more like salespeople than scientists. Real scientists always question their hypotheses. Today, most want to cut off debate to protect their narratives. I don't trust most of them. Climate will change. There will be winners and losers. That, too, is never discussed.

"What can we do, anyway? No one can make it rain during a drought or make the sun shine during a flood. There's too much money being wasted on something we know so little about and is basically out of our control, anyway."

"You seem to have a lot to say for someone with no opinion."

Frederick chuckled. "I usually keep my views to myself, but you asked. Many people would demonize me for my opinions, especially on a college campus. Like many other conservatives, even black conservatives, I have to keep my thoughts to myself. Besides, I have more important things to worry about."

CHAPTER 24

Forty-eight hours after they arrived at the safe house, Seth called Titus.

"How are things?" Seth asked.

"All right so far."

"The Burrus family adapting to the accommodations?"

"They're doing amazingly well. They're great people."

"Splendid."

"How's your search going for another safe house?"

"I'm scouting out a long-term location, but I don't have anything yet."

Titus rubbed a hand over his forehead. "I understand."

"I do have new information that I think might be helpful."

"What's that?"

"It's a bit complicated, but I'll tell you when I work out a few more details. Basically, I have a new assignment for you. You need to come back to DC soon to prepare for it."

"What about Dr. Burrus and his family? They shouldn't be out here alone."

"Charles agreed to watch over them until they can get something longer-term arranged."

"Charles? You mean your IT guy?"

"That's right, but don't worry. He'll be a big help. You'll see. Expect him to come in a white Chevy van. He's on his way already.

He's bringing more food and other supplies. Once he's settled in and gives you the go-ahead, you can return to Washington."

Titus stood in the door, an assault rifle in hand, closely watching a white van come up the drive. Frederick was simultaneously standing near the first-floor window with a shotgun, while Isabella had a rifle trained on the van from a second-story window. They were taking no chances.

The van stopped a little distance from the house, and Charles Newman stepped out.

Titus muttered, "Oh, my God." Charles looked exactly like a stereotypical image of an IT geek. He was tall, thin, with a large head, pointed nose, and wispy gray hair. His thick glasses hung on the end of his long nose. A 22-caliber Ruger handgun hung loosely in a holster at the front of his pants.

Titus knew he shouldn't judge someone only on appearances, but he couldn't help it. As he walked toward Charles, he said softly for the second time, "Oh, my God."

A dark-haired woman in the passenger seat wore aviator shades. She seemed Asian, and Titus worried that Charles was already under control of their enemies.

He kept an eye on her, as he approached the van and said, "I'm Special Agent Titus Warren of the FBI. You can call me Titus."

"Charles Newman, MI-6. So nice to meet you."

After shaking hands, Titus pointed at the woman in the van. "Your friend?"

"Extra protection."

"I see." He pointed at Charles' gun and kept his eyes on the woman. "Your Ruger might be nice for target practice, but I hope you brought a little more firepower than that to protect Dr. Burrus and his family."

Charles smiled without any sign of anxiety. "We'll be fine. I brought some excellent surveillance equipment, too."

"Great. We'll know who's coming before everyone is killed."

Charles laughed. "Don't worry. I brought plenty of firepower, too."

"What did you bring?"

He pointed at the woman who was just getting out of the van. "Her, for starters. She's the most-lethal weapon I have."

Titus saw an attractive, lean woman with long, black hair. She carried a shotgun, as she walked toward them. His instincts didn't register danger.

Coming closer, she looked Titus over. "I'm Ying," she said curtly with a British accent.

"Special Agent Titus Warren, FBI. You can call me Titus." He eyed her impressive compact assault shotgun. "What do you have there?"

"You don't recognize it? This is my 12-gauge pump-action KEL-TEC." She walked back to the van and took out an assault rifle. "This beauty is my AR-10."

Titus was impressed. "Nice."

"I've shown you mine. Now show me yours."

Titus smiled and held up his weapon. "Heckler and Koch MR762A1 sniper and assault rifle."

She reached for it. "May I?"

He eyed her closely, then said, "Sure."

She examined its features, balances, and aimed at the sky. "I like it." She handed it back and went to the van for more equipment. Grunting slightly, she hefted guns, ammunition, and other gear to her shoulder.

"Need help with that?" Titus asked.

"Why would I need help?" she asked bluntly.

He knew better than to respond.

As she walked to the cabin, Titus saw she had a large KA-BAR survival knife attached to a belt in her back. He had one just like it, along with a Gerber LHR 6.87-inch fixed combat blade. He also noticed she had attractive legs.

Charles, paying little attention to the two of them, got his surveillance equipment from the van. Titus picked up a couple of items to examine. "Your surveillance stuff looks pretty nice, and there's plenty of it."

Charles grinned. "It's nothing special, really. Your basic outdoor-vision security cameras, night optics, and motion detectors. Many hunters have the same things or something similar. My indoor monitoring system is top-notch, as you'll soon see."

"I see." After a moment, he asked, "Is Ying MI-6 as well?"

"You would think so, but no. She's my wife."

Titus' head jerked back in surprise. "Your wife?"

"That's right."

"Hell, no offense, Charles, but I figured you to be a socially inept geeky gay intellectual when you got out of the van. Your wife is, well, damn good-looking, if you don't mind my saying so."

Charles laughed. "No offense taken, Old Boy. Actually, I'm quite straight and mingle with non-geeky people quite nicely. That is, when I'm not at my computers."

Titus smiled, glad to see Charles had a sense of humor. He'd been around plenty of intellectuals at the University of Virginia, and he enjoyed teasing them.

"I know I don't look like your typical MI-6 agent, and Ying doesn't look like a woman who would marry someone like me, but she is. I'm MI-6, and she's my wife."

"Well, she looks lovely, in a Rambo sort of way."

Charles laughed again. "You're a funny man, Titus. She *is* lovely, but don't get any ideas. She's my Rambo."

Titus patted his back. "Of course." He added after a pause, "You know I was just messing with you right?"

"Of course. You Americans can be quite obnoxious when you try."

"I deserved that." Titus thought for a moment. "If she's not MI-6, what's the deal? Is she ex-military?"

"Ying knows her way around weapons, and she's a deadly shot, but she's not ex-military, either."

Titus felt increasingly confused. "Is she with some other law-enforcement agency?"

"No. Many people assume that, too, but she's here only as my wife."

Titus, stunned, couldn't let it go. "Here as your wife? At a safe house with killers looking for us, and she's coming here as your wife? This isn't a campout, Charles."

"I know, but Ying insisted. She wouldn't have it any other way. You really shouldn't get worked up about it. She's talented and has been with me on dangerous operations before. If you keep worrying, your blood pressure will be a mess in a few years."

"You Brits have a strange sense of humor. I get that. What's the rest of her story? You're killing me here. You two look like the odd couple, and she's here in a dangerous situation. There has to be a story to this, and I need to know, or she goes back."

Charles smiled patronizingly. "I suppose you're right. I've been stringing you along a bit, an old habit of mine when it comes to Ying, I'm afraid."

Titus waved his hands, motioning Charles to get on with it. "What's the story?"

Charles laid down the equipment and leaned against the van. "We met when I was on assignment. She was married back then to a very wealthy French businessman. They were on holiday in London when she was taken hostage and held for a large ransom. It was a nasty affair that ended with the death of her husband."

"I'm sorry."

"Well, she's not. She describes him as a self-centered, narcissistic ass who was both physically and emotionally abusive to her." He pointed at all his surveillance equipment. "Her inheritance is how I got these toys, by the way. Her ex had no children, so she got everything after he died."

Titus gestured with his hands again. "So how'd you end up to-gether?"

"The authorities discovered where she was being held and killed the three men holding her. However, they found a very complicated explosive device attached to her upper body, which the captors activated before they died. The rescue team couldn't remove it or deactivate it safely, so they called me in. In addition to my IT work, I teach agents how to deactivate explosives at MI-6. I did a lot of explosive work in the Queen's army, you see."

"Go on. This is getting interesting."

"They asked for my help. I deactivated the device right before it would have exploded and killed both of us. There were fifty-seven seconds left on the detonator."

"That's very brave of you, Charles. I'm impressed."

"If you look for it, you'll see she had the number *57* tattooed on her right hand as a reminder of how close she came to losing her life."

"I'll look for it."

"After I got her out of the contraption, she threw herself into my arms and has never let go."

"That's quite a story. She wouldn't leave you?"

"No. I literally couldn't get rid of her."

Titus chuckled. "Poor you."

"I really tried to push her away. I did," he insisted. "I didn't want to take advantage of a beautiful young woman, because I happened to be the one who deactivated the bomb."

Titus stared at him, trying to figure him out. Charles was a dichotomy of many things.

"There are many other people who could have done it. Eventually, I learned she really loved me for who I am. She says she's attracted to my intelligence and character." He smiled and added, "I can't blame her for that, can I?"

Titus grinned. "No, you can't." He was glad Seth sent Charles. As they talked, he was becoming more impressed with the frail-looking man.

"She said she couldn't care less that I'm skinny, knock-kneed, blind, and older. I came to love her, too, so we got married."

Titus patted his back. "Too bad for you."

Charles smiled. "Yes. No one ever thought I'd marry anyone so beautiful and so young."

"And her weapons skills? Where does that come in?"

"The hostage event had an enormous impact on her. It rocked her to her core. Ying was in therapy for a while, but that didn't change her insecurities. Eventually, she decided what she really needed was to know how to defend herself."

"Makes sense." Titus nodded.

"With her money, she hired top-notch instructors who trained her in weapons and hand-to-hand combat. Ying was a talented dancer. She learned quickly and had the physical abilities to excel. Now she's an expert in combat skills and keeps training all the time." After a moment, he added. "I suggest you never cross her. I've seen what she can do."

"Don't worry. I wouldn't dare." Titus patted Charles' shoulder and carried some of his equipment toward the house.

CHAPTER 25

Titus sat on the outside deck early that evening when Seth called. "Did Charles and Ying get there OK?"

"They did. Interesting people. They're getting settled in and oriented to our situation. I like them."

"Splendid. Do you feel better about leaving Dr. Burrus and his family for a few days?"

"I feel better now that I met them." After a short pause, he added, "You could've told me about Ying ahead of time. That was a bit of a surprise."

Seth chuckled. "She's special, isn't she? I thought you needed to meet her yourself. She would've been a hard sell over the phone, and I was afraid you'd insist she couldn't come."

"So you thought to use the old, 'Ask for forgiveness, not permission,' routine?"

"Exactly."

"That's devious of you, but you are probably right. As long as she wants to be here, we certainly can use another gun and pair of eyes. The surveillance and monitoring equipment Charles brought looks state-of-the-art. If anyone comes near us, we'll know about it."

"Excellent."

They spoke at some length about the attack at the restaurant and what it meant.

Eventually, Titus asked, "Do you know how Dr. Lin found out about Dr. Burrus in the first place? That's assuming he was the one who sent the assassins."

"I'm confident it was Dr. Lin who sent them, but no, not yet."

Titus rubbed his forehead. "Are we under surveillance?"

"That's always possible, but I doubt it."

"Why?"

"I'm quite sure we'd both be out of the game by now if that were the case. We'd be dead or in some dark hole, being tortured for information. Dr. Lin's people found Dr. Burrus' whereabouts another way. Charles and I will figure it out. It's only a matter of time. He can work his computer magic from there."

"What's our next move?" He gazed out at the beautiful countryside, as the sun set. "You mentioned something about my going back into the field. What did you have in mind?"

"Dr. Lin is throwing another one of his famous mega-parties at this Texas estate. It's a formal affair. Top-level representatives from countries around the world will be there to discuss climate change and the future of the UN."

"I guess he believes he must personally whip the world leaders into line."

"It appears so."

"The man doesn't lack confidence, does he?"

"Being a billionaire tends to do that to people."

"So how will this party help us."

"I want you to be there?"

"I'd love to meet the guy, but what, exactly, do you want me to do?"

"I'd love to have you abduct him right out of the house for a covert investigation." Seth chuckled. "Given our situation, I just want you to do a little direct surveillance and some eavesdropping. See for yourself what he's all about. It may give us some ideas on how to proceed."

Titus stared out at the setting sun. "Are you sure you want me to do that? There's a lot of exposure and risk with little obvious gain."

"My gut says we need to lay eyes on this snake and perhaps shake things up a bit."

"OK. I hope you're right." He thought for a moment. "How did you plan to get me in? Do I go as a cook, a waiter, a delivery truck driver?"

"He's much too clever and paranoid for that sort of thing. He uses his own staff for everything."

"So how do you expect me to get close?"

"The representatives are allowed to bring a spouse or significant other."

"OK. How does that help?"

"You'll pose as the date of the Ms. Colette Beaulieu, who represents the French government."

"Who is she?"

"She's a wealthy, highly connected, French bureaucrat and a friend of mine. Her family made millions in the French wine business. She's also four times divorced and well-known for being what you might call a cougar. You'll be there as her latest boy-toy."

Titus laughed. "A boy-toy? That's funny. She sounds like an interesting character."

"She is, I assure you. I've known her for many years. She's perfect for our purposes."

Winnie walked up and rubbed her nose against Titus' free hand. He petted her, as he listened.

"The socialist-leaning French government is quite taken by Dr. Lin's babble. She, however, privately share similar concerns that I do about his views and growing influence."

"Has she helped you before?"

"I team up with her now and then on certain projects."

"How much does she know about this?"

"Not much. Nothing about Dr. Burrus or his work. All she really knows is that Dr. Lin is a person of interest to me, and I warned her he's a very dangerous man. She's smart enough to know that it's in everyone's interest that she know as little as possible in case things go, well, don't go as planned."

"OK. So I go in as this Colette's boy-toy. Once there, I spy on Dr. Lin. Sounds reasonable." After a moment, he asked mischievously, "What's the catch with her, Seth? Is she morbidly obese, eighty-something, with horns coming out the sides of her head?"

Seth laughed. "No, no. Not at all. She's actually quite a splendid-looking woman for her age and is only twenty or thirty years your senior."

Grinning, Titus shook his head. "Only twenty or thirty?"

"Remember, you're not on holiday, Old Boy," Seth said with amusement. "I'm not running a bloody dating service. I bet you'll like her."

Winnie brought him a stick. Titus threw it and watched her chase after it. "I was just giving you a hard time. We're lucky to have her help."

"Indeed. I'll provide you with a new identity and a toy or two of your own when I see you."

"A toy or two? Are you getting kinky on me?"

Seth laughed. "You Americans always have sex on your minds. No. I'll give you some of Charles' special surveillance equipment, of course."

"Ah."

"Now get back here soon. We have work to do."

Once back in DC, Titus met Seth at one of his favorite restaurants in Georgetown, a quaint, old, brick home that had been converted into a pub. They sat in the rear, well out of earshot of the other patrons. Titus ordered a grilled, bacon-wrapped scallops with garlic and an arugula salad with balsamic dressing. Seth had lamb chops sizzled with garlic and a side order of oven-roasted asparagus.

"These lamb chops are exquisite," Seth said after two bites. "How'd you find this place? It's so secluded, and the food is wonderful."

"By a lot of trial and error, I assure you."

"I see."

Titus had plenty of questions and immediately got down to business. "I know my cover is to be the new boyfriend of Colette Beaulieu, but specifically, who am I supposed to be? What's my background story?"

Seth smiled. "You, my friend, will be Rodney Clements, the son of a wealthy New York hedge fund manager who died, leaving you more money than you know how to spend."

Titus nodded. "What do I do for a living?"

"Nothing, really. You do a little investing, but you're basically a rich playboy who likes women, alcohol, and exotic travel. You especially like to hang out in Europe and have a taste for French women."

Titus, chewing on a delicious scallop, listened.

"You're obviously in superb shape, so you're also an exercise freak with a huge ego who works out to attract women like Colette for your playboy lifestyle."

"In other words, I'm a complete jerk."

"Precisely." A playful smile came to Seth's lips.

"You really enjoy messing with people, don't you?"

"I'm glad you're catching on, My Friend. Anyway, you met Colette at a gym in Paris several weeks ago and hit it off splendidly. You've had a superficial, hot, sexual fling ever since. I'm having her text all her friends about you to help entrench your cover story in case anyone gets suspicious. Of course, Charles will help me set up all the false documents and phony electronic trails to support your story. He's very good at that sort of thing."

They stopped talking when the waitress stopped by to fill their water glasses. Seth ordered another glass of their best Merlot, while Titus turned down a second glass of Pinot Blanc. After she left, Titus prompted Seth to continue.

"The story is that she's taking you to the Texas gala to show you off to some of her international friends and get to know you better. You'll stay overnight in one of the guest rooms."

"I assume she's comfortable playing lovers and staying overnight in the same room with someone she never met before?"

Seth laughed. "Oh, she's fine with it. She's seen your picture and thinks you're quite handsome. She's filled with fervent anticipation. We told her you're an off-the-books agent for MI-6. She's quite excited abut the entire adventure. She loves every chance she gets to play a little espionage. She thinks of herself as a female James Bond."

Titus grinned. "I know the type."

"Usually, she just provides us with general observations and insights about politicians and other people of interest when she travels, but she finds it exciting. We find her information useful. Here's her bio and picture."

Titus studied the documents. "Hmmm. She's quite attractive for her age."

"Indeed. She's quite a hottie."

Titus laughed. "Quite a hottie? What the hell does that mean?"

"You'll find out." Seth wiped his grinning face with his napkin. "To put it simply, it means she has no problems staying with you, and there are plenty of men who'd love to go in your place."

"Do you have a complete bio on her and my own character for me to get familiar with? I need a lot more details in case there's trouble."

"Yes, of course." Seth handed him a folder. "Here's everything you should need. Of course, destroy it when you're done."

Titus glanced through it. "The more I read, the more I dislike the spoiled rich punk I'm supposed to be."

"I'm afraid that couldn't be helped," Seth replied matter-of-factly. "We wanted to make Rodney Clements plausible as her date, yet as unimportant a person as there could be at the gala. You need to be invisible to Dr. Lin and his gang, which should allow you more opportunity to observe and do your work."

After a few more moments of reading, Titus looked up at Seth. "Thanks for the STD in my medical history."

Seth laughed. "I was hoping you'd notice that little gem. That was Charles' idea, a detail to add to your playboy image. We enjoyed having fun with your character. It makes our work much less boring."

Titus shook his head in amusement.

Seth glanced around the room. After he confirmed no one was looking at their table, he took a tiny device from his pocket.

"What's that?"

"That is an extremely small M-6 microphone and transmitter. It's very sticky, so be careful how you touch it. It attaches easily to clothing and can stay on for many hours without being noticed. Eventually, it falls off and is vacuumed up with the dust."

"Nice."

"It's so tiny, it's difficult to detect even with scanning devices."

Titus picked up the tiny thing with a pair of forceps Seth handed him and studied it. "This is pretty cool."

Seth showed him several ways to attach it to someone without being noticed. "The disadvantage of such a tiny device is that it has a rather short distance of transmission."

"How short?"

"No more than twenty to thirty yards in most cases. Shorter if the person is in another room. Your tiny receiver will be hidden in your belt buckle. When the opportunity presents itself, you can slip receiving buds into your ears."

"Gotcha."

Seth sighed. "By the way, for your information, Charles has discovered something new and rather disturbing about Cheung."

"What's that?"

"I'm afraid the authorities found him dead. He moved to Spain."

"Dead? In Spain?"

"Yes. I assume he took flight after you questioned him."

Titus, looking troubled, didn't speak.

"The Spanish authorities discovered his true identity and that Cheung escaped China. They assume Chinese agents killed him. As far as I can tell, they're clueless about Cheung's connection with Dr. Lin. Given the timing of your visit, I believe Dr. Lin's people found him, questioned him, and tortured him to find out why he ran. I also assume he told them what he knew about you."

Titus nodded solemnly.

"Unless we're very wrong about a lot of things, this tells us just how dangerous and ruthless the people we're up against are." Seth's expression turned very solemn. "They skinned him alive."

Titus' appetite vanished. He said nothing and thought about Dr. Burrus and his family, sincerely hoping they were safe with Charles and Ying."

"You and Colette must be very careful. I tried to explain to her just how powerful and dangerous Dr. Lin is, but I'm not sure she fully understood."

"I'll watch after her," he assured him.

Seth rubbed his chin, thinking of all the things he wanted to say. "You'll have no backup. Abort immediately if there's any sign your or Colette are in danger. If you're caught, it won't go well for either of you, and our hopes to take him down will be lost."

"Why do you say that?"

Seth sighed. "If they're willing to skin people, he'll get what he wants out of Colette quickly, and you, too, eventually, my friend. No one can withstand that kind of thing."

Titus wasn't scared, and he wasn't concerned. "You still think this plan is worth the risk?"

Seth nodded slowly. "We have to tip the scales somehow. This is the only play I can think of. Just be careful."

As usual, Dr. Lin's guests were encouraged to arrive early and enjoy themselves before any of the formal events. Colette and Titus did just that. After settling into their room, they played bocce ball, walked, and socialized with other representatives. The two fell swiftly and painlessly into their roles as playful lovers, holding hands, stealing quick kisses, and subtle touching whenever possible. Titus found Colette to be clever and felt confident he could trust her. She found Titus to be the sort of man she enjoyed dating and relished her role very much.

Even with high expectations, they couldn't believe the opulence of Dr. Lin's estate. It crossed Titus' mind how very different the assignment was from his past Delta missions, which took him into hot Middle Eastern deserts and the cold mountains of Afghanistan. It was also quite a change from his usual FBI work in downtown Washington, DC. The estate's atmosphere was so pleasant, he had to remind himself not to be lulled into thinking they were safe. The mission was every bit as dangerous as all the others, and there was no backup team waiting in the dark or satellite communications to help feed him intel.

Colette knew many of the delegates and mingled easily, as Titus tagged along. As she spoke with a representative from Germany, Titus fidgeted and behaved as if he were totally uninterested in the conversation. He also gave Colette a subtle signal that he wanted to explore the grounds privately.

During a lull in the conversations, she turned to him with a sympathetic expression. "I know this must be quite boring to you, Darling. Why don't you find someone to play tennis with or do something else fun? I'll catch up with you later."

"Are you sure? I could hang out with you some more, if you'd like."

"I'll be fine." She gave him a quick kiss. "Go have some fun."

Titus wasn't sure what he was looking for but wanted to reconnoiter unhindered by delegates stopping him to speak with Colette. Most of the buildings appeared to be staff living quarters, guest apartments, or maintenance buildings of various kinds. He was impressed by the isolated estate's self-sufficiency.

He saw little of interest except for one auxiliary building, a plain, single-story beige thing off to the side. What caught his eye were the guards who protected it and a large *No Trespassing* sign posted clearly in front. His best guess was that it housed their security headquarters, but he couldn't be sure.

As he meandered toward it, a guard approached. Other DGF staff were so pleasant, Titus was surprised when the man pointed an accusatory finger and barked, "You there! What are you doing?"

"Sorry, Man. I'm one of the guests and just walking around." He showed the guest badge that hung from his neck. "I was just curious why this building has a no trespassing sign when the other don't."

"That's none of your business, and you aren't allowed here," the guard growled.

Titus sheepishly raised his hands in defense. "That's cool. I'm going. I've seen a lot of large estates before, but I never saw anything like this place. Is this the security building? I mean, security at a place like this must be extensive."

The annoyed guard gestured for him to leave. "Just go."

"OK, OK. I was just wondering."

The guard watched, as Titus shoved his hands into his pockets and walked away like a spoiled kid who hadn't gotten his way.

On his way back to Colette, he formulated a plan to go back there for a nighttime reconnaissance. He was startled from his thoughts when a DGF golf cart pulled up, driven by an attractive Chinese staff member in tan shorts and a DGF short-sleeved shirt cut low enough to reveal an attractive figure.

"Excuse me, Sir," she asked sweetly. "Are you a guest?"

"I am."

"You look like you might be lost. Can I help you find something?"

"No, I'm fine." He gave an amused smile. "I was just taking a long walk and daydreaming a bit. It's beautiful here."

She got out of the cart and offered her hand. "My name is Lan. I'm a member of the entertainment staff."

As he shook her hand, he noticed she held on a little bit longer than expected. She placed her second hand lightly on top and looked into his eyes somewhat seductively.

"Just let me know if you need anything," she said.

"I will."

As he started to walk away, she asked, "Are you sure I can't give you a ride? I could give you a tour of the estate."

"No. I'd rather get in some exercise, but thanks."

She gave an alluring smile. "OK. Let me know if there's anything I can do for you. I could even give you and your wife a private back massage before tonight's events, if you're interested. Are you here with your wife?"

Titus, surprised by the question, didn't know what to make of it. "No. I'm good."

She waved and drove off.

He didn't wave back. He carefully studied the other entertainment staff. All were young and attractive, and there was no mistaking their seductive body language. What was that all about? Was that the way the superrich entertained guests, or was there something more to it? He wasn't sure, but it seemed odd.

When he caught up with Colette, she was in a beautiful rose garden. Staying in character, he kissed the back of her neck.

She turned, smiled, and kissed him back.

"What a beautiful garden," he said.

"Yes, isn't it lovely? I could stay here for hours."

They sat alone on a garden bench, and he quietly told her what he saw. "We can only speculate about the building until I can take a closer look."

"I agree."

Titus looked around. "What do you think about the staff? Are they a bit too seductive, or is it just my imagination?"

"It's probably nothing, Darling." She ran a hand over his cheek. "I'm sure you have plenty of women come on to you. Dr. Lin is well-known for throwing amazing parties. I'm sure his staff are given free license to be flirtatious, sort of like a playboy club. I've seen it all before—handsome young men and beautiful women entertainers at events like this to energize and please the guests. It's nothing new." After a pause, she added, "One young man even came on to me not long ago."

"He did, did he?" he asked in playful jealousy. "What did you do?"

"Nothing." She grabbed his arm, smiled, and pulled him close. "I'm already with the handsomest man here."

When they returned to their suite, Titus' senses were on high alert. Something wasn't right. Purely on instinct, he subtly searched the room when Colette went to freshen up in the bathroom. It was a fine art to search a room without looking like he was doing it, but his training taught him well. Several minutes later, he spotted it.

It was a tiny, well-hidden camera in an air vent. Either Dr. Lin was on to them, or it could explain the subtle sexual soliciting he noticed by the entertainment staff. Seducing people with prostitutes and recording the encounter had been successfully used to blackmail people since recording devices were invented. While at the FBI, Titus was part of several cases that involved seduction and blackmail. In Washington, powerful players were common targets for such traps.

When Colette came back into the room, Titus pulled her close and gave her a passionate kiss. As he hugged her, he whispered, "We're being watched. There's surveillance equipment in this room."

"OK," she whispered. "Then let's give them a show."

To his surprise, she stepped back, unzipped her floral dress, and let it drop to the floor. His eyebrows shot up. He was momentarily stunned into silence by her action and her beauty.

Colette grabbed his arm and pulled him onto the bed. As she started removing his clothes, he gently stopped her. Actual sex with someone he hardly knew wasn't for him, and doing it while being watched was worse. Then he remembered Seth and Charles' little joke in the file.

"No, no," he said in embarrassment. "I can't. I'm sorry. I should have told you sooner, but I'm afraid I'm having a little herpes outbreak."

Colette, shocked, said honestly, "Well, damn." She couldn't remember the last time she was turned down by a straight man. She wasn't sure if he was being honest, playing his role, or didn't like the idea of being watched. Whatever the reason, she pouted and reluctantly pulled away.

"I hope you understand," he said softly. "I promise to make it up to you another time."

She liked him and moved closer. "OK. Just let me hold you for a while then."

"Sure."

CHAPTER 26

When they arrived at the formal gala that evening, they saw multiple guards, cameras, and a metal detector just before the entrance. Obviously, security would be tight. Dr. Lin stood just inside the large ornate front doors in an elegant foyer with a large crystal chandelier above. Fa Shen was at his side.

Titus felt relieved after he passed through the metal detector, then was greeted by Shen's scrutinizing gaze, as he stood in line.

After Colette's pleasant greeting with the multibillionaire, she said, "And this is my date, Rodney Clements."

Dr. Lin held out his hand. "Nice to meet you, Mr. Clements."

Titus took the hand with both of his and shook it enthusiastically. "It's so great to actually meet you, Dr. Lin. I've heard so much about you. I'm a really, really big fan of yours. Climate change will kill us all if we don't do something fast. This is so special to be able to meet you."

"Thank you. I hope you have a nice evening," Dr. Lin said coolly, pulling his hand away from the goofy admirer. Neither he nor Shen had any idea that Titus just attached a tiny microphone to the back of Dr. Lin's sleeve.

"All go well?" Colette asked softly, as they walked around admiring the elegance of the ballroom.

"Perfectly." After a few minutes, he looked at her as if seeing her for the first time. "May I say that you look very beautiful this evening. That red dress is stunning."

"This old thing?" she replied mischievously. Actually, it cost a fortune, but she had plenty of money from her multiple divorces. "I must say you look quite dashing in your tux."

He grinned. "Thank you." Music starting playing, and several people walked onto the dance floor. "Would you like to dance?"

She smiled warmly. "Of course."

They danced, mingled, and tried to take in as much as they could. Nothing important stood out to Titus. He was impressed, however, by Colette's calm demeanor and how well she played her part.

As the orchestra took a break, Dr. Lin went to the podium to address the crowd. Everyone became quiet. Three camera crews were there, and his message was being sent to all domestic and international outlets.

"Thank you all for coming," he said. "Many of you had a long journey, and I hope you've had a pleasant stay. Let us know if there's anything you need to make your visit more comfortable. I have a wonderful entertainment staff who are devoted to making your stay pleasurable and memorable."

Polite clapping followed his remarks.

"We're gathered here today to mingle, recreate, and discuss ways to combat the terrible problem of climate change."

Heads nodded.

"Recently, I announced a billion-dollar donation from the Dynasty Foundation to the United Nations to fight this deadly problem. As I said at that time, the one-billion donation was only the beginning. I stand behind my words.

He paused and smiled for effect. "Today, I announce the donation of a second billion dollars to fight our world's ever-increasing climate chaos. This time, it comes from my personal funds once again to be spent through United Nations efforts."

The crowd applauded so loudly, he had to wave them back to silence.

"My friends, this, too, is only a drop in the bucket of what it will take to save our planet from destruction. Much, much more money is needed. For this, I ask your help. That's why I gathered you here today. Every nation needs to contribute more money to the United Nations for this cause. After all, we all live on this planet together."

Most heads nodded, and a few people applauded. It was one thing for him to give away his own money but another to solicit from them.

"The United Nations must also have greater authority to tax nations based on their relative wealth, so this vital work can be ongoing. It must be able to enforce its mandatory taxation and regulatory policies. Only with more financing and greater authority can the United Nations monitor and control climate change. These things must be done without hindrance by national or regional authorities. We must begin to act as one people on this one planet."

Some representatives, especially those from poorer countries, clapped loudly.

"As part of its global efforts, the United Nations must be able to set policy, be allowed to police, and better regulate the world's oceans and air. This will be a massive, expensive endeavor. I will offer not only my financial help but also my voice and leadership in these efforts."

Some raised their glasses in approval, but overall, the reaction of the crowd was mixed.

"Great achievements such as these take all our efforts. You must return home and press the governments you represent to work through the UN. It's up to us to save this planet, and, in so doing, we'll unite the world in this common cause. I'll speak to each of you individually about how your nation might contribute to this effort and how your country might be able to use my donation to combat climate change. Thank you so much for coming. We have much important and exciting work ahead to do together."

Dr. Lin knew his speech was received with mixed and generally lukewarm enthusiasm, but he also knew through his well-controlled news media releases and arm-twisting they could go home to an excited populace impressed by his generosity. Clips of the speech would be shown to highlight areas of special interest to each nation. The broadcaster in smaller nations would discuss how this lone man gave away so much of his own money and challenge the larger nations to contribute more. To them, taxation would be for someone else.

He would have broadcasters in the large nations emphasize his generosity, caring about saving the planet, and world unity. The spin in each country would be custom designed for those who heard it—designer propaganda. He knew his worldwide public opinion would skyrocket no matter what the representatives thought. He also knew his backup plans of blackmail, bribery, and threats would leave the results of his efforts in little doubt.

After the speech, Dr. Lin mingled with his guests. Again, tiny, well-hidden microphones were placed by his security staff throughout the room and on the uniforms of staff workers who moved through the crowd. Recordings from public and private areas would be analyzed and used by Dr. Lin and his staff to entice or blackmail people who were reluctant to do his will.

At the first opportunity, Titus excused himself to go to the restroom. He went into an empty stall, saw no surveillance, and placed the listening device in his ear. He didn't turn it on right away, because Seth warned him to use it only for short periods of time to avoid possible detection and wearing out the small power source.

Intermittently, he listened to Dr. Lin's conversations. From what he heard, the meeting between Dr. Lin and the representative from Argentina concerned money going to the South American country. Dr. Lin assured him they'd get their share and asked for continued support for his initiatives. Both seemed agreeable enough, and Titus found the conversation extremely boring.

Later, Titus noticed Dr. Lin and his huge bodyguard slip into a private study off the main room and close the door. Guards came to stand on either side of the entrance. Dr. Lin's staff ushered guests in one-by-one, presumably for private conversations with the philanthropist.

Colette gave Titus a rundown on the people she knew at the gala. The most-interesting one to Titus was Samuel Conners. Titus saw him on TV and was aware that he was President O'Malley's Chief of Staff.

When Titus noticed Conners being led to Dr. Lin's study, he whispered into Colette's ear, "I need to know what Conners and Dr. Lin talk about."

She nodded.

"We need to get closer to the study. I'm out of range here."

They stopped dancing and casually moved in the general direction of Dr. Lin's meeting room. Before they got far, though, Titus stopped, spun Colette around to put her between him and the door, and snuggled up close.

"Do you see the large Chinese man guarding Dr. Lin's study on the side nearest us?" he whispered.

She looked casually over his shoulder. "You mean the one limping?"

"That's the one. He knows me. He and a few of his cronies tried to kill me recently. I thought Dr. Lin sent him. Now I know for sure."

"Why would he want to kill you? Dr. Lin didn't even recognize you."

"I was with someone who was the real target."

"Who?"

"That's best left unsaid. That limp was my doing."

Colette rested her head on his shoulder. "Hmmm. That poses a problem."

"Yeah, to put it mildly. If he identifies me, we'll be running for our lives. I need to get close enough to listen in. Can you distract him while I come in from the other side? I don't recognize that guard."

Colette lifted her head up to smile impishly. "Honey, I've been distracting men and luring them to my wishes since before you were born. How long do you need?"

Titus smiled at her confidence. "I have no idea. Try to keep him occupied as long as I'm near the study. I'll try to be brief."

She nodded subtly.

"I'm a dead man if he sees me, and you'll be in very hot water for bringing me here. If they catch me, you know what to do. You had no idea I was anything but a rich playboy and feel embarrassed that I used you to get me in here, OK?"

"OK, Handsome." She kissed him.

Titus pulled back and looked sternly at her. "Be careful. He's not just a bodyguard. He's an assassin."

She didn't flinch. "Don't worry. I've been around killers and scum my entire adult life." She paused. "Most of them were called lawyers and politicians. He's no different. Men are men. You're all quite predictable."

He smiled at her daring. "Be careful, anyway. Afterward, we need to get out of here as fast as we can. I can probably avoid one guard, but there were others who might recognize me, too." He grinned and added, "If any of them are out of the hospital."

She giggled, staring into his brilliant blue eyes. "You're so conceited."

"That's true."

"I like that about you."

He smiled. "I'd better go."

As he walked away, she moved slowly toward the guard. Quickly formulating a plan, she began toying with the pearls around her neck.

Titus mingled briefly, as he moved to the other side. He had very little time to waste if he wanted to overhear any of the conversation between Conners and Dr. Lin.

As Colette neared the door, her necklace broke, and pearls spilled on the floor. "Oh, my God! My necklace!" she blurted to the nearest guard.

She bent to pick them up and looked up at the man in desperation. "Could you please help me? My pearls are being scattered everywhere. It's a very expensive necklace."

The large man looked down at the woman in the red dress pleading with him. She was much older than he, but he still found her attractive. He glanced at the other guard, who nodded.

"Please?" she asked.

"OK." He looked at the nearby people. "Everyone move away slowly. Watch where you step."

Colette and the guard crawled around on their hands and knees, searching for pearls, She watched his eyes dance back and forth to view her plentiful cleavage. She smiled knowingly. All was going as planned.

What she didn't know was that a member of Dr. Lin's security team was closely monitoring her actions. He was immediately concerned at seeing one of Dr. Lin's personal bodyguards crawling around on the floor. The man should have known better than to leave his post to help her.

He glanced at his supervisor for advice, but he saw him in an intense conversation with another of the monitoring staff. The man decided to just watch for a while. It was probably nothing, and the last thing he wanted was for one of Dr. Lin's guards to be pissed at him for calling attention to a small infraction.

Titus moved closer to the study from the opposite direction of Colette. As he did, he saw an attractive woman standing alone right where he wanted to go. Seeing a waiter walk by, Titus took two martinis off the serving tray.

The man from the underground security team saw Titus, identified him as Rodney Clements, and listened in.

Titus offered a martini to the young woman. "Would you like a drink?"

She looked at him curiously, smiled, and accepted it.

"Enjoying the party?" he asked.

She shrugged. "It's OK."

He offered his best smile. "I'm Rodney. And you?"

"Sharon," she replied, looking him over a little more and liking what she saw.

"What's a beautiful woman like you doing alone in a place like this?"

She sighed. "My husband's too busy to spend time with me tonight." She pointed toward a tall man with salt-and-pepper hair standing on the other side of the room, speaking with two women. After a moment, she asked, "How about you? Are you alone?"

"Pretty much."

She looked at him suspiciously. "I noticed you earlier. I had the impression you were with someone, an older woman, I believe."

Titus laughed. "I am, sort of. You might say we're going our own way tonight."

"Is she your mother?"

He shook his head at the rude question. "No. She's a friend. She needed someone to accompany her to this event, and she asked me. Where are you from?"

As he told Titus about herself, he unobtrusively turned on the listening device and listened to Dr. Lin's conversation. Intermittently, he asked the woman open-ended questions to keep her talking.

The man monitoring Titus eventually lost interest, concluding he left his older date to hit on a pretty young woman.

Titus was upset that he missed some of the conversation. After a few moments, Conners said, "No. I told you, the President won't go that far. He's very concerned about authorizing so much power to the United Nations. He already feels the U.S. gives them too much money."

"Come now, Mr. Conners," Dr. Lin replied. "After all, it's to help the world community. How can anyone object to saving the Earth? As the mainstream media all say, President O'Malley is being too nationalistic and mean-spirited."

Conners coughed. "Don't give me that worn-out line. The President knows the best thing for the world is to keep America strong and economically healthy. That has always been proven to be true.

What you're proposing will lead to more unnecessary regulations, will cost trillions, and will give the United Nations too much power."

"Don't you think you're being a bit paranoid and overly dramatic, Mr. Conners?" Dr. Lin snarled.

"Hell, no. The President isn't stupid, and neither am I. Billions have already been wasted by the previous administrations on similar projects. Do you know how many so-called 'green companies' have gone bankrupt even with huge federal loans and subsidies? They produced nothing of any worth other than filling their own pockets and donating money back to the politicians who funded them."

Dr. Lin didn't reply.

"No," Conners continued. "Feeding the poor, we support. Giving medical assistance to the needy, we support. Being ready for the next pandemic, we support. Keeping water and air cleaner, we support. We can do all those things ourselves, and we can donate to other countries that deserve it, if we wish. We don't need the United Nations or Dynasty Global Foundation to do it for us and claim all the credit."

"Don't you see how fighting climate change will unite the world?"

"Under whose authority, Dr. Lin?" Conners asked sarcastically.

"The only world authority that exists, the United Nations."

"Yeah, and who will control the UN?"

Dr. Lin didn't answer.

"We've noticed how you seem to be actively seeking leadership of that esteemed body," Conners continued. "That would put you in a position of considerable power, wouldn't it? The President and I aren't fools."

Again, Titus heard no reply.

"The President can support you on your global medical efforts, but I don't see President O'Malley spending new money on the global-warming movement. He ran on a campaign to reduce federal waste, not increase it."

"I see. There seems to be no negotiating with you." After a moment, Dr. Lin continued, "Please tell Mr. O'Malley that if he wants to continue to receive his medication from me, he will honor my wishes."

"Come on, Dr. Lin. Is that kind of obvious strong-arming really necessary? We merely have a difference of opinion."

"You can also tell him that he really doesn't want to find out what it's like when someone stops the formula. It isn't pretty."

"What exactly does that mean?"

"He'll see."

Titus heard a loud thunk, as if Conners slammed his hands against a desk or table.

"Are you threatening the President of the United States?"

Dr. Lin chuckled. "Of course not, Mr. Conners. How silly of you to think so." His tone became serious. "There is no other way. If he scratches my back, I will scratch his. I'll achieve my goals with or without his help. America can come onboard and make my task easier, or it will be left behind."

That time, it was Conners who didn't reply.

"Good day, Mr. Conners. We're done here. Shen, see this man out the door."

"I'll tell the President, but he won't like it. I personally don't like the entire situation. Are you saying he'll get ill if he stops the drug?"

"He'll find out soon enough. Now run along like a good lap dog and tell your master what I said."

Titus brought his attention back to Sharon when she asked, "Are you listening to me?"

"What?"

She put both hands on her hips. "I asked if you were listening."

"I'm sorry. I just remembered something very important. I have to go. It was nice meeting you."

She assumed he was just like her husband—a complete jerk.

Moments later, Colette glanced up and saw Titus had moved away. She flirted with the guard a moment longer, as he finished helping her with the necklace. Once Titus was lost in the crowd, she thanked the guard with a kiss and moved on.

When she caught up with him, he said softly, "Time to go."

She became upset. "I don't appreciate your leaving me all alone so long."

"I was just talking with someone," he whined.

"You mean that woman?"

Titus shrugged.

"Well, I feel suddenly ill. We have to go."

He looked extremely disappointed. "Now?"

"Now."

The man monitoring them from the security station heard their heated conversation and smiled. The guy flirted and was caught, and he was paying the price. People were so stupid.

On their way back to their room, Titus whispered into her ear, "Seth was right."

"How's that, Darling?" she whispered back.

"This is big—very big."

"Will you check out that building tonight?"

"No. I have all the information I need."

CHAPTER 27

Soon after he returned to Washington, Titus met Seth at his office at FBI headquarters. As usual, their meeting was scheduled on the pretext of discussing international terrorist activities.

Seth's face lit up with excitement and concern, as Titus described his observations in Texas and the conversation between Conners and Dr. Lin.

"Sorry I didn't get a chance to investigate that building that was off-limits, but I felt we had more than we asked for, so I wanted to get out of there."

"I would have advised the same thing. Bravo to both of you. Your intel is invaluable to us. You and Colette did a first-rate job. I'll have to find a special way to thank her."

Titus said, "Now we know with a great deal of certainty that Dr. Lin's people were involved in the assassination attempt on Dr. Burrus and how extensive this case really is."

"It couldn't be bigger if it goes as high as the President of the United Sates. We're swimming in very dangerous waters, Titus. The number of people we can trust is dwindling to a devastatingly low level."

"It also means we can't count on being covert forever," Titus added. "A member of my FBI team, Special Agent Cynthia Cook, told me last night that Special Agent Russel Clapton has been asking a lot of questions about me. He's a rising star in a different unit and should have little interest in what I do."

Seth rubbed his chin. "Hmmm."

"His questions didn't feel right to her, and she told me about them. She speculated he's after my job, but she wasn't sure. I have no proof, but I'm concern he might be shaking the branches for Dr. Lin."

Seth crossed his arms. "That's of considerable concern. We have to be on guard and assume the worst. As I've told you, Dr. Lin has eyes and ears everywhere."

Titus leaned back in his chair. "That's what I thought. It makes sense Dr. Lin would check into the U.S. intel community for people who might be tailing him."

Seth grimaced. "It does, indeed. What did she tell him?"

"Basically the truth. I've been on special assignment that requires some time away for undercover work concerning suspected terrorists."

Seth nodded. "Good. The truth, or a reasonable facsimile, always holds up best under scrutiny. Hopefully, his asking about you is nothing but internal politics. If he is a mole for Dr. Lin, he's probably just snooping around. I'll have Charles look into this Russel Clapton."

"Sounds like a good idea."

Seth leaned closer to Titus. "But you raised a good point. We need to move with all speed before we're discovered. Not only does this Clapton fellow bother me, but you came dangerously close to being recognized in Texas."

Titus nodded. "Yeah. Don't remind me. That could've gone very badly if he spotted me first."

Seth nodded.

"I think it's time to bring in Deputy Director Otero. We need all the help we can get, and he's about the only person you and I both trust."

Seth considered the suggestion. "All right. He might also be helpful in keeping this Agent Clapton away from us by sending him on his own special assignment."

Titus placed a hand on his desk phone. "Should I call him right now? No sense waiting."

Seth nodded.

Taking a deep breath, Titus picked up the receiver and placed the call. Otero answered on the third ring.

"Yes?"

"Deputy Director, this is Agent Warren."

"How may I help you, Warren?" Before Titus answered, he added, "Did Miles find you? I know he was looking for you."

"He did, Sir. I'm with him now. That's why I'm calling."

"Oh?"

"We'd like to speak with you as soon as possible. It's about the joint project Mr. Miles and I've been working on. We could use your help."

"It's about damn time. I'll be right there."

Otero sat quietly, as Seth and Titus explained everything they knew about Dr. Lin, the Wake Formula, his organization, and the involvement with ambitious and powerful people, including the current President.

Afterward, he said simply, "Holy shit."

"Yes, holy shit," Seth agreed.

Otero shook his head. "This really goes all the way up to the President?"

"Unfortunately, it does," Titus answered.

"At least we know more about the who and what we're up against than before," Seth put in. "We're no longer completely in the dark. We know Dr. Lin is involved for certain, and we understand the basics of what he's up to."

"By that you mean recruiting, manipulating, and sometimes blackmailing powerful people around the world with this drug and lots of money," Otero responded.

"Exactly. He's clearly attempting to gain power through the United Nations," Seth continued. "Have you noticed all the recent news about him and his damned humanitarian Dynasty Global Foundation?'

dation?'

"Who hasn't? It's hard to miss. They present him as some sort of climate hero, but, although I had no idea who you've been investigating, something never smelled right to me about him."

"He's a multibillionaire who owns numerous media outlets who prop him up as a savior," Seth stated.

"And, of course," Titus added, "the other mainstream media outlets go along like idiots."

"He wants to be elected Secretary-General of the United Nations," Seth said. "That's certain. He wants to make it a more-powerful organization than ever before. The power he could wield concerns me a great deal."

Otero nodded. "If it's power he wants, it's a brilliant plan."

"It look like it's up to us to figure out his plan and do something about it," Seth said firmly.

"Why the hell did you wait so long to bring me onboard?" Otero asked, irritated.

"I needed to know more before putting you in harm's way, Raphael," Seth replied. "At first, I just needed a field agent to get some intelligence. Titus did a wonderful job, as you said he would. Now we have to stop a maniac. That's a whole new ballgame."

The Deputy Director patted Seth's shoulder. "You need never protect me, My friend." After a moment, he added, "Right now, I need to visit West Virginia and meet this Dr. Burrus. He sounds like a very interesting man. Together, we'll develop a plan."

"How will we all go to West Virginia without being missed?" Titus asked.

"Don't worry. Seth and I have our ways." He glanced at Seth. "The usual?"

"The usual."

"What are you two talking about?"

Otero chuckled. "As you've probably figured out by now, bureaucrats like to see reports."

Titus chuckled and nodded.

"The more reports they see, the harder they think we're working," Seth added. "So we give them lots of terrorist reports, and all is good. They feel safer and leave us alone."

Otero smiled. "No one will think we have time to take a piss, much less work on an unsanctioned operation, if we provide our superiors with lots of reports to review." He glanced at Seth. "We've done it before, haven't we, Old Friend?"

"Yes, we surely have."

"I see," Titus said with a playful smile. "I have to remember that one, Deputy Director, before my next evaluation."

His superior grinned. "By the way, Warren, when we work on this project, just call me Rafael. There's no rank on this mission."

"Yes, Sir. Just call me Titus."

"I'll do that."

"What about Agent Clapton?" Seth asked. "Can you help get rid of him, Rafael, in case he poses a threat?"

Raphael said, "I hate to think one of our own in the FBI is mixed up with Dr. Lin, and I haven't seen a shred of evidence that he is, but he meets the criteria for the type of person you've described Dr. Lin recruits. Agent Clapton is single, very ambitious, and has risen up the ranks with incredible speed this past year. He's in position as a potential insider, which is valuable to Dr. Lin."

"Can you get him off our scent in case he's involved in all this?" Seth asked.

Raphael hesitated for a moment, then smiled. "Yes, I can. I heard he wants to go undercover, something he's never done and wants to complete as a way of checking all the boxes for advancement. I'll dangle an important undercover assignment in front of him and several others. With his ambition, he'll beg me to be selected. Then I can send him far away on the assignment, and he'll forget all about you, Titus."

The Supreme Council opened their meeting with the usual pomp and ceremony, with all members wearing their imperial robes.

Dr. Lin sat in his throne-like chair in his formal yellow robe. Six guards lined the walls of the meeting room.

Breaking from recent meetings, Dr. Lin's first question was to the Director of Medical Affairs. "How's your research going, Dr. Liu? Do you have an antidote yet for the toxic effects of the Wake Formula?"

"Still no significant breakthroughs at this point, Master Lin, but my research team is working night and day on it."

"How are our long-term seriously ill patients doing?"

"We're getting better at keeping them alive. However, three more have died. Four others are in a coma."

"I see. Who died recently? I'll see they are replaced immediately."

"One was a lawyer from New Orleans who had an unusual reaction to the drug the first week. He died of cardiac arrhythmia. We're still looking into what happened."

"That's most unusual. What do you think happened?"

"We think he was using other drugs, probably crystal meth. That may have led to a lethal combination on his heart."

"I see. I can easily replace him. The others?"

"The others became ill after they stopped the formula. They either came back to us to restart medication too late or never returned for treatment at all. One was a rising professional golfer from India. The other was one of the American congressmen."

"I see."

"They should never have tried to stop their medication. They have only themselves to blame," Dr. Liu added.

"What has become of the other American congressman who stopped his medication?"

"He's in a coma. We're experimenting with various ways to revive him. So far, we've had no luck."

"I see. What have you done with the bodies of those who died?"

"The usual protocol. They're on one of the cargo ships that carries medical supplies. They will be fully autopsied for research purposes before being dumped overboard at sea. Their bodies will never be found."

"Very good. Is production of the drug still going well?"

"Yes. So far, we're keeping up with current demand. I envision the need of a second production facility very soon if demand keeps growing."

"I will give that some thought, but we have other priorities right now."

Dr. Liu nodded.

Dr. Lin turned his gaze to General Chen. "Have acceptable cover stories been made to hide the deaths of the clients Dr. Liu mentioned?"

"Yes, of course. Generous financial gifts to the surviving family members have helped as well. Those who give us any trouble will be threatened or dealt with accordingly."

Next, he looked to his head of Strategic Planning and Propaganda. "Has optimal media coverage been arranged when our cargo ship reaches port and the medications are unloaded in Africa?"

"Yes, they have," Liang Lee replied. "This is the largest donation of medication to Africa in two years. The whole world will know about it."

Dr. Lin nodded. "Good. The enhanced publicity will more than make up for the cost of the cheap antibiotics we give them."

"As you wished, I've arranged for you to be on the front cover of several of the most-prominent magazines in America, England, and France this month, plus the news apps and lesser magazines. You'll be more famous than the Beatles when we're done."

"Very good, Lee. Then all is on schedule, I assume?"

"Yes, Master Lin."

Dr. Lin looked back at his head of Security and Surveillance. "General Chen, what did you find out from my old friend, Cheung? Did he speak to the man who was seen following him?"

"I'm afraid he did, Master."

"What did he tell this man?"

"Cheung told him about his work in China as an industrial spy, about Dr. Burrus, and about his connection to you."

Dr. Lin sat motionless, a cold expression on his features. Inside, he seethed with anger.

"He said he tried not to tell him anything, but the man forced him by breaking one of his fingers and threatening to break more. I saw the broken finger."

"So my old friend gave me up that easily, with just one broken finger?"

"Yes. Fortunately, however, I believe Cheung didn't understand why you were interested in Dr. Burrus' work. He thought Dr. Burrus developed a drug for sleep."

"Are you saying he told the man I bought a medication for insomnia?"

The general chuckled. "Yes. He seemed to have no understanding of the Wake aspect of Dr. Burrus' research. Even under extreme torture, he didn't sway from his story. I believed him."

Dr. Lin nodded. "Cheung never paid attention to details. He only obtained information. It was never his job to analyze the information when he worked for the Chinese government."

General Chen nodded.

"Who interrogated him? Who employed him? Why was he interested in the formula?"

"Unfortunately, Cheung didn't know."

"I see. That *is* unfortunate. Hopefully, this man and those he works for will not be a threat, because Cheung gave him misleading information. Still, we must be on guard, General Lee."

"Of course."

"You're sure you got all the information from Cheung there was to obtain?"

"Quite sure. He was terrified. The pathetic man was no warrior. He squealed like a pig with every slice of skin that came off his body. He would have sold his mother into slavery to make us stop."

"Well done, General. I never wished harm to Cheung, but he deserved such punishment for betraying me."

"Yes, Master."

"What of this man who saved Dr. Burrus from your assassins in Tennessee? Do we know who he is? Was he a police officer or a local redneck with a gun? Was he the same man as in Paris?"

"We don't know, Master Lin."

In a harsher tone than usual, Dr. Lin said, "You don't know very much General. Find out. Also find out where Dr. Burrus is. Use every resource we have. You must locate him again quickly. After interrogating him, kill him and anyone else with him."

"We're analyzing satellite images of the cars leaving that area of Tennessee on the day and time of his escape. It will take time, but I believe we'll find where he went. If the other man is still with him, we'll capture them both, extract the information we need, and kill them."

"Keep me informed of your progress."

CHAPTER 28

After the council meeting, Dr. Lin took a shuttle to his private living area. First on his agenda was a relaxation break with several of his favorite concubines. Afterward, he went to the children's area of the house. Instead of going into their school area, he watched them on monitors. He knew his presence would disrupt their activities, and he was able to observe them, their teachers, and mothers without their knowledge.

Dr. Lin, pleased with what he saw, found his staff of instructors and his children hard at work. Mostly, the mothers stood nearby attentively, helping only when needed. A couple of mothers looked uninterested in their children's instruction, which displeased him. He noted who they were and planned to punish them later. Most of the children were in classrooms, while others had martial arts training.

One of the senior martial arts instructors wasn't pushing his oldest son hard enough, so Dr. Lin immediately called the supervisor of all instructors. "My oldest son's martial arts instructor is too soft on him. He need to be more rigorous in all of his training. One day, he will inherit my empire, and he must be ready in every way."

"But, Dr. Lin, he...."

"There is no but! Replace him by the end of the week."

After another hour, Dr. Lin was satisfied and took his shuttle back to his office to review his financial portfolio.

Three hours later, someone knocked on his door.

"You may enter," he said.

An aide came in. "There is a Ms. Berry here to see you, Master Lin."

"Who is she? Was I expecting a Ms. Berry?"

"No, Master. She wasn't on your schedule but insisted on seeing you today."

"Who is she? Why is she here?"

"Ms. Berry is the lawyer you saw in New York after one of your media events. She refused your generous offer to move up in the Society of Wake, so you stopped her medication."

"Yes, yes. I remember now."

"She is here to tell you she has changed her mind about your offer. Do you want to see her, or should I send her away?"

"Normally, I would make her wait, but I've been working hard and could use a pleasant distraction. Get together the contracts I wanted her to sign. After I review them, you can bring her in."

The aide bowed and returned with the contracts. Dr. Lin looked them over and wrote in several additional requirements. "You may bring her in now."

She came in, escorted by two guards. Two aides were also working in Dr. Lin's office. The attorney looked nothing like before. The once-vibrant lawyer was thinner, pale, and walked like an old woman. There was no vitality or confidence in her facial expression or demeanor.

Dr. Lin stood and pointed to a chair. "Have a seat, Ms. Berry. Are you feeling all right? You look a little peaked."

She slowly moved to the chair and sat. "What have you done to me?"

Dr. Lin moved to a seat across from her. "What do you mean? I have done nothing to you."

"Look at me. I have no energy. I want to sleep all day, and I can barely walk. I'm a laughingstock at work. I was about to become the youngest partner in my firm's history, and now I had to take medical leave before I was fired."

"Why do you come to me with your problems, Ms. Berry? You are no longer a member of the Society of Wake. You had an opportunity to advance in that exclusive club, but instead, you declined my generous offer and departed. Do you remember? It was in New York, I believe."

Ms. Berry coughed. "I remember. I didn't want to leave, but your offer wasn't what I wanted."

"Oh, but you did leave. Now tell me, why have you come all the way from New York to my home to speak to me? I can think of nothing we have to say to one another."

"I've changed my mind," she said desperately. "I need that damn Wake drug of yours, and I need it now. I'm getting worse and worse. I can't go on like this."

"So are you saying you're ready to accept the conditions of my contract?"

"Yes. That's why I'm here."

"Do you accept all my conditions? I added a few. There are penalties for not signing when I asked you."

"That's what I said. Please give me the drug now. I feel horrible. I want my life back."

Dr. Lin motioned to Fa Shen, who brought the contracts for her to sign. Dr. Lin looked at her. "Then sign these agreements."

She was distrustful but accepted the papers. "I'll have to read this thoroughly, of course. My mind is so slow. It's hard for me to even read. If I could have some Wake Formula now, I could read this tonight and bring it back tomorrow."

"No, you may not. You'll have time to read them later once they are signed."

Her eyebrows furrowed. "Are you kidding me? You think I'll sign a contract I haven't read?"

"That's right. It's sort of like the famous words of one of our great political leaders, who said something like, 'We can read the health care bill after we pass it.'" He motioned to Shen to take the contract back from her.

She sat motionless, saying nothing.

"You're either fully in or fully out of my care and organization," Dr. Lin said. "I'm a very busy man. Sign the contracts now or don't sign them. I don't care either way. It's up to you, but don't waste my time any further."

"Why? You have plenty of time."

Dr. Lin laughed. "I like that. You still have some wits about you. There are many other people I can get to do the legal work I had in mind for you. You're merely one cog in my great machine."

"I see."

"I expect, and insist upon, complete loyalty and absolute obedience from members of the Society of Wake." His voice became sterner. "Do you understand?"

"OK, OK. Give me back the damn papers. I'll sign them. I need my medication."

"Then you'll do whatever I ask?"

She rolled her eyes in anger and frustration. "Yes, damn it. Give me the contract."

"What did you say?"

"Yes, I'll do whatever you ask."

He stared at her for a moment, then he said, "Take off your clothes."

She thought she hadn't heard him correctly. "What did you say?"

"It was a simple command. I said take off your clothes."

Her entire body tensed with anger. "Here. Now? Why would you ask me to do such a thing? You realize that's sexual harassment, don't you? I could sue you for that."

Dr. Lin laughed, then he folded his hands in his lap and waited.

"You don't really want me to take off my clothes. I'm a wreck. I'm sick. Can't you see that?"

He didn't reply.

She looked around the room. "You have beautiful women all around you. Do you really need me to take off my clothes?"

He stared at her coldly without speaking.

Seeing no other way out, she stood and unzipped the back of her dress. She almost stumbled to the floor, as she stepped out of it. "May I have the drug now?"

Dr. Lin gestured for her to continue. "Everything off, underclothing, too. You will keep nothing from me. Who knows? You may be hiding a weapon and want to kill me. Do you want to kill me, Ms. Berry?"

"No, of course not," she replied, thinking what a great idea it was.

His stare penetrated hers. "Then take off the rest of your clothes."

"Must I do this in front of all these people? I'll do whatever you want, but can't we have some privacy?"

He waved his hand for her to proceed. "Off now. I won't ask again."

Removing her panties and bra, she stood naked before him, trembling and crossing her arms in front of her small breasts, her head lowered.

"Don't worry. I don't desire you, Ms. Berry. What I desire is your absolute obedience."

"I did what you want. May I put my clothes back on now? Can I get my medication now?"

"First sign the contracts."

She nodded.

He motioned for Fa Shen to bring the contracts to her, then he changed his mind and looked at the frail woman. "That large man over there has your contracts. You can get them from him."

Without a word, she walked slowly toward the big man.

Shen looked down at her but didn't speak, nor did he offer the contracts.

"May I have the contract?" she asked, defeated.

Shen looked at Dr. Lin.

"Do you want her first, Shen? It would be most entertaining for the rest of us if you took her right here."

He looked her over. "She's too sick and skinny. I don't desire her."

Dr. Lin considered other ways to humiliate her, but, after a moment, he said, "Give her the contract."

She quickly snatched the papers from him. Seeing no table to write on, she went to her knees and signed each document on the floor without reading a word. Struggling to stand again, she handed them back to Shen, who passed them to a legal aide.

Berry turned to Dr. Lin. "May I have the medication now?"

He turned to an assistant. "Give her a dose of the Wake Formula now and one month's worth of supplies to take with her.

Grabbing the drug in both hands, she stuffed it into her mouth as quickly as possible, swallowing without water, then she fell to her knees in exhaustion and complete satisfaction.

Dr. Lin looked down at her and smiled. "You made a wise choice, Ms. Berry. You should be able to return to work after two or three weeks of treatment, if my calculations are correct. Had you waited much longer, you might not ever have recovered. Do you understand?"

She stood. "Yes. Thank you."

"Congratulations. You are once again a member of the Society of Wake. We'll supply you with the drug and will expect payment in full."

"Thank you."

He handed her a slip of paper with a name and address on it. "Go to Dr. Dozier. He has an internal medicine office in Northeast Manhattan and is a member of the Society. He'll give you a medical excuse for your poor job performance. His letter will reassure your boss that you've been suffering from a temporary medical condition that made you ill and unable to work. He'll say you had a severe viral infection, but the medical threat is over. Will that work for you and your firm?"

"That...that sounds good. Thank you." After some hesitation, she asked, "May I put my clothes back on now?"

"Oh, I'm sorry. I forgot you were naked. Yes, you may."

It was a somber gathering of minds at the West Virginia safe house. The group sat around the kitchen table, exchanging ideas and concerns. Ying, standing guard from the lookout on the second floor, watched the monitors Charles hid around the grounds. Frederick and Isabella began to realize for the first time that the full weight of the FBI wasn't protecting them.

"I'm so sorry," Titus explained. "Even though Raphael and I are with the FBI, this is all off-the-books."

"For heaven's sake, why?" Isabella asked.

"For your safety," he replied soberly. "Dr. Lin has eyes everywhere. We can't trust anyone. Seth and Charles are in the same boat with MI-6."

"When did you plan to tell us?" Frederick asked.

"As soon as we needed to," Seth said. "Adding to your fears wouldn't have helped. Now we need all cards on the table to figure out how to proceed."

"How can so few people possibly defeat Dr. Lin and his coalition?" Isabella asked in desperation and frustration.

"I agree, he's quite formidable," Seth admitted soberly, "but isn't the perception of invincibility exactly what tyrants want? There appears to be no way to oppose them. They use fear to keep others from even trying. We must not and cannot let that happen to us. We must keep our focus off our fears and on what has to be done."

"We'll find a way," Rafael reassured. "Dr. Lin is only human. He has weaknesses like anyone else. We don't have to beat his entire organization. We just have to take him down. Cut off the head, and the rest of the snake dies."

Isabella sighed and smiled warmly. "Of course. I'm sorry. You're both right. As Isaiah says in the Good Book, 'So do not fear, for I am with you. Do not dismay, for I am your God. I will comfort and protect you. I will uphold you with my righteous right hand.' I have to focus on my faith, not my fear."

Frederick hugged her tightly. "Exactly. God will see us through this."

"Thank you, Sweetheart."

"I think we should get you and the kids far away from me until all of this is over. I'm the one they're after."

"No. I'm not leaving you, Frederick. We're in this together."

"What do you think, Titus?" Frederick asked.

"I hate to say it, but she's right. They'd go after her to get to you. Even if she didn't know where you were, they would assume she did. She's safer with us."

He was terrified by the thought of Isabella and their children in danger. Taking her hand, he said, "Then we stay together."

Charles was quiet until suddenly, he said, "I'm not sure this helps, but I discovered where the leak came from."

"So tell us," Frederick said urgently.

"It came from me."

He cocked his head in confusion. "What? I don't understand."

Charles shuffled in his chair and took a deep breath. "Yes, it was me. It wasn't on purpose. I discovered someone piggybacked my internet searches on Dr. Burrus."

Seth patted Charles' back. "I told you not to blame yourself. I wouldn't be surprised if Dr. Lin has an army of computer geeks constantly searching for anything related to Dr. Burrus and a thousand other things."

Charles shook his head. "I should've covered my tracks better."

Titus rubbed Charles' shoulder. "I'd rather have you on our side than whatever team of computer whiz kids Dr. Lin has. Believe me, you'll be a big part of his downfall."

"Thank you, but he, she, or they were quite clever. They probably set up a sophisticated sentinel program a long time ago to monitor any searches concerning Dr. Burrus. Once they found out what I was doing, they covertly followed right along. When I located Frederick in Sewanee, so did they."

"Why hasn't he come after you and Seth?" Isabella asked.

"Because Charles' system is untraceable," Seth answered before Charles could reply.

Charles nodded. "They were able to see my search results but not the source. Once I found out about them, I sent them on a wild goose chase. I wish I could see their faces when they realize it. It'll take them a long time to figure it out."

Titus laughed. "So now there's a terrible battle going on of mighty geek warriors somewhere out in the cyber clouds?"

Charles laughed with him. "I guess so."

"We have to be more careful than ever," Seth said. "Dr. Lin knows someone is getting close. He's a ruthless chimera and more dangerous than ever. He hasn't found us yet, but I'm sure he's looking. Whatever we do, it must be soon."

"Something else has been bothering me," Titus said.

"What's that?" Rafael asked.

"When I listened in on Dr. Lin's conversation with Connors, he said something like, 'The President doesn't want to find out what will happen if he stops taking his medication.' What was he talking about? Does your drug have some sort of withdrawal symptoms, Frederick?"

Frederick coughed to clear his throat. "I never used it in human trials, but yes, there were significant withdrawal problems from the Wake Formula in my animal studies."

"What sort of problems?" Rafael asked.

"If I withdrew the drug from test animals that used it only a short time, there was no real problem. However, animals taking it for six months or longer became very lethargic and died."

"How many died?"

Frederick sighed. "All of them."

"Holy shit," Titus said. "From what?"

"What goes up must come down," he answered, more matter-of-factly than he felt. "It appears that the animals' brains became dependent on the drug for alertness. Their brain's natural ability to stay alert and awake stopped functioning, and it eventually deteriorated, because the drug did it better than their own neuronal mechanisms. Once the Wake Formula was removed, the dogs drifted into dullness, then a coma, and then they died. Their brainstems weren't active enough to keep them alive."

"What do you mean by brainstems?" Ying asked, looking down from the second floor. She could hear the conversation clearly from up there and intermittently came to the rail to listen even better.

"That's the part of the brain that keeps you alive," Titus called up to her. "It subconsciously keeps you breathing and your heart beating. Turning off the brainstem is what kills people who have a toxic level of alcohol or large amounts of sedatives."

Frederick nodded. "That's right. It was because of that potential lethality that I hesitated to try the Wake Formula on humans—at least not until I solved that problem."

Titus rubbed his head. "Correct me if I'm wrong, but you're saying that the President's life could be in danger when his supply of the Wake Formula runs out, not to mention the danger to my missing congressmen."

Isabella's hands covered her mouth. "Oh, my God. I hadn't thought of that."

"Yes," Frederick replied. "That's quite possible, assuming they haven't improved the formula and that the President has been exposed for an extended period of time."

"If that's true, we could have an international crisis on our hands," Raphael said. "How many other heads of state or leaders of large international corporations are taking the drug?"

"We already have an international crisis on our hands," Seth retorted. "It's just that no one knows about it yet."

"We need a medical solution for that part of the problem," Titus said. "That might act as a fulcrum to help us with other aspects of our situation."

"I don't understand," Rafael said. "What sort of medical solution? What other aspects?"

Titus looked at Frederick. "You need to get back to work, Frederick. You have to find a cure for the lethality of this drug. If you can, it might not only save the President's life but could be used to eliminate Dr. Lin's leverage over his other clients."

Frederick thought about the ramifications, but he honestly didn't see how it could be done.

"Aren't you putting the cart before the horse?" Rafael asked. "We need to stop Dr. Lin. Then we can worry about stopping the medical complications of the drug."

"Actually," Seth said slowly, "Titus' idea makes sense. People associated with the drug are missing. Some may be dying or dead. That would be a logical conclusion from what Frederick just said. More people could become ill, die, and stay under Dr. Lin's control if the drug remains as lethal as it is helpful. Right now, he controls both the carrot and a very hard stick. I must say, it's a brilliant place to begin."

"What do you propose we do?" Rafael asked Titus.

"Frederick is no use here. We need to move him to a secure laboratory facility where he can resume his research. We need him to find a cure for the drug's toxicity."

Frederick remained skeptical. "I understand what you're saying, but how and where could I possibly renew my research?"

"I was thinking somewhere in Washington, DC, so you and your family will be closer and easier for us to protect."

"I agree," Rafael said. "Besides, between NIH, Bethesda Naval Hospital, Walter Reed Army Hospital, Georgetown Medical School, and other research facilities, I'm sure we can find some vacant laboratory space to suit your needs."

"He'll have to work in total secrecy and with security measures in place to protect him," Seth commented. "That won't be easy."

"I'll also need equipment, supplies, and lab animals," Frederick said. "It seems impossible."

"Money isn't everything, but it solves many problems," Charles said. "Ying and I can front the money for the lab, and I can set up security for you anywhere."

"Are you sure?" Frederick asked. "It sounds like a very tall order."

"I'm sure. A lot's at stake here. We have to try."

"You seem hesitant, Frederick," Seth said. "Are you willing to do this?"

Frederick shrugged. "Sure, but setting up an entire secret lab will be very difficult. I don't see how much I can accomplish without samples to work on."

"Can't you make more?" Rafael asked.

Frederick laughed. "You can't get the components of this formula off a pharmacy shelf. It took me years to collect all the materials I needed. Some of them can be bought, others need to be synthesized, and several must be isolated from large amounts of fresh brain tissue."

"He's right," Titus said. "He explained the neurochemistry of sleep to me in some detail. Some of the components of such a formula are bound to be specific biological compounds that are nearly impossible to synthesize. They exist in the brain in such low concentrations that it would take a lot of brain tissue to isolate enough to work with."

"Then I guess we need to think of another way to proceed," Seth said solemnly.

"Not necessarily," Titus said with a little bravado. "Frederick said he can't make more Wake Formula, but there might be a way to get some."

Seth was puzzled. "What do you mean?'

"Perhaps we can steal it from one or two of Dr. Lin's clients."

"Would that be enough, Frederick?" Seth asked.

"I wish it were, but I doubt it. I'll need a lot of it to do the various experiments I have in mind."

Titus, initially disappointed, slowly smiled. "What if we steal what you need from Dr. Lin's pharmaceutical plant?"

"Now you're talking," Frederick said, hope creeping into his voice.

"Great idea, Titus," Rafael said.

"There's another issue to consider," Charles said. "I've been watching Dr. Lin's operation for some time by tapping into MI-6 satellite feeds. I don't think he produces the drug at his pharmaceutical plant."

"Why not?" Rafael asked.

"He goes to a subterranean facility much more often than his pharmaceutical plant, and it's guarded more heavily. My bet is that the Wake Formula is produced at the underground location. It would make sense to keep it in a secret, well-guarded location.

"Where is it?"

"The western corner of his ranch. It seems to be located under a huge slaughterhouse."

"Interesting," Titus said, his mind connecting the dots.

"I've been monitoring people and trucks coming and going from there. They go through a few well-guarded gates, then disappear into the underground facility and re-emerge later. I'm pretty sure that's where he makes the Wake Formula. It's where I'd do it."

"I agree," Frederick said. "It makes perfect sense. Remember, he needs a lot of animal brains to get some of the necessary chemicals, and he has a slaughterhouse there to provide them."

"Would chemicals from cow brains work on the human subjects?" Rafael asked.

"I don't see why not. Most biological chemicals are similar if not identical among species."

"He could easily protect and keep an eye on production when it's on his property," Titus added. "Can you get me more detailed information on that facility, Charles?"

"That won't be too difficult."

Titus smiled. "Then it's settled. I'll break in there and hopefully get enough Wake Formula for Frederick's research."

"It's dangerous," Seth said, "but it might work. How will you go about it?"

"Titus and I will plan the details once we have more intel from Charles," Rafael said. "In the meantime, let's find Frederick a good place to do his research and obtain the equipment he needs."

CHAPTER 29

Just two days before Titus planned to escort the Burrus family to Washington, DC, a paramilitary team armed with AK-47s stealthily approached the West Virginia cabin at three in the morning. Their mission was to assassinate Dr. Burrus, his family, and anyone with them. They parked two miles away, were deadly quiet as they moved, and were almost invisible dressed in black.

Charles' motion detectors and night optics sounded the alarm quickly, as the intruders entered the area. Charles hurriedly woke the others. Unfortunately, Rafael and Seth had returned to DC to make final arrangements for the research facility Dr. Burrus needed.

All cabin lights were off, as Titus, Charles, and the others gathered around the monitors on an interior second-floor room and watched the men approach. They were difficult to see, but Titus and Charles counted four.

"When they get closer," Titus said calmly, "they'll probably surround the cabin to prevent anyone from escaping, then they'll breach the building from all directions."

Isabella tightly grabbed Frederick's hand. He squeezed back warmly.

"Don't worry," he assured them with more confidence than he felt. "We'll be ready. They won't know what hit them until it's all over."

Heads nodded. Titus saw determination in all their faces.

"Isabella, bring Winnie in now," Titus said. "We already know they're coming, and I don't want any barking. We want them to believe they're taking us by total surprise."

Nodding, she ran from the room.

"You all know what to do," he told the others calmly. "We've prepared for this scenario many times, and we'll be fine. Everyone has a job. Just do your job, focus on your part of the plan, and things will work out."

They nodded.

"Gear up. Put on your communications devices and night optics, so you can see in the dark, and we can stay in touch. Remember, they probably have silencers, but we don't. After our first shot, they'll know that we know, so things will happen quickly."

Frederick wiped sweat from his forehead.

"They might be wearing bullet-proof vests, so shoot for the head if you have a clear shot. If not, shoot for the center of mass and hope for the best. That'll be your best chance of hitting someone."

Isabella ran back inside. "Winnie's inside."

"Good. I want you, Winnie, and the children to go into the basement." He handed her a weapon. "Here's the MP5 submachine gun. I showed you how to shoot it. Do you remember?"

"Yes."

"Good. If all goes well, you won't have to use it. Stay connected to me on your com set, but stay off the air unless it's important, OK?"

She looked hesitant. "Are you sure you don't need me up here with Rafael and Seth gone? I can shoot."

Titus gently placed a hand on her shoulder. "If the kids weren't here, it would be different. We need them out of harm's way, and they need you. Now go."

"OK." She stood on her toes to kiss Frederick. "I love you."

He looked into her eyes, wondering if he'd ever see her again. "I love you, too."

As she left, Titus said, "Frederick, take the second-floor window facing south. You know what to do. These men are assassins sent to kill you. Don't hesitate to shoot, but be sure of your target and shoot to kill. Ying and I will be in the tree-stands. You know where they are. Remember, we might not be up there for long depending on how this goes."

Nodding, he walked away.

"Stay alive, Buddy," Titus said.

"You, too, my friend. No matter what happens, thank you."

"Ying, take tree-stand Bravo. I'll start in Alpha. From there, I should be able to take out the guy coming from the west as well as the one in the north. Got it?"

"Got it."

"Stay in touch with me after our initial com check, so we can work like a team, just like we practiced. I might need your help if anything goes sideways."

She nodded, quickly kissed Charles, and left.

Titus looked at Charles. "You're our eyes and ears, Buddy. Stay on the monitors as long as you can. Let us know what they're doing. Once you hear the first shot, flip on the outdoor floodlights. You also have the responsibility of taking out anyone who makes it into the house." He smiled. "Thanks for all your help, and good luck."

"You, too, Yank."

Titus, gathering his equipment, quickly walked to the tree-stand as quietly as possible. He climbed up using the knotted rope he hung there and pulled it up after him. He carefully arranged his camouflage to keep him as unnoticeable as possible and still provide views of the north and west.

Taking a deep breath, he said, "Com check. Report in."

Everyone reported they were in position.

"Are we ready to do this?"

"Ready," they replied.

"Good." After a moment, he added, "I've gotten to know each of you, and you'll do great. Remember, wait for me to take the first shot unless you're fired upon or you see someone about to break into the cabin. I want them to get as close as possible to make them easier targets.

"Once I fire, I want you to fire at your targets immediately before they can react. Keep them in your sights. With a little luck, we'll take all of them out quickly. They think they have us by surprise, but the surprise will be on them. We don't want any of them to escape."

"God be with us," Frederick said.

"Amen," Isabella and Charles said.

Titus crossed himself.

The assassins stealthily moved closer.

As Titus waited, he slipped into the cold, mechanical, mental state of calm alertness he developed from his Delta training and years of combat. His nerves were steady, his mind focused.

As Ying waited, anger burned in her veins. The cold-blooded killers coming at them were no different from those who kidnapped her years earlier. She would have no second thoughts about putting a bullet into as many as she could.

Isabella sat quietly, praying in the dark basement with Winne at her side, and her children in her arms. She knew God heard her prayers, but she also knew not every prayer was answered the way she hoped. Leeza started trembling, and Isabella held her tighter.

Sensing something wrong, Winnie gave a low growl.

"It's OK, Winnie," she said softly. "We'll be all right."

Charles spoke into the com net. "The assailants are fanning out. They're about fifty yards away."

"Stand ready," Titus said gently. "Start taking aim at your targets as soon as they're in sight, but hold your fire."

"They have surrounded the cabin and are moving in," Charles said.

As Titus watched the men creep forward, he said, "Get ready." A few seconds later, he said, "Take aim. On three....one, two, three, fire!"

Titus fired three times in rapid succession. He was certain his first bullet struck his target's head. He wasn't sure if he hit the second target with the next two bullets, as the man dived for cover.

Ying fired right on Titus' heels. Her first shot caught her target in the neck. Her second missed completely, as he fell to his knees, clutching his throat. A third shot caught him square in the forehead, and he crumpled to the ground.

Frederick missed his target completely. He hesitated a second too long after Titus' first shot, and the assassin dived for cover.

Titus watched for movement from his second target but saw none. After waiting as long as he could, he lowered the rope and quietly climbed down for reconnaissance. "I'm out of my stand and searching," he told the others. "Be certain of your targets. I don't want to be hit by friendly fire."

He found the first man easily. His bullet left only small fragments of the man's head. Titus circled to approach the second target from behind. Gunfire continued from other directions, telling him their plan hadn't worked as perfectly as he wished.

A smattering of bullets struck near Frederick's window and entered the room, He ducked, but he wasn't fast enough to evade one that grazed his forearm. The wound startled him at first, then he realized it was superficial.

After a few moments to recover his wits, he returned to the window and fired back. He was so hyped on adrenalin, most of his shots didn't come anywhere near his target.

Eventually, Titus found his second target, sitting on the ground to wrap a bleeding ankle. He must've caught the man's lower leg, as he dived to the ground.

When the assassin finished bandaging his wound, he aimed his rifle at the cabin, waiting for targets to show themselves. With a wound like that, he wasn't going anywhere.

Slowly, Titus slid his Gruber combat knife from its sheath. He quietly crept up behind the wounded man. He could have easily shot the man, but he didn't want to betray his position in case other combatants were near.

At the last second, the man sensed something and twisted quickly around.

Titus leaped. They grappled for a moment, but Titus plunged his knife into the man's left eye. He pulled it out and quickly slit his throat from ear to ear.

When the man stopped shaking, Titus knelt motionless and listened. No sounds came from nearby.

A moment later, he heard gunfire from Frederick's area.

When Frederick's target realized no bullets were coming near him, he moved swiftly to the cabin and returned fire.

Hearing continuing fire from Frederick's position, Charles moved to a nearby window, saw the target, and opened fire. One shot struck the man's leg. The wounded man fell back behind cover, while Charles continued shooting at him.

Taking less fire, Frederick was able to send a few rounds in the general area the combatant was hiding.

"Titus, are you all right?" Ying asked.

He was breathing heavily, but he said, "I'm good."

"What are your orders?"

"There's gunfire from the south side. Frederick might be in trouble. I'm going to help."

"I hear it. Do you want me to come with you? My man is dead."

"Hold tight for now. I'd rather do this alone if I can."

He moved cautiously toward the gunfire, wondering if he should have stayed at Frederick's side. He hoped he wasn't too late.

What he found surprised him. Instead of Frederick being in trouble, the assassin was severely wounded. He held his bloody abdomen, several fingers were missing from one hand, and the lower part of his left leg was barely attached.

He held his AK-47 in his good hand and occasionally managed to fire toward the cabin. Gunfire rained down from Frederick and Charles. Several bullets struck near Titus.

"Hold your fire, Frederick, Charles," Titus said softly. "I'm near your target. He's badly wounded, and I have him in my sights. I need to talk to him."

Gunfire from the cabin ceased, and the man turned when he heard Titus approaching. Before words could be spoken, the man dropped his weapon and clutched his abdomen with both hands.

Titus slung the man's weapon over his shoulder. "Who sent you?"

The Chinese man rocked back and forth in agony without replying.

"I asked who sent you?"

"I won't tell you a damned thing," he said through gritted teeth.

Titus aimed his Glock at the man's forehead. "Who sent you?"

The man started swooning from blood loss and looked ready to faint. When he recovered enough to reply, he said, "Shoot me. I don't care. Just shoot me."

Titus was tempted, but he didn't fire. "No. I won't do you that favor. You can stay there in pain all night if you don't cooperate. Maybe a wolf or a pack of wild dogs will come by to finish you off. You don't deserve any better."

The profusely sweating man looked like he was fading in and out of consciousness.

Titus knew he didn't have long to live. He holstered his Glock and cut pieces of cloth from his own shirt to make a tourniquet.

The assassin waved him away. "No. I don't want to live with a mangled body. Look at me."

The man was in great pain and bleeding out rapidly.

"Kill me. I can't stand the pain!"

"First, tell me who sent you? I already know who it was, but I want to hear it from you. What does it matter now?"

"Master Lin. Now kill me!"

"How'd he find our location?"

"Satellites. He told us satellite images tracked you here."

"How'd he get satellite images?"

"He knows people," the man gasped. "He controls people. He can get anything he wants."

"Are there more of you coming?"

He moaned in pain and said softly, "I don't know." After a moment, he bellowed, "You can't win! He's too smart, too rich, and they say he never sleeps. He's a demon. Even if you survive today, you're as good as dead." He groaned again. "Now kill me. Please, kill me. I told you everything I know."

Titus slowly drew his Glock and looked into the man's eyes. They desperately pleaded for him to fire. There was no way to save the man with wounds like that, and he was clearly in agony. Titus reluctantly aimed and fired a single shot between the man's eyes. The pitiful figure slumped to the ground from his sitting position.

Titus knelt down on one knee, listening carefully for other assailants. He didn't hear anything to concern him. Looking at the corpse, he crossed himself.

"Titus, do you need help?" Ying asked over the com.

Titus took a deep breath before saying, "No. I'm good. I think we got all of them."

"May I come down?"

"Yeah. Meet me at the cabin. I'll grab their weapons and frisk the bodies. I'll be there shortly. Make sure everyone is all right."

CHAPTER 30

Exhausted, Titus entered the cabin and tossed the confiscated weapons and ammo on the table. He was disappointed, but not surprised, that the assassins carried nothing of interest.

Winnie ran up and nudged his leg, wanting attention.

Titus reached down to pet her head. "Hey, Girl. Did you keep everyone safe?"

She barked excitedly.

Titus gazed around the room, seeing only Charles. "Good to see you, Buddy. Where are the others?"

"Upstairs looking after Frederick. I just came down for pain medication for him."

"Is he badly hurt?"

"No. It's just a superficial arm wound, but it definitely scared the hell out of him, and I'm sure it hurts like hell. Isabella and Ying are up there, tending to him."

Before Titus could reach the stairs and check on Frederick, Isabella came to the railing above and looked down at him.

He waved. It was funny to see her with an MP5 slung over one shoulder. He was surprised to see how upset she looked after they just survived a deadly assault.

"What's wrong?" he asked. "Is Frederick all right?"

She crossed her arms in indignation. "I saw what you did from Frederick's window."

Titus' eyebrows furrowed. "You saw what?"

"Did you really have to shoot that poor man? He was unarmed and badly hurt. He needed help. Aren't we supposed to be the good guys?"

He shook his head in frustration. How could he explain what he had to do to someone as sweet and innocent as Isabella? He hated that she saw what happened.

"Can we discuss this another time? Right now, we really have to get out of here. They know we're here. More will be on their way as soon as these guys don't report back."

She didn't move.

"Believe me, I didn't want to shoot him. Part of me still feels bad about it. He was in tremendous pain and wouldn't have lived another fifteen minutes no matter what. He wouldn't let me stop the bleeding and begged me to end it for him." After a moment, he added with more irritation than intended, "Not to mention that he came here to kill your husband."

"Titus is right," Charles said, looking up at her. "He was more merciful to that man than I would have been."

Isabella took a moment to process what they said, then she sighed and nodded. "OK. I guess I'm still shaken up by all the violence. I didn't mean to imply...."

The front door burst open with a loud crack. A man dressed all in black rushed in and sprayed bullets around the room. Gunfire tore into walls and blew out windows.

Titus dived into Charles and knocked him down. Shots rang out over their heads.

Winne leaped and bit down hard on the man's arm, making him scream in pain. Her jaws tightened savagely.

He whipped his wounded arm around wildly, trying to knock her to the floor. After a few swings, she lost her grip and was flung down. She slid across the floor and scrabbled back to her feet.

The assassin fired several rounds into her. She went down a second time, then got up and moved toward him again.

Still on the floor, Titus drew his Glock from its holster. His internal clock warned him he might not be fast enough before the shooter aimed at him again, and he was right.

The man turned toward Titus and Charles to fire. Shots rang out, but, to Titus' surprise, they came from the top of the steps. Most of them missed, but Isabella managed to hit him twice in the body. He fell, then tried to stand again.

Knowing the assassin wore body armor, Titus put a bullet through his head, and he went down for the last time.

Titus ran to the man to make sure, but he was dead. The bullet hit above one of his eyes and out the back of the head. He glanced at Winnie. She'd been hit multiple times. Blood flowed across the floor from both bodies.

Charles struggled to his feet, but Titus tackled him so hard, he completely knocked the wind out of him. Knowing there could be more coming, Titus cautiously went outside to check. After confirming no more immediate threats, he went back inside the cabin.

Charles leaned against a table, rubbing his shoulder and catching his breath. The room was torn to pieces by automatic gunfire. Isabella, kneeling beside Winnie's body, sobbed softly.

Ying and Frederick came down the stairs, weapons ready. Frederick's injured arm was bandaged, but he carried a Glock in his good hand. Ying still had her rifle.

Charles went to Isabella, putting a hand on her shoulder. "I'm so sorry about Winnie. This is my fault. I left the monitors too soon. I thought there were only four."

Pointing to the floor, Titus said, "He must've come in way behind the rest. It wasn't your fault, Charles. All of us thought it was over."

Isabella patted Charles hand. "It's OK. Frederick and I are lucky you're here to protect us. Things would've been much worse without you."

"Winnie was a hero," Titus stated.

Isabella nodded. "She was a good dog."

Charles looked at Titus. "I'd better get upstairs to watch the monitors."

Titus nodded. As Charles left, he looked at the others. "We need to get the hell out of here as fast as we can. More assassins are sure to come. I have no idea how much time we have."

Isabella looked at Titus with pleading eyes. "Can we bury Winnie and the dead men first? It's the right thing to do. If we can't, I understand."

Titus hesitated, then shrugged. "OK. You go bury Winnie. It might be a good idea to get rid of the bodies, anyway. If someone comes along and sees them, they'll call the police for sure, and we don't need that right now."

Isabella hugged him. "Thank you, Titus. I'm sorry for coming down on you. I never should have doubted your integrity."

Titus nodded, then he looked at the dead assassin and grinned. "That was a good shot. You saved Charles and me."

"I was going to return the gun to you, but now, well, I'd like to hang onto it a little longer."

"Keep it as long as you like. Hurry and go bury Winnie." He turned toward the stairs and called, "Charles, stay on the monitors until I tell you to pack it up. Let me know if you see anything."

"Will do!" he called back down.

"Ying, stay on watch upstairs at the window."

"I'm on it." She flew back up the stairs like a gazelle.

"Frederick, is your arm good enough to help me bury these bodies?"

He nodded. "It has to be."

After they finished with the burials and packing the vehicles, Titus called Seth on a burner phone, to explain what happened. "If Dr. Lin can track our cars by satellite from Tennessee to here, I'm sure we won't be able to leave without being seen."

"Don't worry about it," Seth assured him. "Get out of there and head east. Don't stop until you're in Baltimore. At least now we know how extensive his resources are."

"Baltimore? What's the plan?"

"Once you're in Baltimore, you can park in a large underground parking deck to ditch the cars. You'll lose them there. They won't know if you'll hide out in Baltimore or go north to New York or Philly, west toward St. Louis, or back south to Washington, Richmond, or Atlanta. It's a great hub to lose them."

"OK. I know a couple large malls in Baltimore with underground parking."

"Fabulous. From Baltimore, I want you to come to DC as quickly as possible. Rafael and I can meet you there."

"Where in DC?"

"We'll talk about a specific location once you're on your way back."

"Good plan. How's the lab going?"

"Making progress. It's in the basement of an old research building at the National Institutes of Health. We should be able to put Frederick back to work very soon."

CHAPTER 31

Dr. Lin, smiling politely, sat in a news studio for a live, prime-time interview. The large cable network was well-known for stirring up hysteria about climate change, and he planned to take full advantage of that. Several follow-up interviews with other so-called experts on global warming and climate change would follow on the heels of Dr. Lin's interview to drive home the points the network advocated.

After discussing Dr. Lin's huge successes as a businessman and prior contributions to the war on climate change, the interviewer asked, "Is it true, Dr. Lin that you're considered a leading candidate to head the United Nations?"

The billionaire, smiling warmly, looked upward for a moment as if pondering how to answer such a difficult question. "I really have no idea. As you know, I'm not a politician. I'm just a lucky businessman who's been blessed with unexpected success."

The reporter didn't answer, although the camera focused on her enough to show her disappointment at his answer.

As if in empathetic response to her expression, he continued, "However, I've come to realize that the world is facing very dark times. If someone doesn't address global warming and climate change more seriously, more rigorously, and more effectively, disaster will soon fall upon this planet."

She nodded in sad agreement, then she cleared her voice. "Dr. Lin, you're definitely a leader. Everything you've put your mind to accomplish, you've achieved. You've literally gone from a man of simple means to one of the wealthiest people in the world. Don't you think you could be the right someone to lead the world community against such a difficult, important problem?"

Dr. Lin didn't answer at first. Then, with a voice somewhere between a scholarly professor and an inspired priest, he said, "The Earth is clearly facing imminent disaster. I believe it's my obligation to do all I can. If I'm called upon to be the Secretary-General of the United Nations, I will serve proudly and with great energy to solve this horrific problem."

The interviewer smiled broadly, as if she just achieved the impossible. "I have one last question."

"Go ahead."

"With all that you're doing to help fight global warming, does your Dynasty Global Foundation still find the time and the financial means to send medical supplies to needy countries?" She knew the answer to such an easy question, but she felt it would be a good way to prop up Dr. Lin's image even higher if possible.

He smiled and nodded. "Oh, yes. Our efforts to combat climate change have not hindered us in any way from helping sick children in poor countries. I would never allow that. We have two medical supply ships in operation at all times. One takes supplies to Africa, the other to Central and South America." After a poignant pause, he clasped his hands together and added, "I only wish we had more ships, many more. If elected to head the United Nations, I will see to it that even more medical supplies are delivered to Third-World countries."

"You're truly an amazing person," the commentator remarked with awe in her voice. "Thank you so much for being on our show. I, for one, look forward to seeing you lead the United Nations to even greater achievements. Given your history of incredible accomplishments, I have no doubt you'd take it to another level. Thank you again for your heartwarming, humanitarian efforts."

Dr. Lin smiled and nodded.

The cameras turned off, and the two stood and briefly shook hands.

As he started to walk away, she asked, "Dr. Lin, would you be so gracious as to sit with me a little longer to discuss what the rest of us can do to fight global warming? I'd love to hear any suggestions." She knew her interview had greatly enhanced his image, and she wanted to spend more time with him. Such a wealthy, powerful man might provide many opportunities for her somewhere along the line.

To her surprise, he replied blandly, "I do not have time," and left with a bodyguard on either side.

When Dr. Lin and his entourage left the building, a howling rainstorm greeted them. One guard opened a large, black umbrella and held it over his head to keep him dry from the raging weather. As they escorted him swiftly to the curb, a stretch limo arrived to take him to his next interview.

Back in Washington, DC, Rafael and Titus met late into the night at his condo. Over pizza and beer, they studied several photos of Dr. Lin's underground facility and other information Charles provided.

The facility was, indeed, isolated, and it appeared to be very well-guarded. A fifteen-foot electronic fence surrounded the complex, and unmanned electric gate, then a manned gate with armed guards just before entering a tunnel that led underground. Patrols of armed guards watched the grounds constantly. There was little to no traffic in the surrounding area, except for employee vehicles and trucks going in and out.

"Breaking in there won't be a picnic," Rafael said bluntly, "if we can do it at all."

Titus nodded.

"What about those trucks?" Rafael swallowed a bite of pizza. "Maybe those can be a way in."

Titus nodded. "You might be onto something. There's always a turnover of laboratory equipment and chemicals. Then there are standard maintenance supplies that any facility needs."

Rafael scratched his head. "Most of the traffic arrives and leaves during the day. I'm not sure it would be very useful."

"You said 'most.' Is there any regular nighttime traffic at all?"

"A couple delivery trucks arrive one or two nights a week."

Titus took a swig from his beer. "Are you sure?"

Rafael glanced over the photos that were taken in the past two weeks. "I can't be sure, but it seems like it."

"I might catch a ride on one of those trucks. Even with my experience, a direct break-in would be extremely difficult given their level of security. I'd rather be invited in at night when there's only a skeleton staff."

Rafael nodded. "How do you suggest we go about hitching a ride with one of those trucks?"

Titus pondered the question for a few minutes, then grinned. "I'm not sure exactly, but I have an idea. We'll need an attractive female to have any hope of my plan succeeding."

Rafael smiled. "A pretty woman is usually the most-reliable distraction if that's what you're thinking."

"Of course it is."

"Do you have anyone in mind?"

Titus shifted his weight uneasily. "I hate putting her in harm's way again, but I think Ying would be perfect for this."

Rafael considered the idea. "I'd hate to use a nonprofessional for such dangerous work."

"If you've been around her long, or saw her during the attack at the cabin, you'd know that the word 'nonprofessional' doesn't apply. She might be a civilian, but she's tough, smart, and well-trained."

"And pretty."

After discussing the idea in more detail, they agreed on the basic plan. It was late in the evening, but Rafael called Ying and Charles. He wanted both of them to agree to the idea given the potential danger.

After speaking with them, he told Titus, "OK. I laid out the plan for them, and she's in. Charles said Ying live for this kind of thing. He couldn't hold her back even if he wanted to, and he'll help."

CHAPTER 32

Eight days later, a chemical delivery truck driver was fifteen miles away from his destination when he saw a white SUV smashed into a tree on the side of the road. The accident didn't look very severe, but he noticed an Asian woman leaning next to the SUV pressing a bloody rag to her forehead. He couldn't see her face, but what he saw of her tight jeans, long black hair, and tight T-shirt put a smile on his face.

He didn't normally stop for accidents, but it was in the middle of nowhere, and the injured woman seemed quite attractive. Maybe it would be OK just this once.

He pulled over past the SUV, got out, and walked slowly toward her. "Are you all right, Ma'am? How badly are you hurt?"

Before she answered or even lowered the bloody rag from his face, three men with black nylons over their faces stepped from the SUV. All of them aimed weapons at the driver.

"Hands up," one said in a strong Hispanic accent.

The stunned driver was instantly terrified. "Oh, shit," he mumbled. How stupid was he for stopping? Shaking his head, he raised his hands.

"Drop the keys to the truck on the ground, *Amigo.*"

He did.

One of the men took the keys and started the truck, while another pulled a hood over the driver's face. "You're coming with us. Don't struggle, and you won't get hurt."

"What? Why are you taking me? I have nothing of value. Take my wallet."

They pushed him into the SUV without responding.

Once the man was inside, one of the abductors asked, "What's your name?"

"Don. Donald Moss."

"Listen up, Don. We don't want to hurt you. We just need information, and we need to borrow your truck for a few hours. That's all. If you cooperate, we'll let you go unharmed, understand?"

He nodded.

"If you don't cooperate, we'll have to kill you. Do you understand?"

He nodded again.

"What was that, Don?"

"I understand. Just don't hurt me. I have a wife and four kids."

"Then do what you're told, and you'll be together with them later tonight. You'll have an exciting story to tell."

"OK, OK."

They drove off and went to an even more-isolated location off the main road. Charles and Rafael got out to work on modifications to the hijacked truck. The main thing they did was replace the original driver's seat with a hollowed-out bench strong enough for the driver to sit on and big enough inside for Titus to squeeze into.

Titus and Ying stayed with the hooded driver to extract information. Titus pressed the barrel of a pistol against the man's forehead and said, "We need to know the exact procedure you follow when you get to the research facility you're going to."

"What procedure? I just go there, and they let me in."

He grabbed the man's ear and twisted. "Don't lie to me. We already know a lot about the security there. We'll know if you're lying, but we need details."

"OK! Let me go!"

Titus didn't move. "To increase your motivation, you need to understand that your life depends on us getting in and out of that facility without a hitch. Do you understand?"

The man nodded.

"The woman you stopped for will stay with you. If the rest of us don't come back in the next two hours, she'll kill you. Believe me. She will."

"Without hesitation," Ying said with soft malice into his other ear. "Then I'll dump your body where no one can find it and be long gone. Those are my orders."

He started shaking. "OK, OK. I get it. How do I know you'll let me go?"

Titus released the man's ear. "You haven't seen our faces, because we plan to release you if you cooperate. If we planned to kill you, we wouldn't care. That's as much proof we can give."

"Yes. I haven't seen any of your faces, I promise. Not even the woman."

"Good. Listen closely. We intend to break into the lab you were headed to, get what we want, and leave without being detected. It's a simple heist. That's all. We don't plan to hurt anyone. Our success means you live. We get caught, and you die. It's pretty simple. Do you understand?"

"Yes, but that place is very well-guarded. You might not get in even with my help. How can I be responsible for that?"

"You bring up a good point, Don, but sometimes, life isn't fair. Our success means you live. If we're not back in the specified time, you die. Give us every edge you can think of, OK?"

"Yes."

"So how does it go down when you get there? What sort of security do they have? How many guards? Where are they located? What are the exact procedures of your delivery? How can we put suspicious guards at ease when they don't see you and don't recognize us? You need to help us make sure this works in every way if you want to see your family again."

Now fully motivated, Don explained the procedure in great detail. He even added a few useful suggestions. Rafael came over to listen once he finished with the truck alterations.

Afterward, Titus gathered the team together to review the plan. When all was ready, he squeezed into the hidden compartment of the truck. Rafael, sitting behind the wheel, drove toward the factory.

Ying watched them go. Feeling like it was his best chance, the captive struggled against his restraints and managed to get to his feet. Ying knocked him to the ground, and he shrieked in terror and pain.

Ying, grabbing his collar, held a knife against his groin. "Try to escape again, and I'll cut off your balls! Do you understand?"

"OK, OK! I won't try to escape." He almost added, *I think you're a psycho bitch* but thought better of it. "Just don't hurt me, Lady. I'll cooperate. I want to see my wife and three kids again."

"I thought you had four?"

"Yeah, yeah. My four kids."

Rafael drove exactly at the speed limit, dressed as a blue-collar laborer, and his features were so well disguised his own mother wouldn't have known him. Titus felt a bit claustrophobic under the seat, but at least it had adequate ventilation and room.

"You were pretty brutal to that trucker," Rafael commented, hoping small talk would soothe his nerves. "I would've shit my pants if I were that guy."

"That's because you're only an FBI Deputy Director in your day job. If you were a trucker or a real FBI agent, you would've handled it just fine."

Rafael shook his head. "You know, since we aren't on FBI time, I want to say that you're a real ass, you know?"

Titus smiled. He never felt closer to his boss. "Yeah, I know, but to be honest, my bark is worse than my bite. I hated scaring that guy, but if I didn't make him sweat, we'd have a good chance of being dead soon."

"Yeah, I know. You did good. I even wondered for a moment just how serious you were."

"You need to get into the field more often, Rafael. You're getting soft."

Rafael smiled and shook his head. "You're enjoying this off-the-books time together, aren't you? Sometimes, I wonder why the hell I put up with you."

Titus laughed to himself. "I'm no psychiatrist, but my guess is that you have self-destructive tendencies."

Rafael laughed out loud. "Yeah. That must be it."

When the gates were finally in sight, Rafael rapped on the seat. "We're only a few minutes out. Be totally quiet now."

The truck stopped at a closed electronic gate. A camera took a picture of Rafael, as he entered the code the trucker gave them. He held his breath when nothing happened, but then the gate slowly swung open.

He drove slowly into the compound. Fifty yards farther in, he stopped at a second gate. Along the road, he saw guard dogs and small teams of guards on patrol. Titus had been right. This place was locked down tight. It would take a Delta or SEAL team to get in any other way.

Parking beside a guard house, they waited. Eventually, an army guard came out to check on him. Another guard watched from the guardhouse window.

The guard tapped on the driver's side window. When Rafael lowered it, the guard asked, "Who the hell are you?"

"Supply delivery," Rafael replied in a heavy Spanish accent.

"Supply delivery?"

"Yes, Sir. Lab supplies from Dynasty Chemicals Warehouse. I was told the delivery is expected."

The man studied him and the truck. "I haven't seen you here before. Isn't this Don's truck? Where is he?"

"Sick with the flu. Are you Williams or Campbell?"

"Williams. Do I know you?"

"No, but Don said to ask Williams how his baby daughter, Lilly, was doing. He said she was sick last week."

Williams relaxed and smiled. "You tell Don she's doin' just fine. Hasn't had a fever in two days."

"Will do."

"Give me the keys to the back. Wait here until I check the cargo."

Rafael nodded and handed him the keys. Williams went to the rear of the truck, unlocked the door, and pointed a flashlight inside. He saw the usual assortment of supplies Don brought. Going to the front of the truck, he momentarily flashed his light in the front cab, too.

Rafael held his breath until the light went out.

"OK. What'd you say your name was?"

"I didn't. It's Diego Lopez."

"Let me see your ID."

Rafael handed him the phony license Charles prepared.

Williams wrote the name on his clipboard before returning the license. "OK, Diego. You can go on through. As soon as you unload the supplies, you need to leave. I'll be expecting you."

Rafael nodded and turned the key. The engine grumbled without starting, so he tried again. It almost started that time, then it died.

"Damn," he said.

"What's the problem?" Williams asked. "Want me to look under the hood?"

All Rafael wanted was to get moving and avoid letting the man study his disguise for too long. He tried a third time, and the engine turned over, making him sigh softly in relief. "No, I'm good. Just getting used to Don's truck. Thanks."

He drove away as quickly as he could without making it look like he was in a hurry. As expected, the two-lane road quickly reached the entrance of an underground tunnel. He drove inside and went down to a large loading dock on his right.

Rafael looked around. There were no other trucks, and only one dock worker was waiting. He was relieved. If they came in during the day, it would've been much busier. He didn't look for cameras but knew they were there. He also knew Charles would have taken care of them.

As he left the truck, he didn't close the driver's door, so Titus could slip out easily at the right moment. He went to the rear of the truck and threw open the door, then he turned and looked at the dock worker, who sat on some crates, watching.

"Hey, Buddy, mind helping me over here?"

The rotund man stood slowly and walked closer, yawning as if ready to take a nap. "Who are you? Where's Don?"

"I'm Diego. Don's sick. Can you give me a hand unloading this stuff? Don said unloading is your job, not mine."

The man nodded grudgingly.

"I'll help if you want."

The man nodded, but he smiled. "I'd appreciate it."

"No problem. What's your name?"

"Kevin."

"Well, Kevin, I didn't plan to make this run, but I need to get home soon. My old lady said she'd take care of me tonight if she's still awake. You know what I mean?"

Kevin wiped his sleeve across his nose and smiled.

"She rewards me real good when I work overtime."

"I wish my wife was that nice. I practically have to beg her to get anything these days. Before we had kids, she was a wildcat."

Rafael laughed.

After a few minutes of work, Rafael jumped into the truck and took out a six-pack of Budweiser hiding behind a box of sodium bicarbonate. Holding it up to show Kevin, he asked, "You want a beer?"

Kevin smiled and looked around to see if anyone was watching. "Sure." Then he remembered the cameras and climbed into the truck. "We'll have to drink those in here. There are cameras watching the unloading. I don't want to lose my job."

"I understand." Rafael handed him a Bud after he found a place to sit, then Rafael jumped back out. "You can stay in there and hand me stuff while you enjoy the beer. I'll carry them to the dock, and you can organize them later. Have as many beers as you want."

"Thanks, Bro. I appreciate it." The worker handed Rafael several boxes, then he sat down to start drinking.

After the first haul, Rafael saw no one else and walked to the front of the truck, where he knocked lightly three times before walking to the rear again and continue unloading.

Titus cautiously slipped out of his hiding place. When he scanned the area, he saw nothing concerning. Tossing a large backpack over his shoulder, he darted for the dock.

Rafael kept a lookout, as Titus smoothly and quietly hopped onto the dock and into the facility.

Just as Titus disappeared from sight, a guard came around the corner. Rafael's heart jumped, wondering if the man saw Titus. He walked in the same direction Titus went.

Immediately, Rafael dropped a box of test tubes. It struck the floor with a loud crash, and the guard turned suspiciously toward him.

Titus heard it, too, and pressed himself between some boxes. He was thankful to Rafael for warning him. He hadn't seen the security man coming from behind.

The security man walked toward the truck. "What's going on? Everything all right?'

Rafael looked frustrated, standing over the broken glass. "Just some broken test tubes."

Titus quickly moved deeper into the facility when he had the chance.

The guard placed his hand on the butt of his gun and stared at Rafael. "Who are you? Where's Kevin? Isn't this Don's truck?"

Before Rafael could answer, Kevin peeked out the back of the truck. "It's OK, Tony. He's filling in on deliveries tonight. Don's out sick."

"Are you sure about that?"

The last thing Kevin wanted was for the guard to get close enough for him to see or smell the beer. "Yeah, he's good. His name's Diego. I've seen him before. He's even helping me unload. That's more than Don ever did."

The guard nodded but stood his ground.

Rafael's heart beat faster, but he still looked calm. He desperately wanted the guard to move on. Trying a little reverse psychology, he asked, "Hey, Tony, you mind helping me and Kevin clean up this mess?"

The security man sneered. "I don't think so, Diego. Nice try. You have your work, and I have mine." He took another look around the dock area. "Sure you're all right, Kevin?"

"Except for that mess, I'm good."

The guard nodded and headed off.

"Sure you don't want to help us clean up?" Rafael called.

The guard didn't answer.

Rafael glanced around. Titus was nowhere in sight.

CHAPTER 33

Titus moved stealthily deeper into the facility, not knowing what to expect and carrying only his Glock to keep his hands free. He'd never be able to shoot his way out in an all-out fight.

Although it was dark, there was enough night lighting to find his way. He wore a black nylon mask and was dressed completely in black. Overhead cameras were everywhere, but Charles hacked into their security feeds and put the cameras in a benign-looking loop. He prayed that wouldn't be noticed until he was in and out.

The building was larger than expected. It was gigantic. The facility seemed organized into two general areas—one for manufacturing and the other for research. He heard dogs barking from a distant research area and went the other way, hoping to find a stockpile of Wake Formula. He peered into several rooms that looked like offices. Eventually he found an area labeled, *Refrigerated Sample Facility.*

Titus slowly opened the door, cased the area, and quietly entered. The large room was very cold, but there were no signs of stored Wake Formula.

What he saw, though, was amazing. The huge room held frozen, unprocessed cattle brains. He had no idea how many were in the pile, but there were over 300 large boxes. Looking up, he sat a large, stainless-steel chute coming down. That was how they brought the cow brains into the facility once they were removed in the slaughterhouse directly overhead. He envisioned an assembly line where the brains were processed.

The system impressed him. Since some of the components of the Wake Formula had to be extracted from brain tissue, Titus hoped he was getting close to the processing and storage area.

Hearing a noise from the other side of the room, he ducked behind some cover. A security guard walked in and scanned the room. Relaxed, he was apparently just making his rounds. The man shivered, and quickly left the freezing room.

When the way was clear, Titus left the room to continue his search. Figuring he was at the wrong end of the manufacturing area, he walked to the side where the guard just left. Along the way, he saw several working areas where he assumed the brains were processed.

At the far room, he found a room labeled *Pharmaceutical Storage—Authorized Personnel Only.* When he tried the door, it was locked.

Titus was examining the lock to figure out how to bypass the electronic-swiping mechanism when he heard movement behind him.

"Don't move."

Titus froze, angry at himself for being caught so easily.

"Slowly put your hands on the wall in front of you."

Titus did.

"Stay real still." The guard came closer and removed Titus' gun from its holster, then he patted down Titus for more weapons.

Two mistakes went through Titus' mind. First, he hadn't called for backup before coming close. Second, he should've made his prisoner off balance by making him lean forward and spread his legs wider.

The guard continued frisking him. Titus moved so fast, the man never knew what hit him. Titus kicked backward and hard against the man's shin, then he pivoted, as the guard, moaning in pain, reached for his leg. The kick tore through his pants and left a bleeding gash on his leg.

Titus struck the man hard on the side of the head, and he fell unconscious. It was over in two seconds. Titus took the man's weapon, then he stopped to listen. He heard nothing.

The man made a few grunting noises but otherwise didn't move.

Titus knelt and examined him. He found the man's wallet and keys but nothing of interest. He snatched the guard's magnetic badge from his motionless body, muttering, "How convenient," before swiping the badge through the door lock.

The door opened.

Titus dragged the man into the room and took duct tape and plastic ligatures from his backpack. He secured the guard's hands behind his back with plastic ligatures and wrapped them further with duct tape before wrapping the man's legs together and added tape over his mouth while leaving his nose open to breathe.

As he worked, he grinned and thought, *Never leave home without duct tape.*

Once the man was fully secured, Titus searched the room. It was cold, but it wasn't as freezing as the other room. He quickly realized the room housed nothing but Wake Formula. Smiling, he carefully filled his backpack with as much medication as he could. From what Dr. Burrus said, he had exactly what they needed.

After securing the medication, Titus slipped from the room and retraced his steps. Suddenly, he stopped to consider the situation. He had limited time before the guard would be missed, but there was the chance he could secure vital information about the facility. In particular, he wanted to check the research section.

It was a huge gamble, but he took a deep breath and cautiously moved from the manufacturing area toward the research section, hoping and praying he wasn't making a mistake. When he arrived, he saw state-of-the-art centrifuges, distillation equipment, scintillation counters, glass beakers, and all manner of lab equipment, some of which he didn't recognize. There was also an area where he heard barking from caged lab animals.

He detected a faint voice in the distance and quickly ducked down. Staying very still, he listened and heard two distant voices coming from one of the research labs ahead and on the right. Titus, considering his options, decided to move closer.

Being overly cautious after his last blunder, he carefully went forward while staying out of sight.

As he turned a corner, he saw a man in a white lab coat working at a computer, while a guard stood beside him. They were discussing the Dallas Cowboys.

Titus listened carefully, peeking out when he could. The man in the white coat entered data into a computer while they chatted. Titus was excited to see one of Dr. Lin's research computers open and running. It might contain valuable information if he could gain access. The guard was a problem. Titus had to move fast if he wanted to reach the computer before the scientist turned it off.

As he considered ways to subdue both men, the guard said, "I have to get back to my rounds. Catch you later, Doc."

He sighed inwardly. Once the guard was gone, Titus crept up silently on the clueless scientist, carefully listening for the guard or anyone else nearby. He heard nothing.

Once Titus was in an optimal position, he struck the back of the scientist's head. The man fell against his work station. Titus caught him and helped him slump noiselessly to the floor.

The man was unconscious. "Sorry about that," he muttered, securing the man with plastic ligatures and layers of duct tape like the guard. He stashed the body out of sight.

At the work station, he found the computer up and running. Taking out a thumb drive, he slid it into the side of the computer and scrolled through as many documents as he could, copying anything that looked remotely interesting.

In addition to research information, he found many medical records. One in particular caught his eye, a medical report on one of his missing congressmen.

Jackpot, he thought.

He didn't have time to read it but copied that and other documents as long as he dared, then he withdrew the drive and texted Rafael to come get him.

Titus carefully returned to the dock. He saw another guard along the way, but the man didn't pose a problem. The dock worker was napping on a crate when Titus got there. Rafael and his truck were gone. Titus found a secluded spot to wait.

Every minute that passed felt like forever. It was only a matter of time before the fallen guard or scientist was found, and then he would be in big trouble.

The dock worker woke when Rafael's truck returned to the loading dock ten minutes later.

"Hey, what's up?" the man asked. "Why are you back?"

"I lost my cell phone. It must've fallen out of my pocket. Have you seen it?"

"No, I ain't seen no cell phone. Are you sure you lost it here?"

Rafael got out and looked around anxiously. "Not really, but I have to look." He wanted the man to move farther from the truck, so he added, "Would you mind checking by those boxes? I'll look over here."

As the man went to look, Titus slipped back into the truck and crawled under the front seat. A moment later, Rafael pulled his cell from his pocket and held it up.

"Found it," he called. "Thanks for your help, Kevin."

"No problem. Tell Don I hope he feels better soon."

"Will do."

Kevin climbed back onto a crate and lay down out of sight of the cameras.

Rafael slowly drove from the compound.

"What took so long?" Titus whispered.

"The guards almost didn't let me back in. It got a bit hairy for a minute."

Ten minutes after they left the compound, alarms went off in the secret research laboratory.

CHAPTER 34

Two days later, Dr. Lin and his Supreme Council sat in the throne room for an emergency meeting. Tension filled the room. After the traditional, formal opening, Dr. Lin began, "As you may have heard, the Wake laboratory was broken into two days ago. We must discuss this matter thoroughly. General Chen, I generously gave you two days to investigate. What is your report? Have the intruders been apprehended?"

"No, Master. Our security cameras were incapacitated during the intrusion, and the only security guard who saw the intruder was subdued. The intruder's face was covered in nylon, so he wasn't able to give a description."

Dr. Lin's eyes narrowed. "The monitors were incapacitated? What does that mean, exactly, and why was the backup system not activated?"

"We believe our system was hacked from a sophisticated outside source that fed false images to our security personnel. It made it seem as if nothing was wrong. No one monitoring the area noticed a problem until after a bound guard was found. One of our scientists was also subdued and bound."

"How did the intruders enter undetected? What did they do during this break in other than make a mockery of our security?"

General Chen coughed to clear his throat. "I believe the intruder, or intruders, came in on one of the night-delivery trucks."

"How was that possible? We have electronic and manned security measures in place for anyone coming and going from the research and production facility."

"The guards suspected nothing. We now know that one of our regular night delivery drivers was abducted and his truck stolen. Records show that it made a scheduled delivery at the time of the intrusion. The delivery truck was expected, so there was little suspicion."

"Did the intruders have our security code for the electric gate?"

"Yes. The driver was forced to give it to them."

"Was anything in the laboratory destroyed?"

"No, Master Lin."

"Was Wake Formula taken?"

"Yes, Great Master, a great deal, I'm afraid."

The normally calm billionaire slammed his hands on the arms of his majestic chair and stood. "This is outrageous! General Chen, how is this possible? Except for my family's safety, your primary responsibility is to protect the Wake Laboratory."

"I have no excuse, Great Master. I thought the facility was secure."

"Do we know who the intruders were?"

"No. Not really."

Dr. Lin remained standing. "Not really. What does that even mean?"

"No one specific. From our interrogation of the truck driver, we know at least three people were involved. Their faces were covered, but he knew there were at least two males and one who sounded like an Asian female."

"Go on."

"Apparently, the female staged an accident to get the trucker to stop. She had a bloody rag held against her face. Two men came out of her SUV and ambushed the man. They took him prisoner at gunpoint until after their raid on the facility. They let him go, and he reported everything as quickly as he could."

Dr. Lin, sitting down, anxiously tapped the fingers of one hand on his thigh, listening.

"The guard at the security house said the driver of the truck was Hispanic. We have tapes to confirm it. He didn't see anyone else, and he claims he searched the truck. Our investigation later discovered that the front seat was modified to be able to hide someone inside. The driver unloaded the supplies and then left. He never went inside the laboratory, although he returned a second time, saying he lost his cell phone at the loading dock. We believe he dropped off an accomplice and then came back to retrieve him."

"Have you run facial recognition on the truck driver's face?"

"Of course. We have adequate pictures, but no match was found. Our experts believe he may have used a sophisticated disguise to alter his features."

"Could the Asian woman be one of ours?"

"That is highly unlikely. Your staff is very loyal to you, and all female employees have been accounted for by our internal surveillance cameras at the time of the trucker's abduction and laboratory break-in."

"Who are they, then?"

"We don't know, Master Lin."

Dr. Lin closed his eyes to calm himself. He prided himself on his demeanor and had already shown more emotion that he wished. Feeling slightly calmer, he said, "Clearly, they have resources. Perhaps it was a team from the FBI, CIA, or some other agency from abroad."

General Chen scratched his head. "I don't believe it was a government agency, Dr. Lin. If they were, they would have moved fully against us by now."

"Then perhaps it's one of our clients. I believe it came from someone in the Society of Wake. Many have become very wealthy with my help and have the resources to do such a thing."

The general nodded. "That's a more likely possibility. Some of our clients are current or former FBI, CIA, and even military officers who have intelligence capability and access to Black Ops personnel."

Dr. Lin nodded solemnly. "Perhaps one of them wants to destroy me and take over the business. Perhaps they want to steal the drug, so they don't' have to pay me, or perhaps they were cut off from the formula and are desperate enough to send a cover team to steal it. Check into all those possibilities."

General Chen nodded. "Yes, Master."

"What will you do about security at our research and manufacturing facility?"

"I'm personally reviewing every procedure and security measure so such a thing can never happen again. The patrol guards who worked there during the intrusion and those on the monitors will be fired or otherwise removed."

Lian Lee, the Head of Strategic Planning, stood. "Excuse me, Master Lin. I believe we're under a full assault by a powerful organization, not just one client. First, Dr. Burrus shows up alive out of nowhere. Now there is a theft of the Wake Formula out from under our noses. They must be connected. We must make an all-out effort to take control of the United Nations very soon, before anyone can stop us."

Dr. Lin motioned for him to sit down again. "I agree. We must consider all possibilities. What specifically do you have in mind?"

"Every media outlet under our control must run story after story about the severe and immediate dangers of climate change. Social media must scream for something to be done quickly. More data must be given to the media from activists and helpful scientists. Any scientists who question our assertions must be publicly humiliated and labeled as traitors to humanity."

Dr. Lin nodded. "I agree. How can we use our political connections more effectively?"

"We will insist that every politician in the Society of Wake suggest or even publicly demand your leadership at the United Nations to prevent imminent global disaster. Celebrities and other people of influence will be asked to help as well. As you know, they need little prompting, as they love publicity. Wake Formula will be withheld from anyone in the Society who refuses or even hesitates to cooperate with us."

"Your wisdom shows itself clearly once again, Lee."

Lee bowed. "Thank you, Master Lin."

"Gentlemen," Dr. Lin said, "our enemies believe they have severely wounded us. However, they have only motivated us to move up our timetable. Soon, a shift of power will take place that will culminate with our seizing total global authority. Nations will not know what transpired until too late. They will either join our world community or be crushed by it."

Heads nodded around the room.

Dr. Lin looked severely at the general. He showed weakness in his frustration earlier, and it was time to demonstrate his strength. "What has happened is unacceptable, and failure in the Society of Wake cannot be tolerated, General Chen. What has been done?"

The general, anticipating such a reaction, was prepared. "I knew you would want me to take immediate, decisive action, Master Lin." He turned to nod at a guard.

The guard brought him a large bag.

Dr. Lin's brows furrowed. "What is this?"

The general, reaching into the bag, pulled out a severed head. "The truck driver who told the intruders the code to the gate." He placed it at Dr. Lin's feet.

Dr. Lin nodded in approval.

He pulled out more heads one-by-one and placed them on the floor in front of Dr. Lin. "Here are the heads of the guard at the gate who let the intruders in, the guard who was observing the monitors, and the lazy dock worker who allowed the break-in. They weren't just terminated. They were terminated permanently."

Dr. Lin, staring at the heads on the floor, motioned the general back to his seat. Taking a deep breath, he said, "I see only one thing missing."

"What is that, Master Lin?"

He signaled Fa Shen to stand behind the general.

General Chen stared at Dr. Lin and understood. Dr. Lin and Fa Shen were the only men in the world who frightened him. A small trickle of sweat ran down his forehead. He dug deep within himself to find the courage to ask, "Do you require my head as well, Master?"

Dr. Lin let the question linger for a few seconds, then he said, "No, General Chen. You have been my trusted helper for many years."

The general nodded his appreciation.

"However, I require a piece of you for your failings. There must be accountability. Hold out your hand."

The general hesitated, then held out his hand.

Shen grabbed the hand tightly and took out a long, sharp, razor-thin knife.

Before the guard could strike, General Chen said, "My loyalty to you has never faded, and I regret my failing, Great One. May I have the honor of demonstrating my dedication to you?"

Dr. Lin stared at him sternly. "If your loyalty was in question, your head would already be on the floor, General." He considered the request, and his anger began to fade. "But you are a loyal member of my most-trusted inner circle—and my friend." His gaze went to Shen. "Give him the knife."

Shen slowly obeyed, but he remained close enough to intervene if the general tried to use the knife on anyone but himself.

"What do you require of me, Master Lin?"

"I suddenly feel merciful. I no longer require a hand, just a single finger to remind you of your failings."

General Chen was greatly relieved. "Thank you, Great Master."

He placed his hand on the arm of his chair and without hesitation, sliced off the little finger of his left hand.

No one else in the room dared move.

The general, picking up the severed finger, placed it beside the heads on the floor. As he sat down, blood ran onto the chair arm. Some trickled onto his fine robe, but he sat without expression.

Dr. Lin nodded in satisfaction.

No one moved or spoke.

"Get the general a dressing," Dr. Lin told a guard. He looked at General Chen. "Wrap your wound, and let us continue our meeting."

CHAPTER 35

As President Shane O'Malley heard Dr. Lin's demands from his chief of staff, he became increasingly irate. "Did he actually say he would withhold my medication if I don't go along with his crazy plans?"

"He did, Sir," Samuel Conners replied. "He insisted that you publicly and privately push for more spending on global warming, climate change, or whatever else they're calling it this week. He didn't send me back with any more medication, as you hoped. You'll run out in a week or so if you use it at your usual rate."

The president stood and paced. Conners didn't move, knowing it was a bad sign.

The president clenched his fists. "Who the hell does he think he is? Does he really think he can blackmail the President of the United States?"

"I believe he does, Sir. He seemed utterly calm and confident, like a man holding all the cards. What can you do, Sir? You have very little leverage. You can't force him to sell you the medication. If you have him investigated for blackmail, he could exposé your secret use of the drug. Your political enemies would have a field day."

"What sort of field day? It's not illegal. Hell, very few people even know about it. What would be the big deal?"

Conners thought a moment. "I wish it were that simple, Sir, but they'll tell the public you're a cheater. They'll say you can't be trusted. They'll ask what other secrets you're hiding. There may be no way to recover from the accusations your political enemies will surely make, and this time, it won't be fake news, Sir."

The President stopped and eyed him at the insinuation. "Are you implying I've broken the law?"

Conners sat straighter in her chair. He was in dangerous territory. The drug had always been source of contention between them. "No, Sir, of course not."

The President nodded.

"But if you claim you've done nothing wrong, they'll ask why you hid your use of the drug all this time. They'll ask why you didn't share the drug with other Americans. Your legacy could be tarnished forever, and your family could become quite embarrassed by the whole affair. Your wife still doesn't know you use it, correct?"

The President's shoulders slumped. With a sigh, he nodded.

"I'm afraid he's got you by the short hairs, Mr. President. He's warning you to cooperate with his agenda or else."

The President shook his head at the mess he was in. After a moment, he said, "I feel pretty stupid right now, Conners. I never used drugs, not even smoked pot. Here I am, messed up in what feels like a drug deal gone bad."

"I didn't mean to make you feel stupid, Mr. President. I'm just saying we can predict what will happen if your use of a performance-enhancing drug is exposed to the public. He hasn't threatened to expose you yet, but he could. For now, he seems content to just cut off your supply if you don't cooperate with him. Hopefully, that's all he intends."

The President sat down and rubbed his forehead. "To tell the truth, Conners, that damn drug has been an amazing help to me. I hate to think about dealing with everything I have to do without it."

"I understand."

"When Dr. Lin approached me to use his Wake Formula several years ago, I was a rising star in my state. It sounded like a good idea to help get things done faster, like powerful vitamins. I actually had no idea it would work so well. I sure as hell didn't know it could lead to this mess."

Conners said nothing.

After another few minutes of the President stating the obvious, Conners saw in his eyes that he came to a decision.

President O'Malley took a deep breath. "I won't have anything to do with that tyrant any longer. The President of the United States won't be held hostage to him or his damn drug. I'm done."

Conners didn't speak.

"One of the things I told the American people when I ran for this office was that I would do reasonable and prudent things to protect the environment, but I wouldn't be part of the huge waste, fraud, and political corruption that was so often associated with so-called climate change initiatives." He shook his head. "No. I won't do it just to feather my own bed."

"Yes, Sir."

"I'll have to do the job and go to sleep every night like every other President before me." A sly grin crossed his face. "At least, I *think* every other President before me. Some have been amazingly energetic."

Conners laughed. "Yes, Sir. I'm relieved to hear it, Mr. President. To be honest, I never liked your using a performance-enhancing drug in the first place. I haven't enjoyed secretly delivering the PED to you." After a moment, he added reassuringly, "Even though this isn't an illegal drug—not yet, anyway."

The President sat back in his chair. "I don't blame you. I'm sorry I put you in such a position."

"Thank you, Mr. President. I appreciate that, and I wouldn't have done it for anyone else. I believe in you, Sir."

"I'm not sure I deserve your loyalty, but thank you."

"I have to tell you, Dr. Lin gives me the creeps. I sense something truly evil about him. His outrage over global warming is only to attract attention to himself for political purposes. I don't believe he's a climate-change fanatic for a moment. He's too smart. He's in it just for himself."

"He certainly won't be the first, but I have to give him credit. At least in his case, he's more subtle about it than most. Instead of making money off the liberal climate-change agenda, he at least gives generously to the cause. How smart is that?"

"He already has all the money he needs, Sir. He's after power. I can smell it a mile away. The lust for power flows from his pores."

The President nodded. "Of course he does. The same foul odor stinks up the swamp in DC from people like him. Anyway, set up a press conference tomorrow. Dr. Lin will hear my response to his threat loud and clear. My administration will stay the course."

"Do you really want to go public, Sir? The mainstream media will crucify you. Most of them already cast you as some sort of demon. They'll say you're trying to block the good work of a good man. You know how they are."

"I'm sure they'll try. They always do."

Conners didn't answer.

"Someone has to stand up for common sense. We can't afford to continue to waste billions more on meaningless projects that do nothing except circle back to pad the pockets of corrupt politicians. That's the point I'll make to the public. They can decide if they agree or not."

After the successful raid on Dr. Lin's laboratory, there was both a celebration and a lot of work to do. They won a major battle, but the war was far from over. Finding an available research laboratory with the technical accommodations Dr. Burrus needed wasn't easy. With Deputy Director Otero's covert help and connections in Washington, a lab with adequate space and animal facilities was eventually found in the basement of an old, rather isolated building on the National Institute of Health campus. The NIH facility even had room for the Burrus family to live in until the situation was safer.

Ying and Charles supplied the lab with all the equipment and animals Dr. Burrus requested. Charles and Titus set up a state-of-the-art surveillance system around the lab to keep it safe.

The raid on Dr. Lin's lab gave Frederick enough Wake Formula to start research, and he got immediately to work. He enjoyed teaching science at a small liberal arts college, but he was first and foremost a researcher of the highest caliber, and he couldn't help feeling excited about getting back into serious biomedical research. He told Isabella proudly, "I feel like an explorer again without ever leaving my laboratory."

Lab assistants were out of the question, so Isabella worked side-by-side with her husband. The hours were long. It wasn't an ideal situation for either of them, but the important work had to be done fast. Given his science background, Titus provided what help he could. Ying, who wasn't at all scientifically inclined, assisted by babysitting Martin and Condoleeza.

One day, Titus made the mistake of asking Ying, "How's the babysitting going?"

"I don't baby-sit their children," she snarled back. "I'm guarding them. Do you see babysitters carrying around a Sig Sauer P226?"

He laughed. She had a point. Though she never admitted it, he saw how much she enjoyed guarding and babysitting the children.

One morning, soon after the lab was set up, a rotund man in a white lab coat was seen on video cameras snooping around the outside of the old research building.

"Looks like we have a guest," Ying told Dr. Burrus and Isabella.

Dr. Burris watched the man on the monitors. His type looked all too familiar. "I'd better go meet him."

"You're the one Dr. Lin's looking for," Ying reminded him. "Let me see what he wants."

"No. Scientists understand scientists. I'd better do it."

"Then let me," Isabella said before Ying could protest. "I'm also a scientist."

Dr. Burrus smiled but raised one hand to stop the discussion. "He looks innocent enough, but who knows? He might be a bigwig around here. I'll do it. If it's done right, he won't suspect a thing and won't bother us again."

Ying defiantly placed her hands on her hips. "What if he's here to kill you?"

"You can watch over me from the window. Believe me, he looks harmless. I suspect he's just curious."

As Ying protested, Dr. Burrus walked to the door and went straight out to the stranger.

"Hello, there," Dr. Burrus said. "Can I help you?"

The obese man studied him. "Hello. I'm Dr. Sledge from arthritis and rheumatology. You are?"

"Dr. Bill Ray at your service." He shook the man's hand.

Dr. Sledge shoved his hands into his lab coat pockets nervously. "I was just on a morning walk and noticed activity over here. I was surprised. Are you setting up a laboratory in this old building?'

Before Dr. Burrus could reply, Ying marched out with a pistol in the pocket of her coat. She became concerned when the unknown man put his hands in his pockets.

"Dr. Clark, we need you in the lab right away," Ying said.

Dr. Sledge's eyes squinted with uncertainty. "Dr. Clark? I thought you said your name was Dr. Ray."

"Quite so," Dr. Burrus said with a warm smile. "My lab assistant just joined us yesterday and keeps getting my name confused with Dr. Clark's." He leaned over and whispered conspiratorially, "To tell the truth, I'm not sure she'll work out."

Dr. Sledge grinned and nodded, glancing at Ying.

"I'll be there in a minute, Cassidy," Dr. Burrus told Ying. "Remember, I'm Dr. Ray, the good-looking one. Dr. Clark can help you until I return."

Ying realized her blunder but wasn't ready to leave. "Oh, I'm so sorry, Dr. Ray. I'll just wait for you. It's you I need inside."

Dr. Burrus looked at his guest. "Now what were you asking me?"

"I was asking if you're setting up a lab in this building, but it's clear that you are."

"Yes, that's right. Is that a problem?"

Dr. Sledge, looking uncomfortable, rubbed the back of his neck. "Well, actually, it might be. This building hasn't been used in years. I thought it was slated to be torn down. My department was told, unofficially of course, that we would acquire research space in the new building to be put on this site. I've been looking forward to a new research lab, to tell the truth."

Dr. Burrus realized it was just another old-fashioned academic turf war. He patted the man's back reassuringly. "Well, Dr. Sledge, you have nothing to worry about. I'm just a visiting scientist from Germany. I've been given the space only on a temporary basis, since it wasn't in use. I'm sure your long-term plans are still on schedule. I'll probably be out of here in a few months, when my sabbatical is up, and I return to Germany."

Relief showed on Dr. Sledge's face. "Oh, that's good to hear. Do you mind if I come in and take a look around? This building has been locked up tight until now. I'd love to see it out of curiosity. Have you made any progress setting up your temporary lab?"

Ying tensed when Dr. Burrus said, "Yes, it's all set up. You're more than welcome to come in."

"Wonderful."

When Dr. Sledge moved toward the lab, Dr. Burrus raised his hand to make him wait. "Let me see if we have a total body protective suit that will fit you first. What size do you wear?"

"Why would I need a protective laboratory suit?"

"I'm doing viral work in there. The viruses I'm studying are quite lethal in vulnerable people sort of like COVID-19. I think that's why they have me working so far from the rest of the campus and in a building ready to be torn down. We can't be too cautious, you know. What's your size?"

Dr. Sledge froze. "A toxic virus?"

"That's right. It's exciting work. You'll need to shower when you come out, so it might take a little time, but I'm happy to show you everything."

"Well, actually, that's OK. Don't go through all that trouble. I don't have time right now. I have an experiment back at the lab I have to get to." Walking away quickly, he waved. "See you around, Dr. Ray. Good luck with your work."

"Are you sure you don't want to look around the lab?" he called just for fun.

"No, thanks. Got to go."

Ying walked up closer to the professor, then she turned and smiled at him. "Well played, Dr. Burrus."

CHAPTER 36

As soon as the computer files from Dr. Lin's laboratory were thoroughly mined for useful information, a meeting of the entire group took place at Dr. Burrus' kitchen table above the lab. Two bottles of wine stood open on the table, as well as some chips and dip.

"I have to open this meeting of the minds by giving a shout out to all of you for a job well done in obtaining the Wake Formula." Seth raised his wineglass.

The others raised their glasses, too.

"Congratulations."

Everyone drank.

"Titus, your performance went above and beyond by not only obtaining the formula for Frederick's work but by stealing information from their computers, too. "

The others clapped. Titus smiled and nodded.

Seth's gaze went to Frederick. "Have you learned anything clinically useful by going through their research files?"

"The files were very helpful." Frederick smiled. "Interestingly, they've been trying to find a safe antidote to the Wake Formula for over a year. Their previous work will save a lot of time. I won't have to repeat what they already did."

"Did they make any progress?" Rafael asked.

"Not really. However, what's certain from their research is that their Wake Formula clearly has serious withdrawal problems in human subjects as well as research animals."

"What kind of problems?" Titus asked.

"When their clients stopped taking the drug for any reason, they became very tired. If the Wake Formula wasn't restarted in a timely manner, their clients become progressively more lethargic. People who used the Wake Formula for longer periods of time were at greater risk. Once stopped, long-term users often lapsed into comas. Many died. It's also concerning that they had complications just restarting the drug after a long period of abstinence."

Rafael grimaced. "That doesn't sound good."

"What did they do with the ones who died?" Titus asked.

"Good question. You won't like the answer."

Titus waited.

"Apparently they obtain the bodies using one pretext or another and slip them onto a Dynasty Foundation medical supply ship. They take them out to sea and dump them overboard after doing an autopsy for research purposes."

Titus nodded solemnly. "Not a bad way to get rid of evidence."

"Some of their very ill clients were also put on those ships to study them and then dispose of the bodies the same way if they die."

"So they get them out of the country and away from curious eyes and authorities," Seth said.

"That's what it looks like," Frederick replied.

"It's a devious and brilliant plan." Seth paused. "What's your research approach?"

Frederick said, "I've gone in a different direction."

"How's that?" Rafael asked.

"The clinical response to discontinuation of the drug reminds me very much of meth or cocaine withdrawal, only worse. I'm treating the Wake Formula like an addictive drug."

"In other words, you hope to develop a detox protocol," Seth said.

"Exactly. I'm modifying some of the components of the Wake Formula to make its half-life significantly longer for that purpose. As you may know, most medications used for chemical detox are functionally similar to the drug of abuse but have a longer half-life to make the stepping-down process smoother and safer."

"It's like substituting Diazepam or Phenobarbital for Alprazolam or alcohol," Isabella added.

"Do you think you can do it in a reasonable time frame?" Seth asked.

Frederick nodded. "I hope so. I think so."

"I really hope so, too."

Frederick gazed up, thinking. "I'll call the modified formula Wake Formula-LA, for long-acting."

"I'm surprised they haven't tried that already," Titus said.

Frederick nodded. "Me, too. I think the difference is they don't view the Wake Formula as a drug of abuse or addiction. I didn't either when I was experimenting with it. They seem fixated on approaching the subject as an antidote for a toxic side effect."

"I hope you can come up with something to save my congressmen," Titus said bluntly.

"I'll do my best."

"It's in God's hands," Isabella said.

Titus smiled. "You know, Isabella, I've haven't been much on praying since I was a kid, but I've been praying a lot more lately thanks to you and Frederick. We have a lot to pray about right now."

She smiled and nodded. "We absolutely do."

"The records revealed more," Frederick said. "I believe your congressmen are onboard one of the medical ships right now, Titus."

His eyes lit up. "Are you kidding me? I had no idea where either one was. That's nice to know. Are they all right?'

Frederick shook his head. "I'm afraid not."

Titus' brow furrowed. "What do you mean? What's wrong?"

"The one from San Francisco is very ill. They're working on him, but it seems he's in poor shape and could die. The other one from Virginia is already dead."

"Dead?"

"That's what their records say. He died within the last week."

Titus leaned forward in his chair. "And his body is onboard one of their ships right now?"

"According to their database it is. They plan to examine the body and brain tissue to study the drug's lethal effects. Like the others, they'll throw him overboard when the autopsy is complete."

"They've probably done this sort of thing many times," Seth added, "which is why so many mysteriously missing people have never been found."

Titus' face erupted in anger and outrage. "We can't let this happen. We need to find my congressman and the others and get them off that ship. We have some Wake Formula. We can at least keep them alive until a detox protocol can be found, right Frederick?"

"I don't know. As I said, sometimes it's too late."

Rafael was concerned, too. "Do you have any ideas how to get the congressman and the others off that ship, Titus?"

He thought about the problem for a moment. "I have an idea or two. Search and rescue on short notice was my specialty in Delta Force. I've helped extract people in situations much worse than this. Of course, I had the resources of the U.S. Army Special Forces back then, but I think it can be done."

"What do you specifically have in mind?" Charles asked.

"There are several possibilities." His mind raced. "I'll need as much intel on the ship holding them as you can find."

"I'll get on it right away."

After many hours of discussion, Rafael finally said, "I think the yacht idea is our best bet, Titus."

"I agree," Seth said.

"Charles, can you get all the explosives and other equipment we need?" Titus asked. "Do you understand exactly what is needed?"

"I was a commando in the bloody Queen's Navy. I know precisely what we need and how to obtain it. Thanks to Ying's generosity, we have the money to fund this adventure. So yes, I can act as quartermaster for this little mission. It's a brilliant idea, Titus. With some luck, it might even work."

At the press conference, Conners felt great pride when the President faced the hostile group of reporters. It was a source of anguish to him that years earlier, the press mutated from being an unbiased conveyor of news into a partisan, agenda-driven group that helped tear the nation apart.

"I've always been in favor of reasonable, effective measures that support clean water and air," the President began. "However, we've learned from the past how restrictive legislation on energy production in the United States places our country at the mercy of foreign supplies while having little or no impact on energy use or the environment."

Grumbling came from the assembled reporters.

"Such legislation did, however, cost many American jobs and increase the risk of world conflict." After a pause, he continued, "Already there has been billions spent on climate change with little or no impact. What is certain is that the taxpayers' money spent on these projects circled back to fund liberal politicians who pushed the spending through."

He glanced at Conners, who provided him with the next part of his speech. Conners smiled and nodded his encouragement.

"Consider this," the President continued. "If my political opponents really felt that the world was facing imminent and catastrophic danger, wouldn't they be desperately reaching across the aisle to save the world, just as political parties came together after 9/11? Wouldn't they do anything to come together?"

He paused to let that sink in.

"No, that isn't even close to reality, is it? Instead, these politicians try to discredit and slander my party and others who oppose them. Why wouldn't they be turning to God to save our planet rather than attending political fundraisers? Do you remember how people flocked to our churches after 9/11 when they truly felt danger was imminent?"

He gazed over the crowd and then at Conners, who nodded encouragement.

"No, these people don't act like they're fighting for their lives but rather their political power." He took a deep breath. "They still buy their second and third homes on the beaches they say will be flooded soon. They still fly in private jets. They still play golf with donors as often as possible. They don't try to bring the nation together but rather use climate arguments to palliate their base."

The anger rising from certain reporters was palpable. Several tried to interrupt the President, who ignored them.

"Can we really afford to spend hundreds of billions of dollars more at the expense of other problems and our national defense? No. That won't happen during this administration."

The mainstream press exploded with indignation. Questions were shouted from all sides.

"Don't you care about the environment?"

"Don't you care about your children and grandchildren?"

"Don't you care about America?"

After each question, he explained it was because he cared about those things that he stood firm in his policy.

Immediately after the speech, as Conners predicted, the talking heads in the mainstream media vigorously criticized the President. Many referred to him as "the Earth Killer."

Dr. Lin watched the press conference. The more he watched, the angrier he became. He immediately activated his stable of politicians and celebrities to go on talk shows to discuss how embarrassing the President was to the country and how dangerous he was to the planet.

CHAPTER 37

Shortly after the medical supply freighter, *Dynasty Medical Salvation,* entered international waters, the first mate called the captain.

"Sir, we just received an SOS from a nearby vessel."

The captain looked up from his coffee. "From who?"

"A yacht not far off our starboard. It's having an engine malfunction and says it's stranded. They're asking for immediate help."

The captain, raising his binoculars, saw a yacht smoking from the engine. A skinny, tall man waved his arms frantically. Alongside him was an Asian woman in white pants and a red top, also waving desperately.

The first mate scanned the rest of the yacht with his own binoculars and saw nothing remarkable. "What should we do, Captain? That rich dude and his whore look like they need help, but our orders are not to stop for any reason until we've unloaded our human cargo."

"I know the orders," the captain replied with an edge to his voice. "If that man reports we left them stranded to the wrong authorities, we could get attention we don't want or need. With rich people like that, who knows what kind of connections they have?"

"Yes, Sir. What should we do?"

"Let's pull closer and see what he wants."

"Yes, Sir."

The captain ran his hand through his beard. "Still, let's not take any chances. Tell the men to stand by armed and ready. I've been told by the higher-ups to stay on high alert these days. Apparently, there's been some trouble."

"Yes, Captain."

The captain kept his eyes on the yacht, looking for signs of trouble, but he saw none. Shaking his head, he laughed. "Rich people think they can do anything, but they're so stupid, they can't even handle a small boat on a beautiful day."

The first mate laughed. "Yes, Sir. That's for damn sure."

When the ship was alongside the yacht, the captain used a megaphone to call, "Ahoy! What's the problem?"

"Thank you for stopping!" Charles shouted back. "As you can see, we have an engine problem. We're dead in the water." He pointed at the smoke coming from the engine.

"I see the smoke. Nothing serious, I hope."

"We don't know. I'm not an experienced mechanic. The crewman who's usually with us is sick, so we're out here alone."

Ying gave the captain the most-distressed look she could muster. "Can you help us? Please?"

"I'll send my mechanic over to you."

Titus slipped overboard on the opposite side of the yacht, carrying explosives and other equipment.

"Thank you!" Charles shouted.

Titus was deep enough no one could see him from above making his way to the ship's port side.

On the captain's orders, the ship's head mechanic and another crewman got into a dinghy and piloted themselves to the yacht.

When they came aboard, Ying saw both had scruffy beards and multiple tattoos. The mechanic was an unimposing man with gray in his beard. The younger one gave her the creeps. He had a tattoo of a naked woman with large breasts on one forearm and a woman giving a man oral sex on the other. His eyes moved lustfully up and down her body without trying to hide it. He seemed to enjoy making her feel uncomfortable.

Charles didn't like the way the young man stared at his wife but worried even more she'd do something about it before it was time. He tried to ease the tension with small talk.

"Where's your ship headed?" he asked.

"South America," the mechanic answered.

"I see the name on your ship. Are you really one of the Dynasty medical supply ships we heard so much about?" Ying asked with fake enthusiasm.

"That's right. Doing good for the world. That's us."

The younger man, staying quiet, kept looking at Ying, picking his teeth with a toothpick.

"That sounds so exciting," Ying said. "Come this way to the engine area. We're lucky you were the ones who found us."

Charles brought the man to the engine and watched him study it. "What do you think? Can you fix it?"

"Yeah. It's unusual but easily repaired. It shouldn't have happened in the first place. Someone might have messed with your engine before you left dock. I can repair it. It'll take thirty to forty-five minutes or so."

Charles smiled. "Great."

"Hey, you got any beers you can spare?"

"Of course."

"How about some money?" added his partner, who stood behind them. "It looks like you have plenty."

"OK," Charles said sheepishly.

The mechanic settled down to work, while the other man made himself comfortable in a nearby chair.

Charles brought them beers and a hundred-dollar bill apiece. "Will that do?"

"That'll do very well." The mechanic smiled.

"How about another fifty apiece?" the assistant asked gruffly. He glanced at Ying and grinned. "Or fifteen minutes alone with your hooker will do."

Ying tensed and fought to restrain herself. She pulled a thin jacket over her shirt.

Charles glanced at Ying, hoping she would be patient. He forced a chuckle as if the man just made a joke. "Actually, she's my wife."

"Your wife?"

"That's right. Tell you what. There's another hundred bucks for each of you chaps when the work is done. I'll throw in a case of beer to take back to the ship for good measure." After a moment, he added sternly, "But you leave my wife alone."

"We'll take it," the mechanic said quickly.

The younger man chuckled. "Your wife. Right." He scuffed the deck with his boot and said, "OK. Give us the money. I'll leave your wife alone."

Charles wished he could strangle the man, but he simply nodded.

The mechanic got to work, while the crewman kept drinking beer and eyeballing Ying. After ten minutes, the crewman became restless and stood. "I want a look around your boat."

Ying quickly approached him. "I know you're bored. How about I get you another beer?" When he didn't answer right away, she added, "Maybe I'll have one, too."

He grinned. "Yeah. I'll take another beer."

"Great. I'll be right back."

He stared at her butt, as she went to the refrigerator and retrieved two more beers.

When she returned, she sat down directly across from him and noticed he had a gun tucked into his trousers, hidden by his shirt. His stares were unnerving, but he forgot all about looking around the boat.

Suddenly, they heard a loud boom from the ship.

"What was that?" the mechanic yelled.

The crewman ran to the side of the yacht. "There's been an explosion on our ship."

"On our ship?" He ran over beside the man to look.

Seth and Rafael hid on the yacht, waiting for the explosion. When it went off, they slipped into the water with their firearms. Titus felt he'd have a better chance to set off the first explosions alone. After that, though, he needed everyone's help.

Realizing they were set up, the crewman turned menacingly toward Ying and Charles, reaching for his gun.

Before he could draw, Ying pulled out a small pistol and aimed at him. "Pull out your gun and see what happens," she said. "I'd love to put a bullet through that nasty face of yours."

He and the mechanic froze.

"Slowly remove the gun using only two fingers on the butt. Set it on the deck."

He obeyed, his eyes on hers.

"Now kick it toward me."

He kicked it.

Ying bent to pick it up. As she did, the mechanic threw his wrench at her. It struck her shoulder, making her drop her gun and reach for the wound.

Charles dived for the gun, but, as he moved, another explosion went off on the big ship. It rocked in the water, sending waves against the yacht. Falling flat on his face, he slid across the floor away from them.

Ying remained upright, barely keeping her balance. The crewman, who had excellent sea legs, ran toward her.

Ying kicked him in the crotch. There was little force behind it, but at least it stopped him for a few seconds.

The mechanic charged her, too.

Charles, pulling out a rifle, aimed at them both. "Stop or I'll shoot!"

The men froze.

"Both of you flat on the deck! Right now!"

They got down on their stomachs.

Charles walked closer to Ying. "Are you all right?'

She rubbed her shoulder. "I'm OK. It's just a bad bruise."

Charles handed her the rifle. "Watch them." He walked a few steps to pick up the guns. He also found a knife in the crewman's boot. Once they were disarmed, he ordered them into the cabin.

Ying grabbed binoculars and scanned the ship. "I don't see anyone watching us. I assume they're reacting to the explosions. I don't think they saw us."

"Good." Charles turned toward his captors. "Listen carefully. In a few minutes, we're going to your ship using your dinghy. We're all coming over to help, understand?"

No one answered, so he aimed at their legs. "Do you understand, or do I need to blow off someone's kneecap?"

"We heard you," the mechanic said.

"If you do anything suspicious to tip off your ship, it'll be the last thing you ever do. We'll shoot without hesitation. Understand?"

They didn't reply.

Ying aimed at the crewman's crotch.

"We understand!" he said quickly.

Charles ginned. "Now push off, Mates. We have a boat to catch."

CHAPTER 38

Seth and Rafael used a hook-and-ladder device to board the ship. With the crew in chaos, they were able to climb aboard without being seen. They immediately covered their faces with nylon stockings.

Titus, whose face was also hidden, watched them and came to them the moment they were aboard. He noticed some huffing and puffing under Seth's nylon stocking. "You OK there, Old Man. The climb was a little rough, was it?"

"I'm fine, thank you. I just haven't done this sort of thing for a while. Twenty years ago, I was in better shape than you."

Titus didn't believe it, but he smiled. "Let's get moving."

Slowly, they moved through the ship, not getting far before an armed crewman saw them. Though initially confused over their identity, he raised his rifle to shoot.

Titus saw him and fired two silenced shots into the man's chest, sending him down. Moments later, a second armed crewman came around a corner and was shot by Rafael.

"We must be close to something important," Seth said, "or they wouldn't have armed men here while there's a raging fire on the ship."

"Good point," Titus said. "Let's keep looking."

When the dinghy reached the ship, the mechanic called up, "We've come to help. Let us up."

The crewman above them pointed at Charles and Ying. "What are they doing with you? No one but crew is allowed aboard."

"They want to help. The woman's a nurse. The man says he can help her."

"I don't know. I have to ask the captain."

"We don't have time for that," the mechanic said, when Ying poked her concealed gun against his back. "They're here to help. Just let us up. I'll take them straight to the captain myself. They'll be my responsibility."

"OK. Climb aboard." He pointed a finger at Ying and Charles. "You two can't wander around the ship alone."

"Of course," Ying said. "We just want to help."

As they boarded, Ying and Charles pulled out their weapons. The crewman on deck shook his head and sneered at the mechanic.

"They had us at gunpoint," the mechanic said.

"All of you on the deck," Charles said. "Arms behind your backs."

"You, too," Ying told the crewman who let them aboard.

They did as they were told. Charles bound their hands and feet, as Ying watched. He carefully gagged them and then spoke into his mic.

"Onboard," he said. "Three crewmen in custody. What's your status?"

"Two down," Titus replied. "Checking below deck for the medical clinic. Stay out of sight and wait for instructions."

"Ten-four."

Suddenly, shots rang out, and a bullet clipped the top of Seth's right ear. Another bullet barely missed Rafael's head. The three men dived for the floor and came up shooting. The firefight ended with two dead crewmen.

The top of Seth's ear was missing. Blood ran down the side of his face and some inside his ear. He placed a hand against it for pressure to stop the bleeding. "Bloody hell, that hurts."

"Let me look," Titus said. "Rafael, stand watch."

He gently wiped away the blood and patched the wound as best he could with a field dressing Rafael brought.

"Damn," Seth joked between groans. "I hope this won't ruin my good looks. I plan to seduce a wealthy widow and retire from all this someday."

"You never looked better," Rafael told his old friend. "Who knows? Maybe when they fix your ear, you can talk them into a facelift, too."

Seth managed a smile.

"Let's hope that all you two have to worry about by the end of the day," Titus said, finishing the bandage. "Ready to move? We have to go."

"Ready," Seth replied. "No more whining from me. Chin up."

Cautiously and with military precision, they moved forward, examining each room one-by-one. Most were unlocked, so they were able to check them and proceed quickly.

Shaking one door handle, Seth found resistance from a lock. "This might be it. It's locked, and I hear movement inside."

Titus motioned the other two men back, then he shot out the lock.

Rafael knocked in the heavy metal door with a kick and stood back. No gunfire came at them, but they heard movement and muffled voices inside.

Titus used hand signals for them to move on three. As he raised his fingers one at a time, on three, he burst into the room with his gun ready. Movement came from the corner of his eye, and he almost fired, but held back.

Seth and Rafael ran in after Titus, guns raised, but they held their fire, too.

Two nurses and a doctor hovered nervously in a corner, all un-armed.

"Don't shoot!" the doctor said.

The room was lined with hospital beds.

"Hands on your heads!" Rafael said.

"Keep on eye on them while Seth and I search the next room," Titus ordered. On the mission, he had full operational command.

Rafael nodded.

The adjoining room was a clinic that held six patients. All were unconscious with IVs in their arms. In one bed, Titus spotted the congressman from San Francisco.

Found you, he told himself.

"Look over here." Seth saw a metal slab with a woman's body being autopsied.

"Damn." Titus felt disgusted when he saw the top of her skull was removed, and her brain sat at a nearby dissection table. Two more bodies were stored in a nearby cold box. One was the congressman Titus was told was dead.

He could barely contain his anger. "Someone will pay for this," he growled.

Walking back to the doctor, he grabbed his shirt with one hand and shouted, "What have you done to these people?"

"Just doing my job," the man whimpered.

Titus shoved him toward Rafael. "Tie up this 'doctor' before I do something I might regret. Make that all of them."

"Do you have to tie us up? We're no danger to you."

"You bet your ass we are." Rafael looked at the nurse in disgust. "This is an equal-opportunity raid, and you're as guilty as the doctor."

After all prisoners were secured, Seth looked determinedly at Titus. "We've got what we came for. Time to end this."

Titus clicked on his mic. "Charles, Ying, we found and secured the patients. It's time to coordinate our attack and put this hunk of junk out of commission. What's your location?"

There was no response.

"Charles, Ying, what's your location?"

Silence answered him.

Titus took a deep breath. "Something's wrong. They aren't answering "

Suddenly, the com system crackled, and Ying said, "Titus, we need help. We're under heavy assault."

He heard fear in her voice. Gunfire sounded in the background.

"Charles is pinned down," she said. "I'm trying to reach him, but we're outnumbered. I can't get to him!"

"Where are you?"

"Get on deck. You'll know. Just follow the gunfire. Hurry!"

"Stay low, and don't do anything foolish. We're on the way." Titus looked at Seth and Rafael. "Time to go. Charles and Ying are in trouble."

As they moved double-time toward the upper decks, several shots struck near Titus. The three men ducked and returned fire. After several minutes, Rafael wounded the shooter and drove him off.

As they were moving again, Titus said, "We have to change the game plan."

"What do you mean?" Rafael asked. "What's wrong?"

"I don't have a good feeling about this. There are more armed men than expected, and we aren't exactly a well-oiled Special Forces team. Instead of the covert pincher movement I hoped for, we're on a rescue mission. It's no one's fault, but I don't like how this is playing out."

"What should we do?"

"We need to hit them from two directions again. I want you and Seth to make your way to help Charles and Ying. Flank the shooters if you can. I'll try to draw some of them away."

"How?"

"I'm going back to the yacht for more explosives. When I return, I'll come up on the other side of the ship and start more fireworks."

"OK, but don't get yourself killed." He meant it to be funny, but every word was serious. "We'll be in deep shit if you do."

Titus smiled. "Thanks for the concern. You stay alive, too. I mean it. Don't be heroes. Just hold them off until I can do my thing, OK? Then I'll find you."

They nodded, and Seth and Rafael ran off to help Ying and Charles. Titus ran back to where he stashed his gear and slipped overboard.

CHAPTER 39

After retrieving more explosives from the yacht, Titus swam back and boarded the ship, placing several incendiary bombs in strategic locations before finding a safe place for himself. When he was ready, he set them off.

The effect was immediate. The explosions were loud, destructive, and ignited new fires. They created total mayhem on the ship, with several crewmen abandoning the shootout to find the new source of trouble. That left fewer sailors to fight Charles, Ying, and the others.

The damage to the ship was more severe. Crewman ran about frantically, as the captain tried to save the ship.

Titus watched from behind cover for an opportunity to help Charles and Ying. When he saw the captain and two armed crewmen coming his way, he reconsidered his plan, as an opportunity crystallized in his mind.

Ducking out of sight as they passed, he followed them silently. Eventually, the opportunity he hoped for came.

He walked up behind the captain and pressed the barrel of his gun against the man's back. "Drop your weapon, or you'll never walk again."

The stunned captain did as he was told.

When the two crewmen saw what happened, they raised their weapons.

"Tell them to drop their weapons," Titus growled.

The captain hesitated. Titus twisted the man's body between himself and the crewmen and shoved the barrel harder against his back. "Now!"

The captain stiffened but said nothing.

Titus had no time to lose. He aimed at the man's foot and fired. A bullet tore through the end of the captain's right boot. He screamed in pain, as he lost two toes. Blood poured from his shoe onto the deck.

"You bastard!" he shouted.

Titus, seeing one crewman preparing to fire, crouched behind the captain. One bullet entered the crewman's chest, and he was down. The other crewman ran off.

"Drop your weapons!" the captain finally shouted.

No one moved.

Titus pressed the gun harder against the captain's back. "Again."

"Everyone, drop your weapons! That's an order!"

Slowly, the crewmen reluctantly obeyed.

"Tell them to lay on the deck and spread their arms and legs wide apart."

He did, and the men slowly obeyed the order.

"Get on your walkie-talkie and give orders to the rest of the crew. I want all the shooting to stop."

"They won't listen to me."

"They'd better, or I'll shoot the other foot. You're the captain. They have no choice. We won't harm you and your men any further if you surrender."

Compliance was slow, but eventually, the ship grew silent.

"Are you guys all right?" Titus asked over the com net.

"We're OK," Seth replied.

"Have the crew in your area surrendered?"

"They have. What's going on. How'd you do it?"

"A gun to the captain's back and a bullet in his foot helped him decide to surrender."

"Well done, Titus."

"Tie up the prisoners and check for weapons. Work fast. I want off this ship as soon as we can. Have their so-called doctor attend the captain's foot and the other injured crewmen."

After securing his own prisoners, Titus joined the others. At first, they seemed fine. When he took a second look at Ying, she tried hard not to show it, but she held her side and seemed pale.

He walked over to her. "Is something wrong?"

She shook her head.

He saw blood on the lower part of her shirt and the waistband of her white pants. "Ying, you're hit."

"It's not bad. I'll be fine."

Charles was checking prisoners when he overheard Titus' conversation with Ying and ran up to them. "Ying, what's wrong?"

She showed him the stain. "I was hit a little bit."

"What? You didn't tell me you were hurt. Lie down and let me examine you."

She lay on the deck, and both men examined the wound. A bullet went through her side. Fortunately, no major organs were damaged.

"It doesn't look bad," Titus assured her.

She grimaced with pain but said, "I didn't think so. It hurts a bit, though,"

"Why didn't you tell me, Darling?" Charles asked. "When did this happen?'

"When you were pinned down with gunfire. I was trying to reach you. I knew the wound wasn't bad, and I didn't want you to worry about me."

He carefully hugged her and fought back tears. "I love you. Never, ever, do that again."

Managing a smile, she nodded.

Titus and Seth incapacitated the ship's engine, completely destroyed the communication system, and all personal communication devices were thrown overboard. They quickly searched the rest of the ship.

In the captain's quarters, Seth disconnected a computer to confiscate when Titus saw containers that looked like the ones he found at Dr. Lin's laboratory. "Seth, look at this. We just got us some more Wake Formula."

"That's a nice bonus to our trip."

"It sure is. Come on. Let's get this stuff to the deck and onto the yacht. This should make Dr. Burrus happy."

After videoing all patients, living and dead, for evidence and documentation, Rafael and Charles carefully loaded them into the yacht. It was a tight fit, with barely enough room for everyone. The corpses were put on ice for the journey home.

The doctors and nurses helped with the patient transfer.

"Should we take the medical staff with us to care for these people?" Seth asked Titus in private.

"It's tempting, but the patients should be all right long enough for us to get them to shore. Dr. Burrus can take over from there. Besides, there are several wounded crewmen aboard who need medical attention."

Seth didn't protest.

As the medical staff were taken back to the ship to be dropped off, Titus told the doctor. "We've disabled the ship and all communications."

The man seemed ready to protest when Titus said, "We'll make an anonymous call to the Coast Guard in a day or two. You'll be stranded for only a short time. You can release the crew when you get aboard and provide them with any medical assistance they might need. You have food and plenty of medical supplies still aboard."

After they docked the yacht, Frederick and Isabella pulled up with two large vans to take everyone to the NIH clinic. They immediately saw Ying was wounded but that she was doing all right.

"How'd it go?" Frederick asked.

"Better than we could have hoped, except Ying and Seth were wounded," Titus replied.

"I see that."

"We got you more formula, too."

Frederick nodded. "I can always use more."

Once back at the clinic, Dr. Burrus worked frantically to stabilize the new patients, after tending Ying and Seth's wounds.

Two days later, the media was abuzz with breaking news that one of Dynasty Global Foundation's medical supply ships had been found adrift by the Coast Guard after being attacked by modern-day pirates.

As one reporter put it, "Sadly, pirates not only killed and wounded several brave crewmen, but they stole life-saving medications from Dr. Lin's foundation."

Other reporters emphasized how the crew fought back gallantly, but they had few weapons to defend themselves.

"How many pirates were there?" a female commentator asked the captain on a cable news channel.

"It must've been twenty or more. All were heavily armed."

"Were you harmed in any way?"

"I was beaten and then shot in the foot for refusing to show the pirates where the medications were stored. They shot off part of my foot when I refused to cooperate."

She shook her head. "Thank goodness you're alive. The world is proud of you and your crew."

The doctor onboard stated in an interview, "In addition to the physical injuries, almost everyone on the ship suffered severe emotional trauma from the cruel attack."

"Have you heard from Dr. Lin?"

"I have a copy of a written message from Dr. Lin to the surviving crew and their families. I can share it with you, if you like."

"Please do."

The doctor took out a sheet of paper and read it. "My heart is broken for the heroic men and women who were killed or injured onboard one of the Dynasty Global Foundation's medical supply ships recently. I was brought to tears not only for you brave men and women but for your families who have also suffered. I consider the attack by the pirates to be a cowardly act of ultimate brutality and selfishness.

"I am outraged that anyone could steal life-saving medical supplies intended for poor children in underdeveloped countries. However, I promise that you survivors and families of your fallen comrades will be well-compensated for your suffering. I also promise that more medication will be gathered and shipped to the needy children very soon in the name of the fallen.

"Clearly, our world must come together as one family to fight against such cruel aggressors and others who care so little about human life. Thank you again for your sacrifice and service to humanity. With all sincerity, Dr. Dao Lin."

As Frederick watched the TV interviews with Titus, he asked, "What did you do with the medical supplies? You didn't bring them back here."

Titus shook his head. "We didn't do anything with them. We left them on the ship. The crew must've thrown them overboard to weave their sordid tale."

"Ha. Got it."

CHAPTER 40

While Dr. Lin's popularity and notoriety grew exponentially worldwide, President O'Malley's approval rating plummeted equally fast. Protesters drew attention to themselves near the White House and hounded the President wherever he went. World leaders frequently made barely concealed insults about him. The president of the French Republic and the Prime Minister of Canada were particularly harsh.

To make matters worse, the President, who was known for his boundless energy, was noticeably slowing down and looked ill to those around him. TV news footage showed him on three occasions having trouble staying awake during public events. Late-night comedians enjoyed making jokes about a President who would rather nap than confront the Earth's imminent climate disaster. Some mainstream media interviewed psychologists from major universities, who held the theory that the President was suffering from a guilt complex for not supporting Dr. Lin.

One cable TV station quoted an unnamed source from within the White House as saying, "When the world burns to ashes, O'Malley will be just fine, because he's obviously in cahoots with Satan."

Only Conners knew why the President's health declined so rapidly, and he was greatly concerned. At one of their meetings, he felt obligated to say, "President O'Malley, you can't go on like this. Look at yourself. You can hardly keep your eyes open, and it's only ten in the morning."

The President stared at him without speaking.

"You know why this is happening, don't you? Your body got so used to that damn drug, the Wake Formula, that you can't do without it."

The President still didn't reply.

"You need to reverse course and throw your support behind Dr. Lin and his agenda. There's no other way. You need that medication. You look terrible. Everyone knows something's wrong."

President O'Malley's face showed sadness and resolve. "I can't do that, Conners. What he wants to do is against the policies that got me elected. Someone has to stand up to him."

Conners squirmed in his seat. "I respect that, Sir. I really do, but you have no choice. There are so many issues you need to fight for—the economy, antiterrorism, national defense, unborn babies, urban infrastructure. The list goes on and on, but it all goes to hell in a hand basket if you can't do your job. The media is crucifying you on a daily basis."

The President felt overwhelmed and admittedly very sleepy. His eyes kept flicking shut. "We'll see, Conners. I have to take a nap right now. I have to work through the day in small portions." He went to a sofa and lay down.

The next day, the President's personal physician, Dr. Thomas Hubert, was called in. After an examination, he said, "I'm not really sure what's going on with you, Mr. President. I'll need to order a full gamut of blood work and other tests, including a full-body MRI, and see if anything turns up. I also have to investigate the possibility of poisoning."

The President knew nothing would be found, but he agreed.

When all results came back normal, Dr. Hubert brought in several specialists, including a neurologist, a rheumatologist, an endocrinologist, and an infectious disease expert. They proposed one exotic theory after another based on their field of expertise, but no one had a definitive answer.

After all the doctors gave their opinion, Cassandra Washington, a tall Black woman who was the President's primary spokesperson, went to the podium at the White House press room to speak to reporters about the President's status.

The excited room became deadly quiet when she walked in. She saw on their faces that they were ready for a big scoop, but she wasn't about to give that hungry mob what it wanted.

She said evenly, "I'm sad to report that President O'Malley has been ill. Although numerous doctors have been consulted, no definitive diagnosis has been determined. Most seem to agree he's probably suffering from a viral infection of a yet-unidentified strain. It's hoped he will recover soon, but the prognosis isn't certain.

"For now, the President is receiving outpatient care at Walter Reed Hospital. He wanted me to tell you that he remains in good spirits and thanks everyone for their hopes and prayers."

Immediately, questions flew.

"How ill is he?"

"Is he contagious?"

"Is he dying?"

"Does he need to step down from his office until he fully recovers?"

She knew the President's being removed from office was what many of the sharks wanted to hear, but she wasn't going to accommodate them. "Although he feels very ill, we believe he'll be fine," she said with more confidence than she felt. "He has no plans to step down from the work he was elected to do unless his condition becomes much worse. I'll let the medical experts with me answer your specific medical questions."

Five days later, Cassandra Washington was back to give an update at the request of the Chief of Staff. In a worse mood than the previous conference, she hadn't seen the President in two days.

The noisy room quieted when she walked in.

She placed both hands on the podium before she began. "Thank you for coming. There has been no significant change in the President's health. He is at Walter Reed Hospital. We're still optimistic he'll improve soon." She took a deep breath and had to compose herself before continuing. "I'm also here to announce that the President has reversed his stance on climate change."

Noise filled the room, as reporters began asking questions.

She raised her hands to quiet them. In a matter-of-fact tone, she said, "He says he has come to realize that global warming is a severe threat and wants to help. The President wishes to thank Dr. Lin for leading the charge against global disaster, and he supports his nomination as the Secretary-General of the United Nations. He also supports greater authority to be given to the UN to combat global climate change and other serious global problems."

A dubious reporter asked, "Did President O'Malley change his mind because he believes that, or because his approval ratings have tanked dramatically?"

Cassandrea cleared her throat. "I believe the President has seen there is great interest in this area and has decided he didn't want to hold back the good intentions of Dr. Lin and others."

Question after question about the change was directed at her, and she answered each in a positive but vague manner. Eventually, she said, "That's all the questions I can answer today. There will be further follow-ups at another time. Thank you."

As soon as the press conference ended, she walked briskly to Conners' office and entered without bothering to knock.

Conners looked up, a bit startled.

"Did the President really say those things," she demanded, "or was it all bullshit?"

He stopped writing and look up at her. Taking a deep breath, he said, "He did. He feels he has no choice but to go along with Dr. Lin to get the media off his back. He doesn't have the energy or motivation to fight them anymore."

"I don't mean to be insulting, but that doesn't sound like the man I work for. I'm going to the hospital. I want to hear it from him myself before I repeat any of that crap on a million talk shows that will love to have me on."

Conners held up a hand to stop her. "I'm sorry, Cassandra, but he won't see anyone but me, the First Lady, and his doctors right now. Besides, if it's a virus, it could be contagious as well as dangerous. I've been around him so much, I would've caught it already if I were susceptible. He asked that everyone else stay clear for now. I'm his only go-between to his staff."

"Then I'll call him."

"You don't understand. You won't get through. He barely has enough energy to give me instructions. He wants...no, he's ordered...that I alone handle things with his staff until he's better. I'm sorry, but that's the way it is right now."

Crossing her arms, she stared at him.

"You know me, Cassandra. I hate seeing him capitulate to that man, but I care more about the President than I do Dr. Lin."

She didn't believe it. Leaning over the desk, she poked Conners' chest with one finger. "OK, Conners, but if I find out you're lying to me, I'll publicly bury you. I don't like this U-turn policy, and I don't like looking like a fool on national TV."

His face turned red with indignation. "You stab that finger into my chest one more time, and you'll be looking for a new job. You can leave now."

She almost vented her anger again, but she controlled herself. Without a word, she stormed off.

The day after the announcement of President O'Malley's support, Dr. Lin renewed his supply of the Wake Formula.

CHAPTER 41

Withholding information on the rescued congressmen and the others from their superiors and to the missing people's families felt wrong in many ways to Titus and Rafael.

During a meeting, Rafael said, "I feel bad I got you into all of this, Titus. Our jobs are on the line if things don't go the way we hope. We could even be charged with murder or manslaughter if a patient dies in our custody."

Titus nodded. "I know, but I have no regrets. We have no choice but to keep them in safe harbor for now. We still don't know who we can trust. If word about our activities reaches the wrong people, our efforts to stop Dr. Lin will end, and the lives of Frederick and his family will be in even greater danger." He paused and shook his head. "No. Things are as they have to be."

Rafael leaned back in his chair. "Of course you're right. This isn't my usual way of operating, and I feel like time is running out. Dr. Lin's influence is growing, and I don't know how long we can keep our identities secret."

Titus nodded. "No one on the ship could identify you, me, or Seth, but Charles and Ying were seen by several people."

"I know. As with other FBI Deputy Directors, I've been given an artist's drawing of them" He laughed. "They aren't that good, actually. The only thing the crew got right were Ying's legs."

Titus laughed.

"The drawing could be for any of a million people. Charles and Ying have to be more careful than ever. I told them not to be seen in public together and to alter their appearance as best they can. The important thing is that we recovered those poor people on that ship and have video evidence of the situation they were in."

Titus nodded.

"Also, Dr. Burrus is doing his best to cure them. If they recover, we have witnesses."

"*When* they recover," Titus said hopefully. "It's a race from now on."

Frederick and Isabella worked tirelessly in the clinic and the research lab. Keeping the patients alive wasn't easy, but information from the ship's medical logs helped immensely. Each patient had two IVs for basic life support, with a third to test ever-evolving compositions of Wake Formula LA. Isabella spent most of her time acting as a nurse to the patients, but she also assisted in the research lab. Dr. Burrus' time was spent in the opposite manner, with most of his efforts dedicated to the research lab and making rounds only twice a day in the clinic.

Reflecting on everything that transpired, Isabella shook her head in disbelief, as she hung a new IV bag of Wake Formula LA for a patient. "Who would've thought we'd be here, doing this, a couple months ago?" she asked Frederick, as he made his evening rounds.

He chuckled despite their strange, dangerous situation. "Not me. That's for sure. Here I am, making rounds on patients I never really met, don't have a medical license to practice in DC, and have absolutely no authority to do research on these poor people."

Isabella shook her head again in amazement. "God works in mysterious ways. There's a lot at stake, not only for us but for the world. I pray constantly things will work out for the best."

"Me, too."

Her expression became serious. "Do you really think it will? I still don't know how we can stop Dr. Lin even if we save these people."

"There's always hope, Isabella," he said, trying to convince himself as much as her. "We can only do our part and let Titus and the others do theirs. The rest is in God's hands."

Isabella, taking a deep breath, nodded.

"I still think this is pretty crazy," he said. "I'm just thankful we somehow have a medical clinic to take care of these people and a research lab to find some answers. That's a miracle in itself."

She walked over to him and kissed him, wrapping her arms around him. "Yes, it is, my brilliant husband."

As her head rose from his shoulder, she stiffened. "Look!"

"What's wrong?"

She ran to one of the patients. "I'm sure I saw a couple of her fingers move."

They watched together as the woman's left shoulder twitched very slightly.

Frederick quickly brought over EEG equipment. "Let's check her brain activity to see if she's really waking up."

After the machine began testing, they held hands and nervously watched, as the machine spat out its results.

Frederick smiled. "It's not much, but there's a slight change in her brainwaves." He pointed at the reading. "See here? Some alpha waves have appeared."

Isabella hugged him tightly. "You did it, Frederick! Your latest formulation is working!"

"Maybe. Let's wait and see. Praise God, but this might be it!"

At the Supreme Council meeting, Liang Lee began. "I'm greatly concerned, Master Lin. First, Wake Formula was taken from our underground production and storage facility. Now one of our medical-supply ships has been assaulted. Live and dead clients were taken, and more Wake Formula was stolen. I fear we're fully exposed, and the U.S. government is ready to close in on us. Should we cut our losses and disappear? Our escape plans may be needed very soon."

Dr. Lin tapped his fingers on the arm of his chair. "These are indeed very serious matters, Liang. However, we can't panic. I still don't think a government agency is involved, at least not the United States. None of our moles in the CIA, FBI, or Homeland Security have reported any active investigations into us. President O'Malley has far too much to lose than to expose us."

Liang sat solemnly without speaking.

"Besides, if the United States government was involved, we would already have been arrested after they rescued our clients and found the dead bodies on that ship. One of our dead clients was a U.S. congressman. No. Something else is going on."

Liang relaxed a little.

"These attacks on our operations must come from people who have means and want to control the Wake Formula for themselves. Greed is the great motivator, Liang. Finding those with enough greed, motivation, and the means to do these things will lead us to those involved. Then we can stop those who have attacked us."

"Yes, Master Lin. I'm sure you're correct, as usual."

Dr. Lin turned his gaze to General Chen. "Do you have the names of the clients who have the potential ambition, arrogance, and means to attack us, General?"

"All our clients are ambitious enough, Dr. Lin. That's why we recruited them. As to the means, I'm looking closely at those with connections to the military, FBI, CIA, and Homeland Security. I'm also investigating our clients in other countries with contacts to similar agencies. However, it has been very difficult and complicated to follow and investigate so many. Obviously, if it's one of our clients, they are being very careful to hide their tracks."

"Of course they are, but you must find them. Keep searching day and night, General. Use all our resources. As Liang pointed out, we're at great risk right now. If we must, we'll kill the three most-likely traitors, maybe the five most likely."

The general nodded.

"Once I head the United Nations and strengthen its influence, we'll have so much power, no one will be able to stop us." He made a fist. "If any allegations are made toward us, I'll deny them and claim with indignation that far-right nationalists are plotting to stop our efforts to unify the world. The media will defend me, and no nation will have the authority or power to challenge me."

All members of the council nodded.

"When we have power, no one will know that it's really my Supreme Council that rules the world."

"Must your Supreme Council always be in hiding, Great Master?" Fu Wong asked.

Seeing the question took Dr. Lin by surprise, he added, "I seek to stand proudly and openly by your side."

Dr. Lin cleared his throat. "You won't remain in the shadows forever, Fu Wong. In a year or two, after I have obtained supreme power, you'll all be seen at my side. First, I must solidify and grow my own power and that of the United Nations. Just as Julius Caesar was made permanent dictator by those who sought his favor, I will become the permanent head of the United Nations by those who seek favor with me. No one will dare oppose me after that."

All heads nodded.

Dr. Lin felt excited. "Nations will become dependent states. National leaders will be my vassals and retain their power only with my approval. We will create the greatest empire the world has ever known."

Everyone but General Chen was excited. He, however, remained concerned. "But Julius Caesar was killed shortly after he obtained permanent power, Master Lin. We must always stay on guard."

Dr. Lin gazed at his Head of Security and Surveillance. "Yes. You're right, General Lin. The Great Caesar let down his defenses. He didn't have Mark Antony at his side when he should have. I have you and a legion of bodyguards who will always be with me. Do not worry. I will learn from the mistakes of Caesar." He smiled. "Unlike him, I have the Wake Formula."

CHAPTER 42

The pressure to stop Dr. Lin weighed heavily on the minds of Titus, Seth, and the others. At the group's next strategy meeting, Seth said, "We've won some battles, but Dr. Lin is winning the war. Now that President O'Malley supports him, he'll soon be Secretary-General of the United Nations, so he'll be untouchable."

Rafael shook his head. "I couldn't be more disappointed with the President."

"Isn't it funny how his so-called virus went away soon after he committed to support Dr. Lin?" Titus asked. "I'd bet my pension Dr. Lin cut him off until he capitulated."

Charles tapped the butt of a pencil against the table. "No doubt. His endgame to obtain world power by heading a more-powerful UN is pretty obvious." After a pause, he added, "Well, at least obvious to the people in this room."

"Talk about a New World Order," Seth said. "He'll shift money to those who support him, build UN military forces, and crush anyone who gets in his way."

"He sounds like the Antichrist to me," Isabella said.

"He's no Antichrist," Titus said soberly. "I met him. He's just another power-hungry sociopath, and we're going to stop him."

"How?" Rafael asked.

Seth sighed. "That's the questions, isn't it?"

Titus shook his head. "We need to destroy his source of power."

"What do you mean?" Ying asked. "How do you destroy the entire mainstream media?"

Titus laughed. "I didn't mean them, although you have a point. I meant the lab where he produces the Wake Formula. If we destroy his ability to make and distribute the drug, we take away his ability to leverage and control powerful people like the President."

Rafael nodded. "Not a bad thought, but how? I'm sure that lab is an armed fortress. It would take an army of commandos to take it out."

Titus smiled. "I agree, so that's exactly who we'll get."

Seth looked at him curiously. "I don't understand. Where do we get such an army? You aren't thinking our little group can pull off something like that, are you? Our raid on the ship ended up all right, but we were lucky. All of us could have been killed. I'm not sure I want to press my luck any further."

Titus nodded. "I didn't mean us. I mean we get the help only the President of the United States can provide."

Rafael was confused. "President O'Malley? Are you kidding me? That bastard just sold out his country for the damn drug. He's obviously under Dr. Lin's control."

"You're right, but does he want to be? I seriously doubt it."

"What do you mean?" Seth asked.

"I heard Conners arguing with Dr. Lin about his agenda and how the President wouldn't go along. I don't think the President would play Dr. Lin's game if there was any alternative. That's why he got sick. He was coming off the Wake Formula when he refused to cooperate. He might just work with us if we can become his source of the Wake Formula. We have enough to do that, right, Frederick?"

Frederick nodded. "With the extra from the ship, we have more than enough."

"Interesting thought," Rafael said, "but there's no way any of us can get close enough to the President to convince him. Even I would have a hard time getting an audience alone with him."

Titus grinned. "Don't give up so quickly. I have an idea."

Seth rubbed his hands together in excitement. "Let's hear it."

As usual, Sam Conners got home late to his Georgetown town-house from the White House. His dedication and long hours on the job cost him three marriages and estrangement from his two children.

After walking in, he turned off the alarm, bolted the door, and hung his car keys on a hook in the kitchen. He poured a small glass of bourbon. After a few gulps, he took the rest into the bedroom to undress and relax.

As he walked through the bedroom door, a gun touched the back of his head.

"Don't move."

Conners dropped his glass to the floor. It shattered, sending shards of glass and liquor over his shoes, but he didn't move.

"Put your hands against the wall and spread your feet," the masked intruder ordered.

He frisked Conners without finding a weapon.

"What do you want?" Conners asked, panicked.

"Now down on your knees."

Conners complied.

"Put your hands behind your back."

Conners felt flex cuffs snap into place on his wrists, and the masked intruder turned him around.

"What do you want?" he asked fearfully.

"If you scream or try to escape, things won't go well for you, understood?"

Conners began shaking. "Yes. Don't hurt me. What do you want? I don't have much money, but you can take everything I've got."

"Believe it or not, I want to help you."

Conners managed a nervous chuckle. "You want to help me? I'm supposed to believe that after you broke into my home and tied me up?"

The man didn't answer.

"Do you know who I am? Leave now, or I'll have the weight of the United States government on your back for the rest of your life."

"I know who you are. You're Sam Conners, Chief of Staff for President O'Malley. That's why we're talking."

Conners' mind raced. His biggest fear had always been to be captured by a spy and tortured for information to betray his country, then be killed.

"I need you to give a message to the President."

Conners felt a tiny bit of relief. Maybe he would survive after all. He studied the masked man curiously. "What sort of message?"

"Tell him we know about the Wake Formula. Tell him we know he gets it from Dr. Lin."

Conners' expression changed from fear to surprise.

"We also know that Dr. Lin is forcing the President to support a climate-change agenda."

"I don't know what you're talking about."

"I don't have time to play games with you, Conners. You and I both know that's true."

Conners didn't reply.

"We also know you're the go-between. You obtain his performance-enhancing drug from Dr. Lin's suppliers, so you're in this as deep as him. Don't lie to me anymore, understand?"

Perspiration ran down Conners' forehead. "Who are you? Where'd you get your information?"

"All you need to know is that I've been sent from people who want to stop Dr. Lin."

"What people?"

"That's on a need-to-know basis right now."

"Well, I need to know. How can I or the President trust people we don't know?"

"Listen to me carefully, Conners. My group is very, very secretive. Dr. Lin is more dangerous than you realize. A number of powerful people, besides the President, are secretly cooperating with him. He kills people. He tried to kill me and my friends. We have to be very careful until we take him down. Do you understand?"

"Are you the pirates who attacked his ship?"

"You'll learn all about us very soon. What you need to know is that we have a plan to stop Dr. Lin. That's all we want, to stop him. Nothing else, but we need the President's help."

"You broke into my home and tied me up, then you forced me on my knees. Does that sound like the kind of people I'll ask the President of the United States to help?"

"I'm sorry, but we had to do it this way. There was no other way to reach the President or make sure you heard me out."

Conners' brows furrowed, but he didn't speak.

"We desperately hope the President will believe us. We know he's a hostage every bit as much as you are right now. Honestly, we aren't sure what else we can do."

Conners didn't know what to say.

"Did you know that Dr. Lin didn't develop the Wake Formula?"

"What do you mean?"

"He stole it and thought he killed the inventor."

"How do you know this?"

"The scientist who developed the Wake Formula is a member of our group."

Conners cocked his head. "Even if that's true, what does it matter?"

"It means this scientist can help the President get off the drug safely. We strongly suspect the President recently tried to do that, which is why he was ill. Isn't that correct?"

Although Conners was very interested, he refused to admit anything.

"Don't you see? Now the President can be free of that damn stuff safely under the care of the doctor who invented it."

Now very curious, Conners said, "Go on."

"Do you think he'd be interested in getting off the Wake Formula safely?"

"What do you want from him? Is this about money? I won't let you blackmail the President of the United States."

"This isn't extortion. I already told you, we want to stop Dr. Lin. That's it. We know the President is being coerced by Dr. Lin, and we want to help end that. We also want to stop Dr. Lin from obtaining more power through leadership of the United Nations. All he wants is power. He's evil. Do you understand now?"

Conners shook his head. "I don't know. How can I trust you?"

The intruder looked at him closely. "Listen, Conners. We've been risking our lives to bring an end to Dr. Lin for some time. He's very dangerous, and we need the President's help to finish this. Once Dr. Lin is empowered as the UN's Secretary-General, he'll be harder to stop than ever, if it can be done at all. You know that. We have to act decisively right now. Time is of the essence."

Conners took a deep breath. "Just hypothetically, if the President agreed to help you, what would you need him to do?"

"We need him to help us destroy the underground laboratory where Dr. Lin makes the drug. We can show you where it is and give you other details about it."

Conners grinned. "We know where it is. We aren't complete fools. We checked into a few things ourselves, but if we destroy the lab, then the President...." He stopped before completing the thought.

"Then the President can't get his damned drug. We know. We understand. That's why he did an about-face on his climate change policy, right?'

"He didn't capitulate. Hell, he was so sick, he couldn't speak. I made that up to save him from himself. I had to get more Wake Formula from Dr. Lin any way I could. What I did would be called treason by some."

The intruder smiled under his mask. "Thank you for that confession. You have as much at stake as we do. That actually makes me feel a lot better about the President. I thought he sold out his principles to save his own ass."

"No, that was me. He almost fired me for it. The President was furious after he came around. I lied and put him in a very difficult situation. It's hard to believe I still have a job."

The intruder leaned forward. "If it makes you feel any better, you probably saved his life."

Conners almost smiled. "What do you mean?"

"Anyone who stops taking the drug for any reason dies. That's why the doctor who developed it is working on a way to prevent the dangerous withdrawal symptoms. He never tested it on human beings, and he was very upset that Dr. Lin did it once he stole it."

Conners' expression changed to understanding. "OK. I'm beginning to believe you." He wiggled his cuffed hands. "Let me go, and we can talk some more."

After a moment's hesitation, the intruder nodded. "OK, but don't cry out for help or try to run. If you do, you'll regret it. Do you understand?"

"Just get these cuffs off me."

The intruder cautiously removed them.

Conners' stood and wiggled his hands to get blood flowing again. "So now what?"

"Now we go somewhere. I have something to show you."

Conners shook his head. "No way."

"Don't freak out. I'm not kidnapping you. I need you to be totally convinced about what I'm saying and what we plan to do. Telling you about us is one thing. Seeing what the doctor's doing is another. You'll be safe. No harm will come to you. If I wanted to harm you, I could have done it by now."

"Where are you taking me?"

"You'll see. It's not far. I'll get you back here tonight. If you don't believe me after this little trip, then I guess you're done. You can go your way, and we'll go ours. Either way, I won't harm you. The scare tactics are over. We only needed them to get your undivided attention.

The only thing I ask is that we keep your head covered on the way, so we don't reveal our location before you and the President decide what to do."

They drove for an hour and a half, making frequent turns to keep Conners unaware of their location. Finally, they arrived at the lab only a few miles from Conners' house. Still blindfolded, he was led into the old NIH building.

"You can remove the blindfold now," Titus said.

When Conners did, he was amazed to find himself in a hospital ward. Several beds held patients with IVs. Each had a thin cover over the face to conceal his or her identify. The people waiting to talk to him wore nylon stockings over their faces.

Titus saw fear and apprehension in Conners' eyes. He looked almost as frightened as when he'd been ambushed.

"We won't hurt you," Titus said. "We just need you to see what this is all about."

Conners would have bolted for the door had Titus not been in the way. The largest of the others stepped forward.

"I'm the doctor here," Dr. Burrus said behind his covered face.

"What is all this? Are you the scientist who supposedly developed the Wake Formula, or are you torturing these people?"

Frederick chuckled and shrugged. "I'm not torturing them. I'm trying to save them."

"So you did develop the Wake Formula?"

"I did." He waved his hand around the room. "All of this is a medical clinic to care for the people Dr. Lin supplied with that formula and then stopped for one reason or another. Our group found them this way on Dr. Lin's so-called medical supply ship and rescued them from sure death."

"What's wrong with them?" He felt he could guess the answer.

"They're in various stages of coma, although a few are starting to come out of it with our help."

He looked at the scene in disbelief.

"This is what would have happened to the President had you not gotten him more of the Wake Formula in time. You probably saved his life."

Conners grinned and nodded. "Who, exactly, are these people? Why are their faces covered?"

"They're people who have much in common with the President. They're successful people who decided to take a shortcut to be even more successful. We won't reveal their names, because, like the President, we must assume they don't want the world to know what they did."

"Why aren't they in a regular hospital? They look pretty sick to me."

"Because a hospital can't help them. Did the President's doctors or hospitals help him? Other doctors don't have a clue. They have no treatment for this. They don't even have an accurate diagnosis."

"You're right."

"I have a doctorate in neurochemistry and am also a medical doctor. I developed the Wake Formula. I can take better care of these people than anyone in the world."

Conners nodded.

"Think about it," Titus said. "Who can we trust? Dr. Lin's tentacles are everywhere. Who knows how deep they are in the medical community?"

Conners looked puzzled. "Then why did you trust me enough to bring me here?"

"Because we overheard your conversation with Dr. Lin at his banquet," Titus said.

"What? How? Was I bugged?"

Titus smiled. "No. *He* was bugged."

Conners' eyebrows shot up. "I'm impressed. That couldn't have been easy with all of his security. Behind his façade of power, that guy's totally paranoid."

"We're a small group, but we're extremely capable."

"What, specifically, did you hear?"

"We heard enough to know that you wanted nothing to do with the Wake Formula. We also know you have concerns, like we do, about Dr. Lin's growing influence and power."

He nodded. "You're right about both."

"How did the President get involved?" Rafael asked.

"He said he was approached by Dr. Lin at a political fund-raiser when he was a rising young Senator. He had big dreams and was full of ambition. He knew Dr. Lin was extremely successful, so he decided to try the Wake Formula. He said he thought it was just another one of those holistic medicines that don't do anything, but he didn't see any harm in trying. There was nothing illegal about it."

"I see," Rafael replied. "Go on."

"The drug worked better than he ever hoped. With the extra time, he had a huge competitive advantage. Over a period of time, he started using it more and more often."

"So it started off innocently enough, but now he can't get off the damn stuff, right?" Frederick asked.

"Exactly."

Frederick nodded.

Conners stared at him. "Are you really the scientist who developed the Wake Formula?"

"As I said, I'm afraid so."

"For heaven's sake, why?"

He sighed. "It's a long story. Basically, I wanted to develop a new sleep medication by researching how people stay awake."

Conners' head tipped to one side. "What? That sounds weird. In fact, it's so weird, I believe you."

"You should. It's the truth."

Conners rubbed his chin thoughtfully. "So you really think you can help the President get off this drug?"

"Yes, I believe so. I've developed a detox protocol using a variant of the Wake Formula that seems to be working. It looks promising."

Conners waved his hand around the room. "I don't see any of them looking very good."

"These people are slowly improving, I assure you. Their early movements and EEGs prove it. In the meantime, we have enough Wake Formula to stabilize the President until I can optimize the detox protocols."

"What does optimizing it mean?"

"I've developed a long-acting form of the Wake Formula that I call Wake Formula LA. I'm testing various doses and formulations to get the best combination."

"What's involved in making your new version?"

Frederick tried to think of the best way to explain it. "I took a few key components of the original drug and added chemical groups, such as phosphate polymers, to make the components inert until enzymes in the blood slowly cleave off those added chemical groups to reactivate them. Many slow-release medications work that way. It's not new science. Pinpointing the precise components to add to the chemical group and precisely which chemical groups to add is the challenge."

Conners shook his head. "I'm sorry I asked."

Frederick grinned under his mask.

"You think this will work? You're sure you have enough of the regular formula to give the President until you perfect your new formula?"

"Yes. We have enough to supply him for years."

"Do you have it here?"

"We do."

"Show me."

Frederick led him down the hall and showed him their large stores of the Wake Formula.

"That looks like it, all right," Conners said with a smile. "Where'd you get it? Are you making it here?"

"No. That's impossible. It takes a much-bigger operation than we have, but I can modify it, and we have plenty."

"We stole it from Dr. Lin's lab," Titus added.

"Really?" A hint of glee came to Conners' voice. "That's amazing. You stole it from Dr. Lin?"

"We did."

"Wow. For your information, we've had a cover team of scientists trying to duplicate the formula for a while."

"How'd that go?"

"Not well."

"I'm not surprised," Frederick said. "There are too many naturally occurring and complex biological compounds in it. They'd have to obtain them directly from brain tissue, like I originally did—a *lot* of brain tissue. It took me years."

Conners nodded. "I believe you. In fact, I'm impressed. If you're being straight with me, I greatly admire what you're trying to do."

"Thank you," Frederick replied. "Yes, we're being totally straight with you. Are we on the same team?"

"We're getting there."

"Tell you what. I'll show that I trust you." He reached up to remove his nylon hood.

Conners turned away and raised a hand to stop him. "Wait! I don't want to know who you are, at least not yet. Like you said, it's too dangerous. If I don't know who you are, no one can get it out of me. The less I know about the details, the better."

He looked at Titus, whom he assumed was the leader. "I want to help. Where do we go from her? What's the plan?"

Titus explained, with Seth and Rafael adding bits and pieces.

"I know the plan had a lot of moving parts," Titus said at the end, "but if everyone does his job, I think, with the President's help, this will work."

Conners sighed. "OK. I've seen worse plans, but I can't think of any alternative."

"I've done this kind of thing before with Special Forces. I can pull it off with the right team in place."

Conners said, "I trust you, but not enough to take you to the President."

"I don't want to see him," Titus said quickly. "We want you to have a private conversation with him and tell him everything you've seen and heard. Don't tell anyone else. That's why we brought you here, to be our link to the President."

After a moment, Conners nodded. "OK. I'm in."

Titus handed him a folder. "If the President agrees to help us, give him this list of requests. Let me know if he's in or out ASAP."

Seth gave Conners several untraceable burner phones. "Use only one of these to contact us. Confide and trust no one except the President. Stopping Dr. Lin won't be easy. If you can't convince the President to help us, we don't know what we'll do, but you won't hear from us again."

"Don't worry. He'll come onboard. I won't leave the Oval Office until he does. He'll probably be more excited about this than I am."

"Thank you," Rafael said.

"You think your plan will work and keep this from blowing up in the President's face?"

"I hope so," Titus said. "It's not just his life at risk. All our lives depend on it."

"Take some Wake Formula with you," Rafael added, "so he won't be dependent on Dr. Lin. Consider it a gesture of our good faith."

"OK. What about all these sick people whose identity you're hiding from me?"

"That's our problem," Frederick said. "I promise we'll take good care of them."

"You really think you can get the President off that damn drug safely?"

"I do. I'm very close to perfecting the detox protocol. It should be ready soon, and we'll get him on it by the time he needs it. Until then, we'll supply him with Wake Formula."

"We may look like outlaws," Titus added, "but I assure you, we're patriots. We just need the President's help to complete our work. Dr. Lin is a malicious, formidable enemy."

Two days later, Conners called on a burner phone. "He's in. It wasn't easy, believe me. He was initially all over the place about it, but he finally saw the light."

"So he'll cooperate with everything, including the clean-up?"

"Oh, he insisted on that part. He's well aware that what you plan is highly illegal, but it's also the right thing to do. It's the only way to stop Dr. Lin. The President justifies it by labeling the operation a covert antiterrorism action that can be resolved with only limited military force, which I believe it is."

"Thank you, Conners, very much."

"But there are some stipulations."

"What stipulations?"

"First, he won't directly supply ground support on U.S. soil. Cover operations there are up to you. If we can help make certain people available who otherwise wouldn't be, we will. Just give us the names. We won't order anyone to help you."

"Understood."

"Second, casualties should be kept to a minimum and must be absolutely necessary."

"That won't be easy. Dr. Lin's people are armed and dangerous, but we'll do our best."

"Finally, and most importantly, this project is Top Secret. No one is to know about it other than those involved—ever. Is that understood?"

"We understand."

"The President wants a store of Wake Formula now in case we don't see you again."

"You got it."

"And he wants your doctor to personally detox him off the drug when this is over."

"Of course."

After a moment, Conners said, "That's it."

"OK. Then it's a go?" Titus wanted to be absolutely certain.

"It's a go. We have some ideas on what to do about the many people who'll be affected by the loss of the drug. We'll discuss those ideas after we see how things go. As you said before, there are many moving parts to your plan, and you don't have much time."

CHAPTER 43

Conners watched President O'Malley pace the Oval Office, knowing he was trying to muster the nerve to make the phone call. He called the leaders of Russia, China, and many other great nations, but none of them made him as nervous as the present call.

He glanced at Conners, who nodded in encouragement.

Finally, he lifted the receiver of the secure phone and had the call put through. After several rings, it was answered.

"Dr. Lin, this is President O'Malley. I hope I'm not disturbing you."

Dr. Lin was bathing in one of his Jacuzzis with five concubines when the call came through and sat up straighter when he heard it was the President.

His concubines stirred with excitement when Dr. Lin casually said, "Hello, President O'Malley. Yes, I was working, but I suppose I can give you a few minutes of my time. After all, time isn't usually a problem for me."

Fighting the urge to vomit, the President said, "Thank you so much."

Dr. Lin smiled and winked at one of the thrilled concubines. "How can I help the President of the United States today?"

President O'Malley despised the man's mocking tone and forced down his Irish temper. "I wanted to call you personally to let you know I realize that we need to work together on your climate agenda.

The world has clearly voiced its opinion, and it backs your ideas more than mine."

Dr. Lin smiled. "I'm happy to hear you say that to me personally."

"Listen, Dr. Lin. I'm serious about working together with you on this. Since I'm in, I've decided to go all out."

Dr. Lin asked, "What, exactly, does that mean?"

"I've decided to arrange a week-long emergency summit on global warming here at the White House, and I want you to be here."

Dr. Lin squinted in disbelief. "That's quite a turnaround, but I don't know. I really don't have time to come to the White House right now."

The excited women in the Jacuzzi waved their hands, gesturing he should go.

Dr. Lin smiled at them but remained uncommitted. In a nonchalant voice, he said, "I have a very busy schedule. I'll have to think about it."

"It's important that you be there, Dr. Lin. The meeting will be held in your honor, and I hope you'll not only agree to attend the summit but also give the keynote address. I plan to have you lead several committee meetings, if you desire. I'll be there, too, but you'll be the star of the show."

Dr. Lin said nothing.

"I assume you want to maintain your leadership in this area, correct? A conference like this, at the White House with the President of the United States, would be wonderful publicity for both of us. There's nothing like the White House to get the world's attention."

Dr. Lin hesitated. He had mixed emotions. His well-masked but constant paranoia made him prefer to do important things on his own turf, but the White House was special. "I'll consider it. It's an interesting offer."

Conners passed a note to the President that read, *Sweeten the deal now.*

The President nodded. "After the meetings, you and I can make a joint press conference. I'll say you were right all along, and that more data presented at the conference convinced me to support your idea fully on the imminent and severe danger of global warming."

"Hmmm. That sounds compelling."

Conners made encouraging gestures with his hands.

"I'll give you my personal endorsement as Secretary-General of the United Nations. I'll also endorse the UN to have greater authority to place and enforce international transactions and propose significant financial penalties on any country that doesn't comply with the UN's important and internationally binding laws and regulations. We'll make sure the UN has a military that supersedes that of any individual nation."

Dr. Lin's heart raced with excitement. He waved the women to leave, as he no longer felt interested in them. "This is a very different tone, President O'Malley. Are you sure about this?"

"Quite sure. I need your help, and I believe you could use mine as well. It's a win-win."

Dr. Lin had to control his enthusiasm. "How then can I turn down such an honor? I'm happy you see things my way, Mr. President. Yes, I'll take very good care of your medical needs now and in the future."

"Thank you, Dr. Lin. My people will contact yours soon about the details." He hung up.

Conners, smiling broadly, patted the President's back. "You did it. He went for it! Thank you, Mr. President. That couldn't have been easy for you. I'll let our secret group know they have a green light to proceed as planned."

The President gave him a stern look. "This better work, Conners. That conversation almost made me sick to my stomach. This entire operation is being run by people I don't even know. I hope to God this doesn't blow up in my face. If it does, I won't just be removed from office. I could land in jail."

Dr. Lin's helicopter landed on the White House lawn on schedule. Reporters and camera crews from around the world were there to capture the historic moment. They weren't disappointed, as President O'Malley greeted Dr. Lin with all the pomp and ceremony of a visiting foreign leader.

As they shook hands, Dr. Lin smiled at the President. He was in no hurry and wanted as much media coverage of them together as possible. "I'm happy to see you looking so healthy, Mr. President."

President O'Malley smiled back. "I do feel better. Thank you." Slowly, he guided his guest through the special White House entrance.

There Dr. Lin, Fa Shen, and the rest of Dr. Lin's limited staff wee instructed to follow the mandatory security procedure. Dr. Lin's briefcase and luggage were X-rayed and thoroughly searched. The usual inspectors, however, were reassigned, replaced by Charles and Seth.

When Charles examined the contents of Dr. Lin's luggage, he immediately recognized the special vials of the Wake Formula. He nodded to Seth, who respectfully, but slowly, patted down Dr. Lin and his associates. As he did, Charles replaced the vials with identical-looking dummies. Dr. Burris neutralized several vital components of the Wake Formula in the dummies, but otherwise, they were identical.

When Dr. Lin settled into his room, he carefully examined the contents of his luggage and found everything in order. There was nothing to concern him. He also had his staff methodically examine his clothing, luggage, and the room for listening devices or anything suspicious. They found none.

After breakfast meetings, the conference began promptly at noon the following day. Climate specialists, members of the Red Cross, congressmen, UN representatives, and several celebrities were there. Numerous scientific meetings were held to discuss the latest findings on climate change. The theme for most speakers was the imminent crisis of global warming, the need for more legislative restrictions on fossil fuel use, carbon footprint restrictions, enforcement of international climate legislation, and more money for research and enforcement of climate regulations.

Other than the Hollywood celebrities who attended, Dr. Lin was the person everyone wanted to meet, greet, and take selfies with. Some of the celebrities were his clients, but even ones who weren't wanted a minute of his time. In his element, he enjoyed each moment. A few scientists who didn't reiterate that the sky was falling like all the rest were scheduled to speak later in the day.

Dr. Marshall presented satellite images demonstrating that overall temperatures on Earth had been more or less stagnant for many years.

Nobel Laureate Dr. James Beck gave a sophisticated talk on climate cycles. His data emphasized alternating solar warming and cooling trends and predicted that a solar minimum may be on its way, which could lead to global cooling.

"Compared to the influence of the sun," he stated, "all other influences on climate changes are minuscule."

Dr. Kimberly Taylor bravely commented on how climate data had been inconsistently and often unscientifically gathered. She described how the data was often disproportionately collected in micro-high-temperature areas, like large cities and near high-volume traffic. Additionally, climate data had been collected in non-standardized ways around the world, creating questions of accuracy and reliability. Many in the audience were furious, and a bit embarrassed, as she showed how vastly different the data was collected in the U.S., Russia, Africa, Western Europe, the Middle East, and China. Dr. Taylor agitated her hostile audience even more when she flatly sated, "No wonder we've had decades of failed predictions," and called the overall effort of climatologists "embarrassingly poor science compared to other fields of science."

She ended her presentation by describing how she'd been abused verbally and in writing by many of her peers, professional journals, and the mainstream media for challenging the group think. She labeled it as overt prejudice for merely trying to be scientifically honest, comprehensive, and not compromising to peer pressure. She fought back tears when she described how the abuse overflowed onto her children and husband.

In the end, Dr. Taylor called for greater ethical and legal protection for scientific free speech and against future politically motivated abuse.

Outraged that such people were invited to the conference, Dr. Lin pulled the President aside when he could and said softly, "I must speak with you."

The President smiled. "Of course. What's on your mind, Dr. Lin?"

"Not here, please. In private."

He agreed and directed Dr. Lin aside, away from anyone else.

"Why'd you invite scientists to this conference who oppose my climate agenda?" Dr. Lin demanded. "Are you with me or not?"

The President smiled warmly and patted Dr. Lin's shoulder like an old friend. "Don't worry, Dao. It's just practical politics. We need to at least look like we're examining climate change from every perspective. The list of speakers is public knowledge. Showing that we had opposing views presented at the same conference is the best way to silence our critics, don't you think?"

Dr. Lin grimaced. "No, I don't. What if they actually raise doubts among some of the other scientists?"

President O'Malley grinned reassuringly. "Do you really think the scientists who have made their careers pushing the climate-change agenda will alter their opinions now and throw away everything they gained? I don't think so. Like them, we'll simply ignore the opposing view or say their data was paid for by big oil and coal companies. The media will eat it up."

Dr. Lin finally smiled. "Perhaps you're savvier than I gave you credit for, Mr. President."

He smiled again. "I hope to prove that to you, Dr. Lin. I really do."

Dr. Lin coughed to clear his throat. "You'd better be right."

An aide interrupted them to say, "Dr. Lin, you're on in twenty minutes."

When Dr. Lin took the stage, he not only described his anguish over the climate crisis but pushed for greater involvement of the United Nations to save the planet. Without notes or slides, his talk lasted an hour and a half. He closed by reiterating, "One world authority, with a powerful and independent military to enforce international regulations and taxation, is the only way to ensure peace between the self-serving aims of individual nations. A more-powerful United Nations could quickly position itself to fulfill such a role for the good of people around the world."

CHAPTER 44

At three o'clock AM, a covert attack began on Dr. Lin's Texas subterranean Wake Formula production and research facility. All participants were either current or retired Special Forces troops. All fully understood their mission was not only dangerous but unauthorized. If caught, they could be sent to federal prison for the rest of their lives.

They also all understood that the mission was vital to the safety and sovereignty of the United States at the highest levels of government. All were hand-picked by FBI Special Agent Titus Warren, who knew each person's strengths and weaknesses.

As expected, surveillance revealed the facility was even more heavily guarded than the previous time Titus was there. He hoped his intimate knowledge of the layout would make up for the added security.

He divided his team into two group. He commanded Alpha team, and his old friend, Captain Edward Prescott Parker, commanded Bravo.

The assault began when Alpha team blocked all incoming and outgoing communications to the facility. Moments later, Bravo team stealthily approached the slaughterhouse, which sat directly above the hidden underground laboratory. Using tranquilizing rounds, they took down the three guards outside the slaughterhouse and another two inside.

"Brave team in place," Captain Parker said into his mic. "All guards down."

"How many?" Titus asked.

"Five prisoners in custody and sleeping soundly."

Titus looked at his Gamin combat watch. "Are you ready to drop the packages?"

"That's a go. What's your status?"

"Alpha team ready. Proceed with the drop."

Brave team opened the six hatches that led to chutes used to drop cow brains into the cold processing area. A powerful incendiary explosive bomb was dropped down each chute. The team quickly departed without incident. When they were safely away, Captain Parker set off the explosives with a remote detonator.

After six loud explosions, the facility began burning. Captain Parker and his team saw flames rising from the chutes in a magnificent display of light and color.

Inside the facility, alarms screamed, and water sprinklers went off. The drenched, late-shift personal scrambled to get out of the chaotic building to safety, but confusion was everywhere.

Captain Zheng, the head of night security, momentarily stunned by the blasts, barked orders into his coms headset. He was a short, stocky, ex-Marine with a fiery temper.

"Move the supply of Wake Formula from storage to the research area immediately! Except for those on the fire team, all guards stay at their posts. Don't let any personnel leave the ground without my personal approval. Stay on high alert with weapons ready. Search for intruders. Assume we're under attack until we know otherwise. Fire team to the production area!"

Responses quickly came from all guards.

"Has anyone seen anything suspicious?"

"No," the guards reported one after the other.

After waiting for what felt like forever, but was actually only eleven minutes, Alpha team raced down the road toward the compound in two fire trucks with sirens blaring. A third truck, carrying Bravo team, would back them up later.

Alpha team slowed to a stop at the first guardhouse, which was manned by armed guards instead of just an electronic gate with a pass code. A guard raised his hands to stop them, while two others remained on high alert in the guardhouse, watching with their automatic weapons ready.

"We need to get through!" Titus shouted over the sirens.

The guard hesitated.

"There's a fire in your facility! Don't you have a damn clue? We've been called to put it out. Now!"

The guard checked the trucks, then nodded. "Go ahead."

As Titus drove toward the second security station, he reported in. "Bravo team, we're through the first guard gate and moving toward the next."

"Maybe your harebrained scheme will work after all," Parker said.

"It better. As they say, all plans go great until they don't. Stay ready. Follow behind in twenty minutes unless you receive other instructions."

"Copy that."

As expected at the second security point, an armed guard came out to meet the fire trucks. He stood in front of the first one, motioning it to stop. Other guards watched from inside the guardhouse.

Titus, leaning out the window, pointed ahead. "We got a call about a serious fire in your facility. We need to get in."

"I know about it, but no one goes into the facility without permission."

"Then get it!" Titus shouted. "You've got a fire! The longer we sit here, the worse it gets. People could be hurt of killed, for Christ's sake."

The man stared at him without expression, then he said, "Wait here. I'll call my boss. Until I get permission, no one gets by this gate under any circumstances. Sorry. Those are my orders."

Titus nodded.

The guard returning to the guardhouse, placed a call. A few moments later, he came out again shaking his head. "I'm sorry, but permission to go into the facility is denied. You need to leave immediately."

"Are you kidding me? Why?"

"Apparently, outside communications are down, and we don't know why. Captain Zheng said we'll take care of the fire ourselves. You need to leave."

"That's not acceptable. By Texas law, we're obligated to enter any premises where a fire may endanger people or cause property damage. If we have to, we'll call the police. Do you understand?"

The guard didn't reply.

"What is this place, anyway? What's with all the guards and attitude?" He thought it was a natural thing to say, but he regretted it as soon as he asked.

The guard gripped his weapon tighter. "That's none of your business. Just leave before we make you. Those are my orders. We'll take care of the fire ourselves."

Titus struck his fist against the truck door. "We can't do that! It's the law. Lives could be in danger. We're going to put out that fire."

"I can't let you do it."

"Let me speak directly to your Captain Zheng or Zasin or Zin or whatever the hell his name is. Your head of security can't overrule state law. You can get in serious trouble if anyone is hurt, and your insurance company may not pay for damages when I report that your refused us entry to stop the fire. What's your name? You could face legal charges and be sued. Do you realize that? Do you want to face responsibility for this fiasco? Let me hear it from your captain myself. We're wasting valuable time."

After a moment's hesitation, the man said, "OK. Come this way. Not letting you through ain't my decision. I'm just obeying orders."

Titus and another fireman got out of the cab and followed the guard. The guard looked at the extra man and raised a hand, then he pointed at Titus. "Just you. You're in charge, right?"

Titus nodded. "I'm the chief." He signaled his partner to return to the truck.

The ex-Delta did so reluctantly.

The guard took Titus into the guardhouse, where Titus saw two more armed men. One kept a wary eye on Titus, the other watched the fire trucks.

Titus was practically unarmed and outnumbered by three armed men in bulletproof vests. He also knew the head of security would order him to leave once he was asked. Titus' only option was to act quickly.

Just as the guard shouldered his MP5 and picked up the receiver for the internal landline, Titus gave him a lethal blow to the temple. The man crumbled to the floor.

The guard watching Titus rushed him. Titus sidestepped and slammed an elbow into the man's face. He went down, dazed.

The third guard, who'd been watching the fire trucks, frantically raised his Heckler and Koch MP5 and fired.

Fortunately for Titus, the man rushed his shot, and his weapon was set for single fire, not auto. The bullet missed Titus' head, and he dived to the ground. Before the man could adjust aim for another shot, Titus pulled his Ruger from an ankle holster and shot twice at the man's head.

The first only clipped his ear, but the second shot struck the man's forehead. He was dead before he hit the floor.

Titus' senses were on high alert. On his knees, he scanned for the other guards. When the second man recovered enough to raise his MP5, Titus shot him twice in the head.

He looked at the carnage. No one moved, and he momentarily relaxed. Two men burst through the door with weapons drawn.

Titus aimed and prepared to fire when the men raised their hands.

"Don't shoot!" they shouted.

He lowered his weapon in relief. They were his own men. Quickly checking the guards, they saw all were dead. Steven Holloway offered a hand to help Titus to his feet.

"Getting slow there, Warren. You could've taken out three guards twice as fast when you were still in Delta."

Titus grinned and mentally agreed. "Whatever. You two sure took your time getting here. You didn't show your faces until all the work was done. That one over there nearly put a bullet in my head."

"Sorry we missed the fun. We knew we were being watched. After the shooting started, the guard's face disappeared from the window, so we decided we didn't want to sit around being bored any longer. Besides, we figured you were getting your ass kicked."

Titus nodded. "Now that you're finally here, let's destroy all the communication equipment in here in case someone comes by after we leave. Do you think the men in the first guardhouse heard anything?"

Holloway, glancing at the other guardhouse, saw no movement. "I don't think so. The sirens probably covered the noise here. We thought you might like a little background noise, so we kept them on nice and loud."

"Good." He turned toward Murphy. "You stay here and make sure no one other than Bravo team follows our asses into that tunnel."

Murphy nodded.

Once back in the truck, Titus contacted Bravo team. "We secured the second guardhouse and are about to enter the facility. The first guard post let us through, but it's still manned. Secure them when you arrive. Join us down the tunnel."

"Ten-four."

Titus and the others drove the fire trucks through the long tunnel and up to the loading dock.

Three guards were on the dock. One approached the fire trucks, his rifle ready.

"What the hell are you doing here? Who gave you permission to come through that tunnel?" he demanded.

"Are you blind or stupid?" Titus fired back. "We're firemen. We're here to put out your damn fire. We got permission from Captain Zhang, and the guardhouses let us through."

"Captain Zhang? Are you sure? Why wasn't I notified?"

"Hell if I know. Maybe he's a little busy right now. Take it up with him if you have a beef about letting us do our jobs."

The guard wasn't about to question Captain Zhang's orders, and Titus knew it. The man's tension visibly softened, and he waved a hand. "OK. Come with me. We've got a hell of a fire in here, but I have to come with you. No visitors are ever left alone on this property no matter who they are. Those orders aren't negotiable."

"Understood. Show us the way." Titus turned to his men. "Get the hoses and equipment. Hurry. We've had too many delays already."

Titus started into the building with the guard. He was careful not to get too far ahead of his men, who dragged heavy hoses and other equipment.

His well-trained men, prepped for that moment, casually but carefully noted the positions of the armed guards. Several men walked toward them, some were on a catwalk overhead, and one was with the group. Two were left in the loading area.

The ones overhead worried them the most. They had the high ground, and it wouldn't be an easy shot to take them out. Subtly and efficiently, Alpha team spread out in a pattern for optimal attack and defense.

They were forty yards inside the building when three men came up to Titus. The two younger men raised their weapons. The third, in his fifties, appeared to be in charge.

He held up a hand. "Stop. What are you doing in here?"

"Who the hell do you think we are? We're firemen," Titus said, irritated. "We're here to put out your fire, for heaven's sake. Why do we keep getting stopped for doing our job? What's wrong with you people?"

"How'd you get past the guards?"

"They let us through. We're here to put out the fire."

The older man's eyes narrowed. "The guard let you in without my permission? They had clear orders not to let anyone in unless I authorized it."

"So you must be Captain Zhang," Titus said, offering his hand, but Zhang didn't take it. "Yeah, the guard told us Captain Zhang denied entry without his permission, but I told him we have to put out any large fires where people could be in danger or there might be significant property damage. That's state law. He let us through. He didn't have a choice. The law is the law."

"I'm the law here. You have to go."

"I'm afraid state law surpasses any local authority you think you have."

"We have a fire, but we also have a possible security threat. For that reason, I forbid you to come any farther. You must leave now."

"We can't do that. Texas law says...."

Before he finished, Captain Zhang drew his sidearm and pointed it at Titus' chest. The other men aimed at Titus' men.

"These guns say you leave now," Zhang said.

Titus raised his hands in surrender. "Hey, calm down. Are you really threatening to shoot firemen sent here to help? I see flames burning back there."

"We'll shoot anyone who refuses to leave. You're trespassers, and you've been warned. Now go."

"OK, OK. Watch where you point those guns. We'll go."

Captain Zhang lowered his weapon.

"You'll be hearing from the fire department and the police."

"You'll hear from our guns if you don't leave right now."

Titus waved his men to pull back. Acting surprised, they moved back slowly.

Titus watched the situation carefully. As soon as the other two guards lowered their weapons, he said, "Be careful with that."

His men, hearing the signal, went into action.

CHAPTER 45

The two men closest to Titus immediately turned on their hoses and fired a powerful stream of water at Captain Zhang and the two guards with him. All three men flew violently backward across the room, striking a wall. One man on Alpha team put his rifle barrel against the head of the guard who was escorting them inside. Two other men ran back and captured the guards on the loading dock before they knew what was going on. Titus' men didn't want to worry about an attack from the rear. They had enough to worry about in front.

Shots poured down from the overhead guards once they realized what happened. Fortunately, they were confused and hesitated long enough for the Special Forces team to take cover.

When the first opportunity came, Titus' men sent heavy streams of water at the catwalk, wreaking havoc on the shooters and forcing them back.

Titus, crouching under cover, pulled the gun from his ankle holster and scanned the area, firing at any target he could see.

Soon, armed guards from deeper inside the facility ran into the chaos and joined the fight. The ones on the catwalk regrouped and resumed firing. Titus saw one of his men on the far side of the large room go down.

Alpha team pulled out the automatic rifles they concealed in their equipment and returned fire. They didn't have the strategic advantage, but each was an expert marksman.

Captain Zhang was knocked out when he struck the wall. Slowly regaining consciousness knelt, wobbling back and forth, unable to remember what happened. As his mind cleared, he felt severe pain in one arm and realized it was broken. His head, back, and shoulder hurt from hitting the wall.

Zhang looked around and saw the firefight raging. Everything came into focus, and he felt enraged. He quickly crawled a few feet to snatch a semiautomatic handgun with his good hand. Although guns were blazing, no one seemed to notice him.

When Zhang spotted Titus, his adrenalin surged, and his hatred flared to a frenzy at the man who assaulted his facility. Crazy with rage, he stood and ran right at Titus, firing like a madman.

Suddenly, bullets slammed all around Titus. Not knowing where they came from, he ducked behind a freight container for cover. A second later, he readied his weapon and ducked around the container with his head at the floor. Zhang charged at his position, firing rapidly and nearly upon him. Titus aimed and fired three times.

Zhang went down ten feet away, blood running from his head and chest. He was dead.

Titus looked around for other shooters without seeing any. He felt something sticky and saw crimson staining the front of his right pants leg. In the heat of the moment, he didn't realize Zhang hit him. Sharp pain lanced up his thigh. Before he could react, a new round of bullets struck the wall behind him. Titus backed farther into cover only to find himself in someone else's sights.

Sergeant Holloway, who had more combat experience than any of the others, saw Titus was in trouble. He looked for the shooter, found him, aimed, and fired.

The first shot grazed the man's arm, but the second one took him out.

Titus looked up at Holloway and nodded his thanks. Holloway replied with a thumbs-up.

Once out of immediate danger, Titus took a moment to put pressure on his thigh wound. The remaining shooters on the catwalk still had an advantage, but two of Titus' men managed to slip directly under them and shot up at their feet. Immediately, screams of pain sounded, and blood poured from the boots of several shooters. Those not hit scrambled back for safety.

Titus didn't know the extent of his wound, but at least no artery was hit, because the blood flow would have been spurting a lot harder. He pulled a knife from an ankle holster and cut off a piece of his pants leg from his uninjured leg to tie a temporary tourniquet about the wound.

Holloway ran over to Titus. "Are you all right, Sir?"

"I'm fine thanks to you. We need to push harder and end this as quickly as possible."

"True, that. You stay put. We'll take care of it."

Titus nodded, although he had no intention of watching from the sideline.

When Holloway saw an opportunity, he reloaded and ran for a better firing angle. Titus' leg hurt like hell, but he pulled himself to his feet and cautiously moved toward the sound of the greatest gunfire. Normally, he moved quickly in a fight, but the best he could do was inch forward and watch for opportunities to help his men.

To his dismay, Alpha team became steadily outnumbered, as more reinforcements arrived from deeper inside the building. Each side worked at gaining a tactical advantage over the other without any progress.

Titus knew they needed numbers. "Bravo," he said into his mic, "this is Warren. What's your status?"

"Pulling through the second gate now," Captain Parker replied. "What's your status?"

Bullets peppered the floor and walls around Titus' position. "We penetrated the facility and initiated the assault, but we're outnumbered and facing heavy resistance. We need backup stat."

"Roger that. Be there in ten."

Not wanting his men to take unnecessary risks, Titus switched to Alpha team. "Bravo team is on their way. Hold defensive positions."

Bravo team, arriving a few minutes later, charged into the fight.

Dr. Lin's guards were fierce fighters, but they were no match for the combined Special Forces teams once they coordinated their assault. The enemy also had a raging fire at their backs to contend with.

When the remaining guards realized Captain Zhang was dead, and the fire behind them was coming closer. They threw down their weapons, surrendering one at a time. Eventually, all were taken down or surrendered.

Titus wasn't happy that he lost two men, while three others sustained significant injuries. More had minor wounds. He comforted himself by understanding the significance of their mission and that it might have been a lot worse.

An elite medical team, assembled by Conners, was quickly called in, arriving in black, unmarked helicopters. The medics treated the wounded on both sides. Animal transport cages were brought in to remove the surviving research animals. Several other unidentifiable helicopters soon followed to evacuate the prisoners. Titus had no idea where they were being taken and didn't want to know.

Conners and the President came through, Titus reflected, as a medic tended his wounded thigh. The fire smoldered, but it was finally contained.

Under his orders, the men searched the ravaged facility and removed all the Wake Formula and computers they could find. When they finished, Titus called Captain Parker to him.

"Has everything of importance been removed?" Titus asked.

"Yes, Sir."

"Good."

Parker glanced at Titus' wound. "Are you OK?"

He looked down at his bandaged leg and said, "It's not bad. I'll be all right." After a moment, he said, "It's time to remove this place off the face of the Earth. I'm sick of it."

Captain Parker nodded.

"Place the Semtex along the support structures of the facility and the entry tunnel." He pointed at a pair of crutches nearby. "Hand me those, if you don't mind. I'll help select the placements."

When all was ready, and everyone was a safe distance away, Titus pressed the detonator.

"Beautiful," Captain Parker said.

Titus smiled. "Absolutely."

Congratulatory hugs and high-fives spread among the men.

Before they left, Titus thanked each man, making certain the wounded received the best care.

Thanks to Conners, an article ran in nearby newspapers the following day, explaining a pharmaceutical laboratory experienced an accidental explosion and had unfortunately been completely destroyed. People were killed or injured. Helicopters came in to remove injured personnel to regional hospitals.

The report added that the chemical residue from the explosion was highly toxic, so no one except authorized personnel were allowed into the hazmat area. The U.S. Army was keeping people out until the Army Corps of Engineers bulldozed the site and covered it with large amounts of dirt to protect the public.

During the conference, Dr. Lin was treated more like royalty than a business tycoon. It was all orchestrated by Conners and the President to keep the man busy and feed his gigantic ego. Despite the fun he had playing world leader, he wasn't physically his usual, robust self.

On the day the Wake Formula lab was attacked, Dr. Lin was highly occupied at the conference. He didn't feel well. He was certainly bored with all the old global warming and climate change rhetoric, but was he also feeling tired? It was so long that he felt sluggish that he wasn't sure. It left him confused and concerned. Was he coming down with the flu, or was another illness making him feel off? Had be brought along a bad batch of Wake Formula? That never happened before, but it was certainly possible.

To be safe, he doubled his dose the next day.

Dr. Lin was also concerned about his cell phone. He had no signal for nearly two days. When he asked Conners about it, Conners replied, "I'm sorry, Dr. Lin. I'm having trouble, too, as are many others. We're looking into it. Apparently, there's a satellite problem, but it should be fixed soon. I asked them to make it a priority."

In reality, all cell signals were being jammed to prevent Dr. Lin from receiving any news about the laboratory explosive. Urgent email from his staff about the attack on the lab was intercepted and deleted. Phony instructions to do nothing until his return were written by Conners and sent back in Dr. Lin's name. Benign messages from clients and other people who had no idea about the attack were allowed to get through to give Dr. Lin a sense of normalcy.

Feeling even more sluggish, Dr. Lin considered leaving the conference before its completion. After nearly sixty hours of cell disruption, he was informed that coverage had finally been restored.

His first call was to General Chen. "General, this is Dr. Lin. My cell phone service has been down for days. We need to catch up. How have things been going in my absence?"

General Chen, losing control, slammed his coffee cup on the table in front of him hard enough to spill coffee everywhere. "How do you think they've been going? The Wake Laboratory has been destroyed, and you ask how things are going?"

The general immediately regretted his words.

Despite his physical weakness, Dr. Lin jumped to his feet, furious with the general's disrespect and the message. "What do you mean, my laboratory has been destroyed? How do you answer me in such a way? What happened in my absence?"

The general was confused. "You don't know? I explained it in my email to you. The Wake laboratory burned to ashes two days ago. I don't understand why you didn't choose to return immediately."

"I received no email about this! What are you talking about?"

General Chen clenched his fist in rage, knowing something was up. "I sent them to you when I couldn't reach your phone. You replied I should do nothing until you finished your conference. You said the conference superseded everything else."

"What? We've been deceived. Our communications have been intercepted and corrupted. Those weren't my words in the email."

"This is an outrage!"

"Were the stores of Wake Formula saved from the wreckage?"

"No! Nothing is left of the lab, and the Army has secured the site, stating there's a toxic hazard."

"How did this happen, General Chen? Was losing a single finger not penalty enough for your incompetence?"

"I'm most sorry, Master Lin, but I can't be blamed. The facility was heavily guarded by my most-trusted, skilled men. I don't know what happened, and I can't get in to investigate."

Dr. Lin's mind raced, but he said nothing.

"We've been waiting for your orders on how to proceed. Communications to the lab facility were disrupted just before it was destroyed. It had to have been a major assault."

Dr. Lin rubbed a hand against his aching head. "Of course it was, but by whom?"

"It must have a been a well-coordinated military or paramilitary commando group with hundreds of men. There's no other way to explain their success. No one has taken credit for the attack. There were either no survivors, or those who survived were taken away. There is no one left to tell us what happened. Even Captain Zheng is missing and may be dead. The Army keeps everyone out and refuses to answer questions."

"What is the United States Army doing there? This makes no sense. Put everyone we have on highest alert!"

"I already have, Master Lin."

Dr. Lin shook his head. He wasn't thinking as clearly as usual. "Stop all shipments of the Wake Formula to clients immediately. We must save it for me and the Supreme Council until we find out exactly how much we have and can start making more. Many of our clients will have to do without for now."

"Master Lin, do you remember how long it took us to set up the laboratory and produce the drug properly?"

"Of course I do! After we secure all the Wake Formula we can find, we'll calculate how many people can use it and for how long until more can be made. The first time we produced it, we had much to learn. This time, rebuilding the lab will go much faster, and we know exactly how to make it. There will be no more research facilities, only production."

"Yes, Master."

"What time of day was the attack?"

"Late at night or very early in the morning."

"Good."

"Why does that matter, Master Lin?"

"It means most of our scientists and laboratory staff weren't there during the attack. Tell me that is so."

"It is as you say."

"Good. Round them up and keep them on my estate under heavy guard. Tell them we'll get them back to work soon. They should not look for other jobs. We'll pay double their salary while they wait at my estate."

"Yes, Master Lin. That's a very good idea."

"When I get back, we'll devote all our money and resources to producing more Wake Formula at a new, impenetrable production facility. Everything else is insignificant now."

"Yes, Master, but many of our clients will become ill without the Wake Formula. Many will die. Most are very important people. There will be worldwide disasters, as corporations collapse and governments become destabilized. Wars could possibly start. I can't imagine all the consequences."

"That is of no concern to me right now," Dr. Lin replied coldly. "If we have enough formula to sell to others, we can ask a very high price from some carefully selected people. If war or other turmoil develops, we'll use it to secure our global power even faster. I'll argue that one central authority is the only way to combat world chaos and conflict."

"That is brilliant, Master Lin, but we still don't know who our enemy is or what he will do next."

"That is true, General. For now, we suspect everyone, even those on the Supreme Council. The wrath of hell will come down on anyone who has betrayed me. It's your job to find them quickly and destroy them."

"Yes, Master Lin. I will have eyes and ears everywhere."

"Now go and secure all Wake Formula you can before I have one on my bodyguards remove the rest of your fingers for your failures."

The general's eyes squinted in loathing. He once loved Dr. Lin, but he felt only hatred for the man. Had he not secured the production facility in every reasonable way? He thought of killing Dr. Lin, but he still needed the man. Great things might still be achieved, so he simply said, "Yes, Master Lin."

"I'll take my helicopter to the closest medical supply freighter to obtain all the Wake Formula onboard. I need some immediately. The batch I brought with me isn't functioning well."

"Yes, Master. A ship left Baltimore harbor this morning and can't have gone far. I'll give your pilot their coordinates."

"Good."

"Do you think the White House had anything to do with this?" the General asked. "If so, they may try to stop you."

"I rule out nothing at this point. The presence of the Army concerns me, but I don't think the President would make such a bold move. Besides, he needs the drug as badly as we do."

"Surely the timing of all this seems coordinated with your White House visit."

"Yes, of course it was," he replied harshly. "Everyone knew I would be attending the White House conference. It was well-publicized. These events could have been done by anyone with means. I still suspect one of our clients with military connections, and I'm rarely wrong."

"That's true, but you still might be in danger there."

"I agree. One way or another, I'm leaving immediately."

"That's most wise, Master Lin."

"Go secure the scientists, keep my family safe, and find out who our enemy is, or I'll have your head! Start by investigating all our clients in the military or with military connections."

"Yes, Master Lin."

Dr. Lin, exhausted from his short conversation with the General, called for an aide. "Prepare my helicopter for takeoff."

"When do you plan to leave, Master Lin?"

"Immediately. Tell the president I have urgent business to attend to elsewhere."

"Sir, I believe you chair another meeting tonight."

"You have your orders. Now go."

Charles sat back in his chair, smiling, as he removed the headphones after listening to Dr. Lin's conversation with General Chen. He conveyed what he heard to Titus, Seth, and Rafael, who waited nearby.

"Brilliant work, Charles," Seth said, patting Charles' back.

Charles grinned. "Thank you. He's doing exactly what we predicted."

"He is, indeed." Seth turned toward Titus. "It looks like we need to launch your team again for round two."

Titus nodded. "Will do."

Rafael watched Titus limp toward the door. "Are you sure you're up for this? Things could get pretty messy, and that leg doesn't look good. I can lead this one. You've done more than enough already."

"Don't worry. I can manage." Titus chuckled. "Besides, even Seth is going on this one."

Seth rubbed his head. "I don't quite know how to respond to that, Titus. I realize I'm not one of your fit commandos anymore, but I think I can help."

Titus laughed. "I'm just messing with you. Of course you'll be there, and Rafael, too. You're going to be one of the stars of the show." He paused and added, "Who has earned the honor more than you, Seth?"

Seth grinned but didn't reply.

"No one," Titus said firmly. "All of this is because of you. Are you sure you're up to it? You don't have to come. As Rafael said, it could get messy, and you've already done more than your share."

"I wouldn't miss it for the world, Old Boy."

"Bloody good, then. Let's go."

As the black helicopter neared the DGF medical supply ship, the copilot radioed the ship's captain. "This is *Dynasty Copter 1* to *Dynasty Medical Supply Vessel Lin II*. Do you copy?"

"We copy, *Dynasty 1*. This is Captain Wang of *Lin II*. What is your ETA?"

"Our ETA is approximately fifteen minutes. Dr. Lin has ordered an official military-style greeting and inspection ceremony on deck when we land. Do you copy?"

"Copy that. Any other specific requests?"

"Yes. You're to have all armed personnel on deck for inspection when we land. Dr. Lin has very limited time to spend onboard and wants to see the defense team in its entirety."

"Copy that."

"Also, have all senior staff on deck along with all containers of the Wake Formula you have onboard. Plans have changed. The medication is needed elsewhere. Dr. Lin wants to do a quick inspection of the ship's personnel and take the medication with him personally. Do you understand your orders? Dr. Lin will tolerate no delays."

"Yes. However, I'm concerned that we might not have enough time to arrange for all of your requests on such short notice."

"Would you like to tell that to Dr. Lin himself?" the copilot asked, irritated. "I could ask him to the cockpit and let you explain why you can't comply with his orders."

"No, no. We'll be ready."

"You understand your orders, then?"

"Yes. Understood. Tell Dr. Lin we'll be ready, and it will be our honor to have him aboard."

"Excellent. He expects nothing less. Over and out."

Tension onboard the ship was at a fever pitch, as the helicopter came into view. Dr. Lin had never visited the *Lin II* before, but his reputation as a strict taskmaster was well-known.

The first mate scrambled to bring all the Wake Formula to the deck. Other staff and crew hurriedly organized the formal military greeting.

Shortly after the helicopter landed, and its blades slowed, a large Asian man in a black suit and red tie stepped out, carrying an AR-15 and standing guard beside the helicopter. Three more armed men followed and stood beside him, while four others took positions on the other side of the helicopter. That was no surprise to the Captain or his crew, because everyone knew Dr. Lin always had a large contingent of bodyguards wherever he went.

The Captain moved closer to the helicopter, expecting Dr. Lin to emerge next. To his surprise, a tall White man with a patch over one ear came out with a battery-powered megaphone. After him came a Hispanic man and a rugged-looking White man with a shaved head who walked with a limp.

After all took positions, the tall man raised his megaphone and said in a distinctly British accent, "Dr. Lin will join you shortly. In the meantime, we hereby take control of this ship."

The Captain froze, trying to process the words. Did he mean Dr. Lin was personally taking command of the ship, or could he possibly mean they were being hijacked?

The answer came quickly, as all eight armed guards from the chopper dropped to one knee and aimed their automatic weapons at the armed crew standing for inspection.

"Drop your weapons," the British man ordered.

The confused crewmen looked to the Captain and then each other. No one moved.

"Please be good chaps and drop your weapons. I don't want to see anyone hurt."

Still no one moved. Seth didn't like the expressions on some of the men's faces.

"If anyone thinks he'd like to be a hero, raise your weapon and see what happens. These good fellows with me will see to it that it'll be the last thing you ever do on Earth."

No one moved, waiting for the Captain's orders. Finally, the Captain stepped forward. "What's the meaning of this? Is Dr. Lin onboard or not? I must speak to him."

Titus took out his Glock and aimed at the Captain. "Not another step."

The Captain stopped.

"Tell the crew to throw down their weapons, or this won't end well for you," Titus said more forcefully.

"Throw down your weapons," Seth said, "or your Captain will be the first to die."

A few dropped their weapons, but most didn't move. The well-trained men were as afraid of their Captain's wrath as they were of the men they faced. They still had numbers on their side.

Titus moved forward until his gun was jammed against the Captain's forehead. "We won't ask again."

"Throw down your weapons," the Captain said.

More obeyed. A few hesitated, then complied. One man raised his weapon and fired. The shots flew over Seth's head.

The Special Forces team surrounding the helicopter riddled the man's body with bullets. He sank to the deck a bloody mess. The team watched for any other resistance, but the other men quickly dropped their weapons.

"Guard the Captain," Titus said. "The rest of you collect their weapons and secure the prisoners. Handcuff them and take them below after you frisk them for hidden weapons."

Seth and one other man went to take control of the ship's operations and communications areas.

After Titus ordered the helicopter to take off, he led a small team to search the ship for any other possible combatants. Several unarmed crewmen were found below, but they didn't resist once they saw the weapons and realized what happened.

Several of Titus' men, changing into the crewmen's clothing, made themselves look busy on the deck, while others took up hidden sniper positions.

"Lin's helicopter is twenty minutes out," Seth reported to Titus.

Titus nodded, hurrying around the ship as best he could, making sure all looked normal and inviting.

They were ready five minutes before Dr. Lin's helicopter hovered overhead. After it landed, six well-armed bodyguards got out and checked the area. Dr. Lin stepped out, looking lethargic and anxious.

Rafael, dressed as an officer, walked up. "Welcome aboard, Dr. Lin! I'm the ship's first mate. Captain Wang would have greeted you himself, but he broke his ankle last night in an accident and asked if you would meet him in his quarters."

"That is most inconvenient," Dr. Lin growled. "Show me the way." He pointed at one bodyguard. "You stay with the helicopter. The rest of you come with me."

Fa Shen and the other security guards stayed close by Dr. Lin's side, as they walked. Shen was as shrewd as he was gigantic. He watched everyone and everything around him. Sensing something wasn't right, he rested one hand on his gun butt.

Rafael smiled to himself, as he saw how slowly Dr. Lin moved. "Are you feeling all right, Dr. Lin? You look a little pale."

Dr. Lin sneered at him. "That is none of your concern. Has the Wake Formula been prepared for placement on the helicopter?"

"Of course. It's all been collected," he replied enthusiastically.

As planned, Rafael tried carefully to distance himself from Dr. Lin and the others, but Fa Shen noticed and motioned him back to the group.

As soon as the group rounded the first corner, Titus and several of his men came out of hiding with their Heckler and Koch HK416 rifles aimed at Dr. Lin and his guards.

"Stop!" Titus said. "Throw down your weapons!"

Most men would have surrendered when they saw so many guns aimed at them, but not Shen or the other bodyguards. They were fearless, well-trained warriors who were dedicated to their master.

They drew their weapons and fired. Fa Shen stepped in front of Dr. Lin, as he fired at the attackers.

Titus' team held their fire for a moment to give Rafael time to escape, but he didn't get the chance.

Out of the corner of his eye, Shen saw Rafael moving away and grabbed him with a massive hand, pulling him against his body. He swung the man around as a shield between himself and the attackers.

When no one fired, Shen slowly guided Dr. Lin and Rafael back toward the helicopter. "Stay and protect Dr. Lin's retreat," he told the other guards.

A fierce firefight broke out once Rafael was out of the line of fire.

"This isn't going as planned," Titus muttered, knowing Dr. Lin would use Rafael to negotiate his escape and would then kill him. He couldn't let that happen.

He clicked on his com. "I'm going after Dr. Lin and Rafael. The rest of you, take down those men as fast as you can and then join me. No heroics. Cut off their retreat if they try to run."

Titus set down his assault rifle, drew his Glock, and went after Dr. Lin as fast as his injured leg allowed. Fortunately, Dr. Lin moved slowly, too, so Titus soon caught up to them.

When Shen saw Titus coming, he hit the side of Rafael's head with his gun before firing three shots at Titus.

Titus dropped behind cover. Hazarding a quick look, he saw Dr. Lin retreating farther away, while the large Chinese guard skillfully used a dazed, bleeding Rafael as a shield.

Titus carefully moved closer to Dr. Lin and his massive protector, keeping as concealed as possible. When he saw Rafael twist slightly away from the guard, Titus fired twice. Both bullets hit the guard in the chest, and he fell backward.

Titus moved toward Dr. Lin until he was six feet away. Shen, who wore a bulletproof vest, stood and charged Titus.

Titus aimed, but the guard swung a long leg and kicked the gun from his hand before he could shoot. Shen crashed into Titus, tackling him hard to the deck.

They rolled and wrestled savagely, each trying to gain the advantage. Both surged to their feet. Titus was extremely skilled in hand-to-hand combat, but Shen was immensely strong and also very gifted.

Shen slipped around Titus and squeezed him in a bear hug. With his great strength, he began to squeeze the life out of his assailant.

Titus, feeling air leaving his lungs, kicked back hard against Shen's shin. His head whipped back, smashing the man's nose.

In a moment of pain, Shen's grip loosened, and Titus easily twisted away. Titus punched him hard, but his second punch was blocked.

The blow had little effect. Shen swung a big fist hard at Titus' face. Titus twisted his head, letting it glance off his cheek, then he countered with a punch to Shen's face.

Shen returned the blow, but neither man had the power behind their punches to disable his opponent.

After exchanging a few more punches and blocks, Shen lunged toward Titus with his long arms. He grabbed the man and knocked him to the ground, where they wrestled a second time.

Eventually, Shen slid his hands up and around Titus' neck and began squeezing. Titus, feeling light-headed, knew he was in serious trouble. He focused all his efforts on one of Shen's fingers and bent it back with all his remaining strength.

Shen screamed when his finger broke and lay awkwardly to one side, and his grip loosened.

Titus pulled out the combat knife strapped to his calf. Shen tried to take Titus' hand, but he pulled away too fast. Titus twisted and thrust the knife into Shen's side, just below the bulletproof vest. Because he didn't have much leverage or force behind the blow, it didn't penetrate far.

Shen, moaning in pain, shoved Titus away with one huge hand.

Both injured men struggled to their feet, trying to assess their situation. Neither was ready to renew the fight.

Titus coughed, trying to get his lungs fully functional. Seeing the combat knife sticking out of Shen's side, he realized it hadn't penetrated far.

Shen pulled out the knife and smiled menacingly at Titus. Blood seeped down his side, but he ignored it. With the knife ready, he had only one thought—to kill the man in front of him.

Titus had to do something fast, so he attacked. Shen had no time to use the knife blade against Titus, so he came down hard with the hilt against one of Titus' outstretched arms.

Titus grunted, and something broke. Still, with the tackling skills he learned in playing football at West Point, he slammed his shoulder into Shen's gut. The large man buckled slightly, and Titus brought up his head as hard as he could into Shen's jaw.

Shen's head snapped back, his jaw fractured. Titus slammed him with an elbow, then used his good hand against his groin.

Shen grunted and buckled over in pain. Titus kneed him in the face, and he finally fell unconscious.

Titus sank to his knees in exhaustion and pain. Shen looked like a hibernating bear. Titus fought many men before, but he couldn't remember a tougher opponent than the one who lay motionless before him.

Just when he thought it was over, Titus sensed Dr. Lin moving behind him. He never considered the man a threat and almost forgot about him during the brutal fight. He realized that was a mistake.

Dr. Lin, who remained motionless and mesmerized by the fight, picked up Titus' Glock when he saw Fa Shen slump to the ground. He never saw anyone best his bodyguard before. It came as a shock. Dr. Lin had many men killed, but he never fired a gun before. It took a moment to orient himself and fire.

Thanks to Dr. Lin's hesitation, Titus dived to the side and heard the bullet whistle overhead. He got up, ready to fight, when he saw Rafael holding a combat knife against Dr. Lin's neck.

"Don't even think of pulling that trigger," Rafael said, blood slowly running down his face.

Dr. Lin froze. He was a lethal tyrant, but he had no combat skills and had no idea what to do. His hand relaxed, and the gun dropped.

Titus was still catching his breath when he walked up to Dr. Lin. He never was that close to his adversary before, and he stared for a moment. What he saw didn't impress him.

"Are you all right?" Rafael asked Titus.

"I'm OK. Thanks."

"Sorry it took me so long to help. That guy on the ground clobbered me pretty hard with his gun."

Titus nodded. "That's quite a gash on your head." Titus removed his shirt and handed it to him. "Hold this on the wound until we find something better."

Rafael wiped away the blood and pressed gently against his skull. "God, that hurts." He eyed Titus' hand. "That doesn't look good, either."

Titus looked down at his hand for the first time and saw it was swollen and deformed, badly broken. "Yeah. It hurts pretty bad."

Multiple distant gunshots rang out, then stopped.

Titus took the Glock with his good hand. "Secure these two. I'll check on the men."

As Titus walked off, Rafael called, "Don't get used to giving me orders. When this is over, I'll be your boss again."

Titus looked back with a smile. "I wouldn't have it any other way." He walked toward where he heard the last shots.

When Titus arrived, the battle was over. Dr. Lin's guards were dead. His men said they tried to capture them, but they were skilled warriors and never surrendered.

CHAPTER 47

"What's the meaning of this?" Dr. Lin snapped. "Do you know who I am? I own this ship. I give free medical supplies to needy children around the world. You abducted me and killed my security staff. I demand an explanation! All of you will go to prison for this."

Seth calmly looked at Dr. Lin, relishing the moment. He waited a long time for this and risked everything to stop him. "We know who you are, Dr. Lin. We also know what you're really doing here. As for your bodyguards, well, we told them to drop their weapons. They chose not to and opened fire on us. You're our prisoner, and the world, at least as you know it, is over."

Dr. Lin scowled. "I'm the personal friend of the Secretary-General of the United Nations and the President of the United States! You'll pay for this!"

Seth grinned but didn't reply.

Dr. Lin looked closely at Seth, Titus, and Rafael, trying to understand who they were and what happened. He didn't recognize any of them as one of his clients. Could he have been wrong about who he'd been up against? He sneered and asked, "Who are you people? What do you have to do with me?"

"To put it simply," Seth replied, "we're the ones who outsmarted you, Dr. Lin. We've done it even though we have to sleep six to eight hours a night like everyone else."

"What foolishness are you talking about?"

Seth crossed his arms. "We know all about the Wake Formula. We know how you've used it to manipulate people to obtain wealth and power. That's why we had to stop you."

"The President of the United States will hear of this affront to me! Do you know I left the White House only a few hours ago? He'll see to it that all of you are put in federal prison and will never see the light of day again! I'll demand it!"

"About that, Dr. Lin. I'm afraid President O'Malley knows all about our raid and sends his greetings."

"What?" After a moment of bewilderment, Dr. Lin slammed his fist against his thigh. "That deceitful bastard! You can tell President O'Malley that he'll no longer receive drugs from me. Tell him he will die without it. Tell him that!"

Seth and the others smiled at the futile outburst. "I hate to disappoint you, Old Boy, but I doubt he's very worried about that. You see, we confiscated all the Wake Formula from your laboratory and this ship. Soon, we'll have all you have at home and anywhere else it's located. It's over, Dr. Lin. Your monstrous scheme has failed utterly."

Dr. Lin was fuming. He studied their faces, scrutinizing each of them coldly. "So you're the ones who attacked my laboratory and stole my Wake Formula. You're nothing but common thieves."

"I wouldn't call it stealing, Dr. Lin. We were merely retrieving it back for Dr. Burris. We know you stole the formula from him, killed his staff, and tried to kill him, too."

"Listen to me," Dr. Lin said in a more-hospitable tone. "I must have the Wake drug now. I'm sick from a bad batch of the formula. I need some right away, or I'll start slipping into a coma."

Seth smiled. "Actually, Dr. Lin, you haven't had any in days. We exchanged your supply with a placebo at the White House."

Dr. Lin's knees almost buckled, and he felt nauseous with fear. "You bastards. I must have my drug. I feel very, very ill."

"I'm afraid that's not possible," Rafael said. "It's been taken off the ship and is on its way to Washington. We'll use it to help the people whose lives you put in danger."

Dr. Lin's face turned pale, and he seemed truly terrified. "No, no! You didn't. I must have the Wake Formula, or you'll kill me."

"Like you were going to kill the President?" Rafael asked with no sympathy in his voice. "No, we won't kill you, Dr. Lin. We'll just detain you here and refuse to give you the drug that you stole, killed for, and used to usurp power. We'll let happen to you what you planned to let happen to the President of the United States and many others around the world."

Dr. Lin hung his head, realizing they knew everything.

"I'm afraid you'll stay right here on this ship in international waters for a long cruise with us," Seth said matter-of-factly. "Whatever happens to you, you did it to yourself."

Dr. Lin shook his head, trying to process the sudden dramatic change. "You can't do that. I'll pay you money, lots of money. I can make all of you multimillionaires. I have endless amounts of money. Just give me a year's supply of the Wake Formula and let me go. You'll be rich beyond your wildest dreams. You can say I escaped. You can go somewhere that has no extradition treaty with the United States. I know powerful people who can make it happen."

"That's why you have to stay right here," Titus said. "We know you have great power and even greater influence with people around the world. You'd find a way out of this if we gave you the chance. That's why we won't. It's over." He pointed to two of his men. "Take this man below and lock him up."

As Dr. Lin was escorted away, he understood what happened. President O'Malley got him away from his home territory, staff, resources, protection, and medication. These people destroyed his lab and disrupted communications with his people while he was busy at that stupid conference. They somehow deactivated his medication or exchanged it for a placebo. Like Julius Caesar, he let his guard down, and like Caesar, he would pay the price.

Dr. Lin was taken to the first mate's quarters, where he immediately plopped down on the bed. The guards cleared the room of any potentially sharp or dangerous objects. One remained in the room to watch him while the other stood guard outside the door.

Dr. Lin stared at the walls, unable to believe what happened. One minute, he was on top of the world. The next, he was a prisoner on one of his own ships.

"How could I have been such a fool?" he mumbled. "How?" Ignoring the guard's presence, he looked toward the heavens for answers. "Why, my ancestors, did you allow these ordinary men to take my glory from me? Even more glory was to come, glory that I deserved and would have shared with you. Why?"

The following day, Rafael entered the room, glanced at the guard, and motioned him to leave.

Dr. Lin lay in bed and didn't react to his entrance. Rafael pulled up a chair near the bed and sat down. He peered at Dr. Lin.

"What do you want?" Dr. Lin asked eventually. "Did you want to stare at me like a zoo animal?"

Rafael looked into his eyes and held up a vial.

When Dr. Lin saw what he had, he sat up faster than Rafael thought possible. "Have you come to torment me with that, or have you come to give me the Wake Formula I asked for?"

Rafael cocked his head to one side but didn't reply.

"If you give me that and help me escape, I'll make you one of the richest men in the world."

Rafael grinned. "That's not why I'm here."

Dr. Lin sighed. "What then?"

"The President has an offer for you."

Dr. Lin waited.

"Do you want to hear it?"

He took a deep breath. "Go on."

"He wants you to make a video, a confession. He'll give you some Wake Formula this one time if you do that." He wiggled the vial before the desperate man's eyes. "This is actually an extended release derivative of the Wake Formula. It was created by Dr. Burrus to help ease the discomfort of the drug's withdrawal."

Dr. Lin stroked his chin, looking longingly at the vial.

Rafael cleared his throat. "I want to be clear. After this one dose, we won't give you any more and expect you eventually to go into withdrawal and a coma, as you allowed others to do. However, your suffering will be much less than others endured."

Dr. Lin stared at the vial in torment. He wanted it desperately, but he also knew it was only a temporary fix. "What does he want me to say? You offer me so little. I won't admit to the murder of Wake patients or the people in Dr. Burrus' lab, not even for the drug. I won't humiliate my family and ancestors."

"That would be nice, but he doesn't insist on that. He wants you to admit your doomsday declarations about global warming and climate change were for political gain, which, by the way, we both know they were."

Dr. Lin was silent.

Rafael stood. "I see. Well, it was just an idea." He started toward the door.

"Wait! Yes, I'll admit it. I'll admit to my wisdom. That isn't a disgrace."

Rafael was amazed at the man's ignorance.

"I'll admit I used the hysterics around climate change for my own purposes, like so many others before me. I hated speaking like an idiot, but it served my purposes well. It was my hope to unite the world in one great empire through the United Nations."

"Ruled by you," Rafael said in disgust.

"Why not? I'm descended from a royal line. My ancestors will be happy that I corrected the record. I dishonored them by spouting nonsense and acting so melodramatic. I planned to clarify my true thoughts once I had enough power to do so. Anyway, if I must die, I want to go to my ancestors in peace."

"So you'll do it?"

"Yes, just give me the damn vial."

Rafael dangled the vial in the air. "The video first."

CHAPTER 48

President O'Malley waited patiently while he was put through to the British Prime Minister on a secure line. When the call finally went through, he took a deep breath and asked, "Debra, how are you?"

"Quite well, Richard, and you?"

"A bit under the weather but getting better, thank you. I'm calling to let you know that the special operation we recently discussed went over quite well. We have a lot of cleaning up to do here, but our primary threat is over."

"That's wonderful news."

"We have terrorists in custody related to that operation who I'd like to get off American soil. Could you help me with that?"

The PM rubbed the back of her neck. "It could become a sticky wicket, but I believe we can be of some assistance."

He sighed. "Thank you."

"You're quite welcome."

He looked at the long list of things that had to be done quickly. "We also have to deal with the medical phase of this operation. If we don't work fast, we'll have an enormous mess on our hands. Many wealthy, powerful people around the world, including in your country and mine, no longer have access to the drug in question. Very soon, many will become ill. Some might be starting down that road as we speak."

"Yes. I've already heard some disturbing reports along those lines. I have no doubt it will become a huge problem. Many Fortune

500 companies and even financial markets could be gravely affected. We could have a global economic depression."

"Yes. Both of us must keep our eyes on that. Fortunately, only a few people know what's really going on."

"Yes, of course. What do you want me to do?"

"The people who need treatment should be assured that their secret will remain that way. No more drug is available, but they can be detoxed off it. We've obtained the names of all Dr. Lin's clients from his computer records. They'll be contacted and treated immediately if they're willing. I'll send you a list of those in your country and protectorates immediately."

"Sounds like a big project."

"It is. They need to be treated right away. Dr. Burrus has set up a large clinical ward at NIH and will help establish others in England, Japan, and other strategic locations around the world."

"That's wonderful, Richard."

"I'm using military medical personnel to assist him, since they'll be held to a high level of confidentiality. I suggest you do the same."

"Of course."

"If questions arise, our cover story is that a new viral infection has reached many people around the world, but a treatment is available. I'll need you help spreading that story."

"Certainly. Quite a mess we have on our hands."

"That's true, but it would have been much worse if Dr. Lin hadn't been stopped. We have Seth Miles of MI-6 to thank for it."

"I plan to speak to him personally very soon about the whole affair. It's a fascinating story, really."

"Indeed, and our part is only beginning."

It was several days before Dr. Lin slipped into a light coma, then a deeper one. He was still alive, and his withdrawal was eased by the long-acting form of the drug, as promised. Rafael had him flown back to the U.S. to be admitted to a major Texas Medical Center hospital for treatment. The news outlets reported grave concern over his condition.

President O'Malley flew from Washington to Texas several times to check Dr. Lin at his hospital bed. He never opened his eyes. The medical professionals had no idea about the true problem and could only speculate he picked up a strange, deadly virus from one of the many places he visited.

Three weeks after Dr. Lin's admission to the hospital, he passed away. President O'Malley rushed back to Texas and met with several of his doctors. Afterward, they held a press conference.

"I regret to announce that the well-known philanthropist, Dr. Dao Lin, died today of uncertain causes," the President began. "I know the staff here at the medical center did everything they could to save his life. I thank them for their heroic efforts. This is a sad day for his family, friends, and many admirers. I'll speak more on his legacy at another time. For now, I'd like to introduce the medical team who cared for him."

Waving the team members closer, he stood beside them. "I'm sure Dr. Willmore and the others who cared for Dr. Lin will be happy to answer any medical questions you may have."

As the President stepped away, a reporter asked, "Mr. President, I know you've been kept abreast of Dr. Lin's situation and were recently very ill yourself. What have you been told about his cause of death? Could it be related to what you suffered?"

He placed a hand on Dr. Willmore's shoulder. "As I said, I'll leave the medical questions to these smart doctors beside me. However, I can say that yes, many medical professionals I've spoken to believe Dr. Lin was struck down by the same strange illness that made me seriously lethargic not long ago. It seems to be affecting many people around the world. No one is certain of the cause, but some believe it's a new strain of a virus or a virus-like agent."

"Do we know why there seems to be a disproportionate number of world leaders and celebrities struck by this illness?" asked an astute reporter.

"That's a great question, James. The CDC isn't sure why, but it's been suggested that it's because world leaders and celebrities often spend time with one another, which could spread an infection among them. It might be as simple as that, but I really don't know. The CDC epidemiologists are working hard to answer that question."

"You were with Dr. Lin recently at the White House summit on climate change. Could he have caught it from you?"

President O'Malley shrugged. "I really can't say. I hope not. All I know is, I've been totally free of any symptoms for some time."

"How did the conference go?" another reporter asked. "We haven't been given a full report on it yet. Did Dr. Lin persuade you to become even more involved in his climate change programs when you met at the conference?"

"I don't think this is the appropriate time to discuss that."

"Please, Mr. President. We're all curious about Dr. Lin's last days. It'll be part of his amazing legacy."

The President grimaced and took a breath. "Since I know you folks won't leave me alone until you hear something about it, the simple answer is no—quite the contrary, in fact."

"What do you mean?" asked a surprised reporter with indignation.

"Unlike some conferences, this White House gathering of minds brought together scientists from both sides of the debate for a frank and open discussion. Even Dr. Lin agreed in the end that most of the climate models were grossly inaccurate. Some appeared to be based on skewed or even tainted data. Long-term predictions about climate were shown to be difficult, if not impossible, to make."

"What do you mean?" a female reporter asked.

"A strong case was made that there are too many unpredictable variables to determine accurately long-term climate change. Fluctuating changes in the sun's activity seemed to be of greatest concern in that school of thought."

Reporters muttered among themselves, while others called out more questions.

"We'll continue to monitor climate issues but won't participate in knee-jerk, expensive, politically motivated responses to what are probably cyclical trends," the President said.

"So you're back to your old stance?"

The President glanced at Conners, then said, "After hearing all the arguments, I must say I am."

The reporters, forgetting about Dr. Lin for a moment, furiously scribbled notes. Some enjoyed the idea of hanging the President out to dry again in the articles they planned to write. Unfortunately, since he joined the movement so recently, they had no exciting or controversial stories to bash him with.

He raised his hands to quiet the room. "In fact, Dr. Lin told me he would address his change of perspective after the conference. I'm very sad he passed away before he could."

Conners smiled at the President's performance. Most of those very predictable reporters were falling right into their trap, as they knew they would.

"That's very hard to believe, Mr. President," a well-known cable news reporter shouted. "How can we know you're telling the truth, now that Dr. Lin is dead? Are you trying to tarnish his legacy before the poor man's even been buried?"

The President almost didn't answer such a rude question, but he said, "I'm afraid you'll have to take my word on that."

"So you're once again a climate change denier?" a liberal reporter asked.

The President shook his head. "Of course not, Nancy. I never said that. What does that question even mean? People on both sides of the debate are aware that change happens. It always has and always will." He shook his head. "I'm saying that if you examine the data with open eyes, you'll see that climate changes are almost impossible to predict long-term, are almost impossible to control, and that whatever changes occur will surely hurt some people and help others. That's just the way of it."

"So your administration once again cares nothing about the environment?"

"Why do you always assume the worst, Nancy? That simply isn't true. This administration will protect the air, water, and other observable environmental concerns in ways that we know will help, be cost-efficient, and are based on sound information. We won't exaggerate or minimize findings for political gain nor excessively fund ineffective projects for such gain. It's as simple as that."

Several frustrated reporters began shouting questions.

He raised his hands for quiet. "That sort of nonsense has been done far too often in the past, and every dollar wasted is a dollar that could have been used for important purposes such as urban renewal, job growth, poverty, healthcare, infrastructure, and reducing our insane national debt. In fact, I pledge right now that money will be made available to continue the work Dr. Lin started sending medical supplies to needy children around the world."

More questions were called, but he waved them to stop. "I believe we've gotten way off track. Today is about the sad passing of Dr. Lin. I'll answer more questions about my position on policy matters at another time. It's time to hear from the medical staff who cared for Dr. Lin. Thank you."

After the press conference, Conners spoke to President O'Malley in private. "Congratulations, Mr. President. That was well done. The mainstream press hates you once again. All is right in the world."

"Yes, they do, God love them."

"When should I release Dr. Lin's video?"

The President thought a moment. "I haven't decided yet, to tell the truth. I'll let them hang themselves for a week or two with their nasty, elitist articles. It'll be fun." He put his hand on Conners' shoulder. "You know how they are. They never learn."

Conners nodded. "I'll keep a finger on the pulse of it all, but it sounds good to me. I can't wait to see their faces when they can't deny it's Dr. Lin speaking and what he has to say. It'll be a tsunami."

As soon as Air Force One landed in Washington, DC, President O'Malley secretly visited Dr. Burrus' research facility and clinic at NIH.

Conners smiled broadly, as he introduced Dr. Burrus. "This is the doctor, Mr. President, I told you so much about."

President O'Malley shook the scientist's hand enthusiastically. "So you're Dr. Burrus, the doctor who will get me and everyone else out of this Wake Formula mess."

"I am. Have you come to inspect our operation here, or are you ready to start your own detoxification?"

The President smiled. "Both." He glanced around curiously. "Could you show me around your clinic and tell me exactly how you plan to help me?"

"I'd be happy to." He motioned with one hand for the President to follow him. "This way, Mr. President."

After they made their rounds, President O'Malley stopped with his hands on his hips. "I'm impressed, Dr. Burrus. You have an amazing clinic here. Thank you for doing all this."

"It's my pleasure, Sir. We should remember my Wake Formula started this mess in the first place."

"I understand, but I also know the blame doesn't belong to you but to Dr. Lin and those who conspired with him. He got what he deserved, and now he's gone. Those who helped him are either in custody or soon will be."

"Thank you, Mr. President." He held up a hospital gown. "Are you ready to get started?"

"Hell, yes."

CHAPTER 49

Three weeks after initiating the detox protocol, the President lay peacefully in a hospital bed at Walter Reed Hospital. Dr. Burrus moved his entire operation there for greater security for the President, and because the Department of Defense had taken administrative control of the Wake Formula detoxing efforts. The President continued receiving Wake-LA but in ever-decreasing doses.

The President looked tired but alert, when Conners came into his private suite.

"Good morning, Mr. President."

"Good morning, Conners."

"How are you feeling, Sir?"

The President grinned. "Not too bad. Dr. Burrus and his staff are taking good care of me."

"That's great to hear, Sir."

"Have you rounded all of them up?"

Conners smiled. "I have. They're waiting in the hall."

"Wonderful. It's time to bring them in. I can't wait to personally meet and thank all the people I owe so much."

Conners began escorting the guests into the room. First came Special Agent Warren, still limping slightly, with a cast on his hand and wrist. Next came Isabella, followed by Deputy Director Otero. Bruising and stitches adorned one side of his head. Ying Newman sat in a wheelchair pushed by her husband, Charles. Seth Miles came in sporting a small patch on one ear.

The President looked them over. "Where's Dr. Burrus?"

"He's was with the others, Sir," Conners said. "Let me fetch him."

He quickly located the doctor, who strayed to check the vital signs of a patient who was having difficulties. Conners tapped his shoulder. "The President is ready to see you now."

"Yes, of course. Just one minute." Dr. Burrus turned his attention to the Army nurse at his side. "This woman is having more withdrawal than I like. Please slowly increase the Wake-LA IV until her vital signs normalize."

The nurse nodded.

Conners gently took Dr. Burrus' arm. "Please. The President's waiting."

When all the group were in the room, the President sat up straighter in bed and smiled.

Conners cleared his throat and introduced them one at a time. The President smiled and shook their hands, as each approached his bed and happily stood back again.

"So you're the ones I owe so much," the President began. "Many of you look like you went through hell."

"They did, Mr. President," Conners said. "In my opinion, each one is a hero."

He grinned and glanced at them. "My Chief of Staff has told me all about you, and I have to agree with him. You're all heroes. As Winston Churchill once said, 'Never was so much owed by so many to so few.'"

They smiled back, but no one spoke.

"It is very, very nice to meet all of you."

"Thank you, Mr. President," they replied.

Reflecting for a moment he said, "When Conners told me about your plan and what you'd been up to, I found it hard to believe. When I finally did, I wasn't sure whether to give you the help you asked for or have you arrested."

They stood quietly.

Seeing their uncertainty, he said, "Relax, relax. I was just joking. My wife, Eileen, says I'm not very good at jokes. From your expressions, she was right."

Relieved smiles came to their faces.

After a moment, Deputy Director Otero said, "Thank you for your help, Mr. President. I'm not sure we could have stopped Dr. Lin without it. He was a powerful, ruthless man who headed a huge organization."

"No, it's I who must thank all of you. In addition to meeting everyone, that's why I brought you here today. I want to give you my official and personal thanks."

Grins came to their faces.

"Mr. Miles and Mr. Newman, would you please step forward?"

The two men stepped closer to the bed.

"I'm sorry to hear about your ear, Mr. Miles. Can I help arrange for a plastic surgeon to look at it?"

"Thank you, Mr. President, but I already have surgery scheduled in London next week. I'm sure my ear will be fine."

"Good. My sincere thanks to both of you. I was told that it was you, Mr. Miles, who first had concerns about Dr. Lin and rounded up this motley crew when you were stonewalled at MI-6."

"It was really Mr. Newman and I, Mr. President, but we couldn't have stopped him without Special Agent Warren and the others gathered here."

The President glanced briefly at Warren, then back to Miles. "Yes. Of course. I hate to think what would have happened if you hadn't sensed something was wrong to begin with. Excellent work."

"Thank you."

The President looked at Charles. "And you, Mr. Newman, not only helped sniff out Dr. Lin, but I understand your computer skills and bravery were indispensable in taking down Dr. Lin and his organization."

His hands in his pockets, Charles shrugged modestly. "I did what I could, Sir."

The President smiled at his humility. "All I can say is, well done."

Charles nodded.

"Perhaps you could give me your cell number, so I can call you the next time my computer acts up."

He grinned at the joke. "I'd be happy to help any time, Mr. President."

The president smiled. "I want you to know that I told your Prime Minister about both of you. I wouldn't be surprised if she and the King find a special way to honor your incredible efforts. I'm not at liberty to say what they have in mind, but congratulations to you two, Sir Miles and Sir Newman."

The two men grinned.

"Thank you so much, Mr. President," Miles replied.

"Thank you," Charles added.

"She assured me that the people at MI-6 and in other parts of your government who impeded your attempts to investigate Dr. Lin will be investigated and dealt with appropriately."

"That's welcome news," Miles responded.

"As you may know, several members of Dr. Lin's inner circle have already been taken into custody and relocated to special CIA facilities for further questioning. Others are on the run. I'd like both of you to help our interrogation team, as we try to unravel exactly all the things they were up to."

The two men nodded.

"We'd be happy to help," Miles said, knowing Charles felt uncomfortable in the limelight.

The President gestured for Ying and Isabella to come forward. "I'm so thankful for the role you two lovely ladies played in getting us to this point. I know you didn't ask for any of this, Isabella, but you stayed with your husband during very dangerous times and then helped in the lab and the clinic—in addition to being a loving mother to your children. A personal letter of appreciation will reflect my high respect for all you did and are still doing."

"Thank you so much, Mr. President," Isabella replied.

"Mrs. Newman, how are you feeling? I'm sorry you were hurt during the shoot-out on the freighter."

"I'm doing better, Mr. President. I'm sure I'll be on my feet soon."

"She had a second surgery three days ago to repair some post-op bleeding, but she's tough as nails," Charles said proudly.

The President smiled and nodded. "I'm sure she is. You're a civilian who volunteered to put yourself in harms' way several times to topple Dr. Lin. I'm very impressed. You'll be awarded the Presidential Medal of Freedom. Please accept my sincere congratulations."

Ying's hands flew to her mouth in shock. "Thank you, Mr. President. I'd come over and hug you if I could."

The President looked at Conners. "Would you help me up, please?"

After slowly getting to his feet, he went to Ying and hugged her gently. "Thank you again for everything. I pray your wounds will be better soon."

Isabella stepped closer and gave the President a hug, too. "Thank you, Mr. President."

He nodded, then said, "You're up next, Dr. Burrus."

Dr. Burrus stepped forward.

"You're not only a brilliant scientist and physician, you're very compassionate, too. If you agree, I'd like you to continue running this clinic at Walter Reed to train other specially selected doctors around the world in ways to assist patients come off the Wake Formula. I'll also need you to oversee production of Wake-LA until all of Dr. Lin's clients have been successfully treated. It's a lot of work, but I hope you'll say yes."

"I'll be more than happy to help."

"Good." The President added, "I'm sorry to tell you that starting immediately, the Wake Formula and all derivatives of it will be in the custody of the Department of Defense for national security reasons. I'm not sure what we'll do with it in the long run. Maybe nothing, but we certainly don't want it getting into the wrong hands. I hope you understand."

"Of course. I expected that."

"You'll receive a Presidential Letter of Appreciation reflecting my great gratitude for your amazing medical help. Thank you."

"Thank you, Mr. President."

"Special Agent Warren and Deputy Director Otero, would you please step forward?"

They stepped toward the President's bed.

"How's your head feeling, Deputy Director?"

"Still having some headaches but doing better, Sir. Thank you."

"Your assistance in this matter is very much appreciated. The Director of the FBI wasn't pleased that you were involved in a covert operation, but I explained what I could to her, and she understands. She assures me your files will reflect only my appreciation and informs me that she has great plans for you at the FBI."

"Thank you."

The President's gaze went to Warren. "How's that leg and hand doing, Agent Warren?"

"Coming along just fine, Mr. President. Thank you for asking."

"Wonderful. At the advice of Deputy Director Otero, and with my full endorsement, you'll be awarded the FBI Medal of Honor for exceptional acts of courage. You helped save this country from a serious threat that we can never publicly acknowledge, but I know what you did and won't forget it. Congratulations."

"Wow. I'm shocked and humbled. Thank you very much, Mr. President."

A playful expression came to the President's face. "Conners tells me you scared the hell out of him when you broke into his home. Is that right?"

"Guilty as charged, Sir."

The President slapped his thigh. "I wish I could've seen that."

Conners shook his head.

Titus grinned. "It was my pleasure, Sir."

Turning to the entire group, the President said, "I hope you all understand the delicacy of the events that took place. I'm not proud of some of the things I did. In fact, I greatly regret them. I never should've used the Wake Formula and feel ashamed that I did." Staring into the distance for a moment, he grinned. "It reminds me of when my mother called me Shame O'Malley when I got into trouble." He waved away the memories.

The others wanted to reply but didn't know what to say.

"I also hate that Dr. Lin had to die. However, like many other dangerous terrorists before him who had to be taken out, it was the only way." After a pause, he added, "At least he died peacefully and by the same means he used to kill so many others."

Rafael and Seth nodded.

"Although I feel the recent attack on Dr. Lin's compound was justified, there have been American deaths on U.S. soil under my authority. That isn't an easy cross to carry."

They didn't know where he was going, but they felt compassion for him.

"You need to remember that all events regarding the Wake Formula affair are classified Top Secret. In doing that, I'm covering my own ass. I'm not proud of that, but I don't deny it. As far as I'm concerned, Dr. Lin's scheme was an act of national and international terrorism. He intended to covertly gain world power and used lethal force while trying to do so. He had to be stopped."

Heads nodded.

"Consequently, your awards will be for contributions for actions other than toppling Dr. Lin and his organization."

They nodded again in understanding.

"Special Agent Warren, Deputy Chief Otero, Mr. Miles, and Mr. Newman, your awards and recognition will be for bringing down the terrorist group who stole a deadly virus from the Army Research

Institute. It was very good work, and it saved many lives, so it deserves recognition."

They nodded.

"Dr. Burrus, Mrs. Burrus, and Ms. Newman, your awards and recognition will be for your outstanding help in treating this so-called virus epidemic."

The three nodded.

"For the moment, Dr. Lin is a world hero, a martyr of sorts. Very soon, that will change. We won't fully reveal the deadly, manipulative game he was playing, but he made a video just before his death confessing his true motives."

The others smiled.

"Also, the White-Collar division of the FBI has discovered information about money laundering and payoff schemes of the Dynasty Global Foundation, thanks to the help of Deputy Director Otero. When all this information is revealed, the illusion that Dr. Lin was a great humanitarian will collapse. Even the mainstream media, who have so vehemently supported him, will have to change their tune. They will try to move quickly to other matters, but they'll change."

The small group applauded softly.

The President grinned. "That's about it. Thank you all again."

Each of them shook his hand before leaving the room.

In the hallway, high-fives, hugs, and farewells were shared.

Rafael and Seth went off together as old buddies to have a few drinks. The old warhorses were victorious once again, and they knew they had to celebrate immediately, because heaven only knew if they would have more victories to share in the future.

Titus hugged Isabella and shook Frederick's hand. "Well, I must say this little adventure wasn't all fun, but it was been a pleasure getting to know you both."

"I hope this isn't the last we see of you, Titus," Isabella said. "We've both become quite fond of you."

"Yes, I hope not," Frederick answered.

Titus gave them a playful smile. "This certainly won't be the last you see of me." He shook his head. "No way. In fact, my grand plan has worked out perfectly, so I expect you'll see me a lot more."

Isabella was intrigued. She knew Titus was a tease and was messing with them. "Grand plan? Just what grand plan might that be, pray tell?"

"The most-important plan of this entire operation." Titus waggled his eyebrows. "A plan within a plan."

She tipped her head to one side.

His smile broadened. "Don't you see?" he asked dramatically. "Now that you guys will be living in Washington, DC, Frederick can join my softball team this year!"

Frederick howled with laughter.

Isabella smiled and shook her head. "So you manipulated all of these events just to get my husband to play on your silly softball team?'

"Of course. Isn't it obvious? I've got big plans for your husband's athletic career."

She grinned. "You're such a kid."

Titus moved closer to Frederick. "I hope you'll accept my offer, Big Guy. We need that powerful arm of yours in centerfield, especially with me out on injured reserves for the start of the season."

Frederick chuckled. "Sure. I'll play, but first, you have to come help us move."

Titus frowned and pathetically held up his injured hand. "I'd love to, but...."

"Well, you can at least baby-sit or maybe carry little stuff," Isabella said. "Really, I never took you for such a wimp, Titus."

He laughed. "Just tell me when. I'll be there with bells on."

"And I need you to set up a date back at Sewanee," Frederick added.

"A date?"

"Have you forgotten already?" Isabella asked. "Does the name Tammy not ring a bell?"

Titus put a hand to his forehead. "Oh, my God. How is she?"

"Much better now," Frederick replied. "I'll play softball, and you go out with Tammy. Deal?"

Titus offered his good hand to shake. "It's a deal for sure."

After their temporary good-byes, Frederick and Isabella walked back to their work hand-in-hand.

Frederick turned to his wife. "I'm so glad this is finally over, Honey. Now we're free again. I'm Frederick Burrus, and you're Isabella Burrus again."

"Yes, we're truly free!" she exclaimed after kissing him. "No more hiding." Remembering a Biblical quote, she looked up at him. "God shall wipe away all tears from their eyes; and there shall be no more death, neither sorrow, nor crying, neither shall there be any more pain; for the former things are passed away."

Frederick smiled down at his lovely wife. "Yes, they have."